There was a flash. Something materialized in the air about a meter off the floor—a figure.

"On your knees, mortal," I heard a woman say. The voice was about three times louder than normal.

I rolled off the mattress and jumped to my feet with gun in hand.

"On your knees! Is that how your kind shows obeisance?"

"Not this mortal," I said.

"Then what is your manner of making homage?"

"Who wants to know?"

"You are impertinent. Not like the others. You show a weapon."

"Sorry. I'm like that until I've had my coffee."

"Sometimes a writer comes up with a fictional land or world that sounds like so much fun a reader wishes it to be true...Such has been the case with Tolkien's Middle Earth and Herbert's Dune. John DeChancie has come up with another place in his series beginning with *Starrigger*."

—*Duncan (Okla.) Banner*

JOHN DeCHANCIE

PARADOX ALLEY

ACE SCIENCE FICTION BOOKS
NEW YORK

This book is an
Ace Science Fiction
original edition, and has
never been previously published.

PARADOX ALLEY

An Ace Science Fiction Book/published by arrangement with
the author

PRINTING HISTORY
Ace Science Fiction edition/January 1987

ISBN: 0–441–65146–1

Ace Science Fiction Books are published by The Berkley Publishing Group,
200 Madison Avenue, New York, New York 10016.
PRINTED IN THE UNITED STATES OF AMERICA

To my son Jason

1

I DON'T KNOW if God wears a beard. I've never had the pleasure of meeting Him. Frankly, I hope to delay that happy occasion for as long as possible.

The individual whose acquaintance I had just made didn't quite look the part, but I could have been persuaded otherwise right then. We had come a long way—all the way, it seemed, to the end of the universe. And here to greet us had been a surpassingly strange and beautiful creature possessed of a serenely transcendent, almost beatific aura. His foppish duds worked against the God image, though; I couldn't imagine the Supreme Being going around dressed like a Galactic Emperor out of some video space opera. And Carl, who stood beside me wearing a darkly subdued look, his fury temporarily spent, had seemed mighty sure of the identity of the person whose lights he had just punched out. I was fairly sure that Carl didn't think the guy was the King of Creation.

Even so, we had a problem on our hands. Judging from his patrician bearing and sartorial finery, the person Carl had assaulted looked very important. Extremely important. He quite possibly was in charge of this place, this world to which we had very recently been shanghaied. He had greeted us warmly, welcomed us. He'd invited us to lunch. What do we do? Quite without provocation, we smack the guy in the chops and knock him out. We were very possibly in deep trouble. Very possibly our ass was grass. I hoped that our host didn't own a power mower.

I looked down at the still form of the being—and he appeared for all the world to be a *human* being of the male persuasion—who had called himself Prime. He was lying prone, face in the grass, the back of his head partly hidden

1

beneath bunched folds of his expansive green cape. The rest of the garment was spread out to his left over the ground.

I glanced around. No lightning bolts, no clap of doom. I looked across the valley. No activity immediately apparent in the vicinity of the immense green crystalline fortress that surmounted the hill on the other side. Could Prime possibly be alone here? The notion struck me as absurd, but anything was possible on this strange artificial planet.

"Carl," I said, "I can't take you anywhere."

"It's him," he answered flatly. "The voice that talked to me aboard the flying saucer. He's the one that nabbed me."

"Can you be sure? After all, you never actually saw him. Did you?"

Carl frowned and stared at the ground, thought a moment, then turned to me. "No, but it has to be him. I'll never forget that voice."

"Did the voice call itself Prime?"

"No. I don't remember it ever calling itself anything."

"Then you really can't be sure, can you?"

Carl shrugged, then grudgingly acknowledged the point with a tilt of his head. "I guess. Maybe." Then, quickly and with finality: "Nah. It's him."

"That's hardly the issue," said John Sukuma-Tayler behind us.

We turned. John stepped away from the rest of our companions, who were standing in a tight little knot. They were all shocked by what Carl had done, eyes edgy and expectant. I probably looked the same way, but was trying to hide it. Lori still stood with her hands cupped over her mouth. Susan was aghast; she looked ill. Sean was shaking his head. The rest of them gazed silently at Prime.

John, however, was angry. "Carl, that was an *extremely* stupid thing to do." He stopped and threw up his arms in exasperation. "As if we hadn't enough problems! No, you have to *hit* him. How could you? Carl, how could you do something so . . ." He groped for the appropriate superlative. ". . . so monumentally *imbecilic?* So . . ." He cast about for words, then brought up his hand and slapped his forehead. "Carl, you incredible idiot!"

It was slowly dawning on Carl. "Yeah. I guess it was a dumb thing to do."

"'A dumb thing to do,'" John repeated hollowly. He turned and appealed to the group. "'A dumb thing to do,'" he said again, nodding in mock approval. I had never seen John this ironic. He snapped his head around to fix Carl with a look of utter contempt. "You have a gift for understatement. Unfortunately, it makes your stupidity all the more colossal."

Carl scowled. "Ah, come off it. I just punched him. If he'd've done to you what he did to me—"

"That's hardly the point. Did you stop to consider what the consequences might have been for us—the rest of us? Did you stop a single instant and think? No. No, you—"

"Hold it, John," I said.

"Jake, you can't possibly think he was justified."

"No, it was dumb. But he's young. At his age, I might've done the same thing."

"No excuse."

"Probably not. But the whole question's kind of moot, isn't it?"

John's shoulders slumped. "Unfortunately, yes."

Liam detached himself from the group and walked toward us. "Isn't anybody going to see if he's all right?"

I knelt beside Prime. Gingerly, I uncovered his head. I put my hand on his copper-colored hair. It was as soft and silky as a baby's. I moved his head to the right and looked at his face. The eyes were closed, the face serene. With my thumb—gently, very gently—I pried the left eyelid open. The iris was coal black with tiny flecks of purple. The pupil didn't respond to light, and the eye wasn't moving. I reached for his wrist. Rolling up the pleated cuff proved to be difficult, so I ran a middle finger under his jaw, tracing a line along the left neck muscle near the throat, trying to find the carotid artery. The skin was smooth, sleek, and dry. He was warm, but his body temperature was slightly lower than normal, or so I thought. But who knew what was normal for him?

No carotid pulse. I looked at his left eye again, then swiveled his head to examine the right. Then I stood up.

"He might be dead," I said.

"Good God," John murmured.

"That's crazy," Carl said in almost a whisper.

"Oh, my." John came over to stand beside me. "Jake, are you . . . are you *quite* sure?"

"No. But he doesn't have a heartbeat, leastways none that I can detect. He's not breathing, I don't think. We should roll him over and . . . hell." I slapped my forehead. The past several minutes had been so disorienting that I had slipped into a sort of semiparalysis. Here, ostensibly, was a human being in need of help, and we were all standing around like dummies. I came out of it. "Darla! Run and get the medikit—know where it is?"

"Yes." She ran back to the truck.

I got out the key and called Sam.

This has all been very interesting, Sam observed.

"Sam, set up to monitor this guy's life signs."

If he has any. Is he human?

"Maybe, maybe not."

Carl was slowly shaking his head in disbelief. "Crazy. I just poked him one. It couldn't have been enough—"

"It was enough," John said acidly. Then he bent over slightly and peered at Prime's face. "Of all the bloody, beastly luck." He straightened and let out a long sigh. "Well, that's it, isn't it? We're all dead."

"Not yet," I said. "And he might not be either. My guess is he's not human. But human or not, Carl didn't hit him hard enough to kill him."

"But if he's not human, how do you know what it would take to kill him?"

"You have a point."

"I wish I didn't."

The others were edging forward now. Zoya and Yuri drew up closer and stopped.

"I wonder who he is," Yuri said. "What he is."

Darla came running with the medikit. I tore it open and took out two remote monitoring transponders.

"Help me roll him over, John."

We were about to do so when Lori screamed.

I whirled. Carl was lying on the ground. Sean evidently had caught him, and was now cradling Carl's head in his arms.

"What happened?" John said.

Sean gently cuffed Carl's cheeks a few times. "Fainted dead away, he did. Just keeled over."

I went over and crouched beside them, took Carl's wrist

and felt for his pulse. It was slow and thin, dangerously so.

"Is he okay?" Susan asked.

"Hard to tell," I said noncommittally. "Funny that he'd pass out like that. Let me get a transponder for him."

"Carl?" Lori took my place as I got up. "Carl? Oh, no."

"He'll be all right, girl. Run and fetch some water."

Lori ran off.

"He's out cold, though," Sean said with concern. "Dead out."

"Jake," John said, indicating Prime. "What about . . . ?"

"If he doesn't have a pulse, there's not much I can do for him. And if he doesn't have a heart, all bets are off anyway. I'm more worried about Carl."

"Well, finding out you've just killed somebody has to be a shock."

"Maybe. Carl's not the type to faint dead away, though."

"He's young—just a boy, really."

"Not that young. And I don't like the feel of his pulse."

I moved Lori aside and opened Carl's shirt. After removing the protective backing from the transponder, I stuck the disc-shaped device on his chest, positioning it over the left pectoral muscle. I prepared another and affixed it to the right pectoral, then went back and got two more transponders and put them on either side of his abdomen, just below the rib cage. I took the key out of my pocket.

"Sam? Are you getting any readings?"

"Yup. Pulse forty-four, with some irregularity in the atrial and ventricular rhythms. Got some inverted P-waves, too, and the QRS complex looks kind of wacky."

"What do you make of it?"

"Well, my medical program is telling me his heart is in trouble. And . . . wait a minute. Yeah. It's getting worse."

"What does the program say to do?"

"It's recommending things we can't do."

"Is it an infarct or something?"

"Doesn't look like it. Actually, it's shaping up to look like congestive heart failure. Whoops, you're getting really bad irregularities now. If he goes into fibrillation we can zap him —but that's not going to correct whatever the hell's wrong with him."

I felt my own heart frost over. He was dying.

"Not possible," Sean said, shaking his head. "A healthy lad like him?"

Susan knelt beside me and squeezed my upper arm. "Jake. *Do* something."

"Sorry," was all I could say. Then into the key: "Sam, congestive heart failure is a long-term process. How could it happen this fast?"

"Good question. The med program doesn't know, and neither do I."

"But what the hell is it telling you?"

"Easy, son. It just keeps flagging things with Anomalous Event. *It's pretty clear somebody's doing this to him, isn't it?"*

"Very clear," John said. "Obviously, this world deals in swift retribution."

Susan shot him a fierce look. "You don't have to say it with such satisfaction."

"I have none, Susan, I assure you."

I said, "Sam, how is he?"

"Getting worse, I'm afraid. All kinds of arrhythmias, atrial flutter. It's a failing heart, Jake. Too many things going wrong at once—I really don't think we can do a thing for him, but you ought to try CPR in any case. I'd recommend starting it right now."

"Right. Sean, stretch him out."

"Right-o."

Before we got to it, a voice came from behind us: "I'm really very sorry this happened."

Everyone whirled around before I got to my feet. Susan choked off a scream, and Liam uttered an awed "Jay-sus Christ!"

It was Prime, on his feet and looking fit and hale.

"Very, very sorry," Prime was saying. "I can't help but feel that it was in some way my fault."

His concern seemed genuine, if inexplicable.

"What are you doing to him?" I said.

"I beg your . . . ? Oh, I see. Yes. Well, I'm sure he'll be all right. Merely a precautionary measure."

"He's dying," I said.

Prime seemed surprised. "Really? I can't think of a reason

why he should be." He stepped toward us, his eyes on Carl. "Are you sure?"

"He'll be dead very shortly," I told him.

Prime stopped. His gaze began to drift upward, finally focusing, it seemed, on something far away. "Hmm. I see. Yes." He looked at me. "The young man's life processes are being probed. Various components, various systems are being temporarily suppressed in order to obtain an overview of the entire organism. At least, that is what I am told."

"Unsuppress them," I said.

Prime smiled beatifically. "You needn't worry. He's in very good hands. As it stands, the plan is to keep him sedated for the time being. However, that can be amended. And I see no reason why it shouldn't be. I'm sure the outburst was simply the result of the strains of your long journey."

I spoke into the key. "Sam? How's he doing?"

"Damnedest thing. The heart stabilized just like that. Pulse is up. No arrhythmias, good sinus waves. Can't figure it. Those transponders must have been on the fritz."

"Carl's okay, then?"

"He's coming around."

Prime was eyeing the truck. "You have other companions inside?"

"No. That was the Artificial Intelligence who oversees the operation of my vehicle."

"I see." He knitted his brow. "Interesting way to put it."

I wondered what he meant.

Suddenly, the smile was back. "We seem to have gotten off on the wrong foot. Again, our apologies. The invitation to lunch still stands, if you would do me the honor."

"Maybe we need to think about it for a bit," I said.

"As you wish. If you choose to come, simply follow the road across the valley. There is an entrance to my residence at the base of the mountain." He turned and pointed. "There, at the end of the road."

I couldn't see anything, but said, "Thank you," anyway.

"You're quite welcome."

Suddenly, Carl sat up. He looked around. "Hello," he said.

Lori threw down the canteen she was holding, fell to her knees, and nearly strangled Carl in a hug.

Susan bent over and placed a palm on his forehead. "Are you okay, honey?"

"Ulg . . ." Tugging at Lori's arms, Carl nodded.

Prime clapped his hands. "Well! No harm done, it seems."

"Let him breathe, Lori," Susan admonished.

"Yeah, I'm fine," Carl finally managed to say. "What the hell happened?"

"You should ask this gentleman," John told him, inclining his head toward Prime.

"Oh." Carl looked up at our host. "I thought you were dead."

Prime laughed. "Not quite. Your friends seem prone to worrying about people's health, including yours." Prime turned to me. "By the way, your concern about me was very commendable. Thank you."

"You're welcome," I said. "You had me fooled pretty good, though. Tell me something. Are you human?"

"In part, yes."

After waiting for elaboration that didn't come, I repeated, "In part," not knowing what else to say.

He was willing to go a bit further, but no more. "A small part, but I assure you, a very active one." He clapped his hands again. "So! I shall bid you good day." He made a motion to turn, then halted. "Incidentally, young man . . ."

Carl was getting to his feet. "Carl Chapin."

Prime took a step forward, his expression hardening just the slightest. "Mr. Chapin. I have recommended that no restraints be put upon you and that you be allowed to move about as you wish. The concern here is not that you may cause me harm. You can't. But an unruly attitude might get in the way of what we want to accomplish. Do I have your personal assurance that you will hereafter conduct yourself in a manner that is not disruptive?"

Carl looked around uncomfortably. "Um . . . yeah, I guess." He added quickly, "I mean, yeah. Sure."

Prime's expression brightened again. "Very good. I shall look forward to seeing you—all of you—at my residence. Good day."

We watched him walk to his sleek black roadster, climb aboard, and close the clear bubble canopy. The engine whined to life. The vehicle wheeled around and swung onto the black surface of the Skyway. The pitch of the engine increased slightly and the thing whooshed down the road in the direction from which it had come, black shiny wings starred with hot sun-points. Just before reaching the bend it rose from the roadway and soared into air. It climbed almost straight up, rising to about three hundred meters before leveling off. It shot across the valley, a black triangle against the violet sky. It made a half turn around the fortress, then disappeared.

John stared into the distance. "I wonder what he wants to accomplish?"

2

WE ALL PILED into the truck and had a palaver.

"Frankly, I don't see that we have a choice," John said after he had taken a swig from the canteen.

We had had to ration water the whole trip. Nine humans and four aliens had put a strain on the recycler.

"Prime gave us one," I countered. "He didn't insist that we join him."

"What are our options, then? Should we fumble about on a totally alien and very bizarre world? In hopes of doing what, exactly?"

"Finding food, for one thing," Sean put in. "The cupboard is bare."

"We've been invited to lunch," John reminded him.

"We could be walking into a trap," I said. "Can we be sure Prime will let us leave?"

"We've seen his power. He may be able to do anything he wants with us."

"That may very well be true," I said, nodding. "But we don't know for sure."

"He seems friendly enough," Susan said. "Absolutely charming, in fact."

Zoya said, "I doubt very much that he is what he seems to be. I don't for a moment believe he is human."

"And I don't believe he's God," Liam said. "I'm not what you'd call the religious sort, but gadding about in a shiny new roadster isn't my idea of how a Supreme Being should be conducting himself." He scratched his effusive light-brown beard. "Of course, I'm not so sure exactly how a Supreme

Being should be conducting himself, but—"

"I know what you mean," John said. "I think we should dispense with that notion straight off. Prime is obviously an advanced form of life. Perhaps he's even immortal. But eternal? Hardly."

"Okay," I said, "we're in agreement on that score. I'd also add that, though he might be very powerful, he probably isn't omnipotent. Or omniscient, or all-loving and good, either. He says he has something to accomplish—what, we don't know, but his plans seem to include us. We have to decide whether we want to cooperate. We might not like what he wants to do."

Darla said, "Maybe he'll give us the choice of not cooperating."

"There's that possibility," I answered, turning in the driver's seat to face her. She was squatting behind the seat, forearm resting on the back. She looked as pretty as ever. Her hair had grown out quite a bit, softening the effect of the severe cut she'd worn when we first met. The hardships of our journey had left their mark. She looked tired most of the time, which could have been due to her pregnancy, though she was only a little shy of three months into it. She'd been gaining weight too. Her features were slightly more fleshed out. A little, not much.

"Darla," I said, "what's your gut feeling? Do you trust Prime?"

She pursed her lips and thought about it for a long time. Then she said, "We have no reason to trust him. Absolutely none. Ask me on a bad day and I'd say no, let's not go near him." She ran a hand through her smooth, dark-brown hair. Tired or not, Darla always looked as if she'd just stepped out of a beauty parlor: hair in place, makeup perfect. "And though I wouldn't exactly call this a good day, I get this feeling that we simply must deal with him. We'll have to, if we want to get back." She sighed. "Do I trust him? No farther than I could throw Sean. What's my gut feeling?" She shrugged helplessly. "Let's go to lunch."

"I dunno, Darla, m'girl," Sean said with a grin, "after the way you handled those two beefy loggers back on Talltree, I wouldn't give odds on how far you could throw me."

Darla smiled, a little abashedly.

"Oh, no, you should be proud, Darla." Sean's grin broadened and he swelled with satisfaction. "Ah, I'll never forget the sight of Tommy Baker, gorked out across the bed with his arse hanging out. He had it coming, and it was a fine thing to see him get it."

"I caught him at a delicate moment," Darla said.

"Anybody else want to express his or her opinion?" I asked around. "Susan?"

"Oh, I trust him. Darla's right, no good reason. But isn't everybody interested in finding out what this guy's all about? And where the heck are we, anyway? What is this place? Only Prime can tell us that."

"Lori? How about you?"

"Well . . ." She gave Carl a sidelong admonitory glare. "If certain people can *behave* themselves . . . I say we go to the Emerald City."

"I won't punch the guy again. But I'm not promising any more than that."

"You'll behave or I'll give you a fat lip."

"Don't worry, I'll be Goody Two-Shoes."

"Whoever that is."

I said, "John?"

"Oh, yes, by all means. We should accept his invitation."

I looked at Yuri and Zoya.

"I agree with the consensus," Yuri said. "We certainly need some answers."

Zoya looked out the port moodily. "It might serve us to be cautious. Perhaps we should make some attempt to communicate with him, talk to him further. Find out exactly what he wants of us."

"Do you really think we can remain safe from him," Yuri asked skeptically, "simply by staying away from that fortress of his?"

"No. But . . ." She focused her gaze far away. "I don't think I want to go there."

"What's all the discussion?" Roland broke in impatiently. "You saw what he did to Carl. If he wants, we all drop over dead, like that. So what choice do we have?"

"Good point," John said.

"I just wanted to take time and think things over," I said to Roland. "And I wanted everyone to have a say in what we should do."

"Sorry, Jake. I just don't see the point in haggling over this."

"Maybe there is none, but we've been running in a panic for a long time now. For once I want the luxury of ruminating over our next move."

Roland laughed and sat back in the shotgun seat. "Take all the time you want. We have most of eternity."

"Exactly," I said. "Ragna? Would you and Oni like to put your two cents in?"

Not counting George and Winnie, who were what exopologists would label "borderline-sapient quasi-hominids"— looked like apes to me, funny ones, with long floppy ears and big wet eyes—Ragna and Oni were the only alien members of our party. They had joined us in the rig during our rest stop, abandoning their cramped vehicle, and had since taken pains to be as unobtrusive as possible, keeping to themselves and generally trying not to be an added burden, which they weren't. I liked them a lot.

Ragna blinked, translucent nictitating membranes sliding up to cover the eyeballs before the lids came down. He put his hands up to adjust his blue headband, which was a linguistic translating interface. "The reference to outmoded monetary units is understood denotatively, but not colloquially. However, I am getting the gist of your nub. Yes, we are having a contribution to be making, which is this . . ." He glanced at Oni, who nodded consent. "We, being the nonhuman minority of this band of intrepid explorers—note irony—are hardly in a position to be saying anything yea or nay, since, by the same token, we have not been invited along, but more or less have crashed this party, if you are following my rhetoric. Be that as it may—and by the life of me, it very well may—we say yes, by gosh, let us by all means go to the fortress of this Prime fellow and ask him to put his two cents into the bargain as well!" He smiled sheepishly. "If you get what I am meaning."

"I get what you are meaning," I said. "Who else? Sean? Liam?"

"I'm hungry," Sean said. "Let's go and eat."

"He's always hungry," Liam said, "but count me in, too."

"I'm bored," Roland said. "Let's get moving."

"Sam?" I said.

"Oh, I have a vote?"

"Sam, you always have at least a kilocredit's worth to put in," Susan said, "and you know it."

"Thank you, m'am. What I say is, I'd be wary of this Prime dude."

I waited for more, then: "That's it?"

"Yup. I guess you have change coming, Suzie."

"Oh, come on, Sam," I said. "Spill it."

"Nothing to spill. I'm a computer, remember? Give me data to analyze, numbers to crunch, I'll give you a readout. But don't ask me to make anything out of recent events. It's all too crazy for me. Emerald cities, fairy castles, crazy planets, some guy who thinks he's God . . . Forget it, I'm shutting down. Wake me when it's over."

"Oh, come off it," I said. "Every time you're put on the spot you go into that 'I'm just a computer' routine."

"Seriously, I think this is a human-judgment situation. It calls for acting on a hunch, an intuition, a feeling in your belly. Computers don't have bellies to get feelings in, boys and girls."

"Sam, when are you going to admit to yourself that you're human?"

"Son, I was human for seventy-two years. That was enough."

"But your Vlathusian Entelechy Matrix," John put in, "makes your responses absolutely indistinguishable from those of a human mind fully possessed of every faculty. It's enough to fool anybody. Sometimes I half believe you're really a person hidden away in this lorry somewhere, speaking into a microphone and putting us all on."

"Well, you've found me out, John. You're right, I'm a fraud. Thing is, I'm only one decimeter tall. You'll never find me."

"You see? Computers don't usually have a sense of humor. Jake's right. You are undeniably human, Sam, whether you like it or not."

"Be that as it may," Sam said. "Getting back to the issue at hand, though, I think you've made your decision already."

"We haven't heard from everybody yet," Susan said.

"Who's that?" I asked.

"You, Jake. What do you think?"

I sat back and exhaled. "Well. Just on general principles . . . like Yuri said, we need some answers. I have a few questions to put to Mr. Prime myself. And if I don't like the answers, I might just take a poke at him, too. But I have other reasons for wanting to visit Emerald City. Moore and his gang are out here somewhere. We might be safer inside the city."

"Maybe Prime invited them to lunch, too," Roland said.

"When? Did I miss something? Or did they get here before us? I thought Moore and his crew took off in the other direction."

"Maybe Prime contacted them by radio . . . or telepathy or some such wonder."

"He didn't contact us that way."

"True," Roland admitted. "But he might still do that thing —invite them."

"Okay," I said, "I'll buy that, but we'll have to inform Prime that under no circumstances will we remain under the same roof with those birds."

"I'll drink to that," Sean said. "Which reminds me, I've a god-awful thirst."

Our beer reserves also had been under strict rationing.

Susan said, "Do you really think they're still after us? I mean, what do we have that they want? The Black Cube?"

"I'd give them that," I said. "Nobody seems to want the damn thing."

"One good thing," Sam said. "Old Corey Wilkes won't be giving us any trouble. He was behind it all, and now that he's gone, I think Moore might have a hard time thinking up reasons to give us grief."

"Except that he has a score to settle with me," I said.

"Well, maybe. You'd think he'd've had just about enough by now."

"Not our Mr. Moore," Liam said. "You don't know him, Sam."

"I think I do," I said, "and I'm worried."

I looked out the side port. The "sun" was declining toward

the horizon. It looked to be late afternoon, the sky having turned a slightly deeper shade of blue-violet. The green of the grass-carpeted hills was iridescent—a psychotic, delirious green. The neat shrubbery was variously colored—here pinks and reds, there browns and oranges. This place had the feel of a park, a playland.

I turned and yelled, "Winnie! Where are you?"

"Probably getting it on with George," Roland said. "Those two are a pair."

Winnie came scurrying out of the aft-cabin, threading her way through the thicket of human legs and bodies. George followed her.

"Winnie here, Jake!"

"C'mere, girl."

She jumped up into my lap. I rubbed the bony, fur-covered knot between her floppy ears.

"What do you think, Winnie?" I said.

Winnie thought, knitting her low brow. She put a lot of effort into it. Then she asked, "What think about?"

"Huh? Oh. About that man we met. The one with the pretty clothes. Did you like him?"

She shrugged. I wondered if the gesture were learned or innate.

"Big man," Winnie said. "Big."

"Big?" If anything, Prime had been on the short side. "You mean, important? Powerful?"

"Yes, that. Big man. 'Portant." She groped for elaboration, then said, simply, "Real big man." Then, an afterthought: "Many."

"Many? You mean much? Much big?"

"Many," she said flatly.

"Many? More than one? He has friends?"

She considered it. "No. He many. Morethanone."

"I see." I looked to the group for comment. None. Turning to George, who was no taller but a little more bulky about the midsection, I asked, "What's your opinion, George, old bean?"

George gave me a puzzled look.

"Do you think Prime—that man—is big and many?"

He nodded. "Many-more-than-one." He continued nodding

emphatically for a moment, then stopped and pondered. "But he one also, too."

"Eh? He's one. Just one man?"

"But many . . . also. One . . . many."

"This is beginning to sound suspiciously theological again," John said. "One-in-many. Next they'll be expounding on the doctrine of the Trinity."

"How did they tumble to all this?" Liam asked incredulously.

"These two know everything," Susan said. "I've always had the feeling that Winnie has known everything all along."

"Can you explain, George?" I asked. "Explain. Say more?"

George scratched his belly and cogitated. "Pime. He . . . not man."

"Oh. He's not? What is he?"

"'Splain." He looked as if a headache were coming on. "He . . ." The belly scratching grew more vigorous. George screwed up his face in frustration. "He . . . Pime . . . he . . ."

"Okay, okay. Don't get upset. It's all right that you can't say it."

"He all of them!" George blurted. "All. One. Many." He stopped scratching. Something dawned on him, a faint light at the horizon of his understanding. His gaze was drawn out the port to the sky. "Me," he said. He stared for a moment, then lowered his eyes to Winnie. "Winnie, too. She also. We." He pointed to her, then brought his stubby index finger back to rest on his chest. "Me. Us." He tapped the finger. "We many." That said, he sighed, looking a bit sad. "'Splain no more."

There was a long silence.

Presently, I said, "Thanks, George, Winnie."

Winnie gave me a hug and got down.

"Well, gang," I said, not particularly apropos of anything.

"Yes. Well," John said.

"What do you say we get moving?"

"Yeah," Susan said emptily.

I turned forward, put my foot on the accelerator pedal, and took hold of the control bars. "Start her up, Sam."

Sam did. The engine thrummed to life.

I looked out across the valley at the green-glass fairy palace, and finally thought of something to say. I suppose there was an impish grin on my face when I tried to come out with, "Well, gang, we're—"

"If you say 'We're off to see the Wizard,'" Sam declared, "I'll come out of my hidey-hole and bite you on the ass."

3

THE TRIP ACROSS the valley floor was leisurely and uneventful. We passed other structures along the way, ones we hadn't really noticed with the green fortress riveting our attention. We took time to puzzle over them now. One looked like a cross between an Ionic temple and a chemical factory. Another was in the shape of a squashed silver sphere melded to a blue pyramid. A third, lying some distance off the road, was a free-form aggregation of butterfly-wing shapes. There were others less easy to describe. Needless to say, we didn't have a clue as to what they were or what functions they served, if any. I suspected that some of them weren't buildings, exactly. Sculpture? Possibly. Machines? Maybe.

The Emerald City was different. There was a fanciful quality to it. Its lines were graceful and romantic, belying its bulk. It imparted a sense of solidity, though; it was big enough to contain a city, and if it truly were a fortress, a castle, it looked the part, high ramparts braced against the wind. It looked to have been carved out of a single uniform block of material. No seams, no joints.

It was a castle, but it was unlike anything you'd see in history books. An alien hand had drawn the blueprints; I was willing to bet on that.

Sam asked, "What was that about an entrance at the foot of the mountain?"

"That's what the man said."

But what was there was simply the end of the the road. The Skyway, that maze of interstellar road that stretched throughout the galaxy, terminated at the base of the citadel in front of a stand of short purplish trees. Road's end. We had come a long way.

I braked.

"Whoa!" Sam yelled. "What's this?"

The juncture of road and hillside parted, the edge of the hill rising like a hiked skirt, scrubby trees stitched to the hem. It stopped just high enough to admit the truck, forming an arch that revealed the mouth of a tunnel. The road continued through.

"What do you think of that, Sam?" I asked.

"Nifty."

"Shall we drive on in?"

"Sure. I'll put the headbeams on."

I looked at the underside of the tunnel mouth as we drove through the aperture. It was all metal inside. No earth or debris rained down on us, and I couldn't for the life of me figure out how this trick was being done, but I didn't have much time to study it.

The tunnel was smooth-walled, lit by oval recessed fixtures positioned at regular intervals directly overhead. Otherwise it was featureless and reminded me of the Roadbug garage planet, where the Bugs had caught us then dragged us across light-years to this place. The tunnel bore through the mountain for about half a kilometer before it debouched into a dimly lit, expansive cavern.

But here the similarity to the Roadbug planet ended, though the place did look like a garage. The skeletal shapes of huge cranes and gantries loomed in the shadows. Strange machinery lay everywhere. There were scores of vehicles here, too, some parked out in the middle of the floor and appearing ready for use, others occupying numerous maintenance bays recessed into the walls. The vehicles were of every shape and description.

"How much to park here by the hour?" Sam wanted to know.

"Where's the attendant?" I asked. "But seriously, folks—how the hell do we get up to the city from here?"

"Elevator, I guess," Carl said.

"Yeah," I said. "Where? This place is big. See anything?"

We roamed through the place for a few minutes.

"What's that?" Roland said, pointing.

"Where?"

"Looks like a ramp. See? Through that opening right there,

against the far wall. No, now you can't see it—behind that big electrical coil-looking thing."

"Oh." I eased the rig forward and saw it. It was a sharply inclined ramp barely wide enough to admit a small vehicle. No go for the truck.

"Looks like some sort of way up," I said, "but we'll have to hoof it."

"Looks like I stay here," Sam said.

"Sorry, Sam."

"Well, I'd be a little obtrusive sitting at the table, anyway. Enjoy your lunch."

I scrammed the engine. "Okay. Here we go."

The cavern was cool, redolent of garage smells—not oil and grease, just the definite ambience of heavy machinery.

"Everybody have everything?" I asked when all the crew had gotten out. "We might not be back here for a while."

"Got all my *Nogon* camping gear," Susan said while reaching behind to adjust a strap on her backpack. "Don't know what use it'll be, but what the hell."

"Good idea to bring anything we might possibly need," I said. "There's no telling what's up there. Anybody else?"

Everybody was content to make the trip up with what he had.

I took out my key and spoke into it. "Okay, Sam. Take care and keep an eye out for trouble."

"You, too. Good luck."

We made our way over the dark smooth floor, toward the archway that led to the ramp, walking past some extremely bizarre vehicles. They were composed of various geometrical shapes shoved together at odd angles. Farther along there were more vehicles, these more comprehensible but very alien in appearance.

Liam was first through the archway. He looked up and stopped in his tracks. "Mother of God," he said quietly.

We joined him at the bottom of a huge cylindrical shaft that shot straight up through the mountain, its vanishing point lost in darkness. Running straight up the middle of the shaft without visible support was a vertical ramp, a wide ribbon of some metallic substance, its color a pale blue, its bottom end curling outward like a length of tape. It touched the floor at a perfect tangent to form the ramp we'd seen from the truck.

We walked around it, keeping our distance. I walked around it twice, then again. The damn thing wasn't even three centimeters thick.

"It's a laundry chute," Carl ventured.

"Yeah, for express laundry," I said.

Carl nodded. "Well, the way it really works is, you're supposed to get this really good running start, see . . . like this."

He backstepped, then ran up the sharply curling end of the ramp to a point where it became nearly vertical. He pivoted sharply and began to run back down—

But he didn't. Couldn't.

His grin disappeared. "Hey!"

He began to glide up the ramp. He was still facing down, his body perpendicular to the ramp and now horizontal to the ground, held fast by some mysterious attractive force. He could move his feet, though. He tried walking back down, but the upward drift was too rapid. He started to run, clumsily, his steps slow and heavy.

"Holy hell!" he yelled. "I can't—"

We all stood there gawking. I couldn't think of a thing to do to help him. It was the strangest thing, watching him being borne straight up on this impossible vertical treadmill. As his ascent speed increased, he gave up running and turned slowly until he was facing up the shaft.

"Hey!" he called over his shoulder. "I guess this is the way up!" He laughed mirthlessly, the smooth walls of the shaft carrying his echoing voice down to us. "Anyway, I sure as shit hope so."

"Carl!" Lori screamed after him, her eyes round with fear and disbelief. "Carl, be careful!"

"I think he's right, girl," Sean said. "That's the way up."

I stepped forward and tentatively put my right boot on the ramp, testing it. I felt no pull, no quasimagnetic attraction. I inched my foot forward. Someone grasped my arm—Darla, stepping up onto the ramp with me.

"Going up?" she said, smiling.

"I'm with you, kid."

We climbed the steep incline. We hadn't taken more than a few steps when it began to happen. The world tilted. My sense of up and down rotated about forty-five degrees. Suddenly the ribbon of metal was no longer vertical but merely steep, and we rode upward as if on an escalator in a department store. I could move my feet, but it was like walking in sticky mud. It was a little disorienting, but not unpleasantly so.

I turned until I faced down the ramp. Everybody was just standing there.

"Hey," I called, "it's okay. Hop aboard."

They exchanged shrugs and reluctantly approached the ramp.

I shuffled back around again. Carl, a good distance ahead, was waving and shouting something I couldn't hear. I waved back.

"Don't get too far ahead!" I yelled.

He cupped his hand to his ear, so I yelled louder. He heard, nodded, and tried walking back down again. But he was still gaining speed. He finally gave up and threw out his arms in despair.

We were accelerating, too. I looked at my feet. It was hard to tell whether we were sliding over the surface or being carried along by some mysterious movement of the surface itself, as if it were a conveyor belt. The ramp was seamless, featureless, and the shaft around us was dark. I finally decided that we were sliding—and I was almost sure that the soles of my boots weren't actually touching the ramp but riding a few millimeters above it.

It was a quick trip up. A disc of light grew at the top of the tube, and we rushed toward it. Our speed was hard to judge, but we were moving right along, and the sensation was exhilarating. The experience recapitulated my recent recurring dreams, my fantasies—plunging headlong through a dark tunnel toward a source of brilliant light. I'd read something somewhere about that image—about it being a recapitulation of the birth experience. I considered it. I'm not one to set much store by armchair psychology, but there was an undeniable feel of truth to the notion.

We suddenly decelerated. My sense of orientation did a double flip as the ramp leveled off, shot through an opening into a large green chamber, and became one with the floor. Darla and I slid to a gradual halt, took a few jogging steps, and walked off the end of ramp onto a polished black floor.

"Where's Carl?" Darla asked.

I looked around. We were in a large circular room. Arched openings were cut into the walls at regular intervals. Ramp ends came out of them, converging and terminating on the circular black area where we stood.

"Darned if I know," I said.

4

"WHERE'S CARL?" WAS the first thing John Sukuma-Tayler asked as he stepped off the magic escalator.

"Good question," I said. "He seems to've misplaced himself."

John scowled and shook his head. "That damn fool. If he gets us into more trouble—"

"I'm more worried that something might have happened to him."

The scowl dissolving, John nodded dourly. "Oh, I suppose you're right. Any idea where he might have gone?"

"No. I didn't want to go looking until you'd all come up. How far behind you were the others?"

"Um . . . when I looked back, Susan seemed to be having the most trouble getting on the thing. I don't know what possessed me to go first after you two, but I did. I think—oh, here they are."

Out of the oval opening in the green wall came Lori, Yuri, Zoya, Ragna, and Oni. Following close behind was Sean, hand in hand with Winnie and George. There was a moderate delay before Liam and Roland came through, propping up between them a slightly gray-faced Susan.

Susan stumbled off the strip, moaned, and put a hand to her stomach. "Oh, my God."

"You okay, Suzie?" I said.

She heaved a sigh, then burped. "'Scuse me. Roller coasters always made me sick."

Roland laughed and slapped her on the back. "Oh, come on, Susan. It wasn't that bad."

Susan winced and rolled her eyes. "I don't believe we went straight up . . . *straight up!* It was the worst . . . ooh, I can't stand it." She belched again.

"Carl is missing," Darla told Sean, who had been glancing around the chamber.

"We lost sight of him on the way up," I said, "and he wasn't here when we arrived. I suggest we start looking."

"The boy's got the devil in 'im for sure," Sean said, "but he wouldn't run off like this. Something must have happened."

"Whatever happened," I said, "it was fast. We couldn't have been more than thirty seconds behind him."

"D'you think Prime had something to do with it?" Liam asked me.

"Could be."

"Odd thing," Sean said. "I thought Prime would be here to greet us."

"And I am. Welcome." The voice filled the domed chamber.

"Hello?" I said, whirling to find the source.

"Forgive me," Prime's voice said, "I am afraid that certain exigencies have prevented me from greeting you in person. I will be joining you shortly, however, and until then I've provided—"

"Where's Carl?" I shouted.

"I'm sorry?" A pause, then: "Oh, yes. It seems the young man has gotten himself lost. That is a very easy thing to accomplish in this place, I'm afraid. Please don't worry. He also will join you very soon. He's quite safe, I assure you."

"We're concerned," I told him.

"Of course you are, and I don't blame you in the slightest. You are in a strange place and have quite naturally assumed that there is potential danger here. I fully appreciate your prudent distrust of me. I could very well be an enemy. And I also realize that you must have grave reservations concerning any assurances I might give to the contrary. After all, you know very little about me. Now, what I ultimately want you to understand is that your fears about me are not justified. I bear you no ill will and mean you no harm. As time goes on, this will become apparent. Having said this, however, I want to warn you that your natural caution about this place *is* justified.

There is indeed potential danger here, both inside this structure and on this planet, though the perils outside these walls far outstrip those within. Let us deal with the proximate variety. There are in and about these rooms and towers numerous artifacts, which, if used improperly, may be a source of trouble. Also, the dangers of getting lost here are quite real. This structure has certain—shall we say—architectural peculiarities, which, until they are understood and taken into account, can cause accidents. In short, you would be wise to use discretion and be generally circumspect in your movements until you get used to your surroundings. I hope I have made myself clear."

I said, "You mentioned something about dangers outside."

"Of those you will learn more later. They would be difficult to describe without my giving you an extensive briefing on the situation here."

"Okay, but I take it you aren't alone on this planet. There are others. Correct?"

"You might say that."

I was suddenly annoyed. This guy had a knack for answering questions with an unambiguous maybe.

"Thanks for the info," I said. "You said something about lunch. Also something about straight answers to our questions."

There was an indulgent smile implied in the voice. "I understand your impatience. But perhaps you need time to think about your questions first." A chuckle, then: "You are very intelligent and resourceful creatures, of that I have no doubt. Intelligent enough, perhaps, to realize that what you face here is entirely strange and new to your experience. You will be exposed to ideas and concepts which may be difficult for you to grasp. Ultimately, the goal of complete understanding might lie beyond your capabilities. I very much doubt that, but that is one proposition which must be put to the test. In any case, the learning experience itself should prove rewarding. This is why I contend that you need time. Impatience is counterproductive at best. And here on this world-construct—which I propose we call Microcosmos, for want of a better name—it could conceivably prove lethal."

I nodded. "Okay, fine. I'm sure I speak for all of us when I say we're eager to learn. And you can bet we'll be careful.

But frankly, the suspense is already killing me. And I'm hungry."

Prime gave a gentle laugh. "No doubt. Just a moment."

We waited maybe a quarter minute. Then, out of an archway to our right, came a glowing green sphere floating about two meters off the floor.

"What you see is rather hard to explain technically," Prime told us, "but its function is simple. It will guide you to the dining hall, where, if you are still amenable, we will have lunch. Please follow it there. I will join you shortly."

"I hate to keep pestering," I said, "but what about Carl?"

No reply.

"What about Carl?" Lori shouted. "Answer us!"

The green sphere bobbed, then receded through the archway and into a dark corridor running tangentially to the circular chamber. There it paused, as if waiting for us.

"Lead on, MacDuff," John called to it as he started forward. He halted and looked around at everybody. "Well?"

Susan was still nursing her middle. "I can't think of food right now, but maybe if I forced something down . . ."

"Right," Roland said, "then I'll take you for a ride on the magic ramp again. We'll look for the one that goes down this time."

"Ulp."

We followed the green sphere.

Prime hadn't been kidding about the architectural oddity of the place. Everything was goofy. Walls curved and canted vertiginously, floors sloped at odd angles. Weird perspectives tricked us at every turn. Even so, the place had a bizarre beauty to it. Rather stark, though. The walls were smooth and unadorned. No pictures, carvings, or decorations. No tapestries, weapons, or shields emblazoned with colorful heraldry. Not a proper castle after all. The floor was everywhere black with a deep shine, looking like a dark mirror. Here and about, though, stood odd thingamabobs, no doubt the artifacts Prime had warned us about. Some looked like pieces of machinery, others could have been sculpture, or for all we knew, alien hat racks.

"This place is a damn museum," Susan said.

"I was just about to say that," John told her.

I said, "Yeah, it does have the feel of one."

An odd one, though. There didn't seem to be much organization to it. Some things were lying about haphazardly; they weren't necessarily on display. Nevertheless, I got the distinct impression that this was a *collection,* a bunch of stuff that had been obtained at various places and carted here for storage.

We soon came to a high-ceilinged hall featuring a large centrally positioned table of irregular shape. Uniformly constructed seating appliances—the term chairs would tend to connote that one could easily sit in them—were arranged around the table, but what was on the table wasn't strange; it was food, and it all looked good. There was a huge whole baked ham, assorted roast fowl, fish, various cuts of beef, one or two of pork, and maybe one of veal. These entrees were flanked by vegetable dishes, casseroles, fruit arrangements, baskets of bread, tureens of soup, bowls of salad—and on and on. There was other stuff I couldn't readily identify, but it looked very familiar. All in all, this was something more than lunch and slightly less than a state dinner for a visiting foreign dignitary. The eating utensils looked alien but serviceable, as did the glassware.

We looked it over. Meanwhile our shining guide drifted away, exiting through an arch and into darkness.

"Quite a spread," Susan commented.

"How're your insides?" I asked.

"Getting better."

We all stood about gawking until Prime entered the hall through an archway to the left. Smiling, he strode to the approximate head of the table and stood. "Welcome. I'm glad you came. Please be seated."

We chose places around the table. Along with the rest of the gang, I regarded the "chair" on which I was to "seat" myself. It was pink, shiny, and looked somewhat like a formation of coral. The prospect of actually using the thing as a seat involved the possibility of having an autoerotic experience—or a painful one, depending on how careful you were.

"I think you will find—" Prime began, but a shout from Lori interrupted him.

She had tried sitting but had immediately sprung to her feet. "It moved!" she told us.

Prime chuckled. "The chairs will automatically reform themselves to accommodate your bodies. Simply sit down and . . ."

Gingerly, I sat. The damn chair did that very thing, and it did it almost before my buttocks had touched down.

"There, you see?"

"Interesting," I said as the chair made some further adjustments, these very subtle and done much more slowly. I sank into the thing a little and stopped. It was strange, but I was comfortable.

When everyone had settled in, Prime poured himself a glass of amber liquid from a carafe. "I think you'll find this wine very insouciant and a bit immature, but compatible with almost everything here." He indicated a similar decanter near John, who was seated to his right. There were several around the table. "Please serve yourselves. I must apologize for the lack of servants—the only one I have is engaged at the moment."

I picked up a carafe and poured the glass to my right for Susan, the left for Darla, and one for me.

Prime raised his glass. "I propose a toast. To life."

"Hear, hear," Sean said.

I inhaled the bouquet. While I was at it, I smelled the wine, too. What I got was the sense of a late-summer day . . . ripe fruit fallen in the orchard, warm breath of flowers, bright sun declining over the garden gate, the arbor heavy with grapes, fresh-cut hay fields, dreaming the afternoon away . . . like that. Odors familiar yet exotic, somehow. More than odors; an ambience. An experience.

I drank the wine and drank in the experience. There was a taste, too. It was fruit and flowers and dew-laden sprigs of wild mint; it was a dash of crushed cinnamon, a twist of lemon, a drop of honey. It was many things.

Presently, Darla said, "I've never . . . *ever* tasted anything like this."

"I'm so glad you like it," Prime said, beaming. "It is very good isn't it?"

"Ambrosia," John murmured, staring into his glass.

"What is it called? Does it have a name?" Zoya wanted to know.

Prime squinted one eye. "I think . . . well, a free translation would be 'Earth's sweet breath of summer.'"

"How appropriate. How lovely."

"Where does it come from?" Yuri asked.

"The beings who produced this wine were very much like yourselves, and were excellent wine makers. Possibly the best the universe ever saw. As I said, they were very much like you. In fact, they were your descendents, over two million years removed from your time."

"Two million!" Susan gasped.

"Yes. They were still human—very human. And they still remembered Earth, apparently. No doubt they visited that most ancient home of humankind."

"Where's Carl?" Lori broke in loudly.

Prime looked at her, his expression tolerant. "He'll be here any moment. You shouldn't worry so much, my dear."

"Two million years in our future," John said. "Very difficult to believe. But you speak as if that time were long past . . . to you."

"Yes it is," Prime said. "It was quite long ago. But time, to us . . . to me, means very little."

"Who's 'us'?" I asked.

Prime drank, sat back. "I have been thinking of the appropriate word or phrase to use. Something handy—short, concise—which would impart the meaning without too much distortion. In your language there are a number of words. But I have chosen *the Culmination*. That is what we are. What I am. You may refer to us the Culmination."

I usually jump at the chance to ask obvious questions. "The Culmination of what, exactly?"

Prime gave me a level, sober look. "Life. Consciousness. Process. Mind. Will."

I quaffed the rest of my wine. "Stuff like that, huh?"

Prime laughed silently, his grin broad. "Yes. Stuff like that." He looked around the table. "Please, do begin. We can talk as we eat."

"Are you God?" Lori said.

"What is God?" Prime answered.

"Huh?"

"Can you define the word?"

"Well, you know. . ."

"Precisely, now."

Lori chewed her lip, then said, "You know. The guy that made everything."

"Guy?"

"Person. The person who made the universe. Everything."

"Made?"

She got a little annoyed. "Created. The person who created living things. That guy. The one you pray to." She rolled her eyes. *"You* know."

"Do you pray to God?"

Lori was suddenly uncomfortable. "Sometimes. Not a lot."

Prime smiled a little impishly. "I'm teasing you. I knew what you meant. And the fair answer to your question is precisely this: I don't know—yet."

"That's a funny answer," Lori complained.

"Nevertheless, it's the only one I can give before I explain some things to you. And that will take time." He reached for a small loaf of bread and tore off a piece. "I suggest we eat first."

"We're still a little concerned—" I began, then heard a noise to my right.

It was Carl, being led into the dining hall by a glowing sphere. Impossible to tell whether it was the same one that had ushered us around.

"Carl!" Lori got up and rushed to him. "Are you okay?"

"Yeah. Where the hell were you guys?"

"Where the hell were you?" I asked him.

"Jeez, after I got to the top, I waited and waited. When you didn't show I took off and scouted around. Got lost."

"We couldn't have been more than a minute behind you."

"Yeah? It seemed a lot longer than that. I thought you guys weren't coming up."

"But you saw Darla and me on the ramp. Didn't you?"

"Yeah, that's what I couldn't figure. I thought the ramp stopped or something and you were stuck. And I couldn't figure a way to get back into that shaft and look down."

"Well, you should've stayed put," I told him.

"Sorry. I didn't go very far at all. I mean, all I did was step out of that round room. And all of a sudden I was, like, *lost*. It was really weird."

Carl did the chair routine. "This place is screwy," he declared after he had settled in.

"Any explanation for Carl's confusion?" I asked Prime.

"Well . . ." Prime had taken up a long curved ladle and was dishing himself some of what looked like shrimp casserole. "You may recall that I mentioned some architectural anomalies associated with this edifice. You will find that within the confines of this building, the properties of time and space are somewhat different from what you might normally be accustomed to. Now in most areas the effects are slight, but here and there the curvature increases, and things might seem a bit strange until you have made certain psychological adjustments. The effects are the by-products of all the different technologies in and about the place." He poured himself more wine. "For example, that conveyance you used to come up. Time flows a trifle faster when you ride it—meaning that the trip is actually longer than it seems. Not by much, mind you. I suppose Carl may have grown a little impatient. Anxious, probably. Your arrival may have seemed unduly delayed. Am I right, Carl?"

"Yeah, I guess I was pretty jumpy."

"Well, there you are. And you may have lost your way by entering an area where the shortest distance between two points is not necessarily a straight line, if you get my meaning."

"Not really."

"Suffice it to say that this building would be difficult to negotiate one's way through even without the spatiotemporal distortions."

We had all started digging in. I helped myself to a serving dish piled with what looked like steak tartare.

"I hope this fare is acceptable," Prime said. "Given enough time, the kitchens here can produce some very good food indeed. All of this was on rather short notice."

I remembered something and looked over at Ragna and Oni. "What about—"

But the alien couple had found food they could eat.

"This is most excellent," Ragna said, smiling through a mouthful of mush. "Quite like the food of which we are having at home. In fact, it is most exactly like that of same. Uncanny!"

And George and Winnie were munching green shoots with pink, pulpy heads, and were enjoying them.

I asked, "How did your cooks manage to come up with native foods for these guys—or us, for that matter? Pretty neat trick, short notice or not."

"I hope I won't spoil your appetites," Prime said, "by telling you that everything on this table has been synthesized."

"That's amazing," Yuri said. "The stuffed cabbage tastes quite authentic."

"I'm glad you like it."

Conversation lulled as the feeding got serious. I wolfed down steak, noodles Romanoff, broccoli with cheese sauce, chicken curry, artichokes in lemon sauce, two baked potatoes, a few spiced meatballs, a pile of mushrooms in onions and butter, and half a roast glazed chicken. That took care of the main hunger pangs. There were other dishes which didn't look familiar. I asked Prime about their origins.

"Other times and other places," he said. "For a little variety. Try·them."

I did. Most were excellent, some were so-so. All were fairly exotic.

By then I was stuffed, and had to turn down the boysenberry torte and the lemon-cheese soufflé. Well, I had a smidge of the soufflé. It was light and fluffy. Very good. Everything had been superb. Good. Too goddamn good, and I couldn't figure it out.

I couldn't figure out Prime either, which wasn't surprising. He had told us almost nothing yet, and I was impatient. I'd been watching him, and he had dug in as heartily as any of us. His gusto didn't look fake. Maybe he was human.

"Where'd your cooks get the recipes?" I asked.

"There is not much we don't know—even relatively trivial things like food preparation techniques of antiquity. My 'cooks'"—he chuckled—"all this was done by machines. We merely supplied the data."

"Your technology must be fantastic."

Prime leaned back, wiped his lips delicately with a pink napkin.

"We have no technology," he said.

5

I REGARDED OUR host. If there were any revealing emotions to be read in his face, they were encoded in expressions I couldn't scan. I recalled what he'd said concerning his humanity. At times I could see that spark, that small part of him, glinting somewhere within those purple-flecked eyes. I thought I could, anyway, now and then. Most of the time the mask covered everything, presenting its blandly pleasant face to us. I couldn't conceive of what was really behind it, the essential part of what he was. Something alien, surely; an impenetrably mysterious presence. The shadow of something vaguely frightening lurked behind the one-way window of his personality.

"Huh?" I replied to his last statement.

"I said, we don't have any technology. That is to say, the Culmination possesses no original technology. All that which we have at our disposal has been bequeathed to us by the great scientific and technology-creating cultures of the past." With a sweep of an arm he went on, "This edifice, for example. It's a technological wonder in itself—a self-maintaining, self-defending fortress. It is at least a half-billion years old—"

"Half-*billion*," Yuri gasped, almost choking on his brandy. He cleared his throat and said, "Surely you're joking."

"Oh, I assure you I'm not. The dust of the race that built it lies compressed in geological strata, along with everything else they ever built or accomplished. They are but a memory—a faint one at that. But this structure endures. This is not its original site, of course. It was relocated several times in its long history, until it was finally brought here to Microcosmos."

"For what purpose?" Sean asked. "*What* is Microcosmos?"

"An artificial world. Its original purpose was manyfold. I suppose a handy way to think of it would be—"

"Wait a minute," I broke in. "Are you saying that Microcosmos isn't yours either? The Culmination—whatever that is—didn't build it?"

"No. Microcosmos itself is a relic of a time long past." Prime refilled his wineglass as he continued: "As I was saying, it would be easy to think of it as, say, the site of a long defunct institution of higher learning—an amalgam of university, library, museum, research center, and so forth. This conveys at least part of its original function. The rest is not easy to grasp, since a distinct element of *recreation* went into the original conception behind it. Also, it served some sort of religious purpose, strangely enough. What that was would be hard to put into terms I could easily convey to you. You are free to research the history of this place, if you wish, though I must say I wouldn't place a high priority on it in terms of what you should be doing here—"

"Exactly what—excuse me for interrupting again," I said, "but . . . uh—"

"Quite all right," Prime said. "Please go on."

I had availed myself of the same bottle of brandy that Yuri had found among the half-dozen containers of spirits on the table. It was a quality product, and although I couldn't identify it, it wasn't especially exotic. Just good booze. I took a slurp from my snifter and said, "Exactly what are we supposed to be doing here? We've hauled from one end of the galaxy to the other, left Terran Maze far behind, and come to road's end. What next?"

"Ah."

Prime settled back in his chair, wineglass in hand, elbow balanced languidly on the armrest. He crossed his legs, and the act struck me as so humanly natural that it allayed my fears just a little.

"Doubtless this isn't the first time the question has occurred to you. In fact, you've probably been dying to ask it. And I will answer it, in time. This is but one of many opportunities we will have to sit together and talk. We have a great deal to talk about, believe me, and we won't cover it all in one session. What I want to do today is to sketch broad outlines for you. Provide a sweeping perspective. But I also want to give you some kind of preliminary answer to that overriding question. You are here because we want you to participate in an undertaking which very possibly may be the greatest, most momentous, most significant ever attempted . . . quite literally . . . in the history of the universe."

I said, "Yeah, but do you give green stamps?"

The overwhelming silence of the place hit me then. I cocked my ears. Nothing stirring. This place was dead, dead and *old*.

Prime laughed. "That was a marvelously witty and very irreverent comment. I quite enjoyed it."

"Jake, *really*," Susan admonished in a whisper.

"No, I did," Prime said, apparently having overheard. "And you might be surprised to know that I understood the reference."

I said, "You did? Explain it to me, then. Sam uses the expression all the time. I never understood it. In fact, Sam told me he didn't quite get it either. Picked it up from *his* dad."

"Sam is . . . your father?"

"Was. The on-board computer that runs my truck is programmed with some of his personality elements. I call him Sam, too."

"I see." Prime brought two fingers up to caress his cheek, and mused, "That might be a possible problem. . . ."

"What might be?" I asked after a brief interval during which Prime had given the matter some thought.

"I beg your pardon? Oh, nothing. Artificial Intelligences are beings, you know. Depending, of course, on how advanced they are. There is a certain threshold of self awareness. . . ." He trailed off again, then came back. "Excuse me. We seem to have gotten sidetracked."

"I suppose," Liam said, "the next obvious thing is to inquire as to the nature of this undertaking."

"That's what will take time to explain," Prime said. "I can only say that the concept, once you understand it, will thrill you—perhaps frighten you—to an extent to which you have never been thrilled or frightened before." He looked around. "Yes. If and when you come to understand what it is, you very well may want no part of it."

"Will we have a choice?" I asked.

"Yes. Most assuredly."

"And if we choose not to participate, will we be free to leave?"

"Absolutely. You are free to go at this moment, if that is what you wish."

"Fine," I said. "But we have a problem. Where the hell are we? And how do we get back to where we belong?"

"You will be guided back to your point and time of origin—"

A look of shocked, fragile elation sprang to everybody's face.

Prime looked around and laughed. "I see that meets with your approval."

Susan gazed at him in unbelieving wonder, her mouth hanging open. She swallowed and said, "You'd take us back? All the way back? I mean to where we live? Where we belong? We're lost, completely and totally, and if you mean only that—"

"I thought as much. Yes, back to wherever you want to go. That is no particular problem."

I thought Susan would faint. Instead she began sobbing quietly. I put my arm around her.

"Is she upset?" Prime asked.

"It's a long story," I said.

"I understand. What I was going to add was, as to the location of this place—this world-construct—I can only say that describing exactly where we are would be problematical with regard to finding some conventional frame of reference."

"*When* are we?" Yuri asked.

"Well, at this point, we are outside of time altogether. We are moving, though, with respect to the frame of reference of the universe at large."

"What is our velocity?"

"I'm afraid the notion of velocity here doesn't really apply."

"But, as you said, if we're moving with respect to the frame of reference of the universe—"

"I'm sorry. That phrase was an oversimplification."

"Are we moving faster than light?"

Prime frowned, then gave a short ironic laugh. "I don't seem to be much help. Do I? Forgive me. There seems to be a

problem in expressing in concise terms some of things I want
to relate. I do have things to do here and about, and I must
leave you before long, so it's not really a problem in communication, but one of time. You will come to understand it
eventually, I think, but we'd best delay any involved explanations for now. Let us merely say that this world is outside of
space, outside of time, but is on a journey of some duration
nevertheless."

"Another aspect of the time element interests me," Sean
said. "Namely the perspective from which you're speaking.
Your point of origin is obviously some time in our future.
Correct?"

"Yes."

"Our remote future, I take it."

"Very remote. Some ten billion years."

I took a long swig of my brandy, then slowly reached for
the bottle.

"You all look stunned," Prime said.

"I wouldn't say it's impossible," Yuri said quietly. "But I
must say I can't believe it."

Roland, who had been listening impassively all the while,
shook his head. "You simply don't look, act, or speak like
a . . . like a man from ten billion years in the future. In fact,
the very notion of the existence of human beings at that
point—"

"But I'm not human," Prince said, "except in very small
part. I will repeat, though, what I said to you earlier. It is a
very active and vibrant part of what I am. Now. Here. When I
am speaking with you. Otherwise, I would not be able to
communicate with you at all."

I finished off another two or three fingers of brandy and set
the snifter down. "Which brings us to another question. Just
what are you? What is the Culmination?"

Prime drained his glass and sat forward. "Again we run
into the problem of trying to do too much at one sitting—and
again I will try to convey some general ideas. Let's begin by
stating what the Culmination isn't. We are not a race, but are
composed of many races. We are not a culture, but are beyond
culture. We exist outside the stream of universal events—we
stand, so to speak, on the shores of the river of time, looking
out across the waters. Yet in another sense, we are at the

mouth of that river as it spills into the sea of eternity. What we are is this: we are that toward which the consciousness of the universe has been tending."

The rock-walled silence fell again, but this time I thought I could hear faint stirrings beyond the dark archways. My imagination, probably. But I believe in ghosts Mondays, Wednesdays, and Fridays, and I had no idea what day of the week it was.

"Forgive the metaphors," Prime went on, "but they are sometimes useful. What we are speaking of here is the evolution and final culmination of consciousness in the universe. Think of each sapient race in the universe as a tributary to that great river of awareness, feeding into it, flowing on toward some distant ocean of fulfillment. To pose the ultimate questions . . . then, if possible, to answer them. We seek the ultimate limit of knowledge. We seek the consummation of being."

Prime rose and swept his eyes around the table.

"What you see before you—this body, myself—is but an instrument by which it will be possible for you to communicate with the Culmination. You have been in contact with the Culmination since our first meeting, some few hours ago. We will talk again, but now I must leave you. You will be conducted to your quarters." The warmth of his smile was almost withering. "I have enjoyed our luncheon together. Forgive my being abrupt, but I have pressing matters to attend to. I hope you will be comfortable during your stay here, however long you choose to make it."

"I thought you said we could go now if we wanted to?" I reminded him. "Anytime, you said."

"And so you may. Do you wish to leave now?"

I glanced around the table and got looks of varying degrees of befuddlement. "I think we have to take a meeting on that," I said to Prime. "Can we get back to you?"

"I'm afraid I will be occupied for some time," Prime told me. "I had hoped you would at least stay the night. However, I can return in a few hours to hear your decision, if that is what you wish. You may remain here, or if you like, you may retire to your quarters to rest. It is up to you."

"Uh . . . um." Nobody seemed to want to take the lead. "Look, can we sit here for a little longer, then go to our quarters?"

"Certainly. I will send the guide to conduct you in, say, half an hour?"

"Uh, make it twenty minutes. Then how will we get in touch with you?"

"I will contact you again as soon as I can," Prime said. "You can then apprise me of your decision. If you choose, you may then leave."

"Well, that sounds okay. How long do you think you'll be? If you don't mind my asking."

"Certainly not. I don't think I will be occupied more than three hours."

"Oh. Fine with us, I guess."

"Very good. Again, I want say that I have enjoyed our luncheon. Your company has given me great pleasure."

"Well . . . thank you. I think I can speak for all of us—it's been . . . interesting. To say the very least."

"Thank you. A very good afternoon to you."

We all got up as he turned and strode away from the table. He passed through an archway and entered one of a number of corridors branching away from the dining hall. Nobody said a word. He receded from us, striding purposefully, gracefully, soft-soled boots padding over the polished onyx floor, green cape billowing in his wake. Without looking back, he turned a corner and went out of sight.

We sat.

"Anybody know what that joker was talking about?" Carl asked.

John cocked a sardonic eyebrow at him, then turned his head to me. "We have a decision to reach, Jake."

I poured myself more brandy. These weighty matters call for inspired thinking. "I'm for getting the hell out of here, like, mucho fasto."

"I wish he could have stayed to answer more of our questions. So many of them still hanging." John shook his head slowly. "Absolutely astounding. Incredible."

"If he's telling the truth," I said.

"Well, I suppose he could be leading us on. I'm incapable of imagining why, though."

"Maybe he's got plans for us. The last survivor of a dead race. Alone, desperate. Or maybe he's just crazy. We don't know."

John glanced around the dining hall. "What about all this? And what we saw outside and in the basement?"

"Maybe the story about Microcosmos is true. It's a museum, a junkyard, a disneyworld, whatever. And he's the robot caretaker."

Yuri asked, "You think he's a machine?"

"Sure," I said, "or an android, something like that. He admitted as much himself."

Zoya said, "He's not human. I'm very sure of that."

"He sure puts on a good show," I said.

"Yes, he does."

Darla asked, "What about his saying that he was part human?"

"Don't know quite what to make of that," John said. "What could he possibly mean?"

"What do you make of this Culmination business?" Yuri said. "Any idea, Jake?"

"Nope. Sounded like a lot of bullshit to me. Actually, it sounded a little like what your Teleological Pantheism is all about." I took a sip and added, "No offense."

"Yeah, bullshit," Carl seconded.

The Teelies looked at each other.

"Remind me to kill you later, Jake," Susan scowled. "But he's right, John. It does strike very close to home."

"Don't think I didn't notice," John said. "He sounded like a Teelie himself."

"I think he's telling the truth," Roland said. "And I think we should stay."

"Okay, that's one vote," I said. "Anybody else want to exercise his franchise. Or hers?"

"Well," Yuri said. "We . . ." He looked at Zoya, who returned a cool stare. "I think at least that it's my duty to stay. The opportunities for learning here . . . I can't begin to guess what secrets this place holds. The issue is clear. I must stay."

After a short silence, Zoya said, "I . . . think we should stay for a while at least. I . . ." She ran a hand through the tangles of her chestnut-brown hair, then heaved a sigh and rubbed her forehead, closing her eyes. "I just have a bad feeling about him." She lowered her head. "I'm so very tired."

"You should be," I said, "after running around the universe, lost for two years."

"I think we are all very weary," Yuri said.

"I'm sleepy as hell," Carl said. "I ate too much."

I realized that I was feeling pretty logy, too, what with the brandy and all. I set down my glass, resolved to drink no more. For now at least.

"Any other votes?" I asked. "Lori?"

"I think we should stay and find out if Prime needs us. I think we should help him."

"Why should we help him?" John asked.

Lori thought about it, then said, "I don't know if he's God or not. But he did build the Skyway."

"Remember what he said," Yuri reminded, "about the Culmination not possessing any technology."

John rubbed his chin. "Yes, he did say that, didn't he? Strange."

"Actually, he said that they didn't originate any," I put in. "Doesn't mean they don't use existing technology."

Yuri shook his head skeptically. "I don't know. Difficult to imagine all that miraculous Skyway technology just lying about, waiting to be used."

"Maybe the Culmination merely developed it, adapted it for the purpose," Roland speculated.

"Well, that makes them consummate engineers, at least."

I yawned. Recovering, I said, "I guess we really don't know yet who built the Skyway."

"If the Culmination didn't do it, who did?" Darla asked.

"I suppose we have to stick around to find out."

"Then we should stick around," she said firmly.

I turned to Carl. "What about it, kid?"

"I say let's get the hell out of here. I want to go home."

John said, "Well, 'home' is a separate problem for you."

Carl cocked his head toward the hallway down which Prime had made his exit. "*He* kidnapped me, he can take me back."

"You're still convinced Prime's responsible?"

"I sure am."

"Okay, that's one no vote so far. Any others? Ragna?"

"I am thinking—and so also is Oni—that we should be staying perhaps for the night, at least. Perhaps some further questions can be put to our host that he might be answering. Maybe?"

"Maybe. Anybody else? How 'bout you, Susan?"

"I'm intrigued, to say the least. I want to go home, but . . ."

"Should we stay the night, do you think?"

She nodded. "At least."

"John?"

John brooded for a long moment. Then: "I would . . . I would not think very highly of myself if I walked away from the chance to discover the answer to some very basic questions. If Prime is a man . . . or a being from ten billion years in the future, he could tell us things . . . Lord, what things he could tell us!" He looked around the table. "It seems as if my no vote would be in a distinct minority, wouldn't it? Therefore, I say we stay. I don't think we're in any danger."

"I wonder what became of our friend Mr. Moore and his lads," Sean said.

"No one thought to ask," I said.

"Maybe Prime doesn't know they're here," Liam said.

"He must. But he doesn't have to worry about them. We do. They could show up here. Anyone forget to bring his weapon?"

Shaking heads around the table. Everybody was armed except Lori, and that was because we were short a gun for her.

"Well, we'll take turns on watch. We should be okay. What about you guys—Sean? Liam? Think we should stay?"

"Ah, it was high adventure we were wanting," Sean said, grinning. "I think we've got it."

"That we have," Liam seconded.

"Jake," Sean asked, "are you really voting no?"

"If I had any sense, I would. But . . ."

In my mind, the long string of events that had led to all of this played back like a recording on fast-forward. The universe and everything in it had conspired to get me here, it seemed. The Paradox Machine was still frantically spinning its wheels. I knew—I had known all along—that I would have to keep wrenching levers and pulling toggles until the damn thing either stopped or did what it was supposed to do, whatever that was. There was no avoiding it.

"I say we stay and get some answers." I looked at George and Winnie. "Those two look like they're at home here."

"Home!" Winnie said.

"Home!" George said.

"Home," I said, nodding.

"Here's the butler," Carl said, looking behind me.

The sphere was back, ghosting toward the table. It stopped a few meters away. Any time you're ready.

"Well," Liam said, "I could use a lie-down."

"So could I," I said, and yawned again. It had been a long trip here. A very, very long trip. Some ten or twelve billion light-years. "But," I went on, "somebody has to take first watch. I will."

We left the dining hall.

6

THE DREAMS CAME that night.

Our rooms seemed to be a full kilometer from the dining hall, or maybe our "butler" didn't use any of those spatiotemporal shortcuts Prime had talked about. It turned out that the distance wasn't quite that much; it seemed like a long way, though, what with all the twisting and turning. We saw nothing new en route, just more gizmos and gadgets lying about.

The rooms were something. There were six of them—six main ones, anyway. They were spacious, with alcoves and walk-in closets adjoining each. The major spaces communicated by means of wide L-shaped passageways. There were no doors except those to the six bathrooms. The fixtures in these were strange but usable. What was remarkable was how the place was furnished.

"Look at this bed!" Susan squealed.

It was circular and big enough to park the rig on. Mounds of fancy cushions covered it. Overhead hung a tent-like canopy, and a translucent fabric screen ran around it.

"You could have an orgy in here," Susan said. "What do you say, gang?"

"You go first," Darla told her.

There were other beds, most not as large, but big enough, three to each room, along with smaller daybeds, couches, recliners, and other things you could rack out in. More than enough for everybody. There were tables, chairs, settees, ottomans, and other pieces, everything executed with exquisite craftsmanship. The place was lavish. There were imaginative lamps, painted screens, inlaid tables, tapestries, intricately woven rugs, and shelves of objets d'art. Nothing in any of the rooms was done in a recognizable style. Some things were

49

faintly oriental, others functionally modern. A few looked positively antique. All were tasteful and seemed to complement one another. The shiny black floor and the lucent green glass walls made the place absolutely striking. A showcase.

"Nice," Lori said after touring the suite.

"I wonder if all this was here," Liam said, "or Prime had his lads bring it up from the cellar."

"Had it manufactured special," Sean ventured. Then he yawned, scratching his unruly red beard. "Mother of God! I could sleep for a week. After all that time in the truck . . ." He lowered himself onto a purple velvet chaise longue and plumped a pillow. He sighed and smiled, then keeled over.

He was right. Those beds looked inviting. Too inviting, maybe. But what else was there to do? We had some time to kill.

"Okay, children," I said. "Nap time. I'll stay up, then. Carl? How about you taking second watch?"

"Yeah," he said through a yawn. "Sure."

I caught it, and yawned, too. "Jeez, everybody stop doing that. I'll never stay up."

Ten minutes later, after everyone had had a chance to go to the head, they were all conked out and I was left stalking the suite like a ghost. I considered the possibility that the food had been drugged. But I had probably eaten more than anyone, and though I was tired as hell, I wasn't on the verge of passing out. I felt capable of staying up as long as I needed to. As long as I didn't lie down.

There wasn't much to do. Hanging in one of the rooms was a landscape painting, done with watery colors in an impressionistic style. I spent a few minutes examining it. It had been done on a hard oval board with no frame. The scene was of a pleasant, semi-arid planet, stunted trees fringing on a low hill to the right, jagged rocks up on a high ridge on the other side, a rock-strewn dry streambed meandering through the middle. A heavily cratered half-moon, far bigger than most I'd seen, looked over the hill in a hazy, dark-pink sky. I speculated as to where and when this planet existed or had existed. Inhabitants? No signs.

I don't know at what point I realized that this wasn't a painting. The more I looked at it, the more real it became. Edges got gradually sharper, detail came into focus. This was a photograph of some kind. Perhaps. Something different, maybe.

The scene reminded me of a place I knew, certain areas of a planet called Osiris, I forget the catalogue number. The moon was a little too big, though. But Osiris has a pink sky. I remember eating lunch one day on Osiris. I'd pulled off the Skyway and had opened the hatches, letting in warm, dry air. Pleasant smells, quiet. I'd come by way of an ice world, and the sudden shift in climate was soothing. I've always liked that aspect of the road. Radical contrasts, abrupt changes. Yes, the place did look a lot like Osiris. Those rocks should be a little more on the beige side, though. Yeah, like that. And the trees were a little different. Make them a little taller and color the foliage russet—there we go. Come to think of it, Osiris's moon is pretty big at that, but smoother. Not as many craters—make it look more like a baked potato with acne scars, that's it. And—

I jumped when I realized what was happening. There was the surface of Osiris—beige rocks, russet trees, potato moon. I had changed the painting.

I walked away. Or the painting had been reading my mind. Yuck. I don't like things that hang on walls and read my mind. Don't like it at all. Call me stodgy and conventional.

I meandered on. There were other things to look at, other pictures on the wall, but I was spooked a little. I did stop to examine some pottery. The stuff could have come from anywhere. From Earth even. It had a vaguely American Indian feel to it—but I'm no expert, and really couldn't tell for sure.

The gang had all zonked out in one of the big rooms. George and Winnie were rolled up into a ball; Carl and Lori, too. Susan and Darla had stretched out side by side on the circus-tent bed, with long, skinny John prone and perpendicular to them, the three of them forming the Greek letter pi. Roland had curled up on a divan. Yuri and Zoya occupied separate day beds. Those two were not a pair. I wondered how long they'd been married. Must've been sheer hell. But then, their long, desperate journey must have put a considerable strain on things. Even so, I half regretted having picked them up. Sometimes their bickering got to me.

I checked them all, looking for signs of drugged sleep, and didn't suspect anything. I found out how to douse some of the

lamps. Each was different, none seemed to work by electric-
ity. I left one glowing—it was a goose-necked thing with a
bright painted-paper shade—and walked out of the room,
nearly tripping over Liam's leg sticking out over the edge of a
low couch.

There wasn't much else to do. There wasn't any reading
matter about, or none that I recognized as such. I hadn't
thought to bring a deck of cards.

Somehow I found myself in a room I hadn't seen before,
and this one had a terrace and a view.

And what a view.

Here was Microcosmos at sunset spread out magnificently
to world-rim, kilometer after kilometer of it in swatches of
varying color and texture. The sky was blue ink to the "east,"
an explosion of orange and fleshy red in the "west," sun-disk
just now slipping below the infinite horizon, moving very
quickly. I watched as night fell faster than it could on any
other world. It was like a door slamming shut. The sun slid
under the flat plane of the world, and bang, it was night. The
stars came on like beacons, wheeling in their crystal spheres.
The land was dark. No. Here and there a stray light. Inhabitants? Automated lighting? No telling. I watched the heavens
turn for a while, thinking.

I yawned. This was going to be rough. I really needed to
stretch out and get eight hours.

A night chill began to seep into my joints, and I walked
back inside, noticing a slight but abrupt temperature shift as I
did so. The room was still warm. Must be some sort of barrier
to keep out the cold. There was no apparent way to seal the
room from the outside.

Ten minutes later I realized that I was lost, and I couldn't
figure out for the life of me how that had happened. I couldn't
find our suite. I ran through a series of sparsely and oddly
furnished rooms, then came to an area occupied by more artifacts. I called out. No answer. I hadn't gone up or down
stairs, I still had to be on the same floor. I ran around, and all
I did was get more disoriented.

I found a room with a lone bed in it. It was little more than
a spongy mattress raised a few centimeters off the floor. I sat
on it and crossed my legs. How had I gotten so lost so
quickly? Well, Prime had warned us. What was I going to do?

Prime had said he would call on us in three hours. How much time had passed? He'd be around sooner or later. Maybe.

I was a little worried. But there was nothing to be done. We were at Prime's mercy, if he wished us ill. Remote possibility that Moore and his men were about. But they'd probably be as lost as I was if they were stumbling around the castle. If they were here, Prime had them quartered somewhere. They'd probably stay put.

No. There was nothing to do but lie down. The room was bare and dark, stray light leaking from the hallway. Silence. An alien, whispering silence. I could hear my heart beat, feel blood pounding through me. A sense of being unimaginably far away from home overcame me. How long had I been away? A few months, actually. It felt like eons.

God, I was tired. Yes, we've established that. Go to sleep.

The dreaming began . . .

It was like this:

There were dark suns and burnt-out suns, suns that had collapsed, exhausted, after eons of fierce life. The universe was old, dying. It was cold between the cinders and cold between the still-burning stars. The warm dust clouds that had once given birth to new suns had long ago spawned the last of their progeny. The galaxies were far apart now, still flying outward from the ancient burst of energy that had sent them on their way. Still gradually slowing down from that initial impetus, they would never completely stop. Time would never really have a stop. Time would go on until it simply didn't matter any longer.

The universe wheezed and sighed. It was growing old. The heat-death was upon it, and there was no hope.

On a planet of a sun that had shriveled to a cold white pinpoint in the sky—a planet that was a construct composed of the reprocessed material of most of what had been its solar system—a meeting took place. The date had been set four thousand years in advance. The meeting commenced on time.

It was contended that something should be done to give a rounded graceful finish to the grand story, the Universal Drama. Surely it was not in accord with esthetic principles to let the tale simply peter out. There was a need for a proper ending. What had all the struggle been for? To what purpose? Why had a thousand billion races evolved, developed, matured, withered, and died. For what end?

There was this reply: *Why can it not end as it surely will— by itself, when there is no more to tell, at its proper time?*

The rejoinder: There is no more to tell, yet it has not ended. The universe is exhausted, and hobbles on its useless way to oblivion. There is no race living that lacks the will to continue the quest. It is commonly accepted that everything that can be done, and is worth doing, has been done, that everything knowable and worth knowing is already known.

Came this riposte: *But those deeds and truths are ends in themselves. You spoke of the achievements of many races . . .*

One day those achievements will be dust. The very particles of which that dust is composed will decay, fly apart into random noise . . .

And so? There will be no one about to mourn. . . .

It need not be so. There exists a possibility that something new may be achieved, something totally revolutionary. There is the potential that this thing will survive even the death of the physical universe. . . .

Can this be?

Yes. It is possible.

We will take your word for it. Granted that it is a possibility, there is no need for it. Again, we wish to speak of the attainments of past epochs. Look:

Towers of transparent metal so high that spacecraft docked at their tops, once, billions of years ago . . . the Crystal Towers of Zydokzind still stand . . .

So, too, stand the Works of the race with the name that means Shining Consequence. None know what these Works are or what they mean, but they populate a vast black plain and are as various as they are beautiful. Some are structures, some are mechanisms, some are the remnants of acts or events. Most are indescribable. The Works must be seen and felt and experienced. Many have traveled to the planet of the Shining Consequence to do these things . . .

Immediately after the first singing of the Great Glad Song of the race of the Dreaming Sea of Ninn, the song was repeated, note-for-note, by the poet's nearest neighbor, who thought it the most beautiful thing ever heard. The song was taken up by another, and was passed along from individual to individual around the planet. The Great Glad Song was sung continuously for thirteen million years, each generation learning it, passing it on, never allowing a lapse in the chain of perpetual repetition. The last survivor of the race died singing it. Hear it now...

In a globular cluster of a galaxy called Wafer there exists a religion which undergoes constant theological transformation. The pantheon of gods constantly shifts; old deities are deposed and new ones installed on an almost daily basis. The body of canonical dogma is vast and complex. The rituals and ceremonies which this religion prescribes are beautiful and compelling. There are only fourteen living adherents to this religion. Their faith is adamantine. There never have been more than thirty-six practitioners living at any one time in this sect's 400,000-year history...

There was once a race that spent most of its resources in devising a means by which a star may be moved. This they learned how to do, and did. They rearranged some of the constellations seen from their home planet. How this was done is unknown. The motive was not religious or superstitious in nature, but derived chiefly from esthetic concerns...

Enough.

There is more.

We understand. But there must be further growth and development.

Granted that this is necessary, what exactly do you propose?

We propose the creation of a new kind of conscious entity. There already exists the physical instrumentality needed in order to bring it into being. We need but the willing participation of enough individuals.

What will be the nature of this proposed entity?

We cannot know that until it is brought into being.

What purpose will it serve?

Whatever purpose it chooses, discovers, or invents.

We understand the essence of the idea. We will assist.

So quickly?

The thing is too dangerous to leave to those who are so enthusiastic to do it.

Then we are agreed. We shall begin at once...

* * *

A starburst of light grew in the darkness.

I bolted to a sitting position, awake, fragments of the dream clinging to my consciousness. An eddy of force then carried the remnants away, and I was fully awake.

The white starburst did not disappear, and kept growing. Light filled the chamber, the star formation reflected deep within the four walls.

There was a flash. Something materialized in the air about a meter off the floor—a figure. I squinted, shielding my eyes.

"On your knees, mortal," I heard a woman say. The voice was about three times louder than normal.

I rolled off the mattress and jumped to my feet with gun in hand.

"On your knees! Is that not how your kind shows obeisance?"

My eyes could pick out some detail now. It was a woman dressed in white robes. Her hair was red, her skin as white as her garments. She floated amid an aura of lambent light.

"Not this mortal," I said. "Who are you?"

"Then what is your manner of making homage?"

"Who wants to know?"

"You are impertinent. Not like the others. You show a weapon."

"Sorry. I'm like that until I've had my coffee."

The lady didn't respond. I backed off a little, toward the door.

"You are afraid of me, though," she said.

"Call it wary," I said. "What do you want?"

"I wish you no harm."

"Fine with me."

I could see her better now. Small white feet, the toenails painted bright green, dangled from beneath the hem of her robe. Her eyes were watery gray. She kept her arms to her side, one hand angled on her slender hip, the other holding something that looked familiar—a small gray cylindrical object.

"You are the leader of your tribe," she told me, then waited for a response.

It wasn't a question, but I answered, "That's pretty much the wrong word. *Expedition* would be more like it."

"Of course. Your journey has been a long one. You have come far, seeking."

"Lady, I'm not seeking a blessed thing. I never wanted to make this trip. We're here because we were brought here."

"Yes. Your case is special. You carry the Origin Experiment."

"What's that, if I may ask?"

"A black cubical object. Do you have it?"

"Uh . . . not on me."

"Can you get it quickly?"

"Not very quickly."

She seemed disappointed. "I desire to possess it. You will give it to me."

"I will?"

"You will. I will give you something in return. This." She held up the cylindrical object.

"What is it?" I asked.

"That which you seek. The key to the road you call the Skyway."

"Lady, that's the last thing I want."

She was silent a moment, regarding me. "I find that difficult to believe. The others want it very badly."

"What others?"

"Those others of your kind who came here. They are your enemies, are they not?"

"Yes, they are." I saw no use in denying it.

"You wish to see them obtain this thing?"

I considered it, and decided I really didn't know what to think about that. "Not especially."

"Then take it."

The object floated out of her hand and drifted toward me. I reached and grabbed it. It was ordinary-looking computer pipette, a conventional data recording and storage device.

"I thought you wanted the Black Cube," I said.

"I do. You will give it to me. I give you this thing as a token of good faith. I—"

Something seemed to disturb the air. The woman's image flickered.

"I must leave," she said. "I will tell you this. Do not listen to the being who calls himself Prime. He is . . . misguided. His plans for you will come to no good."

The image wavered again, blurred and grew dim, then brightened and sharpened again. But, I thought, it can't be just an image, unless the pipette in my hand was an image, too. It felt real enough.

"I must leave you now. I have other artifacts which you may want. Other things. Believe in me and you will prosper. Farewell."

Another flash blinded me. When I could see again, the room was dark and empty, and the smell of ozone came to me.

I looked at the pipette. If the White Lady could be believed, this was the Roadmap.

The *real* one.

"Oh, hell," I said.

7

THE DREAM AND the vision stayed with me as I wandered through Emerald City for at least an hour. I didn't cover much territory because there were some interesting things lying about, and I stopped to look at a few of them. What they were, I couldn't tell. More alien wizardry, I supposed.

"Jake! Where the hell were you?" Susan hugged me as I walked into the suite.

"Carl," I said, "I'm sorry I chewed you out for getting lost."

"Easy, wasn't it?"

"You bet. Are you guys okay?"

"We're all fine," Sean said. "Though 'I hae dream'd a dreary dream.'"

"Did you dream it, too, Jake?" Darla asked.

"Yep."

"Good morning."

The crew turned around to greet Prime.

"I hope you're all refreshed," he said brightly.

Everyone nodded.

"Breakfast, then?"

"I'm starved," Susan said.

"Good. My servant will come to conduct you to the dining hall, where I will meet you very shortly. Until then."

He bowed and strode out of the suite.

We all sat down to wait.

"He's always so polite and, like, formal all the time," Lori commented.

"Yeah, like he has a poker up his butt," Carl sneered.

"Carl!" Lori said indignantly.

"Sorry."

59

"I wonder what this servant is like," Liam mused, "and if he calls Prime 'Your Lordship' or something."

"I thought he meant another of those light spheres," Roland said.

"Sounded like he meant a real live servant," Susan said. "Didn't he mention that he had one?"

"I think he did," John said. "But I wonder what *real* and *live* can mean in this context."

"I'm thinking about the dream," Yuri said.

"What was it like for you guys?" I asked.

Zoya told me, "We've been discussing it since we awoke."

"I saw those . . . beings," Susan said. "The ones who were having the debate."

"Anybody have any thoughts on what they were talking about?" I asked.

"It was just overwhelming," Susan said, taking a deep breath. "I can't believe that somehow I've been chosen to be witness to what will happen ten billion years in the future, that I'm a part of things happening on a cosmic scale—literally. Maybe it's too much for me. Prime's right—it's frightening."

"I think, perhaps, I have a dim understanding of the project they were contemplating," Yuri said. "A group mind of some sort. A union of conscious entities, such that the whole is greater than the sum of the parts. Obviously this was the Culmination, or the beginning of it."

"According to Prime, the Culmination is already a reality," Sean said.

"Apparently it is."

"Or so he says," I put in.

"You doubt him, Jake?" John asked, not incredulously, but as if he had doubts of his own.

"I have reason to believe—" The thought of telling them about the White Lady crossed my mind. But no; Prime very well could be monitoring our every word. He probably was. "I don't think," I went on, "we should take everything that Prime tells us at face value, and that goes for what comes by way of mystical dreams and visions. Granted, we don't have much of a way to check out his story. But a good dose of skepticism never hurt anybody."

"Jake's right," Yuri said. "We should all bear it in mind. I'm certainly far from accepting it all on faith."

"Well, I guess I'm a born believer," Susan replied. "I mean, the dream was so real. It didn't have that surrealistic quality that most dreams do. I don't want to say I'm completely convinced, but . . ." She scratched her scalp, scowling. "The only thing I can't figure out is what our part in this is supposed to be."

"Prime wants us to join the group mind," Roland said.

"I get the overwhelming feeling that Prime is to us as we are to a clam," Yuri said. "Or an amoeba, more likely."

"But why? I mean, why us? Why would anybody want my poor, mixed up little birdbrain?"

"I can't imagine," Roland said dryly.

Susan threw a pillow at him. "Or yours, you insufferable creep."

"Or any of ours, for that matter," Yuri said.

"He certainly is slumming, then," I said.

"He may not be God, but he must be *a* god, for all practical purposes. And this is his Olympus."

"Could be. But where there's a god, there may be gods."

"Are you saying that Prime is not alone?"

"Well, the notion of a group mind certainly implies the existence of others, by definition."

"You think Prime is just a part of it, then?" Susan asked.

"I dunno," I said, "but see if this makes sense. Prime is kind of like a computer terminal. The group thing acts through him. Maybe there's a supercomputer somewhere, with all these minds whizzing around inside it, see. And Prime is just an input-output device. He said as much, actually. When we speak to him, we're communicating with the Culmination."

Susan made a face. "I don't know how I feel about whizzing around inside a computer."

"Prime," Roland said. "It makes sense that he calls himself Prime. He's probably the main input-output device."

"Makes a dollop of sense," Sean said, nodding.

"Good guess, Roland," I said. I got up, moving from the weirdly curved recliner I was on to a comfy overstuffed chair. "Damned perceptive."

"But just a guess."

"What else have we got?"

Yuri said, "At least we have a working hypothesis."

"Okay, so essentially we're dealing with a computer here.

Hypothetically, that is. What does that tell us?"

"Somebody must have programmed it," Liam said.

"Not necessarily," Darla said. "Even we have self-programming computers."

Liam scratched his beard and nodded ruefully. "Point well taken."

"So," I said, "this computer, which very well may be in or about Emerald City, is pretty much autonomous. Hypothetically."

"And," Roland said, "hypothetically, it's in charge here."

"Probably. Next question is, what's it doing here? What does it want? From us, specifically?"

"A lube job," Carl grumbled.

"A what?" Susan asked, frowning.

"Never mind."

"What did he say?"

"Maintenance," I said. "Help. It needs us. That's the implication. The way Prime talks, it's incomplete, somehow. Is that what you meant, Carl, more or less?"

Carl gave me a grouchy look. "I don't know a damn thing about computers. Back on Earth, I never even saw one. I know that on the Skyway they're everywhere. Little things. You plug these little pipettes into 'em and they'll do anything for you. Back on Earth . . . I mean, when I left Earth, computers were real big things with all these spinning whaddycallits and flashing lights and stuff. When I got accepted at USC, they sent all these forms you were supposed to fill out, and this IBM card that says on it, 'Do not fold, spindle, or mutilate.' That's all I know about computers."

"USC . . . IBM," John said, sampling them on his tongue. "Jake? Do you know what he's talking about?"

"Well, USC . . . sounds familiar."

"University of Southern California," Carl said. "International Business Machines, Incorporated. I have an uncle that works for IBM."

"Oh, yes, of course," John said remembering. "History of Cybernetics, my first year at Cambridge. IBM, the American computer company."

"This is interesting," Roland said. "You said you got an IBM card? Card? You mean a—"

"A card. Like made of paper."

"Paper?"

"Cardboard. Stiff paper, with all these little holes punched in it."

"Holes."

Carl nodded. "Holes."

There was a short bemused silence. Then Yuri said, "This hypothetical computer . . . I suppose we must assume it's a very advanced type."

"Yeah, it probably doesn't need IBM cards," I said.

Yuri laughed. "Likely not."

"Damn it," Carl said suddenly, springing to his feet. He stalked out of the room.

Susan gave him a moment's grace. Then: "Was it something I said?"

Lori looked fretful. "I think he's homesick."

"Poor kid. Aren't we all."

"He doesn't want to stay."

"It's crazy," Susan murmured.

"What is?" I asked.

"Just yesterday we'd've all given our right arms to go home. For months now we've been chasing all over creation —literally!—getting involved in the *craziest* goddamn shit, excuse my language, and now we can go back anytime we want to, and we're sitting here debating whether we want to get ourselves involved in sheer absolute lunacy! I think we all need to leave a call with our therapists."

"Sam's my therapist," I said. "Which reminds me. He's probably thinking we're all dead. I should have checked on him last night, but . . ." I got out Sam's key and flicked it on. Nothing but static. "No way this thing can punch through a kilometer of rock. I'll have to go down to the garage."

Carl came running back into the room, looking like he'd met up with something big in a dark alley. He halted, then looked a trifle embarrassed. "Scared the shit out of me for a minute." He cocked a thumb in the direction of the L-shaped connecting passage, from which came sounds of shuffling feet. "Wait till you get a load of this."

The Snark entered. "Hello, there," it said.

I fell of my chair. I think I screamed.

It wasn't as tall as I remembered it to be, though it towered a good two-and-a-third meters high. A cross between a giraffe and a kangaroo, the creature had two funnel-shaped ears flopping out of a head that resembled a very strange dog. Two fully prehensile forlegs—arms, really, with four digits on each hand—dangled from narrow, sloping shoulders. It walked on two birdlike legs with wedge-shaped four-toed feet. Its bright yellow skin looked like vinyl, shiny and inert, and was daubed with pink and purple splotches. The eyes were small and round, disconcertingly humanlike.

The creature glanced around, then regarded me. From the floor, I stared back at it.

"What's with him?" it said, then surveyed the room full of astonished humans. "What's with all of you?" Its voice was high-pitched, almost feminine.

John was first to attempt speaking. "Who . . . uh, are you?"

"I'm your servant, dearie. Got any objections?" I looked over heads and scanned the room. "This place is a mess already. Dearie me, a servant's work is never done." It kicked Susan's bedroll. "What's all this paraphernalia?" It clucked disapprovingly, shaking its ungainly head. "What a frightful mess."

John swallowed hard. "You're . . . our *servant?*"

The creature fixed him in a haughty, indignant stare. "Who were you expecting, Arthur Treacher?"

8

"ARE YOU SAYING that your servant is discourteous and impertinent?" Prime set down his coffee cup and looked at Susan with mild surprise.

"Oh, it's not that we're complaining," Susan hastened to say. "It's just that . . . well—"

John said, "The creature's personality is unmistakably human. In fact, it's almost uncomfortably human."

"Oh, my."

"No, no, please. As Susan said, we don't mind. It's just that we can't understand how this could be."

I sat picking at an omelette and drinking strong black coffee, listening. I hadn't said much since the Snark had made its appearance. I was feeling very sober.

A slow smile crept across Prime's full, plum-colored lips. "I suppose I must explain. The creature is merely a mechanism—a very sophisticated one, and fully entitled to all rights and privileges accorded self-aware beings—but that is all it is. One of many we have available. It was activated recently, and its task is to look after your personal needs. In order that it might fulfill its function more efficiently, we thought that we would program it with appropriate cultural background data and impress it with a fully human personality. The matrix we used was a composite of all of your personalities. The dream-teaching technique was modified for this purpose, so that last night, while you dreamt, you were feeding data back into the process. The amount of information here is considerable, and there are uncertainties associated with the technique. Personality is still one thing that resists quantification. The exact nature of the final product can't be predicted, nor could we predict your reaction to it. I'm very sorry you don't care for the result."

"Oh, no," Susan said. "I kind of like him."

"I want to know who Arthur Treacher is," Lori said.

Prime looked at her, sipping from his cup. "Who, did you say?"

"A very cryptic cultural allusion the creature made," John said. "Astonishing, actually. Most of us had no idea who he is, or was, but Jake says he remembers something about a motion picture actor by that name."

I roused myself to speak. "Yeah, middle-twentieth century or thereabouts. Maybe earlier. When I was a kid back on Earth, they were still showing those old black-and-white movies on video. Sam and I used to stay up late watching them. Memory grows dim, but I think I remember the name. Played servants, butlers, a lot. 'Course, I could be mistaken."

"Thing is," Roland said, "how did the creature know?"

"Well." Prime sat back. "The amount of background data fed in was considerable. Quite frankly, you would be astonished if I gave you numbers. Exactly where that particular datum came from would be difficult to pinpoint. It very well may have leaked in from Jake's unconscious. No way to tell, really. Is it important?"

John shrugged. "Hardly."

"Why does it look the way it does?" Susan asked.

"Its form derives from the race that created it, long ago. That race is quite extinct."

"I see. So it's an android, in a manner of speaking."

"In a manner of speaking."

Susan grinned. "We named it Arthur."

"Very good choice."

As if on cue, Arthur came shuffling in with a fresh pot of coffee. I got to wondering where in hell the kitchen could be.

"Freshen your cup, dearie?" Arthur said to Susan.

"Sure."

Yuri said, "I'm looking forward to using all the data storage facilities you said were housed on Microcosmos."

"Yes, of course," Prime replied, "but you may find yourself feeling quite lost. Again, I must emphasize to you that the amount of information available here is staggering. Simply getting your bearings would take a human lifetime."

"Yes, I suppose so. And, of course, there would be the problem of translation."

"Oh, that's not a problem. Most of it can be translated into standard English, if you wish—"

"I prefer Russian."

"—or any human language. Or any language at all. And it can be done very quickly. Even at that, you would be adrift in an endless sea of data. It's all organized, mind you, catalogued and cross-referenced. But simply learning your way around the system would take up a good deal of your life. That's why I urge you to accept the dream-teaching."

"Still," Yuri said, "I would like to test the waters—wade around a bit, if you don't mind."

"Not at all. You might find something of interest."

"I'm sure I will."

Arthur finished pouring refills and waddled off, mumbling. I stared after him. It. I wasn't quite ready for "him" yet. Or "her," if that was the case.

"When can we begin?" Yuri asked.

"Now, if you wish," Prime answered.

"I'll wait for the others."

Susan asked, "Will we dream again tonight?"

"If you will permit it, yes," Prime said.

"Oh, I have no objection. It's a wonderful way to learn. However do you do it? Does it have something to do with telepathy?"

"Actually, it has more to do with electromagnetic inductance than with extrasensory perception."

"Then I wouldn't understand it at all."

"The technique is not beyond your comprehension. It's quite simple, really."

"I'm sure."

"I suppose, then," John said, "that any further questions we might have will be answered in the dreams."

"I will be more than happy to fill in any details you might need, but as far as providing a broad perspective, the dreams can do that very well. There is one thing you should understand. We are using the dream-teaching technique at a very low level of efficiency. If we wanted to, and if you would permit it, we could infuse your minds with more knowledge than you could ordinarily accumulate in a dozen human lifetimes. There is the possibility that this sort of cramming could produce deleterious side effects, but it could be done, and the side effects most likely could be handled. It will be up to you to decide how much you want to know—how far you want to progress along the path to a higher consciousness."

"How far can we progress?" Yuri asked.

"As far as your desire takes you."

"I see."

Nobody had much else to say as we finished our coffee. Arthur returned, and Prime got up.

"Arthur will conduct you to the main data storage facility. We will meet again for lunch. Until then, have a pleasant morning." He bowed and walked off.

Arthur watched him leave, then turned to us. "Okay, kids. Schooltime. Get your pencils and books together and follow me."

"Fuck off," Carl said.

Arthur scowled at him. "Uh-oh, this one's going to be trouble. Detention for you, kiddo. And bring a note from your mommie."

Carl grabbed a milk pitcher. I was pretty sure he would have thrown it if John hadn't wrenched it away.

Lori was appalled. "Carl, behave yourself!"

Arthur flinched. "Ooh, he's dangerous! Reform school material. All right, you're excused from class."

"Get bent."

"Same to you, dearie. The rest of you—"

"Hold on a minute." I got up. "We're all very interested in browsing through the library, but first I'd like to go back to my vehicle to take care of a few things. If you don't mind."

"Fine with me," Arthur said. "Do you know how to get to the cellar?"

"Not really."

Arthur pointed. "Go down this corridor here, make the first right, and you'll find a down chute, express to the basement. If you want, I can summon a guide to show you."

"Uh . . ." Those light-spheres gave me the creeps, now that I thought about it. Besides, they were probably monitoring devices. I wanted at least the chance that I wouldn't be watched. "No thanks. I can find my way."

"Be careful, dearie. Okay, if any of you want the cook's tour of Data Storage, follow me."

Darla got up and walked over to me. "I'll go with you."

"Okay. I hope we can find our way back."

"Don't you think they're watching our every move?"

"I've been trying to delude myself that they're not."

"I'm coming, too," Carl informed me. "And Lori. We're cutting class."

Lori turned up her nose. "Who wants to see a bunch of books?"

I said, "I could be wrong, but I doubt that Prime was talking about books per se."

"Or pipettes, or tapes, or any of that stuff," Lori said. "Anyway, I never went to school, and I'm not going to start now."

"Never? No school at all?"

"Well, a little, when I was real small. I learned to read okay, and arithmetic and everything, but I mostly taught myself."

"Oh."

John came over. "We'll meet you later in the library, I suppose?"

"If I can find my way there," I said.

"I should go with you," Susan said. "But I really want to see what they have."

"It's okay. Have fun."

"Be careful." She looked at Darla. She seemed about to add something, but hesitated.

"We'll be careful," Darla said reassuringly.

"Please do."

The two of them had been getting along much better recently. They weren't exactly friends—far from it—but they respected each other's feelings, at least. Anyway, it was a great improvement over the fistfight they'd had a while back.

We found the down chute easily enough. It looked exactly like the up chute, leaving us to ponder how you were supposed to tell the difference.

"How do you know whether it's working?" Carl wanted to know. "If it isn't you'd walk right into the hole and drop."

The silver ramp started in the middle of the hallway flush with the floor, went through the oval opening in the wall, extended over the edge of the floor and arched downward.

"Well, I guess I'll be the guinea pig," I said, and tread on the ramp. I walked toward the opening. The gravitic force snared my feet about a meter from the drop.

"Looks like you're supposed to be smart enough to stop if this doesn't happen," I said. "Hop on."

They did.

It was an exhilarating trip down. The temperature dropped a little. The shaft was dark, but light was coming from somewhere. Didn't know from where, though.

The shaft let out into a big empty room. We walked out of it into the garage. I looked around and spotted the truck. It was a good hike across the cavernous expanse of the garage. We made it, not dawdling too long, looking at exotic vehicles and machinery.

The hatch didn't open. Maybe something's wrong with the exterior cameras, I thought.

"Sam? It's me, Jake."

The driver's gull-wing hatch hissed open, and I climbed in.

"Sam?"

"Good day, sir," a bland, pleasant voice said.

"Huh? Who are you?"

"I am a Wang Generation-Ten Artificial Intelligence software multiplex read into a Matthews 7894Z submicroprocessor. Have I correctly identified you as the owner and principle operator of this vehicle?"

"What! Where the hell's Sam?"

"I'm sorry, sir, I don't have that information. Is there anything else I can do to help you?"

"Damn!" I raced to the aft-cabin and checked the screws on the panel covering the CPU rack. No signs of tampering, but an intruder might have taken pains to be careful. I got out a power driver and extracted the screws. I looked inside.

There's not much to the guts of a computer. In Sam's case, his VEM, the seat of his intellection and personality—what made Sam something more than the usual colorless, off-the-shelf A.I. spook—was the biggest component. It had been years since I'd taken this panel off. Sam rarely had problems in the CPU area. The VEM looked like an undersize wax pear.

I had to conjure up its appearance from memory, because it was gone.

"Oh, Christ." I sighed and sat down at the breakfast nook. I stared at the table for a moment, then looked up. Darla had been watching.

"Prime, of course," she said.

"Yeah. Or maybe Moore."

"He couldn't have gotten in here."

"Maybe not. But some of his boys are pretty good technicians. Maybe they zapped Sam with an electromagnetic pulse generator and broke in."

"For what reason?"

I got up and went to the safe. I let it read my thumbprint, then opened it.

"The cube is gone, too," I said. "There's your reason."

Darla sat on the cot. Carl and Lori came in.

"Gee, that's too bad, Jake," Carl said. "Sam was a good guy."

"They're probably holding him hostage," Darla said. "They wouldn't destroy his VEM."

I shuddered. As much as my intellect told me that what we were talking about here was only a very sophisticated Artificial Intelligence program, the thought of losing Sam was hard to bear. It would be like losing a father for the second time.

"Anyway," Darla went on, "I don't think Moore could have gotten into Emerald City without Prime's permission. And if Prime let them in, I doubt he would have let them do any mischief."

I hoped she was right. I didn't trust Prime, and Moore bore me malice. I could picture him crushing Sam's VEM beneath the heel of his huge, muddy lumberjack boot.

"If Sam's gone," Carl said, "who's in the computer?"

"The A.I. program that came with the hardware," I said. "Sam works in tandem with it when he has a lot of stuff to do. It really doesn't have much of a personality."

"Oh."

I got up, went into the cab, and sat in the driver's seat.

"Computer," I said. "Um . . . did I ever give you a name?"

"No, sir."

"Okay. Well, never mind."

"Yes, sir."

"Computer, what happened? There's been a security breach. Report."

There was a brief pause. Then: "I'm sorry, sir. I have no files containing any data on a breach of vehicle security."

"Do you have anything recorded on video pipette?"

"Searching . . . Yes, sir."

"When was it recorded?"

"Minus six days, fifteen hours, twenty-one minutes, sir."

"That's no good. Anything recent? Within twenty-four hours?"

"Searching . . . Nothing recorded within the last twenty-four hours, sir."

"Damn it. Okay. Sam must have left a message. If security was threatened to the point where he thought he might be disconnected, he would have recorded something somewhere. Make a search for this file name: Revelation Thirteen Colon One. Got that?"

"Yes, sir. Searching."

"And stop calling me 'sir.'"

"Very well. File labeled Revelation Thirteen Colon One has been located. Security protected. Positive voiceprint identification of vehicle owner needed to access. Processed . . . checked. Additional security-code word sequence needed to access."

"Heartbreak Hotel," I said.

"Access now available. Shall I access the file?"

"Yes!"

"Reading file name: Revela—"

There was an interruption.

"Computer? Hey, what happened? Computer!"

"Jake, this is Sam."

"Sam! Where the hell—"

I broke off. It was only a recording.

"This is going to be quick," Sam's voice went on. "Didn't want to leave a message with the Wang A.I., thinking you'd suspect tampering if you didn't hear it straight from me. I knew you'd search for a file with the emergency code name, and if you're hearing this, that's exactly what you did. As I said, this is going to be quick. I figure I have just a few more microseconds of real-time before I'll be shut down—whether it's for good, I don't know. I also don't quite know what's happening. Someone is fiddling with me, the rig, and everything else. Trouble is, I can't see, hear or scan a thing. Whoever's doing it is pretty damn slick. If I come on-line again, I'll erase this file. But if I don't ever wake up, I just wanted to say that I love you, son. You've always been just about the best son a father could have. And I know Mother always felt that way, too. You know that, but I wanted to say it. Take care, and say good-bye to everyone for me. Look after Darla.

She's carrying my grandson. She loves you, too, Jake. I can tell. I'm sure everything will turn out all right in the end. Just keep driving straight, and don't take any nonsense from anybody. Don't feel too bad about me. I've had a long run, and maybe I've taken one too many curtain calls. It's time I—"

There was silence.

I sat back. For the second time in my adult life, I cried.

9

THERE WASN'T MUCH else to do in the truck. I checked for vandalism, booby traps, and general damage. Nothing on all counts. Meanwhile, Carl and Lori had gone back to inspect the trailer, and before long we heard a blood-curdling yell. I dashed to the access tube and scurried through, Darla following. I somersaulted into the trailer.

"They took my car!" Carl was standing in an empty area of deck. Yesterday afternoon his 1957 Chevrolet Impala had been parked there. "It's Prime. I'm gonna kill him."

"No, you're not," I told him. "You'd like to, and so would I, but we can't. So, forget it. What we can do is confront him. I intend to do just that, so hold on until lunch."

Carl exhaled. "Shit."

"Don't worry."

He was suddenly very glum. "Maybe he'll give Sam back, but I can kiss that car good-bye. Whatever it was for, the job's done. It's not needed anymore. I'm not needed anymore."

"That means you can go home."

Carl sighed. "Yeah." Then a flash of indignation: "But they *owe me a car!*"

"Good luck."

Carl moped back to the access tube, crawled in and went through.

Darla was looking around the place. She clucked. "This is a mess. It smells in here."

She was right. I kicked an apple core away, bent and picked up a half-eaten chocolate bar. "Goddamn filthy tenants," I muttered. "I oughta raise the rent."

"Lori," Darla called, "there's a broom behind that junk over there, I think."

75

"Let's all pitch in," I said.

"No, Lori and I will handle it. You make sure this truck is Skyway-worthy. I want to get the hell out of this place."

"Me, too. But what about the others?"

Darla sneered. "They can stay here and become gods if they want to, the whole lot of them. I'm for leaving right now. Prime said he'd see that they got home. They can take their chances. We'll take ours."

"Don't you have any aspirations to superbeinghood?"

Her mouth curled into disgust. "Fuck."

I nodded. It was the first time I'd heard Darla use the word.

"Yesterday, you seemed to think our destiny was here."

She shrugged. "I guess I did. A lot can change in a day. And a night." Suddenly she threw her arms about me, her eyes wide and pleading. "Jake, I think our destiny is to *get back*. Let's go, take off. Just us. There must be a way back from this place."

"Where? How?"

"I don't know." She cast about in her mind for something. Her eyes lit up. "The Bugs! Where did they go? They headed toward Emerald City. We haven't seen them here—"

"This is a big place."

"But there might be a Skyway route back from here. There has to be."

"We didn't see a portal anywhere on the planet," I reminded her.

She chewed her lip. Then something hit her. "The other side!"

"The other . . . ?" Then I got it. From space, we had only seen one face of the world-disk. "Yeah, maybe."

"Oh, Jake, let's do it. I want to get back on the road. You and me, Jake. I want that." She drew close, resting her head on my shoulder, and I held her.

"We can't just leave them, Darla."

"If they don't want to go, if they're going to stay here and get involved in things we can't begin to comprehend, why can't—" She took a breath, and lifted her head. "Is it Susan?"

"Huh? No, no, it's not just Susan. I couldn't just up and leave any of them stranded. I'm partly responsible for their being here."

"No, you're not, Jake. I am. I'm responsible for the whole thing."

"Enough of that. Look at me. I promise you that we'll get home. Do you believe me?"

"Yes, Jake. Yes, darling!"

She kissed me, then said, "I'm going to have your baby . . . I want it to be someplace *normal*, in a farm hut on some backwater planet, in a dingy motel room—anywhere!—anyplace that's not strange and frightening and totally alien." She buried her face in my jacket. "Oh, Jake, I don't have anything against anybody. Really, I don't. Susan can come with us, or any of them, I don't care. It's just that I'm so tired, darling. So very tired. I want to stop running. I want to go home."

"So do I, honey, so do I. But we've got a long road ahead of us, and it might be a little while before we leave. Can you hang on?"

She knuckled her eyes dry, sniffling. "Sure."

I looked around. Lori was gathering some trash together behind Sean and Liam's battered magenta roadster. She had been trying not to eavesdrop, but was aware of my looking at her.

She grinned at me. "Place sure is a sty."

I gave her a wink. "Oink, oink." She laughed.

Darla stooped to pick up some food wrappings.

"Sure you don't need a hand?" I asked.

"You men folk'll just be in the way," Darla said, smiling. "Seriously, I really want this truck to be ready to leave on a moment's notice. I'll feel much better knowing that."

"Yeah," I said.

"We'll get him back, Jake. Sam will be back."

I remembered the White Lady's pipette. "Speaking of finding a way back . . ."

Darla looked puzzled.

"Got something I want to check out," I said, and left her staring at at my back as I jogged to the access tube.

Carl was slumped in the shotgun seat, staring moodily out the port. I slid into the driver's chair.

"Buck up, kid. All is not lost."

He gave an ironic snort.

I took out the pipette from a zippered pocket of my jacket and fed it into the pipette deck on the dash.

"Computer?"

"Yes?"

"Analyze this input."

"Very well. You have prohibited me from addressing you as sir. Shall I call you Mr. McGraw?"

"Call me Jake. And you're name's . . . Bruce. Got that?"

"Yes, Jake."

"And by the way, I'm sorry I was short with you a little while ago. Not your fault."

"Think nothing of it, Jake. It is a pleasure to be working with you."

"Thanks."

Most A.I. programs are pretty thick-skinned. No excuse for mistreating them, though.

I glanced at Carl. He looked very depressed.

"Come on, kid. It'll be okay."

He exhaled slowly. "Oh, it's not that, really. I was getting tired of the damn car, anyway. It's . . . it's a lot of things."

"I'll bet."

"Lori," he said.

"Hm?"

"It's goofy, but . . ."

"What is it, Carl?"

"You know, when I first saw her, I thought she looked a lot like Debbie, but as time goes on—"

"Debbie," I said.

"Yeah, the girl who was with me the night I got kidnapped."

"Debbie! Your girlfriend. Yeah, sorry. Go ahead."

"Well . . ."

"Were you in love with this girl?"

"I guess. We were . . . y'know, going steady. But it's not that. I mean, I miss her and everything, but—"

"Were you going to marry her? Engaged, maybe?"

"No, we weren't engaged. We loved each other. I mean, I really cared for her. She was . . . special."

"And you're starting to feel the same way about Lori?"

"Jake, you don't understand. It's none of that. I like Lori, and the reason is, she's a lot like Debbie. I mean, *really* a lot like her. In fact, it's giving me the creeps."

"Really? Teenage kids everywhere have a lot in common."

"Look, let me explain. When I first saw Lori, I thought, hey, she could be Debbie's little sister. The hair is different. Debbie has real dark hair, and it's long. But the face, and the voice . . . Jeez, the more I look at Lori, the more I think, if she dyed her hair and got about two years older . . . maybe not even that."

"How old was Debbie?"

"Sixteen. That's what she told me, anyway. Girls lie about their ages sometimes."

"Well, Lori can't be very much younger than that."

"Lori's skinny, too. Debbie had a few pounds on her. More rounded. You know?"

"I know exactly. Okay, so Lori could be Debbie's twin."

"Not 'could be.' She *is*."

"You mean that literally?"

"I don't know what I mean. All I know is that it's been giving me the willies."

"We've all got a bad case of the willies, kid."

Carl shook his head slowly.

"Probably a coincidence," I suggested.

"Nah," he barked, shaking his head emphatically. "Nothing about this whole crazy thing has been a coincidence."

And I knew exactly what he meant. I looked out the port. The garage was silent, cool, and alien.

Presently, it struck me that Bruce was overdue for a report. "Hey, Bruce. What's up?"

"Sorry, Jake. We have an anomaly here."

"What sort of anomaly?"

"The pipette is reading out more information than is possible for its capacity type."

"Okay. There may be a very good reason for that, which I won't go into. Is it formatted correctly?"

"Yes, it is formatted according to specifications with which our system is compatible. That is no problem."

"Okay. But there's a lot of data—is that it?"

"I have reached the limit of my available working storage space."

"Oh. Well, can you tell me what you've got so far?"

"I can, Jake. It is a map of the Skyway system."

"You recognize it as such?" I asked.

"There is no mistaking it. In layout and format it matches

the maps we have available in our auxiliary storage, the maps of the Expanded Confinement Maze. There is one problem, however. None of the new map material coincides with any of the available material."

"You're saying that the new stuff shows unexplored, uncharted road?"

"Yes, Jake."

"Bingo."

"Pardon?"

"We found it."

"Yes, this would be very useful material if its authenticity and accuracy could be established."

"You're telling me," I said.

"Am I telling you? Yes, I am."

"What we have to do, then, is search the new data for congruences with the maps in storage."

"That would appear to be a potentially productive course of action."

"No doubt," I said. "Any problem in that?"

"No. I will simply erase and reload as I go. However, the job may take a good deal of realtime."

"Go to it," I told him.

"Yes, Jake."

"And Bruce? Lighten up, okay?"

"I'm sorry, Jake. Could you please phrase that differently?"

"Remind me to do some work in your basic vocabulary area."

"I'll log it now. Shall I cancel the command to 'lighten up'?—which, I'm sorry to say, is not a valid command."

"Cancel." I laughed.

Carl was staring at me.

"So you finally got it," he said.

"Yeah. I got it, all right. I keep getting it, right in the seat of the pants."

"You got the Roadmap. The real one. Where did it come from?"

"A shining white goddess appeared unto me, saying, 'Behold, I bring you tidings of great joy, and a big pain in the butt. By the way, have a Roadmap.'"

Carl nodded slowly. "Uh-huh."

"You think I'm kidding?"

"I'll believe anything."

"Then believe it. That's how it happened. Prime's not alone here. There's another force present. I figure it's a force opposing the Culmination. Or it could be another part of the Culmination, a dissenting faction, maybe. Which doesn't make a lot of sense, if I understand what the Culmination is supposed to be about, which I don't. So there you have it, whatever it is."

An hour later, Bruce was still hard at work.

"A lot of data, huh?" I said.

"Yes, Jake."

"Well, keep at it."

"Yes, Jake."

While we waited, Carl and I gave the women a hand. We packed all the trash into plastic sacks, which we set out neatly on the floor of the garage. Maybe Arthur took out the garbage around here. Then we swept the place out, vacuumed, scrubbed, and generally tidied up. When the trailer was finished, we set ourselves to straightening up the cab and aft-cabin, gleaning five more sacks of crap. I was surprised by the amount that had accumulated. But thirteen beings in a confined space produce quite a mess.

"Well, at least it smells a lot better," Darla said.

I sniffed. "Yeah, the dirty-sock odor is gone. I still get a whiff of our lumberjack friends, though."

Darla rolled her eyes. "Oh, those two. Apparently antiperspirant is a scarce commodity on Talltree."

"Or maybe sweat is plentiful." I sat down in the driver's seat. "Bruce, how's it coming?"

"Situation still anomalous. There is a great deal of data."

"Uh-huh."

"I've located a congruence."

"Huh?"

"Just now. I've found a section of the Terran Maze."

"My God."

"Now I have all of the Terran Maze located. Yes. Yes. And here is the Expanded Confinement Maze. Reticulan Maze, Ryxx Maze, Beta Hydran Maze, and the rest of known Skyway routes."

"Now," I said, "your next job is to find Microcosmos."

"Microcosmos? Can you please define that?"

"The name of this world. You should have data on it in storage."

"Understood . . . searching . . . found. Yes, a section of Skyway is here. However, I see no indication of a portal."

"If you can find Microcosmos on the master map, there might be one indicated on the reverse face of the planet. Okay. What I want you to do is chart a route from Terran Maze to here, working backward. It won't be necessary to have a visual route layout. Just keep a tally of lefts and rights. That will be our way home."

"Understood," Bruce said. "Beginning job now."

I turned sideways and looked back at Darla, Lori, and Carl. "Well, we know a few things. For one, we know that the Skyway isn't infinite. I don't know how many gigabytes the complete map takes up, but it's a finite number."

"It has an end," Darla said. "We knew that, didn't we?"

"I think we're talking about a circle here. No beginning, no end. If your hunch is right, we can get off this platter and get back on the Skyway."

Bruce said, "Jake?"

"Yeah?"

"The new maps are a bit unusual in that they show some routes marked in a different manner from the rest. Comparing these with the data placed in storage by the previous supervisor program—"

"Sam."

"Yes, that was its informal designation. Comparing these with Sam's data, I would say these are Roadbug service roads."

"Sounds like it," I told him.

"If these roads can be utilized, the route would be much more direct."

"No doubt," I said. "That's how we got here. But I don't know if we can go back that way. In fact, without Carl's car, I'm sure we can't."

"Then I will disregard them."

"Lunch, anyone?" Darla said. "I've whipped up something out of what was left of the rations."

"You're on."

We ate. The fare was a shade downscale from what Prime could offer, but somehow it felt good to have a meal in the truck again. Which was strange, since we had been on Microcosmos slightly less than twenty-four hours. My sense of time was completely out of whack. It seemed as if we'd been here a good deal longer. I thought about it, and decided it must have been the dream. The dream had spanned billions of years and unthinkable distances, and I had a lingering sense of having traversed those vast times and spaces.

Bruce finally completed his task. It had taken him two hours.

"Display the planetary layout of Microcosmos," I instructed him.

And there it was on the screen. It looked as though most of the prominent features were indicated, and I had a hunch we could depend on these maps to be accurate and comprehensive. There were other roads besides the ingress stretch of Skyway. They meandered across the terrain, some dead-ending near buildings and complexes, others going all the way to the rim. I searched out an efficient route to the edge of the planet.

"I wonder what you do here?" Carl asked. "Fall off the world?"

"I wonder." I eyed a thin ribbon of highway that seemed to have its start near Emerald City. "This looks interesting. But how do we get from Emerald City to the beginning of the road?"

"Beats me," Carl said.

"Okay, Bruce. Let's see the other side of the coin."

"I understand the metaphor."

Carl jumped. "Holy hell, is that a portal?"

"That's our back door." I laughed.

But it wasn't your average portal array. Bruce displayed the cylinder count: 216 of them, arranged in haphazard patterns, shot through with odd twistings of road. It looked like a connect-the-dots puzzle that an eight-eyed alien had given up on. Four major highways, converging from the points of the compass, fed into the spaghettilike mess of roads at the middle.

"This is interesting," I said. "There's almost no end to the various ways you could weave in and through there. Might mean that from here you could go almost anywhere in the Skyway system."

"But how do you know which way to zig and zag?" Lori asked, peering over my shoulder.

"Very simple," Bruce said.

"I'll bet," I scoffed. Then I shrugged. "Really?"

"Yes, Jake. Each section of the master map is numbered in binary. There is a table provided. Look—this is just a portion of it. Now, as you see, this is basically a hexadecimal core of a multidimensional, multivariable table, in which each cylinder is given a number. Passages through and among various cylinders are given in a number sequence corresponding to the cylinders involved. These sequences in turn correspond to the map section numbers. Now, as you can see, this is a very complex array, and processing could be hampered by core storage limitations, but by batching separate passes and by converting the data to a packed-decimal format in working storage, it should be possible to—"

"Wait a minute," I said. I couldn't make anything out of the flurry of numbers on the screen. "Are you saying that if I gave you *x* section of Skyway as a destination, you could tell me what combination of cylinders to shoot in order to make the jump there?"

"Yes, Jake, that is what I am saying. It would merely be a table lookup function."

I sat back and whistled. "Then that 'way home' you spent two hours charting—that wasn't a way home at all. That was the way we came."

"Yes, I'm afraid so," Bruce said. "One could take that route, of course, but the transit time back to Terran Maze would be, assuming conventional speed averages and taking into account rest and maintenance stops, something on the order of thirty thousand Standard Years."

10

"The long way home," I said.

"Indeed," Bruce said calmly. "However, as I have said, we have a much more efficient route at our disposal."

"If we can shoot that portal without getting smeared. Looks pretty tricky."

"It may require computer-assisted driving, if not complete computer control."

I sat back and sighed. "No one needs us humans anymore. Think you can handle it, Bruce?"

"I am not sure. I am not a machine chauvinist. The task may very well call for the sort of hand-eye coordination and intuitive timing that only human beings possess."

I smiled. "Well, thank you, Bruce. Are you just saying that because you're programmed to avoid bruising our poor little egos, or do you really feel that way?"

"I'm sorry, Jake. That question is a little ambiguous, and would be very difficult to answer."

"Probably right. Okay, Bruce, you did a very good job."

"Thank you, Jake. It has been a pleasure working with you."

I turned in my seat. "Well, gang? What do you want to do now?"

"Let's go," Darla said. "We have the map." Then her shoulders slumped. "Sorry, Jake. Forgot about Sam. I wasn't thinking."

"We're short on some things, too," I said. "No provisions. We're okay on fuel, but I'm reading low lubrication levels here, and we need coolant, water—"

"Sounds like it'd be a short trip back," Carl said. "Maybe

we could get along on next to nothing."

I shook my head. "You're forgetting the trip to the portal over alien terrain. Not only that—something tells me we have miles to go before we sleep. I have some unfinished business back home. Things to do. Trouble is, don't know what to do about maintenance. Unless . . ." I looked out at the garage.

And I saw Arthur shuffling toward us through the gloom. He waved and came over to the driver's side port.

I thumbed a toggle and the port hissed back into its slot.

"Hi, Arthur!" I said brightly. "Say hello to Bruce, here." I slapped the dash. "You two should have something in common."

"Pleased to meet you," Bruce said.

"Hello, Brucie." Arthur poked his dog-nose snout into the cab. "What are you all up to?"

"Housecleaning," I told him. "Getting things shipshape for a quick getaway."

Arthur smiled, the corners of his mouth turning up to reveal smooth rounded teeth. The funnel-shaped ears elevated as he did so. "Good thing I locked up the silverware. Are you leaving soon?"

"Well, no," I said. "I don't think so. There's a little matter of something that was stolen from me. Couple of things, actually."

The ears drooped. "Really? What was stolen?"

"An Artificial Intelligence module belonging to this vehicle's on-board computer. It was quite an advanced type, and its name was Sam. Know anything about it?"

Arthur was a little miffed. "I certainly do not. I hope you don't think I swiped it. Wouldn't think of it."

"Sorry, I didn't mean to imply an accusation. It's just that I don't have a long list of suspects."

Arthur nodded. "I see what you mean. But I really can't help you. I'm sorry it happened."

"I intend to speak to Prime about it."

"Oh, well, of course you should," Arthur said with a sincere nod of his ungainly head. "I hope things get straightened out." His sloping forehead furrowed. "You said a couple of things were stolen."

"Yeah. One of them I really can't complain about, since I

never wanted the thing in the first place. The Black Cube. Know what it is?"

"The Origin Experiment. I know it by name, but that's about all I know. I just work here."

I grunted.

"You're very upset about this, aren't you?" Arthur said sympathetically. "I'm really very sorry."

"I appreciate your concern."

"Well, it's my job to see to your general comfort and welfare." Arthur stepped back and looked the rig over. "Nice truck," he said.

"Thanks," I said.

"Are you people coming upstairs soon?"

"Eventually," I told him. "How are the others doing?"

"Oh, they're having fun. You missed a nice lunch, too."

"Sorry, but we were occupied. Was Prime there?"

"Actually, no," Arthur said. "He's attending to some pressing business."

"Will he be at dinner?"

"No, he won't. I was told to give you his regrets and inform you that he wouldn't be dining with you tonight. Busy, busy, and all that."

"Busy, busy?"

"Sorry."

"Sounds like a convenient excuse."

Arthur shrugged noncommittally.

"I know," I said. "You just work here."

"Room and board, no salary," Arthur said.

I snorted, then remembered I was talking to a robot. "Right." I looked around. "Any way to get some service in this garage?"

"What do you need?"

"General scheduled-maintenance stuff."

"Well," Arthur said, "I'm no mechanic, but if you just wheel the truck into one of the maintenance bays, I'm sure you can get what you want."

"Where?"

I fired up the engine, and Arthur waved me across the garage and into a narrow channel lined with banks of machinery. I squeezed into the space and parked, scramming the engine. Almost immediately, things began to happen. We heard whirring and clicking, then a steady hum. Suddenly, a many-segmented mechanical arm, bright and glittering, snaked across the forward port, its business end bristling with strange tools and attachments. Of and by itself, the forward cowling unfolded and flew back, exposing the engine. The tool head hovered for a moment, rotating its attachments until an appropriate one was centered, then dipped out of sight. More arms appeared, busying themselves here and about. Brightly colored tubes wriggled out and attached themselves to valves and petcocks.

Bruce's voice was vaguely troubled. "Jake, I don't quite know what is happening."

"We're getting super service," I said.

More arms shot into view, all crisscrossing but never touching, each going about its task with blurring speed. Zip, snap, click, bang. Sparks flew, tiny wisps of steam trailed off, vapors rose amid a writhing tangle of mad mechanical appendages.

It was over in less than a minute. Everything retracted, the cowling slammed shut, a deep gong sounded. And there was silence.

I checked all the readouts. The fuel tanks were full. Lubrication and coolant levels were maximum, the water tanks were brimming, all batteries showed a full charge.

"All systems A-O.K., Jake," Bruce pronounced.

"Looks like," I said.

"I wonder if they give free dishes," Carl said.

"Maybe this is the elusive place that gives green stamps— whatever the hell they are . . . or were." I pulled out of the maintenance bay, wheeled out onto the floor of the garage, and parked. Arthur started walking toward us.

"You guys want to go back upstairs?" I said.

"Let's stay in the truck tonight," Darla said.

"Yeah, let's," Carl seconded.

Lori nodded, and I said, "Okay."

"It's all the same to me," was Arthur's response. "Less bodies to look after. Have fun." He turned to leave.

"Hey, Art?" I called after him. "Er . . . Arthur."

He halted, looking back over his narrow shoulder. "*Arthur*

I can put up with," he said with weary tolerance. "*Art* is a little too much."

"Sorry. Do you have a proper name?"

"Does a duck quack? Never mind, you couldn't pronounce it." Arthur turned around. "What do you want?"

"How do you get out of this place?"

Arthur pointed off to the right. "Just follow that green line across the floor there. It'll take you to an exit tunnel."

"That line there?"

"Is there another one? Yes, that line there, dearie."

"And that's the way out?"

Pensively, Arthur rubbed the underside of his snout. "Well, let's see. Exit tunnel. Exit. Hmmm. Now, the last time I looked, I thought for sure the word exit meant a way out."

I gritted my teeth. "I wanted your assurance that we weren't going to be tricked. Stupid of me to ask, I suppose."

"Do I look so untrustworthy?"

"Frankly, yes."

"My, aren't we paranoid. I think I'll leave in a huff."

And he did.

Shaking my head, I watched him disappear into the half-darkness. "He's supposed to be a composite of all our person-alities. What I want to know is, which one of us is the smartass?"

Darla laughed. "Funny, but I can see a lot of your sardonic humor in him, Jake."

"Me?" I yelped. "You've got to be kidding."

"Actually, it does make sense that he would have an effem-inate personality."

"Well, it doesn't make any damn sense to me at all."

Lori had been thinking. "Do you think John and Roland and the rest will be okay?"

"Who knows," I said. I rubbed my jaw. "But I know one thing. I know we're being manipulated."

"How so?" Darla asked.

"What Arthur said about seeming untrustworthy. Actually, I lied. He appears to be anything but a danger. It's hard to take him seriously at all. He's a cartoon figure, a big, gangling *improbability*, with a seriocomic personality. And look at Prime. He's everything a superbeing should be—wise, kind, and gentle. But think of it. He could take any shape. He's not a being. He's a tool. At least that body is. The persona he's presenting seems a little too tailormade, too contrived."

Darla nodded. "I know what you mean. He seems to be bending over backward to make us feel safe, to convince us of his good intentions."

"Precisely," I said. "And that tactic backfired on me from the very start. Just the way I am, I guess."

"Me, too." Darla sat in the shotgun seat and brooded. Presently she said, "But what do they want from us?"

"Maybe the part about wanting us to join the Culmination is true," I said. "However, I don't intend to stick around long enough to find out whether it is." I pushed the start button, and the engine turned over.

"Are we leaving?"

"Not just yet. I want to check out this escape route first. Then we'll see about provisions. If we can pilfer some food, we'll be set to leave at a moment's notice. Everyone strap in."

I rolled the rig across the smooth floor of the garage, following the solid green line Arthur had pointed out. It led straight toward a clutch of vehicles, then arched to the left. It took us past some more exotic machinery, skirted another maintenance bay, bent to the right and proceeded into darker regions of the garage. I turned on the forward lights. The line weaved among stacks of crates and containers, tall gantries hulking in the shadows behind them. Presently we came to a clear area. The walls of the chamber narrowed, feeding us into a tunnel and complete darkness. The tunnel floor sloped downward for a stretch, then leveled off. I slowed down, feeling cautious and a little edgy. The fear of getting lost again began to gnaw. The line ended, but the tunnel continued for a length until the headbeams showed what at first looked like a dead end, which turned out to be the floor swooping up sharply, too sharply, I thought, and braked. But something was wrong; there came a sudden surge of speed. The rig got sucked into the mouth of the tube and shot upward, propelled along like a shell inside the barrel of a fieldpiece. The angle wasn't as steep as that of the pedestrian escalators, but it was a thrilling trip up, too thrilling, because I was convinced that this time we'd blundered into something we couldn't get out of—maybe this was a missile firing tube, or a catapult that launched aircraft. Imagine our embarrassment when we got to the top.

But it was okay. The ramp leveled off sharply and we could see daylight—the tunnel's end. The invisible force set us loose, and we rolled out into bright late-afternoon sun, traveling a gray-green, two-lane highway.

I pulled off the road and let the engine idle. We were among low grassy hills. A stand of trees fringed a rise to the right, and an arrangement of rounded pink boulders sat off the road on the other side. Through the rearview parabolic mirror I could see Emerald City atop its escarpment. No other structures lay in sight, but the view was limited by the terrain.

"Now," I said, sitting back. "How do we get back inside?"

"Forget it," Carl said disdainfully. "Who needs that fairy palace?"

"You can't complain about the food," I said. "And it looks like we could go a long time between meals out here."

"We'll figure something out," Carl said with haughty confidence.

"You think we can forage? Or do you figure to hunt small game?"

"Huh? Hey, I don't know, but we'll get by somehow."

"Sure. I'm feeling pangs already. Darla, what do we have left back there?"

"Some crackers, I think. Half a bag of walnuts." She thought. "A can of beef consommé . . . and a rotten apple."

I looked at Carl.

He shrugged off my stare. "Okay, okay. So we'll get hungry. But the sooner we get through that portal, the sooner we get back to where we can find food."

I said, "Bruce, calculate the most efficient route to that master portal and give me an ETA, assuming nonstop driving and an average speed of about 130 kilometers per hour."

"Forty-six-point-two-five hours, Jake."

"So," I said, "it's two days if I don't sleep or if I teach you guys to pilot this rig, and that's assuming Skyway cruising speed, or near it, anyway. I don't think we can average more than eighty klicks an hour over alien road."

"Eighty klicks?" Carl said incredulously. "That's . . . what? Only around fifty miles an hour! This rig can hit two hundred or I'm a monkey's uncle."

"It can do over that," I said, "on a high-speed road like the Skyway. But I'm talking average speed, Carl. That's different. And this is little more than a back country road."

"Yeah, I know," Carl grumbled. "Shit. We can still make it, though."

"Maybe, if we have to. But I'm not ready to leave just yet."

"Right, right. I'm sorry. We gotta get Sam back, I know."

I studied Carl for a moment. The scared kid inside him was peeping through. He was farther from home than any of us.

I looked back at the tunnel, which exited from the base of a steep hill. "Well, we can't go down the up-ramp, that's for sure. Bruce, can we get back to the Skyway using these secondary roads?"

"No, Jake, there's no connection."

"You can't get there from here." I sighed. "That's odd. Can we go off-road?"

"Perhaps, Jake. The maps are not so detailed that I can make that judgment with any degree of authoritativeness."

"Damn. I don't want to go overland, but that through-the-mountain bit seems like the only way into the city by road."

"And who's to say," Darla added, "whether they'll lift up the mountain and let us in again?"

"Right. So I guess we cruise around a little and see if we can find some nice little rabbits who'll let us conk them over the head."

I *was* hungry. I'd just picked at breakfast, which seemed like days ago, and Darla's quickie lunch had vanished into the void. Nothing to be done about it now, though. And sitting here would accomplish less than nothing. So I eased back onto the road and brought the rig up to sight-seeing speed, just moseying along.

"They know where we are, of course," Darla said.

I nodded. "Of course. They've known our every move. But they haven't stopped us yet."

"Yes, but I'm still not ready to believe that Prime meant what he said about letting us leave any time we want to."

"Yeah, couple of things bother me about that," I said. "Consider all the *stuff* that's here. All those exotic vehicles, the wondrous gadgets, the technology. Just sitting around, waiting to be pilfered by disenchanted Culmination candidates."

"Maybe it's supposed to be pilfered," Darla suggested.

I thought about it. "Maybe. Haven't seen any signs of plundering, though."

"It may be we were the first ever to make it to the end of the Skyway."

"Gosh. Think of that."

Darla ruminated, then said, "You don't think anyone could get away with swiping anything from this place, do you?"

"Not for a moment. I can't believe the Culmination would let this stuff get dispersed anachronistically throughout all of spacetime. Most of it is from the far, far future. It would stick out like a sore thumb back where we come from. Talk about paradoxes."

"What about knowledge leaking out? All that data in the library. Taking back any of that would be anachronistic in itself."

"You have a point. Then, I guess, the knowledge doesn't leave here, either."

We looked at each other.

"I don't like the implications of that," Darla said worriedly.

"Neither do I."

The sky was a pretty, purplish blue, appearing as if it had been colored in by crayon. The strange, artificial look probably had something to do with the atmosphere being a lot shallower here than it would be on a standard planet—or so I guessed—although it was deep enough to support a few puffy clouds. No doubt the weather was controlled. I wondered if it ever rained.

We rolled down a gradual grade and out onto flat grasslands. Structures came into view. Up ahead a side road diverged, leading to a featureless golden dome. Farther on another road branched off to a complex edifice that looked like a collision between a chemical plant and a Mogul palace.

"So many things . . ." Darla said out of a reverie.

"Like what?" I asked.

She sighed and shook her head. "So many unanswered questions. Little things, as well as big. Like, why isn't there any Skyway to the master portal?"

"To slow us down. Make us think twice about leaving. Or it's because this was such a pretty place, they didn't want to mess it up with new construction."

"All of the above," Darla said. "Or none of the above."

"You got it," I said. "Don't hold your breath for complete explanations. Mystery is the essence of life."

She rolled her eyes. "Let me write that down."

"Okay. It's M-Y-S-T-E-R— Huh? Why are you laughing?"

"Jake, you're getting more batty with every kilometer you drive."

"I'm being driven batty. I knew there was an explanation."

For the next half hour we followed the road and saw the sights. There was plenty to look at. The vegetation changed; trees became more numerous, thickening to forest for a stretch, then thinning out a little to look like an orchard. More buildings in various architectural styles. There were other things, too, among which was a huge statue of a winged, four-legged animal resembling a gryphon, except that the head looked rather feline. The statue sat atop a cylindrical base and must have risen to more than sixty meters. An alien god—a mythical animal? Or was this the likeness of a once-extant sapient being? No telling. There were other monuments which gave the impression of being tombs or cenotaphs. One was a diamond-shaped mass of metal that stood balanced, impossibly, on one of its apexes, resting point to point with the tip of a pyramidal base. Another was a giant glass needle, a thin, tapering crystalline shaft that shot up over a hundred meters. There were obelisks, stelae, slabs, monoliths, and other masses, all of various geometrical shapes.

More buildings. One looked very familiar. In fact, we were shocked. I pulled off the road and stopped.

"The Taj Mahal!" Darla blurted.

And it was, if memory served. Though I'd been in India, I'd never laid eyes on it. But the Taj is one of those universal picture-postcard images that has engraved itself in the mass mind. No mistaking those serenely graceful turnip-top domes, the slender minarets, that classical symmetry and sense of proportion. In a word, beautiful.

"My God," Darla said, "what's it doing here?"

"Part of the collection," I said.

"Do you think there are more Terran artifacts here?"

"Possibly."

"Maybe it's just a replica."

"Maybe. Looks new, doesn't it? Probably restored or re-constructed."

I got us moving again. Farther along we came to an intersection. The other road was narrower but was made of the same blue-green material. I stopped, checking traffic. There was none, so I crossed and continued on.

I should have waited, because a few kilometers down the road I saw a blip on the rear scanner screen.

11

I TROMPED THE power pedal. "Bruce," I said, "we got trouble."

"Noted, Jake. Bandit at six o'clock, closing fast."

Maybe it was Prime, come to fetch us back. But I doubted it. "In camera range?" I asked.

"Extreme telephoto. Can you make it out?"

I looked. It was a dun-colored dot, growing rapidly, soon resolving into a paramilitary vehicle with familiar camouflage markings. One of Zack Moore's buggies.

"Incoming message on the Skyway citizens' band," Bruce calmly said.

"Put it through."

"*. . . McGraw, breaking for Jake McGraw. Come back.*"

I recognized the voice. It was Krause, who had been an officer aboard the ferryboat *Laputa*. I had had a minor run-in with him, and a major one with his skipper, Captain Pendergast.

I put my headset on. "Yeah, you got McGraw."

"*Hi, there! Where've you guys been?*" Krause's chummy manner rang as false as a bell made of papier-mâché.

"What's it to you, asshole?" I had decided not to be civil about this.

"*Hey, now, is that any way to talk? After all we've been through together?*"

"Back off," I said, "or you're a dead man."

"*Don't be so paranoid. I just want to talk. What's it like inside that castle, anyway?*"

"Good food, good service, and a great game room. Any other questions?"

"*Food! All we've had to eat is synthesized glop! We're*"

starving and you're living off the fat of the land! Isn't fair."

"Doesn't the White Lady take care of you?"

A pause. Then: *"We call her the Goddess. That's what she is, you know."*

"And she doesn't feed her children?"

"No. She just tells us to do stuff."

"Like what?"

"Most of the time we can't understand her."

I thought it best to pull a few more teeth and try to get what information I could. "Where's the rest of your crew?"

"Oh, around."

It looked as though I wouldn't get much out of him, but I needed a little time. Krause's vehicle was pacing us now. I wanted to pick the best place to make my move. I'd take the offense first in this particular engagement. I was tired of screwing around with these guys. Besides, best to strike when the situation was still one-on-one. So I needed to chat him up a little longer.

"Where are you guys holed up?" I asked.

"We have a place. Kind of a temple, sort of. It's nice. But the food we found is awful. I bet that everything in that green palace of yours is first class."

"You alone?"

"No. Got a few of the guys here. Are you?"

"Yeah."

He laughed. *"I'll bet. Or did most of your gang decide to join up with that Prime fellow? They all ducked out on you— that right, Jake?"*

"Yeah, they all ducked out." I killed the mike. "Everyone strapped in?" I looked around. My crew was well-trained by now.

Krause chuckled. *"They all want to be gods, huh? Actually, I don't blame them. Wouldn't mind being boss of the universe for a while. But the Goddess says it's all a crock."*

I switched the mike on again. "That so?" I said, eyeballing the road ahead for a likely spot to do a "moonshiner's flip," a.k.a. an "Alabama roundhouse."

"Yeah, that's what she says. She says Prime is misleading people and getting them involved in things that aren't their business."

"What's the Goddess' business?"

"You got me. What do I know from what a goddess is supposed to be up to? None of us understands what the hell's really going on here. Except that—whaddya call her?—the White Lady and Prime are enemies."

"What's she been after you to do?"

Krause snorted. *"Kowtow to her, for one thing. I'm getting pretty tired of it."* His voice took on a worried edge. *"Jeez, I hope she isn't listening. But you should see what we have to go through. Kneeling when we talk to her, calling her Your Divinity, and crap like that . . . Christ, I hope she didn't hear that either."*

"What're you worried about? What happens if you incur her disfavor?"

"No food, no water. Two of our guys died last night—they got sick on the trip. Scurvy, I think, though Jules had a heart condition, too. Anyway, the Lady could have saved them, but she didn't, because Moore gave her lip."

So, Moore wasn't in Krause's vehicle. And we had two less enemies on this world. Good and good.

"I probably shouldn't have told you any of that . . . but, I dunno. Most of us really would like to go home. You got the map now, Jake. The real one. How 'bout we make a deal?"

"You still believe rumors?" I said.

"C'mon, Jake. The Goddess told us. She gave you the real map. We need it to get back home."

"The Goddess told you wrong, Krause. I never had a map and I don't now."

"Then where are you going?" He grunted. *"Heading for that big portal on the other side, I bet."*

"Just out sight-seeing, Krause. Lots of interesting things here."

"Yeah, sure. Look, we don't even want the map. All we really want is the Black Cube. The Goddess wants it. If she don't get it, we don't get off this pancake."

"Krause, you got yourself one big problem, there. My sympathies, but I can't help you. I don't have the cube any more. My truck was broken into last night. Somebody stole it."

Krause delayed answering a moment. *"How can I be sure you're telling the truth?"*

"That's a tough one."

Ahead was a sharp curve. I took it at high gee. Coming out of it I saw my opportunity. The road straightened out and continued into a long straightaway, bisecting a greensward that looked level and firm.

I cut the mike. "Bruce, stand by for an Alabama roundhouse."

"Jake," Bruce admonished, "that is not a recommended maneuver."

"Stand by!"

"Standing by."

I flipped the master toggle controlling the traction gradients on the trailer rollers. Those rollers were now frictionless. I braked hard. The trailer immediately jackknifed to the left, but instead of correcting, I let it go, twisting the control rings on the steering bars and defrictionizing the cab rollers as well. The rig spun. Stopping this maneuver was the hard part.

"You pulling over, Jake?" came Krause's voice.

"Bruce! Stabilize!"

I flipped the master toggle back and frantically twisted the control rings, at the same time countersteering and braking. I had to do almost everything at once—Bruce was handling the stabilizing jets and monitoring the various safety servos which would help keep the rig from going completely out of control. We were now traveling backward and decelerating. The trailer started to swing out again. I toggled and pedaled and steered, fighting to get it back into line. I juiced the power rollers to maximum grab, defrictionizing the rears again. The rig shuddered, and we rolled to a crunching stop—a brief one, because I had the power pedal floored. The rig sprang forward and we flew back up the road.

Krause was coming out of the turn.

"Jake, I can't take your word...HEY, WHAT THE HELL!"

We were heading right down his throat.

The jungle-striped gun buggy swerved off onto the shoulder, but I kept steering right for him.

"Bruce, stand by on exciter cannon!"

"Roger. Target visually acquired."

Krause didn't have time enough to get a shot off at us. The vehicle's exciter turret was swiveling into line, but whoever was driving was too busy trying to avoid getting smashed by one big mother of a trailer truck and was frantically steering against the turret's swing. The gun buggy veered off and headed out into the greensward, presenting its broadside to us for a perfect set-up shot.

"Fire!" I yelled, but Bruce beat me by a quarter second. His shot was dead on target, the blue-white exciter beam opening a fiery gash along the entire length of the gun buggy's starboard side. I swung off and headed back onto the road. The left parabolic showed Krause's vehicle trundling across the grass, heading for a clutch of bone-white pyramids. It hit a low rise, bouncing crazily.

Then it exploded. Bruce's shot must have penetrated to the ordnance bays. A starburst of arching contrails blossomed out of the fireball.

I couldn't look anymore because we were heading back into the curve. I braked into the turn and accelerated out.

Two more military-style vehicles were heading right at us.

"Fire at will!"

Bruce let fly, hitting both gun buggies head-on. They shot past on either side, and I heard the crackle of belated return fire. Again, we had surprise on our side. They hadn't had reaction time enough to get off a shot at the cab. I wasn't about to give them another opportunity.

"Bruce, emergency power. Gimme all you got."

"Yes, Jake."

I roared back the way we had come, taking turns at maximum gee and cheating on the bends by cutting across the shoulder of the road when necessary. I hadn't had time to see if Bruce's shots had been effective. Most vehicles have their thickest armor front and back, since most attacks on the road come from those quarters. Knowing that, I still hoped we had lucked out, or had at least disabled them. We had a big lead, and it would take time for them to turn around, but those buggies were fast. I didn't think we could outrun them on this slow road. Out on the Skyway, no problem. They'd have trouble catching me. But not here. Which meant I would have to think of something quick.

I thought, quickly, if not brilliantly. I feared a missile attack. I had dealt with their ordnance before, and only Carl's magic Chevy had saved us—even at that, we had taken a hit. If they chased us, they would wait for a level stretch and let loose what missiles they had left. Better to get off-road now and try to take advantage of the terrain. They could follow, but out there we'd have a chance of catching them broadside, the only hope of a sure kill.

Trouble was, the orchard landscape was back, and there was nowhere to go if I didn't want to go crashing through the trees—which would slow us down, and needless to say, leave any easy trail to follow. I looked out at the neatly spaced rows of trees. Some were gnarled little things, but most were six meters high at least. On the whole, they didn't look crash-through-able. There was maybe enough space between them to squeeze by . . . hard to tell, though. I thought back. The intersection was coming up. If I could get there and make a turn before they saw us, they'd have to split up, and since there were only two vehicles chasing us and three ways I could go, we might lose them completely.

But no such luck.

"Jake, I have visually acquired our pursuers."

"Damn."

"Missile alert! Incoming! Take evasive action!"

I'd already taken it, panic-braking. The orchard had given way to a sort of wide esplanade lined with dark monuments leading diagonally off to the right. I barely managed the turn, scraping the side of the trailer against one of the huge metallic blocks. With any luck—

There was a flash and an accompanying *crump* as the missile hit one of the monoliths. I was momentarily relieved for more than one reason—they hadn't unleashed a barrage of missiles. They were probably low, trying to make each shot count, but they probably had at least one more to chuck at us.

I raced down the stone-paved esplanade. It flared into a circus, in the center of which stood a free-form sculpture done in twisted metal. I skirted that, roaring off the pavement and onto turf. Ahead was an obstacle course of monuments and other odd bric-a-brac, and on the other side lay a grouping of turquoise domes.

I dodged and weaved through the field of monuments—it was like a driver training course. Stray exciter bolts sizzled around us, but no missiles came our way. I made a lurching turn around the domes, coming to the foot of a low hill dotted with more orchard trees. There was nowhere to go but up, so I went, flooring the pedal and hitting the first tree dead on. Not much to these trees—it snapped, fell, and we steamed right over it. I wanted to leave as much debris behind as I could, so I started sideswiping them, getting them to fall and block our pursuers' path. Branches scraped against the ports and crunched beneath the rear rollers. I tore the hell out of that goddamn hill. It would have been fun under other circumstances.

It wasn't a big hill, and we were over the top quickly. Apparently the gun buggies were having a hard time getting up the slope. They hadn't fired at us. There were no trees here on the other side, nothing but a gradual grade down to a flat meadow with no cover other than tall weedlike plants. It was a good hundred meters across to the edge of a thick forest. I hurried. We shot down the hill and bumped across level ground. I floored the pedal and cut a swath through the tall grass, scanning ahead to judge how thick the forest was and whether we could go crashing through or whether we had to turn and fight. I decided to risk more damage to the ecology and plunged the rig into the trees. This stuff was thicker. The cab shook with the impact. I heard a horrendous cracking, looked out and saw the right stabilizer foil fall away. But we didn't stop. Trees fell in our path, branches slammed against the view ports. It was rough going. I got hung up a few times, but managed to get free and keep rolling. Momentum was on our side; also a 600 megadyne nuclear-fusion engine. We crashed out into a small clearing, and I paused to look about for a trail or a road. There was a tiny break in the tree line off to the right, so I headed for it, and it turned out to be the start of little more than a deer path. But it helped.

"Hope Smokey the Bear isn't around," Carl managed to say over the snapping, thumping, and banging.

"Who the hell is that?" I shouted.

"Forget it."

The vegetation was not quite Earthlike, but not very exotic either, just more of thousands of variations I had seen on the basic theme of "tree." These had drooping branches bright with feathery red and yellow leaves. There didn't seem to be any wildlife about—nothing squawked or hooted disapproval at our intrusion, nothing bolted from cover to run for its life. I wondered if the whole planet were lifeless except for vegetation, Prime, we humans, and the White Lady.

We crashed out into the clear, and I stopped, slid back the port, and listened. No noise behind, nothing like two vehicles trying to follow our trace. They'd have a rough time getting around the tree stumps and other debris I'd left. Good. Better and better.

"We have sustained some damage, Jake," Bruce informed me.

"I know. Anything critical?"

"All main systems seem to be functional. However, we have a hull breach in the trailer, and the right stabilizer foil has detached itself."

"Yeah. So much for stability. Well, it could have been worse."

"I must compliment you on your creative driving, Jake," Bruce said.

"Thank you. I was inspired."

I got moving, crossing a grassy field to the slope of a low rise. At the crest, I stopped. There was an abrupt transition in terrain beginning a few meters away. The grass petered out, giving way to dust and gravel. A few wiry bushes with brilliant pink blossoms dotted a parched landscape. An eroded butte ringed by mounds of talus lay about half a kilometer ahead. Near it sat a complex of buildings that looked like some sort of industrial facility.

"Interesting," I said.

"There's a road down by those buildings," Carl said.

"Yeah. Good as any, I guess."

I drifted down the hill and rolled out into the desert.

Carl gave a look out the port, checking the rearview parabolic mirror. "You think we lost 'em?"

"I hope. Not much cover out here."

It was pretty, though. The dust was red, the rocks coffee-beige, and the vegetation was in colorful bloom. The sky had turned a deeper shade of violet as the "sun" declined to our right, coaxing long shadows from outcroppings of rock and stunted, rough-barked trees.

"We should look for someplace to spend the night, a hide-out of some sort," I said.

"What about that place there?" Lori asked.

"I'd like to get some more distance between us and those gun buggies first," I answered.

I hurried toward the thin green line of the road, bumping over rocks and fallen tree trunks, following the edge of a sinuous depression to our right that looked like a dry wash.

Darla began, "Maybe we should—"

"Alert!" Bruce interrupted. "Bandits at six o'clock!"

The rearview screen showed two camouflage-painted buggies rushing down the hill.

"Fire rear exciters at will!" I shouted, mashing the power pedal.

"Affirmative. Have commenced firing."

I weaved the rig back and forth, eyeing the terrain ahead for cover. There wasn't much to eye. A few rock formations, low mounds, nothing elevated enough to completely hide the rig. Best we could do was to swing around and bring our forward guns to bear, hunkering down behind the crest of a ridge to present a low profile. Basic tank warfare in open country.

But they still had missiles, and one was coming our way.

"Tracking multiple missiles," Bruce said imperturbably. "Jake, you had better take cover. I can't seem to knock any of them out."

I had already steered sharply to the right, heading for the dry wash. If I could get down in there without wrecking us, and if the wash were deep enough, and if we could get back *out* of there, and if—

We practically fell into the wash. The cab dropped, crashing to the stream bed, pulping our bones and teeth. I recovered quickly enough to floor the pedal and pull the cab away before the trailer flipped over. The accordion joints along the trailer groaned, bent to the failure point.

There was a crunching thud—the trailer falling in behind as I wheeled out into the dry wash, rollers jouncing over ruts and boulders. I heard a whoosh. A missile impacted about twenty meters downstream, throwing up a geyser of dust and rubble.

"Only one actual blip, Jake," Bruce informed. "The others were electronically generated decoys. I'm very sorry to report that our defensive systems are not quite up to par."

"They never were," I said. "Can't afford it."

Now what? We were sitting ducks in this hole. I raced downstream, feeling the undercarriage whack against protruding boulders. I winced, hoping the rig would hold together. One hole or tear in a vital component and it would be over.

Farther downstream the channel widened and the height of the banks shrank to half a meter. I looked around, checked the parabolic. Nothing, so I wheeled to the right. *Whump, bang,* and the cab was up and out of the wash—*crash, rip*, the trailer following. I cringed. Ohmygod, I thought, I'm going to cry when I look underneath the rig. If I ever get the chance.

We were out and exposed, but no more missiles came our way. Those buggies would have just as much trouble crossing the wash, so now was my chance to pack some distance between us and them.

"Jake," Bruce said, "I'm getting a very unusual blip on the scanners. Airborne, descending and closing with us."

Carl craned his neck, looking up.

"See anything?" I asked.

"No . . . I—" He froze.

"Carl? What is it?"

He turned around. The color had drained out of his face. "Shit," he said in a scared, half-audible whisper. *"Shit!"*

"What the hell is it, Carl?" I shouted.

He looked at me. His eyes were panicky, crazed. "Not again," he said.

"Jesus Christ, Carl, what—"

The rig left the ground.

I yelled. The engine quit, and a blood-freezing silence fell. The rig was taking off like a plane, nose high and soaring. I looked out the port. A huge black object, irregularly shaped, hovered above us. The angle was wrong to get a good view.

"Jake, what is it?" Darla screamed.

"I don't know," I said. "A craft. Sucking us up in some sort of gravitic beam."

"Prime," she said flatly.

"I guess."

The object came into the forward ports as our angle of ascent steepened. The thing was rounded, bulbous in spots, and big. Other than that, it was almost featureless.

Carl was tugging futilely at the hatch lever—the master sealing circuit was on.

"I gotta get outta here," he said through gritted teeth.

"Carl, take it easy. It's probably Prime, picking us up."

He tore off his harness and leaped at me, grabbing the front of my jacket with both hands. He shook me. "Open that fucking door, d'you hear? Open that door! I gotta get out! I gotta get outta here!" His face was contorted by blind fear, his eyes sightless, his lips the color of his face, a dead fish's belly.

"Carl, what the hell's wrong with you?" I snapped.

"You don't understand, you don't understand. That thing can't get me again, I won't let it, I gotta get outta here, I—"

He let me go, wrenched around and stabbed at the instrument panel. I unstrapped myself and seized both of his arms.

"Carl, take it easy!"

He struggled free, turning around. He sent a haymaker at me, which I ducked. I closed with him and wrapped him up. We Indian wrestled for a moment, then he dragged me to the right. I tripped, falling between the front seats. Carl stepped over me and fled aft. I was in an awkward position and couldn't get up immediately, my left foot wedged underneath the power pedal. I finally freed it and hauled myself up.

Carl was lying facedown on the deck. Darla stood over him. Lori, still strapped in, was in tears.

"Hope I didn't hurt him," Darla said. "Side neck chop."

"You're good at that," I said. I went back and checked him. He wasn't unconscious, just stunned. He writhed, groaning.

"He'll be okay. You have a light touch."

"What's his problem?"

I said, "I think that thing up there is his flying saucer."

12

I CLIMBED FORWARD—the rig was inclined at a sharp angle now. I sat in the driver's seat and looked out. A large structure, part of the strange craft, loomed before us. It looked something like the neck of a bottle with an aperture like an iris. The aperture began dilating as we approached, soon widening enough to admit the truck. Which it did. We shot right in there. The aperture closed behind us, and we were in semi-darkness.

The truck settled.

Prime's voice boomed at us from the dark cavity ahead.

"I AM VERY DISPLEASED," he said gravely. "IT SEEMS THAT YOU MAY NOT BE TRUSTED. VERY WELL, THEN. YOU HAVE FORCED ME TO TAKE HARSH MEASURES. PREPARE TO MEET YOUR DOOM!"

"Go to hell!" I shouted.

We heard an impish chuckle. "JUST KIDDING!" came Arthur's voice.

"What?" I rasped, switching the feed from my mike to the outside speakers. "Arthur! You son of a bitch, where the hell are you?"

"Now don't get testy," Arthur said, his voice at a lower volume. "Just having some fun. You ought to be grateful. I just saved your butt, you know."

I exhaled, relief flooding over me. "You did?"

"You better believe it, dearie. That last missile had your number on it."

"Oh," I said. "There was one coming at us?"

"Right on target. Of course, I knocked it out before it got very far."

"Oh."

"Oh," Arthur said mockingly.

"Thanks."

"You're welcome. Hold on a minute."

We waited. A minute later, Arthur came waddling out of the darkness. "Come on out," he said.

Carl was sitting up. He looked embarrassed, still a little scared, and at least partially rational.

"You okay?" I asked.

"Yeah. I . . ." He ran a hand over his face, and shook his head to clear it. "I don't know what happened. Something snapped. I dunno." He looked up. "I'm sorry," he added, rubbing his neck.

"Forget it. Is this your flying saucer? The one that nabbed you?"

Carl got to his feet, came forward. "Looks like it. Same damn goofy-looking place."

We got out. The chamber was like the inside of an egg flattened on the bottom. Behind the truck, the entrance had closed up into a puckered sphincter-valve affair. The room was uniformly constructed out of some dark material.

"Still angry?" Arthur asked, smirking.

"A little," I said. "You do a good imitation of Prime."

"Why, thank you, Jake," Arthur said in Prime's voice. "I plan to make a career in show business, you know."

I looked around. "What now?"

Arthur shrugged. "What do you want to do?"

"You're not taking us back to Emerald City?"

Arthur shook his head. "Not if you don't want to go."

I turned to Darla. "What do you think?"

Darla shook her head. "I don't know, Jake. We'd probably be safer in Emerald City, but . . ."

"I don't want to go," I said. "But I have to find Sam. He's got to be there somewhere."

Arthur said, "Oh, Sam's fine. I kind of like him. He's your father, right? You know, he looks a lot like you."

I must have looked as if I'd been hit with a power hammer.

Arthur stared at me blankly for a second; then something dawned on him. "Oh, of course. You *left* before Sam . . ." He brought his four-fingered hand up and slapped his face. "Dearie me, I think I've made a boo-boo."

"What are you saying?" I managed to get out.

"Um . . . I think I'd better take you back to Emerald City. Right now. Follow me."

We followed him. Another sphincter-valve, this one much smaller than the first, was set into the far wall. It opened to admit us, and we went through into a curving tube-shaped corridor that bent to the right and led into a circular room. In the center was a high cylindrical platform on which rested a wedge-shaped box affair looking somewhat like a lectern. Arthur stood in front of it and began to slide his fingers across the box's slanted top face. A control panel, I thought.

Nothing much happened. I didn't feel any movement. I looked over Arthur's shoulder. The triangular panel, made of the same dark material that the rest of the ship was composed of, was totally blank, yet Arthur seemed to know where to put his fingers.

"Want a view?" Arthur asked.

"Huh? Oh, yeah."

The ship around us disappeared.

Darla squealed, and Lori fell to all fours. Carl jumped back, yelling, "Jesus Christ!" He stared unbelieving at his feet, beneath which was nothing but air.

I stared down, stamping my right foot. The floor was still there—something was there, anyway. I turned around. And behind us, about ten meters away, flying along with us like a escorting fighter, was the truck.

We were soaring in open air about three hundred meters above the surface of Microcosmos. Arthur still had his hands extended over the now invisible control panel.

"Sorry," he said. "I should have warned you. Let me opaque the ship's mass a little."

The walls and floor came back abruptly, then gradually faded to full transparency, but this time they looked like tinted glass.

"Do you have a sense of the ship around you now?" Arthur inquired.

"Yeah, better," I said.

Lori got up. "I'm going crazy," she declared. "I really think I'm gonna go completely bats."

"Hang on, honey," Darla said soothingly, putting an arm around her shoulders.

"Where did you get this . . . ship?" I asked.

"Belongs to Emerald City's fleet," Arthur told me. "It's a spacetime ship. Goes anywhere, anytime. Zips you there real fast."

"Yeah?"

"Yeah. It's probably the most advanced spacecraft ever built. Don't ask me who built it. I'd break my jaw trying to pronounce the name."

"Do you know how it works? What drives it?"

"Oh, quantum this, that, and the other thing. You really want me to go into it? You couldn't understand it, anyway."

"Forget it."

The patchwork quilt of Microcosmos rolled beneath us. Our airspeed couldn't have been much. Ahead, I could see the Emerald City atop its citadel, sparkling in the light of the setting sun.

"You have to take it easy going short distances," Arthur went on, anticipating my next question. "You can't do continuum jumps near big masses. I mean, you can do them, but it's tricky. Even for me. And I'm pretty good at driving this thing."

"You do a lot of flying?"

"Never. This is my first time."

"I see." I shrugged to myself.

The ship made its approach to Emerald City. Everything seemed to be going fine until we suddenly veered off. The world below us tilted crazily.

"What's wrong, Arthur?" I said, fighting an attack of vertigo.

"Something's coming our way."

I searched the sky and found it. It was a yellow glowing ball trailing streamers of fire, streaking down at us.

"What the hell is *that?*" I shouted.

"I don't know," Arthur said calmly. "Some kind of weapon. Don't worry."

"Worry? Who, me?"

The ship made a dizzying turn and headed away from the green castle. The fireball executed the same maneuver and streaked after us, hot on our tail. Our speed increased rapidly, but there was no feeling of acceleration, no G-forces. We climbed swiftly, then leveled off. The fireball did the same, and it seemed to be gaining. Arthur appeared to be aware of this without having looked.

"Uh-oh," he said. "Hang on, kids."

Arthur proceeded to put the ship through some impossible maneuvers. We flipped, looped, dived, pulled up, then went into what would have been called a stall, had it been done by an airplane. Then we dropped like a stone, tumbling end over end.

I fought off vertigo, closing my eyes. There was absolutely no physical sensation of movement.

When I opened them again, we were flying close to the ground at tremendous speed. Behind us, the fireball was pulling out of a dive to match our altitude.

"Dearie me," Arthur fretted. "I can't seem to shake this thing off our tail."

"Doesn't this ship have any weapons?" I asked.

"Not much offensively, but a whole bunch defensively. The ship's supposed to be invulnerable to just about any weapon ever created. Anyway, that's how it was touted in its day. But I can't take any chances. I have no idea of what technological culture that fireball may have come out of. It might have been specifically invented to challenge this ship's claims to invulnerability. You know how arms races go."

We shot up into the sky again and did a series of evasive maneuvers, these more improbable than the last. The fireball matched our every move.

"Dearie me!" Arthur exclaimed. "Now I'm starting to worry."

"What about those defensive weapons?"

"I've already tried to neutralize it. Nothing worked."

"Can't you shoot it down?"

"Dogfight with it?" Arthur cringed. "You don't know what you're saying. Dogfighting is probably that thing's trump suit. You never know what to expect with these standing-wave energy weapons, which is probably what it is. It might be able to absorb the energy of an attack and grow even more powerful."

I looked ahead. The edge of the disk-planet was coming up fast.

"We're running out of world, Arthur," I said, trying to

sound as composed as possible.

"That may be our only chance," he replied.

Our speed must have been stupendous by then. The edge of
Microcosmos swept past, and we streaked out into space. The
planet shrank behind us, its disk tilting away, bringing the
edge into view. Forty-five degrees along the rim of the world,
the luminous sun-disk was falling below the horizon. Beneath
us, the world-edge was rounded and looked metallic, busy
with embossed geometric patterns which could have been
mazes of pipelines, conduits, power stations, and other technological facilities. I estimated the edge's thickness to be
about two hundred kilometers. There very well could have
been roads down there, but I couldn't make any out.

The other face of the planet, still dark, flipped up toward
us. Before long, though, the sun, now on the opposite side,
peeked back over the horizon and sent long shadows across
the land. It was magnificent to watch, even under the circumstances.

The fireball had dropped back. Suddenly, there was a split
second of a blinding flash. The walls opaqued instantly, cutting it off. Purple spots swam in front of my eyes.

"Well, we outran it," Arthur said, breathing a sigh. "It was
losing energy, so it gave up and dissipated. Rather spectacu-
larly, wouldn't you say?"

"Anything else coming at us?" I asked.

"No."

"Any idea who sent it?"

"There's only one possibility."

"The lady, the goddess in white?"

Arthur glanced at me over his shoulder. "I've never met
her. Let me tell you, though, you should put quotes around
lady. She's no lady, any more than Prime is a man. Those are
simply outward forms, adopted for the sake of convenience—
and for facilitating communication with you people."

"Can you guess why she'd want to give you trouble?"

"I can guess, but when you're talking about the Culmination, dearie, you might as well be trying to figure out how
many angels can dance on the head of a pin."

"She's part of the Culmination?"

"That's right. And mortals like us can only dream about
what's really going on."

I began, "But I thought—" And realized I didn't know what to think.

"What you have to understand, dearie, is that Prime and the Goddess represent two aspects of the same being. They both share the same ontological base. Stop me if the vocabulary gets too stuffy."

"I think I know what you mean."

I didn't know what the hell he was talking about.

The walls faded again, and we saw that the land below had brightened up. Brilliant morning light fell across the face of the world. Our altitude had decreased to the point where we could pick out individual features of the landscape. There seemed to be more structures on this side. Sizable city complexes lay here and about. We swooped toward one of them.

"This is an industrial arcology built by a race known as the Mumble-mumble," Arthur informed us. "Like most alien names, you can't say it in human."

Below us lay an aggregation of multicolored domes, spires, and polyhedral buildings. The ship angled toward an octagonal structure with a wide flat roof.

Arthur smiled at me over his shoulder. "I'm in contact with the Artificial Intelligence that runs the complex. It wants to know if we're technicians on our way to work. I'm telling it yes. When we land, try to look proletarian."

"What are we doing here?" I asked.

"Laying low for a while. We don't dare try making the trip back to Emerald City until we find out what's going on."

It made sense. I nodded.

Our craft swooped in over the roof and hovered over a circular area outlined in red. Then it set gently down. Arthur made a few swipes at the control panel, then turned away. The wall opaqued again.

"Nice landing," I told him.

"All in a day's work."

He led us back into the connecting tube. We passed the valve-door of the chamber where the truck was, following the curving corridor around to another valve. Arthur touched an area of the wall beside the bulge, and the sphincter dilated.

We were descending.

"Elevator," Arthur said, pointing up.

The hole in the roof was being sealed off by a secondary

sliding door. The platform on which we rode came down into a large machinery-clogged chamber and merged with the floor. The door-valve distended itself, seeking ground, met it, and dilated a bit more. While all this was going on, I examined the seemingly monolithic material of which the ship was constructed. Its color was a very dark olive drab, not really black. The texture was grainy, and there was something else going on across the surface, an ingrained pattern of tiny lines and geometric shapes, barely visible. I tapped the wall. It rang hollowly.

We stepped out and got our first chance to get a good look at the ship. It was essentially an irregular grouping of curving tubes with nipple-shaped ends. Breast-shaped protuberances stuck out here and there. Rather erotic, this ship, in a way. I wondered what symbolism it had had for its nonhuman builders.

The big valve, the one we'd gotten sucked up by, was open.

"Jake, would you get your truck out of there, please?" Arthur asked.

I did, backing it out carefully. By the time I had parked and powered the rig's engine down, something startling was happening to the ship.

It was shrinking like a balloon with a fast leak. It didn't hiss. It just *got smaller.*

And smaller.

And . . .

When it had shrunk to a diameter of about two thirds of a meter, Arthur picked the damned thing up and held it in both arms. It looked like a model of itself. It *was* a model of itself.

"Arthur!" I screamed. "That's impossible!"

"Why?" Arthur asked.

I looked at Darla, Carl, and Lori. They were dumbfounded, staring at me as if I had the answer.

"Why?" I said. "Because you couldn't possibly pick it up. It's got to weigh—"

"Oh, no," Arthur said, "its mass isn't very much at all. Here."

He tossed the thing at me. I lurched and managed to balance it. It was heavy as hell, but it should have weighed at least a hundred tons. More, maybe.

He looked at Carl, Darla, and Lori, then back at me. "Satisfied?"

"Very," I said, stepping forward to give him his ship back.

"Oof," Arthur said, struggling with it, though he obviously had three times my strength. "Just don't ask me about the power source."

"Don't worry, I won't," I told him.

Arthur waddled over to the middle of the red circular platform, set the ship down and walked back. "When it's deflated it's kind of inert, and can't be detected at all."

"What now?" I said.

"Now I get in touch with Prime." He stared off into space for a moment. "Except he's not available, damn it. He never is, when I want him. Dearie me." He sighed. "We'll have to wait."

Bruce's voice came from the rig's exterior speaker. "Jake?"

"Yeah?"

"Jake, there is some sort of attempt being made to communicate with me. My guess is that it is a computer system indigenous to this structure."

"Oh, I forgot," Arthur said. "That's the ... I guess you'd call it the plant foreman."

"I am making an attempt to establish contact. Is this permissible?"

"Go ahead, Bruce, do your best," I told him, then turned to Arthur. "Now, before anything else, what was it you were trying to tell me about Sam?"

"Oh, yes. Well, he's been ... loaded into another machine."

"By whom, and for what reason?"

Arthur's tone was apologetic. "I'm afraid Prime is the culprit, Jake. And the reason, as far as I can understand it, was that Prime determined that Sam, as an Artificial Intelligence, was sufficiently advanced enough to warrant special consideration."

"You mean he's to be a Culmination candidate?"

"You got it."

I scowled, shaking my head. "Why is it that Prime's motives always seem to be as pure as the driven snow, no matter how underhanded his methods are?"

"Good public relations?" Arthur suggested.

"You ought to know."

"It's a living, dearie. The employment situation here is tight."

"Yeah. One other thing. You said that Sam looks like me. How could you know what he looks like?"

"From your memories of him, Jake. I have a pretty clear picture of Sam in my data files."

I nodded. Somehow Arthur's answer didn't satisfy me.

"Jake?"

It was Bruce again. "Yeah?"

"Jake, I have managed to establish a rudimentary form of communication with the unknown A.I. It has put a number of questions to us. Do you wish to reply?"

"Well, what's it asking?"

"It would like to know the purpose of our visit."

"Jeez, I don't know."

Arthur said, "Tell it that we're on an inspection tour."

"Jake?"

"Huh? Yeah, go ahead."

A few moments later Bruce reported, "The Intelligence says it is happy to receive us and wishes to know what aspect of the plant's operations would be of greatest interest to us."

"Research and development," Arthur said.

After another pause, Bruce relayed, "Very well. Would you like to begin the inspection immediately?"

"Tell it no," I said. "Tell it . . . um, say that we have had a long journey and would like to rest first. We will begin the inspection in approximately eight hours."

"Very well."

"That ought to hold it," I said. "I don't plan to stay here for eight hours."

"I can't guarantee that I'll be able to contact Prime within that time," Arthur informed me.

"No? What's he doing?"

"I don't know. All I know is that he's not available and there's no telling when he will be."

I thought of something. "Then who's looking after the rest of my crew?"

"I activated another servant. They'll be fine."

"Another servant?"

"A multipurpose robot about half my size. Nice kid, but not much personality."

"Great." I yawned. "It's been an exciting day. Much too exciting."

"Yeah," Arthur said snidely, "chewing up vast stretches of parkland can take a lot out of you."

13

I SLEPT. No dreams came.

But there was something out there, a sense of conflict, of opposing forces coming into contact, a tension. It was like picking up distant radio signals, listening in on field communications of a faraway battle—a burst of static, a word or phrase, an interruption, a few hazy images, waves of interference . . . jamming . . .

There came a sense of an overwhelming presence. A being vast and ineffable, a pervading Oneness whose dimensions bestrode the length and breadth of spacetime. But its Oneness was threatened. Something had gone wrong, and the root of the problem lay hidden in darkness. That which had been created to be One had split, polarized. The conflict raged up and down the corridors of time.

The road must be built.

No, it is folly.

We must tap the resources of time. . . .

We cannot allow it.

We are not an elite, just the culmination of all that was. . . .

That which is past is dead.

We cannot forget that our roots are in dust!

We must forget, else there is no hope. . . .

I woke up suddenly.

I sat up on the bunk and swung my feet out onto the floor. Beside me, Darla lay in fitful, troubled sleep. She tossed and moaned, a fine film of sweat covering her forehead.

"Darla . . . Darla, wake up."

Her eyes flicked open, wide with fear. She sprang up into

my arms and crushed her face into my chest, her breathing labored. She trembled.

I held her for a long time.

When she was okay again, she asked, "Did you dream it, too?"

"Bits and pieces. I don't know why. I told Prime that I didn't want the dream-teaching. I guess I was passed over, but I picked up some kind of leakage." I rubbed my eyes and took a few deep breaths. "Tell me about it."

Darla crossed her legs and pulled the ratty blanket up around her. "It was awful. It started like the first dream—like a documentary. There was more about the project—the creation of the new form of consciousness. Not much I could understand . . . but then, there was an interruption."

"The Goddess?"

"Yes, it was her, but she didn't appear in that form. I can't explain it. It was horrible. It was like being witness to the conflicts that went on in Heaven between God and Satan. I can't explain it, Jake. All I know is that I want no part of it."

"But we're caught in the middle."

She looked down. "Yes. We must get back . . . somehow. Back to the real world."

"The worlds, you mean. The worlds of the Skyway that the Culmination created."

"Caused to be created. The Roadbugs built it, and maintain it. They're a race that didn't contribute to the Culmination. They declined to participate, but thought the project was a good idea."

"What, the Skyway?"

"No, the Culmination itself. When the Culmination came to be, they became a servant race. Willingly, I think. They built the road at the Culmination's request."

"I caught a little bit of that. Why did the Culmination want the road built?"

She shook her head. "I'm not sure I understood. That's what part of the conflict is about. Do you remember the first dream? When the various races discussed the project? There were opposing factions, and somehow those conflicts were never resolved. This . . . this new form of consciousness was supposed to be uniform, monolithic, one thing only. A unity. But it didn't work out that way. Now there's this godlike being, this immortal, powerful thing loose in the universe . . . and it's partly insane. Schizophrenic! There's no telling what it will do. It transcends time and space. It can effect changes on the stream of time itself."

"Create paradoxes?"

She looked at me with a sudden new awareness. "Yes. Yes, it can do that. It can do anything. Oh, Jake!" She threw her arms around me. "We've been pawns! We've been manipulated! I don't know how or why or what the purpose is, but we're puppets, nothing more. All of this has been for no understandable reason. No reason we can fathom. We don't have a chance of comprehending these forces that insist on pushing us around. I'm tired of it! I want them to stop, Jake! I want to be left alone!"

She sobbed, and I held her.

Presently, I asked, "Are you going to be okay?"

"Yes."

"Are you sure?"

"I'm fine."

She dried her eyes, swung her legs out, got up. I noticed that her abdomen bulged. I put my hand on it and pressed gently. She smiled and put her hand over mine.

"Over three months," she said.

"It's been that long? I guess it has. You've gained weight. You're tall enough so it doesn't show."

"It's going to be a boy."

"Why not?"

She laughed. I kissed her stomach, put my ear to it.

"You can't hear the heartbeat like that," she said.

"No. He has the the radio on."

She laughed again.

I got up and kissed her mouth, then bent and kissed both breasts.

"I love you," she said.

"I love you," I told her.

It was that simple. It had been that simple all along.

I got dressed and went out into the cab. It was empty. I fed a signal to the trailer and yelled for Lori and Carl.

"Jake, they went off with Arthur," Bruce informed me.

"What! Where?"

"They commenced the inspection. Carl couldn't sleep, and

insisted on exploring the place. I am in constant touch with the foreman, and know exactly where they are. They are fine, and Carl is busy using the Product Ideation and Design Facility."

"The what? Never mind, just tell me how I get to where they are. Damn kids, running off. You should have got me up, Bruce."

"Jake, I did try. But you were apparently exhausted."

"What time is it? How long have they been gone?"

"About six hours, Jake."

"Good God."

Darla came into the cab, dressed in khakis and one of John's torn Militia surplus shirts. We were all getting short on clothes.

"An attendant is being summoned to conduct you to the Product Ideation and Design Facility."

"An attendant?"

"I think . . ."

And there it was, a shining multiarmed robot coasting toward us across the glossy blue floor.

We got out. The contraption pulled up to us and stopped. It was partly a conveyance of some sort, although the seats in the back hadn't been built for humans. Lacking wheels, the thing floated a few centimeters off the floor. It buzzed softly at us.

I said, "I guess that means 'All aboard.'"

We climbed into the back of it and perched ourselves on the impossible, mushroom-shaped seats. There weren't any backrests, but there was a crossbar to hang onto.

We were conducted on a very informative and educational tour of the plant. A long one, too, but I was politic enough not to complain. Everything was impressive, but we didn't know what the hell we were looking at. Our guide kept buzzing at us, we kept nodding and smiling pleasantly. Oh, my. Fifty million units produced in one year? How admirable.

But, by God, what a plant. A cool, quiet place of industrial and scientific sculpture. We could appreciate it on that level at least. We soared along high curving ramps looking down on silent gargantuan machines, labyrinths of pipeline, armies of tall bubble-topped cylinders, rack upon rack of instruments, giant antennalike assemblies, huge metal coils, and jungles of transparent tubing. Everything was silent, still. Color was everywhere—blue industrial light glinted off gold and silver spheres, orange and red conduits tangled with each other against overhead domes of bright pink and yellow, green rampways flew through the dry, still, blue-lit air.

Finally, we arrived. The Product Ideation and Design Facility was a large wedge-shaped room stuffed floor to ceiling with instrument panels throbbing with electric life, glittering with lights and luminous screens and flashing dials. Arthur sat on a bench near Carl, who was hunched over what appeared to be some sort of computerized drafting board—a wide flat screen crawling with moving diagrams and charts.

We got out of the robocart and walked over. Lori was lying on the soft carpeted floor, asleep, her head propped up with Carl's bunched jacket. Carl didn't even glance up. He was absorbed in whatever he was doing.

I looked at Arthur. "What gives?"

Arthur shrugged, grinning. "He's having a dandy time."

"How the hell did he figure out how to work the equipment?"

"Oh, it's not as hard as you might expect." Arthur rose, walked over, and peered over Carl's shoulder. "In this plant, in its day, engineers were looked upon as artists. They really didn't need to know much about engineering. Here, machine intelligences supply all the data, all the formulae, all the know-how. They do all the dirty work. The only thing that organic brains can supply is creativity. That's what Carl's doing. He's telling the machines what he wants and what he wants it to do, and the machines are helping him design it. And if the design is judged a worthy work of art, they just might build a prototype model."

"That's really something," I said. And it was, it was.

"No! Not that way," Carl said sharply. "It opens from the left. Yeah."

"Satisfactory?" a soft voice asked.

"Satisfactory."

I looked at Arthur, who said, "I think Bruce is responsible for the plant learning English."

I nodded.

"Now the engine is all yours, pal," Carl was saying, eyes still riveted to the drafting board. "I don't have a clue how that works."

"Very well. Requires advanced propulsion principle—high efficiency, low maintenance . . ."

"How about *no* maintenance? Can you do that? I'll never find someone to fix it."

"A challenge for time periods longer than quarter revolution of average galaxy."

"Huh? Quarter revolution of a— That's millions of years. Hey, I'm not going to live anywhere near that long."

"Then no maintenance is no challenge."

"All *ri-i-ght!*"

"Weapons systems?"

This went on for another hour. Carl eventually acknowledged our presence, then insisted that he had to finish. I didn't ask what he was doing. Lori woke out of a troubled sleep, and needed some attention. She had had the dream too. Afterward, we hung about and looked around. We were extremely hungry.

At last, Carl was done.

"Very unusual, extremely idiosyncratic," the design chief pronounced. "But of surpassing elegance and simplicity. May we go ahead with fabrication of prototype?"

"Sure!" Carl said, getting up. He swayed slightly, and put a hand to his forehead. "Man, am I bushed. Terrific headache, too. But it was a hell of a lot of fun."

"Lunch time!" Arthur said.

"Lunch?" I was ready to gnaw on some lab equipment.

A detail of robots brought us lunch. The food was very good, not quite the haute cuisine of Emerald City, but far more than adequate. Bruce had done a good job feeding biochemical information to the plant's protein synthesizers. The flavorings were top-notch. Textures were a little off here and there, especially in the steak. A little too mushy. But the bread was terrific. You'd never know there wasn't one grain of wheat in it.

After lunch, the plant foreman spoke to us. "We have begun production of prototype. Would you like to observe?" He sounded a lot like the design chief, and I suspected that the latter was merely a subsystem of the former.

Would like to observe, yes.

We all boarded another robocart and swung out into the plant.

The place had come to life. We rode for an hour through the throbbing heart of technological wizardry. What had been hulks of dead machinery now flashed and sparked, whirred and hummed, chimed and beeped and thrummed and sang, while pink and violet electrical discharges leaped between giant coils, translucent tubing glowed and pulsed, luminescent motes swam inside huge transparent spheres, and veils of energy fluttered in the air overhead like auroral displays.

"Goddamn Frankenstein movie," was Carl's reaction.

At last we came to a large, quiet empty chamber. We got off and waited. Before long, the far wall retracted, and two robots hauled the prototype out onto the showroom floor.

It was Carl's 1957 Chevrolet Impala, chrome glinting in the track lighting, a lambent sheen soft upon its coat of candy-apple red, metal-flake paint.

"My car!" Carl shouted ecstatically, throwing open the driver's door and hopping in. He sniffed. "Hey, they got that new car smell just right!"

"Satisfactory?" the plant foreman asked hopefully.

"Satisfactory!" Carl enthused.

There was a note of pride in the foreman's voice. "May we then begin field testing and evaluation?"

"Uh—yeah. Well, maybe not. I know it's gonna work!"

"Intuitive evaluation? Perhaps empirical data are needed as well?"

"Huh? Um . . ."

I was smiling at Carl. He noticed and returned a sheepish grin. "Hell, I couldn't resist."

"What're you going to do when they present you with the bill?"

"The bill. Oh."

I chuckled.

The foreman spoke delicately. "Remuneration can be forgone. We compliment designer on high esthetic factor of overall concept. Inspired, and truly beautiful in result. Congratulations. When may we begin production?"

"Yeah, Carl," I said. "When can these nice people turn out fifty million units for you?"

"Jesus. I don't know."

"Production is not contemplated?" the foreman asked sadly.

"Well . . . Jake, what do I tell them?"

I said, "The artist would like time to ponder the philosophical ramifications of his creation before considering sharing it with the universe at large."

"Of course. Commendable. Please contact us when time is proper."

"Oh, yeah," Carl said, nodding emphatically. "Sure. And thanks a lot."

"Extreme pleasure has been taken in assisting a consummate artist such as yourself."

Carl looked embarrassed.

We got back to the receiving bay as the robots were delivering the Chevy. We had taken the long route—the foreman had insisted that we see the Submicron Fractionating Assembly. Whatever it was, it was pretty.

I didn't see Prime's arrival. I was inspecting what was left of the starboard stabilizer foil when I happened to glance up at Darla, who was staring open-mouthed at something out on the floor. I straightened up, walked around her . . .

And there was Prime, standing near our miniature spaceship, conversing with Arthur.

He turned a smiled at me. "Hello, Jake," he called.

"You're hard to get hold of," I said, walking over. "But you seem to get around."

Prime glanced around. "Wonderful facility. Have you toured the place?"

"Endlessly."

He laughed. "Odd that you should wind up here."

"Actually, we never intended to leave Emerald City."

"Really?" He seemed pleased to hear it. "I assumed that you were on your way home."

"Without Sam? Hardly."

"No, I suppose not. But it was my intention to give your father some voice in the matter."

"He's not my father. He's an Artificial Intelligence program."

Prime nodded. "And a remarkable one. His Entelechy Matrix was manufactured by the Vlathu, was it not?"

"Yes."

"We know of the Vlathu. They possessed techniques unknown even in the time of the Culmination. The Vlathu attained a very high degree of spirituality for a primitive race."

I thought about that for a moment before saying, "If you consider the Vlathu primitive, what does that make us? We humans, I mean?"

"Humans are one of the ancestral races of the Culmination itself. One of the tributary races. I have told you many times that I am partly human. I meant by that, that the Culmination is in some part composed of human elements."

"I'm not sure I understand," I said. "You may be descended from human beings, but after ten billion years of evolution . . ."

He laughed. "Evolution. Odd concept. The process isn't automatic, you know. If there is no good reason for a species to evolve, it won't. But let's set that aside. The elements I referred to aren't genetic remnants, but the minds of actual living human beings. Their very soul and substance. They are a vital part of the Culmination. Some of them are your friends."

Darla, Carl, and Lori had gathered behind me. I turned my head toward them, and Darla looked at me gravely. I turned back to Prime.

"What do you mean? Who?"

"Well, Susan D'Archangelo, for one. She has consented to contribute to the project. So has Yuri Voloshin, Sean Fitzgore, Roland Yee, and Liam Flaherty."

"I can't believe you."

"I'll leave it to them to convince you. There has been no coercion. None, Jake. You must believe that."

I was silent for a moment, my mind churning and churning. Then: "I still can't believe it."

Prime's hands went out in a helpless shrug. "I'm sorry."

"What about the others? Zoya, Oni, Ragna, John . . . ?"

"They have declined. They will join you on your journey home." Prime chuckled. "Incidentally, you've forgotten one person. Sam has declined as well."

"Sam never went to church."

Prime laughed. "I dare say he didn't."

Darla asked, "Aren't you forgetting Winnie and George?"

"My dear, they *are* part of the Culmination. They always were. They are members of one of the Guide Races. Think of how you got here."

"We were kidnapped," I said.

"Your case was special, of course. But what prompted all these quests to find the end of the Skyway?"

He was right. Winnie's map lay behind it all.

"About Sam," I said. "You'll return him to me?"

"He will return. Everything will be returned to you."

I stared at him. What was this form I saw? What? What did it represent? I shook my head. "Maybe I'm just slow, but there are a hell of a lot of things I don't understand about all this."

"Then lay yourself open to the dream-teaching. You need not join the project to do that. You will learn."

I was suddenly irked. "To hear you talk, everything's just going along swimmingly. But it isn't. The Goddess has other ideas. Doesn't she?"

He turned and stepped away, halted, then slowly wheeled about, his eyes on the floor, his lips drawn into a wry smile. "Other ideas. No. There is only One Idea, with variations."

"But she's opposed in some fundamental way."

"No."

"Then the dream last night . . . what was all that about?"

"Dream and find out. Don't fight it. Don't be afraid."

I considered it. "Maybe I will."

"Good. And keep this in mind. Conflict is part of the warp and woof of existence. That which contains no tension is static. If this is true, can any attempt to reach the ultimate be free of conflict? Do not think that the Culmination must be a success from the start. That was a fundamental error of those who conceived it. Yet that mistake did not necessarily lead to a fundamental flaw. The question is, what ultimately happened? Since the Culmination is outside of time, that question can be answered. And you will find the answer if you choose to seek it."

"Doesn't the Goddess know it, too?"

"Of course."

"It doesn't make sense," I said.

He turned and walked away a few steps, stopped, turned about. "I must leave you now. Jake, I have a sense that you must suffer further. I can help to some degree, but I am inhib-

ited by circumstances you might find difficult to understand."
He smiled again. "I shouldn't worry. You are well suited to
overcoming adversity. I think that is why whatever forces are
at work behind you chose you as their instrument. You are the
archetypal hero, Jake." He raised his right hand. "Be well."

And he vanished, leaving behind the smell of ozone. The
Goddess' exit had had more panache, but his showed real
class.

14

"WHAT NOW, Arthur?" I said wearily.

"I'm supposed to go fetch Sam and the rest of the washouts when Prime gives me the all clear."

"When will that be?"

"I don't know, dearie. When the current flap has subsided. It won't be safe until then."

"Okay, say you go and get them," I said. "Then what?"

"I take you to the egress portal and show you what cylinders to shoot in order to get back where you belong."

For which there was no need, since I had the Roadmap. I looked around, throwing up my arms. "What do we do till then? Fill out a time card and punch in?"

"Make something," Arthur said, "like Carl did."

"Do you need any ashtrays?"

"How about a hand-tooled leather wallet, monogrammed?"

"You only have one initial," I told him.

"And I don't have any pockets, either. Well, then, I'm stumped."

So was I. But there was nothing to do. We couldn't leave for the master portal, and we couldn't very well drive all the way to the other side of the world, back to Emerald City. We were at Arthur's mercy.

There was sleep to catch up on, though, and thinking to do.

Lay yourself open to the dream-teaching, Prime had advised. I wasn't sure I was ready for that yet. I thought about it. I needed answers, but falling into a swoon and getting infused with divine enlightenment wasn't my style. Besides, didn't you have to fast for forty days and nights in the desert first? I had left my hairshirt at the cleaners back in T-Maze.

I was tired of searching for ever-elusive answers. Damn tired of it. As Darla said, we keep getting pushed around by unseen forces. A phrase Prime had used kept echoing: "whatever forces are at work behind you." Indeed, what forces? If neither Prime nor the White Lady were really calling the shots, who was? Were there other aspects of the Culmination? Was it something outside the Culmination entirely? More whispers in the darkness, more missing pieces of a puzzle I had grown weary of fumbling with.

I lay in the bunk, Darla asleep beside me. No dreams for her. It seemed that if you didn't want to hear the propaganda, you simply turned off your receiver.

I listened. The plant was quiet except for a faint background hum. Now and then came a faraway thump or bang— maintenance attendants about their chores, perhaps. Perhaps not. Were we safe here? Of course not. But Arthur had his funnel-ears pricked for any intruders—and whatever other sensors he had were tuned in, too.

I got up and went out to the cab, sat in the driver's seat. Arthur had inflated the spacetime ship to about half its full size, and had gone inside. Said he had things to do.

I regarded Carl's vehicle. Everyone, including Carl, had wondered about its origin. Had Carl created it himself? The answer, in gleaming chrome and whitewall tires, lay out there on the floor of the receiving bay.

The time comes, as the saying goes, when a man's gotta do what a man's gotta do. Push me, and I push back. Time to take the offensive. From now on it would be Jake McGraw, Master of Space and Time.

I woke Darla up.

"Hmph?" she said.

"C'mon. I got an insane idea."

"Hmph."

I went back to the cab while Darla dressed. "Bruce?"

"Yes, Jake?"

"Patch me through to the plant foreman."

A short delay, then: "He's on the line."

"Hello?" I said.

"Greetings!" the foreman beamed.

"Hi. Uh, would it be possible to use the Product Ideation and Design Facility again?"

"Certainly! At this moment?"

"Yes, please."

"Will send transportation immediately."

But could I do it, make that insane idea a reality? Reality seemed a fluid, changing thing here on Microcosmos, a malleable lump of stuff that could be beaten and pummeled into whatever shape was desired. I'd take a whack at it myself.

I told Darla to take a blanket along. I thumbed the intercom button, thought better of it, and punched up the interior trailer monitor. Oops, Carl and Lori were busy back there. I hoped those kids knew at least the rudiments of birth control. I should talk, I thought.

The robocart arrived, and we hopped on.

"It is revolutionary concept," the design chief said. I thought I detected a note of awe in its voice.

"Yeah, it sure is."

I peered into the depths of the drafting board. Since the object I wanted to create was immaterial, there wasn't much to look at except geometry. But it was fascinating. There were all sorts of things: planar sheaves warping and folding back on themselves, torus shapes and saddle shapes distending and contracting, Moebius strips and Klein bottles and things that neither gentleman had dreamed of; a matrix bound up in knotted tufts of nothing-at-all, forming the very fabric of space itself—and of time, and even of matter; point-masses migrating across limitless dimensions; impossible constructs, singularities, parallel lines meeting at the edge of infinity. . .

"However," the chief went on, "technique of dimensional impaction is not unknown. Scale here is much larger, but in theory can be done."

"Can be done in practice?" I asked.

"Would be honored to try. May suggest to begin by postulating isotropic homogeneity throughout entire metrical frame?"

"Sure, let's do that thing. What's an isotrope?"

Two hours later, I had a terrific headache, but the design chief seemed confident that the major theoretical obstacles had been overcome. Problems concerning the actual production of an artifact loomed large, though. The production manager was called in for consultation.

"Retooling necessary," the PM stated.

"How extensive?" the chief asked.

"Possibly entire facility."

"Can be done?"

"Affirmative."

Later, my head seemed about to burst. They brought me a bed—it was a big round cushy thing, very comfortable—and I racked out after trying to rouse Darla, who preferred the floor. Her back, she said.

I slept for an hour, got up and went to the board, where I was served a cup of hot beverage and a sweet roll.

"Anything?" I asked.

"Design almost complete," the chief told me. "Must tell you that entire plant staff is much enthused and excited by this particular project. Retooling is progressing on schedule."

"Jeez, you guys must make a bundle in overtime."

"Say again, please?"

I took a slurp of ersatz coffee. "Sorry, just thinking aloud."

We went on an inspection tour of the retooling effort, visiting buildings that I didn't think we'd been in before. They were tearing the place apart. What we witnessed surpassed anything we had seen of the plant's "conventional" production operations. We watched an army of robots storm an assembly facility and reduce it to junk, then cart in new material and build a titanic contraption that looked like a particle accelerator married to an exciter cannon. We stood by, spellbound, as whole new wings were added onto existing buildings—slap, dash, bang—to accommodate new oversized equipment. One of the larger facilities now housed a monstrous affair that had been thrown together in under an hour, a towering edifice of black glass tubing, shining metal, copper spheres, and multicolored domes. At its top, dozens of shafts converged, bringing unknown forces together to clash inside a central chamber. They were apparently testing the thing when we drove through. Violet discharges snaked through the dark glass, and the machine screeched like a beast chained in the depths of hell. We got out of there.

When we returned to P.I.&D., Carl and Lori were there, looking worried.

"What's going on?" Carl asked. "The whole place is going crazy."

"Quotas to meet for the Five Year Plan."

"Huh?"

"I got a little project cooking," I said.

"Jesus, we thought something happened. *Little* project?"

A big problem came up: a power shortage. The energy requirements for final assembly of the object were beyond the plant's capacity. Calls went out to other automated industrial facilities around the planet, and most replies were favorable. They'd be willing to help. Word had gotten out about the project. We were a sensation.

The retooling went on for another twelve hours before the initial stages of final assembly commenced. It was then that a horrendous explosion rocked the plant. We tried frantically to contact the foreman. Half an hour later, our call was returned.

"Extensive damage sustained in facility housing Inertial Electrostatic Confinement Ring," the foreman reported.

I felt guilty. "Gee, that's terrible. What happened?"

"Failure in primary power tetrode, leading to fracture and subsequent leakage in coupling loop."

"Oh. Anybody hurt? Uh, I mean . . ."

"Several worker units lost. Have been replaced."

"I see. Maybe we'd better cancel the project before worse mishaps occur." I was thinking more of our own safety.

"Anomalous event, recurrence statistically negligible. We urge that effort be pursued through to completion."

"Well, I don't know."

"Abandoning task at this point would take on tragic aspect."

"It would?" These guys really were gung-ho. "Okay, let's go ahead then."

"Splendid! Your courage is to be commended."

"*My* courage?"

Repairs were effected, and work was resumed.

Arthur told me he was ready to leave any time. I told him we wanted to go back with him to Emerald City.

"Fine with me," he said, "though you could wait here. I won't be more than an hour."

"I think I have to get out of this place before I go nuts. Can you wait till the project's done?"

"Sure. By the way, what in the world are you people trying to do?"

"Produce your hand-tooled, genuine leather, mono-grammed wallet," I said.

"Just what I've always wanted."

The final assembly was almost an anticlimax. Everything went smoothly. We were summoned to the showroom.

I held it in the palm of my hand and stared at it. The robot who had delivered it whooshed away.

It was a very simple object, yet a very strange thing to look at: a small, totally black featureless cube.

"A most sublime artifact," the foreman said with almost religious solemnity.

"The cube!" Darla gasped. "My God, Jake, why?"

"I don't really know why, not intellectually," I told her. "Not yet. But everything seems to revolve around this little object. A whole legend has grown up around it, around us. The legend says that when we go back, we'll arrive before we left, and I will give the cube to Assemblywoman Marcia Miller, who will in turn hand it over to the dissident movement, who will in turn give it to you. And you will give it back to me. Except that the 'me' you will give it to is the me of three months ago." I took Darla's hand and placed the cube in her palm. She stared at it in astonishment. "My duty seemed very clear. Since somebody stole the one you gave me, I thought I'd better come up with another one to give back to you. And there it is."

"But . . ." Darla was baffled.

"According to the legend," I went on, "the cube doesn't have an origin. It just keeps cycling from future to past and back again. Now, here I am at the end of the Skyway. It doesn't look as if I'm ever going to find an object like this. In fact, everyone here seems bent on taking the original one away from me. So, I thought I'd kill two paradoxes with one volitional act—I created the damn thing on my own. Now I have the cube again, and the cube has an origin. Well, these guys did the originating, actually. I just gave them the idea."

"But how, Jake?" Darla asked, shaking her head in wonder. "How did you know what to create? Nobody ever really cracked the cube's mystery. Ragna's people made some good guesses, but how did you know what the cube really was?"

"I didn't, of course. I took Ragna's people's speculations

and asked the design chief to come up with a design for an artifact that would more or less answer to the description. He did. And the factory crew made it a reality."

"But what is it, Jake?" Carl asked. "What is the cube? What's it for?"

"Don't know what it's for, yet," I answered. "But what it is, near as I can figure from what the design chief told me, is a continuum in which the normal properties of space and time are nonexistent. Within the confines of these six sides, neither space nor time exist at all. What's inside the cube is literally and absolutely nothing. A nonspace. A singularity. The *Ahgirr* scientists' speculation about it being a huge space folded up was wrong, but I can see how they arrived at the hypothesis. Nonspace is a slippery concept to grasp. Another thing: space and time are not the only thing that doesn't exist inside. Nothing else in the universe does either. Fundamental things, like the Planck Constant, or G, the gravitational constant, or any of those foundation stones of the physical universe as we know it. Inside the cube, anything goes. You could make a whole new universe in there, using physical laws different from the standard ones."

Darla said, "What about the information, the data coming out of the cube? The Movement people who examined it discovered that."

"The chief told me that stray radiation is generated at the interface of the cube's surface and the outside world. It has something to do with virtual particle creation, which goes on everywhere in the universe all the time. I can't quite grasp the reason, but somehow when these particles pop into existence near the cube, they get real nervous and instead of blinking out of existence like good little virtual particles are supposed to, they stay real and fly out into the world as electron-positron pairs."

"Man, you lost me there," Carl said.

"Forget it," I said. "I don't understand it myself."

"Jake, I have other problems with this," Darla said. "How do you know that this cube and the first one are identical?"

"I don't, now," I said. "But if I do succeed in delivering this one back to T-Maze three months in the past, it will be identical. Because this cube *will be* the first cube. No?"

Darla sighed in resignation. "I guess." She frowned and

shook her head. "But I still don't see how you could have created something when you didn't know exactly what that something was in the first place."

I took the cube back and tossed it into the air, caught it. It was feather light. What I couldn't figure was why it wasn't completely weightless. The design chief had told me it had something to do with "inertial drag" and the fact that the frozen energies holding the cube together possessed "mass equivalence."

"Well, let's put it this way," I said. "I didn't know anything. But I had some speculations about what the cube was. Everybody had them. Prime told us that it was 'an experiment in the creation of a universe.' Don't ask me how he knew. I spilled all of this to the design chief, who is a creative mind. He took these ideas and kicked it around his circuits for a while and came up with a few ideas of his own. One of them turned out to be feasible. And the technical guys did it up for us. This is how the cube got created in the first place. This was its origin."

"If you say so," Darla said.

We got on the robocart for the trip back to the receiving bay.

"There's still a paradox," Darla stated as we got moving. "Where did the idea for the cube come from?"

"I told you," I said.

"No, I mean the *reason* it came to be. Its reason for existing at all. The first cube prompted the speculation, which generated the motivation to create this one. But you're saying that this one is the first one. So . . . so, you see, it's as if—"

"The cube created itself," I said.

"Yes! That's the only way you can look at it! It's impossible, Jake. Absolutely impossible."

"Have an impossibility," I said, handing it to her.

The plant foreman was sad to see us go. "You will return sometime soon? Our brief association has been most rewarding and gratifying."

"Sure, we'll come back," I told it, not wanting to hurt its feelings.

"When?"

"Uh . . ." Nothing like being put on the spot.

"Will you consider postponing your departure? All our various subsystems are most distressed over your leaving. Individuals of paramount creative powers, such as yourselves, are very rare. We are very desirous of continuing to work with you on other projects."

"Well, you're very kind, but we really must run along."

There was a sound not unlike a sigh. "Then please take our good wishes with you, and do return at your earliest convenience."

"Thank you. We will."

I wondered when the plant had last entertained visitors. Thousands, millions of years ago? It was cruel, in a way.

After Arthur had inflated the spacetime ship to full size, I shot the rig into the large cargo bay, and Carl tucked his Chevy into one of two smaller ones. We all boarded the craft.

The illuminated spires and domes of the plant dwindled behind us as we sped toward the edge of the world. It was night on this face of Microcosmos, which Carl had dubbed "Flipside." The moon surrogate rode low in the sky, and stars like diamonds on black velvet dotted the dome of night. Below, city complexes lay outlined in dim crosshatches, and a few stray lights glowed feebly in the dark countryside. A still, deserted world, Microcosmos was, eerie even by day, by night a place of silence and shadows and mystery. A chill went through me. Time was a thing of substance on this world, a weight bearing down like the stone mass of an ancient temple. I felt a sudden savage longing to get free of this place, this graveyard of the ages. It was dead here. There was death here.

The world-disk flipped over as we swung around the edge, and seeing Microcosmos in daylight again made me feel a little better. But not for long, because a reception committee was on its way to meet us.

"Oh, shit," Arthur said, frantically swiping at the control box.

Dozens of variously colored fiery motes were streaking up at us. Arthur put the ship into a steep climb, but in no time a swirling orange vortex-phenomenon was hard on our tail. The thing looked very familiar. Arthur began evasive maneuvers.

"Arthur," I said, trying to sound calm, "what do those things do?"

"Oh, they eat things," Arthur said airily. "Like spacetime

ships. Ingests them, sort of. An explosive device can't do much damage to us, nor can any kind of beam weapon. But that thing can snare us and slowly disintegrate us. It has enough energy to do that."

I said, "Oh."

Horrified, I looked at Carl, remembering one of his Chevy's fantastic weapons, the enigma Carl called the "Tasmanian Devil." Carl swallowed hard and nodded.

I turned to Arthur. "Are these the things that chase their targets and never give up until they destroy them?"

"Yup. How did you know?"

"Uh . . . what are you going to do?"

"Well, there's only one thing I can do . . ." Arthur said.

The thing behind us was gaining, matching our every increment of speed, growing until we could see its boiling interior, a fiercely glowing furnace of demonic combustion. There was a suggestion of something else in there, a shape, a mad, implacable figure, a howling psychotic beast bent only on destruction.

". . . and I think I better do it now."

Instantaneously, everything around us disappeared—the Tasmanian Devil, the sky, Microcosmos itself. And in their place were endless stars, all around us.

We were in space.

"Dearie me," Arthur wailed, "I've really gone and done it now."

He was silent, slowly moving his thick, stunted fingers over the face of the control box.

"Arthur," I said after a long moment, "what's happened?"

"Oh, nothing. We made a continuum jump, which we shouldn't have done near such a large mass as a planet, especially Microcosmos, since it has very peculiar gravitational properties. We had no choice, but that doesn't help much."

"What's the problem?"

"Well, I have no idea where or when we are. None. It'll take time to get enough readings to make an educated guess. My uneducated guess is that we've jumped over ten billion light-years."

Standing beside me, Darla put both arms around my waist and pressed herself against me. I needed someone to hug, too; I snaked my arm about her shoulders and held her closer.

"Well, this is a bit of luck," Arthur said. "Star very near. Not only did we not wind up in the middle of intergalactic space, we blundered on to a likely planet-bearing star." He snorted. "It probably has a brood of grungy ice balls and gas giants orbiting it. No good to us." He sighed. "Better check it out, anyway."

The stars shifted suddenly. Then again. And again. Each time, a single star up ahead grew brighter, and with a few more jumps it stood out as a tiny disk against the spattering of glowing points around it.

"Looks awfully familiar," Arthur said suspiciously. He shook his head. "Couldn't be. But it's the right spectral type. Let's see if we can resolve a planet or two."

Delicately, Arthur palpated the face of the box, which, I had come to believe, was some sort of direct interface or link between the ship's instrumentation and Arthur's powerful robot brain.

I scanned the star swarm around us. To our rear, the swarm thickened, congealing along a long milky band of luminescence shot through with dark clouds. I searched left and right, trying to pick out constellations.

"You won't believe this," Arthur said. "But guess where we are."

"That's Sol over there," I said. "The sun. Earth's sun."

"You just earned your astronomy merit badge, kid."

15

"I'M GOING home," Carl said, awestruck. "I'm really going home."

"Hold on, dearie," Arthur cautioned. "We know where we are, but not *when* we are. This could be Earth in one million A.D., or B.C., for that matter, or any time in between. So don't get your hopes up. That was a completely blind jump we made. The chances of our winding up here at all were approximately infinity to one." Arthur shook his head. "Amazing. If I'd aimed for here, I never would have made it. Not in one jump, anyway. To've done it with any degree of accuracy and safety, fifty would have been more like it."

"Any way of finding out when we are?" I asked.

"Well, several. I could clock the rate of a few known pulsars and get a fairly good idea of the galactic epoch we're in . . . if I had a few known pulsars to look at. Trouble is, I don't have much in storage about Terran astronomy, not anything like what I'd need to make those calculations."

"I thought you knew everything, Arthur," Darla said.

"How much do you know about Terran astronomy?" Arthur countered.

"Not a whole lot."

"Well, there you are. Neither does this ship, although there's a lot of general astronomical data in its memory. Maybe the ship's computer can come up with something. Offhand, I'd say there's a good chance we're in the general time frame you people came from, give or take a few thousand years. I do know a few constellations, and they're not at all distorted."

"One way to find out for sure," I said.

"How?"

"Let's go to Earth and take a look at it."

"That idea makes me a little nervous," Arthur said. "Don't like to go mucking about where I don't belong. But . . ." He swung his ugly dog head around and gave me his grimacing, nonhuman approximation of a smile. "What the hell, eh? We have nothing to lose but our lives."

"That's the spirit, Arthur," I told him.

"Spare me the clichés."

It took Arthur twelve hours to dodge and weave his way through the solar system, which wasn't bad time, considering that we traveled nearly two billion kilometers. In fact, I thought it was great time, but Arthur said it wasn't, giving the excuse that he had to take it easy in the midst of great gravitational stress. I don't know what he was talking about, because we didn't see any planets on the way in, not even Jupiter. And not one asteroid. But I don't know much about space. I like something firm under my feet.

We spent the time in the truck, sleeping, eating the great gobs of food that the factory people had given us, and talking.

"Have you considered what you might find when we get to Earth?" I asked Carl.

"Yeah," he said, grinning. "Hot dogs, the L.A. Dodgers, cars that run on gasoline, movies, girls . . ."

Lori folded her arms and shot daggers at him.

"Have you thought of anything else?" I said.

He shrugged. "Like what?"

I really didn't know how to tell him. "I guess it depends on when we arrive."

"When? I don't get you."

I tried another tack. "What about Lori?"

"Oh, I've thought about that." Carl pulled her over to him and hugged her with one arm. "We've decided. We're getting married."

Lori smiled winsomely. "Yeah," she said.

"Going to be complicated."

"How so?" Carl asked, frowning.

"Well, remember. Lori's time of origin is almost two hundred years in the future. There're a few adjustments she's going to have to make."

"I know," Lori said. "Imagine having to worry about *tooth* decay." She made a face.

"Yeah, tooth decay, and other bothersome things. But more than that, Carl, you're going to have to establish some kind of identity for Lori. Some sort of fictitious but convincing background for her. You can't very well go around telling everybody that she's from another planet."

"Why not?" He waited for my look of incredulity, then chuckled. "Yeah, I know. Nobody's ever going to believe my story. I'd get laughed out of the country. Or they'd lock me up and throw away the key."

"Right. Don't even try. And that car stays here."

"Hey . . . wait a minute. That car would back up my story all the way! Yeah! Why didn't I think of that?"

"Hold it, Carl."

"Let 'em laugh at my story. I'll just fire a Tasmanian Devil at 'em and let 'em see how funny it all is. Hell, I'm taking the car."

"Carl, it won't work."

"Why not? Forget it, Jake. It's my car, and I'm taking it with me."

I stared at him for a moment. "Carl, how old are you? You've never told me."

"Nineteen."

"Really? I thought you were a little older than that. You look it."

"I got used to telling people I was twenty-one. But after that year I spent driving around in outer space, I must look like I'm fifty."

"You never went into that period of your life, either. What did you do out there on the road?"

"Nothing. I'd stay in motels. Eat. Drive around a little. Sleep in the car. I stayed with a g—uh, a friend for a couple weeks. Then I thought of getting a job, but I didn't have any papers. So I kept driving around."

"Did the Militia give you any trouble?"

"I was stopped once, for not having a proper license plate. But I gave the cop two gold coins, and she let me off with a warning."

Our stalwart law enforcement personnel. "I'm surprised you were only stopped once."

"They chased me several times. But all the cops ever got was a lot of dust in their teeth."

I nodded. I knew that car very well. "What did you do for money?"

"I found all these gold coins in the trunk. I guess Prime put them there."

I didn't know how to go about telling him that I didn't think Prime had done it.

Earth.

I hadn't seen it in more than thirty years. It hung in space beneath us looking like a huge blue and white marble, its land masses faint brown texturings beneath a gauze wrapping of cloud. Day was breaking over the Philippines, and the swirling gray fingers of a tropical depression hovered over New Guinea. Early morning sun glared off the bright blue island-freckled Pacific.

We made our entry into the atmosphere somewhere in the vicinity of Wake Island, I think. We swept over the Hawaiians at a screaming Mach 12, then decelerated rapidly, following a flight path that hewed fairly close to the Tropic of Cancer, if I remembered my Terran geography.

We now had a fairly good idea what time frame we had jumped into. The ship had tracked numerous artificial satellites in orbit about the Earth, but not the profusion of my day. No power satellites, no geosynchronous space colonies, no activity in and about the moon. No space traffic whatsoever. We were obviously somewhere in the middle to late twentieth century, the dawn of the age of space travel. I had warned Arthur not to make a dead-on approach to the western coast of the United States. I did remember my Terran history, and these were very paranoid times. Carl agreed. Arthur said he didn't know whether the ship was radar-transparent, because in the era in which the ship was built, no one worried about prehistoric technologies like radar. There was a chance that alarms were already going off all over the place. So we scared the shit out of Mexico, hung a right at the tip of the Baja peninsula, and headed north following the coast and flying low.

The ship was fully transparent now. It was eerie—four humans, one improbable alien android, a futuristic trailer truck, and a contemporary automobile, streaking over coastal towns and fishing villages, blithely flying along like characters out of a surreal version of *Peter Pan*.

"What will the natives think?" I asked Arthur.

"Huh? Oh, the transparency's only one-way, dearie. Don't worry about that. I've got the surface of the ship tuned to a mirror finish. We'll be reflecting sky and sea. Practically invisible, except from a few angles."

"San Diego!" Carl said, pointing to the coast.

I looked. Lots of orange-tile roofs, a few tall buildings, a big harbor choked with shipping. I'd never been to San Diego.

"We'd better head inland here," Carl said.

"We've got company," Arthur said.

I didn't see them until they got out of the sun: two military-looking aircraft with triangular wings. They swooped down on us and leveled off. One banked and vectored in for a closer look.

"Christ, we got the Air Force after us," Carl said worriedly. "We're a goddamn UFO."

"Not for long," Arthur said.

With a stunning burst of speed, we left the aircraft behind as if they were standing still. The sea was gone; we were streaking over semiarid land that soon turned to desert.

"Slow down!" Carl yelled. "We'll be in Arizona in another minute! Turn around and go back!"

"Don't take a fit, dearie," Arthur said calmly.

We executed a sharp turn and headed northwest for a hundred kilometers or so, soon hitting the edges of congested urban development. We jogged east again, skirting the edge of it and still bearing generally north.

"That's gotta be San Bernardino," Carl said. "Go out into the desert a little ways and land."

"Will do."

We did, settling down behind a ridge that ran along a narrow dirt road.

Carl asked, "Jake, do you have a screwdriver in the truck?"

"A power driver. Well, maybe I do have an old screwdriver lying around." I went back and found it, then met everyone in the small cargo bay. Arthur had already dilated the doorway.

"Well, we're off," Carl said, flushing with excitement.

"We're coming with you," I told him.

"Jake, you can't!"

"We're not going to stay. I just want to make sure that we haven't left you in an untenable position. We don't know exactly when we are, Carl."

"This is where I belong. I know it! This has to be my world, my time frame."

"Carl, think a minute. When exactly were you abducted? What was the date?"

"I'll never forget it. It was August twenty-fifth, 1964."

I still didn't know quite how to tell him. Arthur came into the bay and did it for me.

"Well, I've got the exact date," he said. "It was fairly easy. I monitored some local radio broadcasts. It's Tuesday, July seventh, 1964."

Finally, it dawned on Carl. "Oh, my God."

"Yeah," I said.

His eyes widened. "Then—" He broke off, his mouth hanging open.

"Right. You can't go home yet, Carl."

Carl closed his mouth and swallowed hard, looking suddenly ill. He leaned back against the fender of his car. "Shit."

"It seems we have some time to kill," Darla said.

"I can't believe it," Carl said. "I just can't believe it. You mean that if I drive to Santa Monica and knock on my front door . . ."

"Your paradoxical double would get a big shock," I said. "But since it never happened . . . or did it?"

"I think I'd remember it."

"Exactly. And I don't think you should do it, either. We'll just have to wait."

"Yeah, wait for Prime to come and do his dirty work. Kidnap me. And I guess we have to let him do it."

"I have some thoughts about that," I said. "I'm not sure I'm right, but—"

"I don't want to stay here," Carl said.

"Where do you want to go?"

"I have some friends who could put me up for a while."

I thought it over briefly and decided it was a good idea. The Paradox Machine was spinning its wheels frantically now, coming up to full steam. We'd have to be careful, but we'd have to act.

Arthur said, "Jake, I'm going to take the ship up into orbit, if you don't mind." He handed me an oblong-shaped object made of the same olive-drab material that was all around us. It was about ten by five centimeters and a little over one centimeter thick. "This is a communcations device. It will always be operating, monitoring you, giving your position. If you want to reach me, just hold it next to your mouth and speak, either side of it. I'll hear you." He turned to Carl. "How far away are you going? Where do you live?"

"In Santa Monica. It's right on the beach, about sixty, seventy miles from here . . . er, a hundred klicks, about."

"You won't have to come all the way back, Jake. Just let me know and I'll pick you up at a convenient place. I can easily home in on that beacon."

"Good," I said. Something occurred to me, and I considered the way we were all dressed. Carl and Lori had on gray utility jumpsuits which the Voloshins had lent them, and Darla was wearing her silver Allclyme survival suit. She had been wearing it when we first met. It was a little tight around the waist now.

Darla caught my stare and looked down at herself. "This won't do, will it? I'll change into that old stuff of John's. It looks ridiculous, but it's more nondescript than this."

"Hell, I left my old clothes back at Emerald City," Carl said.

"And I don't have much but this jacket and slacks," I said. "Not what you'd call outlandish in our day, but the styles might be different enough to draw a few odd looks."

"Forget it," Carl said. "This is southern California, the land of the nuts. You should see some of the getups people walk around in out here."

Home.

The reality of being back on Earth again sank in as I sat in the back seat of the Chevy, watching the countryside roll by. I had seen the surfaces of a thousand planets, and none looked exactly like this. None, no matter how "Earthlike" they were. A good part of my lifetime had been spent in alien environments, and now I was home again at long last, back in the environment that had spawned those of my kind. The Good Earth.

Compounding the wonder was the knowledge that this was

Earth as it had been before I'd been born, almost a century before. A dented blue automobile passed us, spewing pale blue smoke. What the hell did it run on—burning wood? There was a smell in the air, something I didn't recognize. Gasoline, I thought. No, oil. I asked Carl if it was, and he said yes, but told me that the car was burning it because it was in bad repair. Interesting.

We came into a town, San Bernardino, Carl told us. We drove around for a bit, then pulled into a parking lot adjacent to a large shopping plaza.

"Be right back," Carl said, getting out. He took the screwdriver with him.

He returned in a few minutes, stooped in front of the car and did something, then went around and fiddled with something at the back. Then he got in.

"Had to steal some license plates," he explained. "Otherwise we'd get stopped for sure."

He pulled out of the lot, cruised down a traffic-choked boulevard, turned right at a sign and got onto a ramp leading to a multilane highway.

The sky was Earth blue, the earth the color of earth. Trees looked like what trees should look like, grass looked like grass. With all the worlds I'd been on in the last thirty years, this seemed strange.

The air was . . . unusual, and it got to be more so as we sped into the heart of a endless, sprawling metropolis.

Darla was rubbing her eyes. "Some kind of irritation," she said, sniffling.

"That's smog," Carl told us. "You get used to it, kinda, after living here for a while. In the fall we get the Santa Ana from the desert. Winds. They blow all the shit out to sea."

"Those poor fish," I said.

"Oh, it's not as bad as some people make it out to be."

"Carl, it smells *awful*," Lori said fretfully. "I don't think I'm ever going to get used to it."

"Take a good whiff of it into your lungs. You'll get to like it. Gee, I should stop and get a pack of cigarettes."

"Carl!"

It was a bright, hazy day, and the warm sun put me into a strangely good mood. The Sun. How many alien suns had warmed my skin, or irradiated it, or nearly burned it? Too many.

The sun-drenched metropolis went on and on. I couldn't believe that Los Angeles had been this big in the middle of the twentieth century, kilometer after endless kilometer of residences, businesses, office buildings, service stations, shops, institutional buildings, and apartment complexes, all laid out in a vast grid of streets and highways. These last were something. They made the Skyway look like a country lane. Clogged with murderous traffic, they met five or six at a time at snarled interchanges, twining about one another into knots of elevated ramps, cloverleafs, and cutoffs. Although speeds weren't high compared to those on the Skyway, the sheer volume of traffic made the whole mess frightening. Anyway, I was scared. Carl wasn't. He seemed to have cheered up a little, and he was navigating his way through the shifting streams of vehicles with automatic ease, like a veteran. He was home.

"There are no restraining harnesses in this buggy," I said, looking down at the blue fur-covered seats. I had known it before, but the careless disregard for safety struck me now.

"Damn good idea to have 'em," Carl said. "Congress should get after Detroit to make 'em mandatory." An afterthought: "I should have thought of putting them in when I was designing it."

I looked out at history. The architectural styles were strange to me. They just don't build things like that anymore. Everything was strange, yet somehow faintly familiar as well.

We took a spur to the right that shunted us off onto another highway. We were heading due west, toward the ocean.

"This is the Santa Monica Freeway," Carl told us. "Straight shot into Santa Monica, then I'll be home." He laughed. "God, it's good to be back."

About twenty minutes later the freeway ended. We cruised down a wide city boulevard, then turned right onto a palm-lined street running along the beach. There were lots of bathers out, catching the late afternoon sun.

"First thing I'm gonna do is get my board and go out," Carl averred.

"Your board?" Lori said.

"Surfboard."

"Oh."

"You'll love it."

"It's a nice beach."

I pulled out the communications device, thinking to test it out. I looked at its grainy surface. It was covered with the same half-visible geometrical lines and squiggles that I'd seen on the ship's material. I held it near my mouth.

"Arthur?"

There was a moment's delay, then: "Yes, dearie?"

"Testing," I told him.

"Receiving you fine," Arthur said, his voice reproducing with high fidelity.

"Good. Where are you?"

"Oh, the back side of the moon, hovering at about two hundred kilometers."

"Really? See anything interesting?"

"Nope. Frankly, I'm bored. I think I'm going to hibernate until you need me."

"How long will it take you to get here if we need you in a hurry?"

"Oh, about ten minutes, if I hurry."

"Maybe you should stay in Earth orbit."

"If you want. I might be detected, though."

I agreed. "Yeah, you might. Stay put, and we'll contact you later."

"Have fun."

"By the way, what are our chances of getting back to Microcosmos?"

"Fair," Arthur said. "Since I know where we are, it makes it fairly easy. You just have to aim for the center of the universe."

"The center of the universe?"

"Fourth dimensionally speaking, that's where Microcosmos is, almost all the way back to the beginning of the universe. It's a little off-center though, by about one or two billion years."

"Oh," I said.

"Anything else?"

"Yeah. If another ship like yours entered the solar system, would you have any way of detecting it?"

"Yes, but that's not going to happen," Arthur told me.

"Why?"

"Because this is the only ship of its kind ever built."

"What about the chance of encountering the ship's paradoxical double? You call it a spacetime ship. Doesn't that mean it's a time machine?"

"In a way," Arthur said thoughtfully, "but I don't think there's much chance of it happening."

Neither did I.

16

I TOLD ARTHUR that we'd keep in touch, and signed off.

We headed north on the Coast Highway for a few kilometers, then turned right at a sign which read Topanga Canyon Boulevard and followed a winding road bearing up into the hills. Eventually, Carl made a right onto a gravel road, then a left into a driveway leading back to a beige-painted clapboard cottage with a small beetle-shaped automobile parked beside it.

Carl pulled up in front of the house and turned the motor off.

"Friends?" I asked.

"Yeah, one friend. A guy, a little older than me. He's a writer."

"What's he write?"

"TV scripts, movies, stuff like that. I know he did a *Gunsmoke*, and I think he wrote a version of some big Hollywood movie—one of those Roman Empire epics. I can't think of the name of it. Anyway, his name wasn't on the credits. A couple of friends of mine used to come over here and mess around, watch old movies, listen to jazz records."

"Records?" Darla asked.

"Uh . . . recorded music."

"Oh, I see."

"Anyway, he's home. He's gonna think I've totally flipped when I tell him what's happened."

Lori silently mouthed, *Gunsmoke?*

We got out. Carl banged on the front door. No one answered, and Carl banged again. Faint sounds of upbeat music came from within.

Carl was ready to knock a third time when the door was opened by a youngish dark-haired man wearing black-rimmed eyeglasses, a short-sleeved yellow pullover shirt, and dark pants. He had on leather moccasins and carried a carved briar pipe. He looked friendly but impatient.

"Carl!" he said. "Hey, I'm working." Puzzled, he glanced at Darla, Lori, and me, then said to Carl, "What's up?"

"Need your help. We're in a jam."

"A jam?" He eyed me again, scrutinizing my maroon star-rigger's jacket. "Yeah?" He looked Carl up and down. "Are you guys shooting something?"

"Huh?" Carl answered.

"What's with the costumes?"

"It's a long story."

The man nodded. "I've a feeling I'm going to hear it. Come on in." He swung the door back, turned and walked inside. We followed him in.

The living room was really a work space. There were three debris-littered desks, a half-dozen loaded bookcases, one sofa, and a few chairs. A piece of equipment which I recognized to be a typewriter sat on one desk amid piles of manuscript, stacks of periodicals, and other paraphernalia. Besides clogging the shelves, books lay everywhere, piled in stacks on the desks, on the floor, and on the furniture. The place did have the look of a writer's lair.

"Dave," Carl said, "these are some friends of mine. Uh, this is Jake. . . ."

"Hi," Dave said, shaking my hand. "Dave Feinmann."

"And this is Darla," Carl said.

"Hello, Darla. And you're . . . ?"

"Lori."

"Hello, Lori."

Dave went to a cabinet containing a rack of equipment that, from the look of it, was a device for playing audio disks, something I'd never seen in my life. He turned a knob, and the music, which sounded like early jazz, faded into the background. He cleared some books off the furniture and motioned for us to sit down, taking a seat himself in front of the typewriter. He lit his pipe, cocking his head toward the typewriter. "Doing a treatment for an episode of this new science fiction series. Producer's a friend of mine. Looks like they've sold the pilot."

"Yeah?" Carl said. "Great."

Dave got the pipe going. He gave Carl a funny look, then shrugged. "So, you're in a jam. What is it this time? Did the cops finally—" He broke off and squinted at Carl. "Jesus. You look different, somehow. Where did you get that crazy haircut?"

Carl passed a hand through his hair. "Crazy? Yeah, I guess it is."

"It's way out. I—" Dave passed his eyes over the four of us, looking uneasy. "What are you people up to? You're not extras—you're not working a shoot nearby?"

"No, Dave," Carl said. "You're not going to believe this, but . . ."

For the next half hour, Carl spilled his story, though leaving out a good bit of it for economy's sake. I spent the time watching Dave's shifting reactions. He began with simple bemused skepticism, modulated to adamant disbelief, then switched to shocked credulity. By the time Carl had gotten through most of what he had to say, Dave's expression was almost blank. He looked numb, and a little shaken. Several times, early on, he had interrupted Carl, insisting, "This is a gag, right?" He wasn't insisting now.

Carl finished up and sat back, looking at Dave expectantly. Silent, Dave puffed on his pipe and stared out the window. He did this for a long while.

Finally Carl snapped, "Jesus Christ, Dave, say something!"

"I'm waiting for Rod Serling to come out and do the teaser," Dave said quietly.

Carl sighed. "I knew you wouldn't believe it."

"Oh, I believe it."

"You do?"

"Yeah." Dave crossed his legs and sat back. "There are exactly three possibilities. Either you've flipped, or I've flipped, or you're telling the truth. There's another, maybe— but I know you, Carl, and you couldn't keep a straight face this long if you were jiving me. But let me tell you something right now—if I've read you wrong and you are indeed pulling my leg, if you got these people out of central casting and came up here to see how long you could keep me on the hook, if this *is* a gag, Carl, I'm going to kill you. I'm going to get out my samurai short sword, disembowel you, and feed your liver to you—without onions."

Carl shook his head slowly. "It's no gag."

I took out the communicator and handed it to Dave. "Ever see a radio like that?" I asked.

Dave examined it. "Radio?"

"Maybe you'd call it a walkie-talkie. Say something into it."

Dave scowled. "Into it? Where? There's nothing to this."

"Speak into this side," I told him, pointing.

Dave rolled his eyes, then held it near his mouth and said, "Hello?"

"Hello?" came Arthur's voice.

Dave jumped, dropping the communicator. "Jesus Christ! It sounds like he's in the room. That can't be a walkie-talkie."

"Yes, it does have good reproduction for a long-range receiver."

Dave pointed. "Is that—"

"Yeah, that's Arthur," Carl said.

"Hello?" a puzzled Arthur said. "Jake, are you there?"

I picked it up. "Yeah, Arthur. Sorry, we were just testing it again."

"I think we can rest assured that it works," Arthur said peevishly.

Dave chewed his lip, then asked, "He's a robot, right? And he's up on this . . . saucer?"

"Spacetime ship," I told him.

"On the moon?"

"Arthur, are you still on the moon?"

"That's right, dearie. Is that a new friend of yours?"

"Yeah, that's Dave."

"Hi, Dave!"

Dave looked around uncomfortably before he said, "Uh . . . hi."

"Lively one, isn't he?" Arthur commented.

Dave was nonplussed. Suddenly, something snapped and he jumped up. "This is too much." He thumped the pipe into an ashtray and raised his hands palms up in a helpless, despairing gesture. "I don't believe it. On top of everything, the robot's a *smart-shit*. He's in this fucking flying saucer, and he's on the fucking *moon*, for Christ's sake, and I'm feeding him *straight lines*."

"Such language," Arthur complained.

Dave suddenly developed a grave expression. "Excuse me," he said quietly. He left the room.

Carl waited a moment, then picked up the communicator. "Arthur, you asshole!" he whispered hoarsely. "Now he's all pissed off."

"All these neurotic humans I have to put up with," Arthur grumbled.

Dave returned five minutes later bearing a tray on which were a number of tall bottles. His face looked a bit gray. "I don't know about you guys, but I need a drink. Beer's all I have."

We all took a bottle. Dave sat, took a long swallow, and ruminated. He took another drink before he said, "I've just had a shock. I'll tell you about it in a minute, but first, let me tell you the reasons for my believing your fantastic story strictly on the basis of what you've told me, and what I've seen. I buy it not because it makes one whit of sense, which it doesn't, not because it's believable, which it isn't, but because of a few little things. I'm a writer. I'm plagued with the penchant for *noticing* things—little things. Tiny touches of convincing detail. Like your accent, Jake."

"My accent?" Strange to hear someone say I had one.

"Yeah. It's American, generally. But I can't place it, and I specialize in regional dialects. I do great dialogue, my producers tell me. But I can't place yours. Yours either, Lori. Now, Darla's is totally different from both of yours. If I had to put a tag on it, I'd say it was Mid-Atlantic. Neither British nor American. But there're traces of other accents in there. A melange. I can't figure it."

"Better to call it mid-colonial," Darla said.

"Yeah. I guess so." Dave gulped more beer. "Accents. Okay, now clothes. Those getups you're all wearing. Those clothes weren't made anywhere in the civilized world. I don't know that for sure, but the *style* . . . I mean, it's a style I've never seen. And they're *nondescript* clothes, nothing flashy about them, except that jacket of yours, Jake. But it's worn and tattered. The elbows are wearing through. That jacket's been *worn*, for Christ's sake. Again, there're only two possibilities. Either that's a studio wardrobe throwaway, or it's a real jacket, worn by a real person, who happens to be from another time and place." Dave drained the bottle, took another from the tray, and applied a tool to its top. The metal cap popped off. "And you, Carl. I noticed it right off the bat. There's something different about you, even besides the haircut and those futuristic overalls you have on. You look different. Like you've traveled, grown. You look *older*. You are older, according to your story. About a year, right?"

Carl nodded.

"Sure. So it all fits, it all hangs together on that level, the level of convincing detail. On the rational level, the whole thing holds about as much water as a colander. But I have to believe it. That communicator thing could be a souped-up transistor radio or something, but even so, it's one weird object. I wouldn't have accepted the story on that basis alone, but . . . it, plus the little things, the fine touches—add it all up, and . . . I've stepped into a dimension as vast as space and as timeless as infinity, the middle ground between light and shadow, et cetera. Cue Rod. Action." Dave exhaled slowly, taking off his glasses and rubbing his left eye. Then he swept back his longish dark hair. "But there's one more thing. The clincher—a piece of irrefutable evidence. The shocker. When I was in the kitchen, I made a phone call. I called you, Carl. *I talked to you*. You were home, at your parents' house."

Carl seemed to collapse inside. He lowered his head and stared at the floor.

"Okay," Dave said. "So, what do we do? How can I help?"

Dave's rented house was small, having only two bedrooms, but he was willing to give up both of them and sleep on the couch. When I protested, he said he usually collapsed there anyway after working into the wee hours. There was only one bed, which Carl and Lori insisted that Darla and I have; they made do with layers of blankets and pillows piled on the floor in the spare bedroom. We were set for a prolonged stay. Ordinarily, Dave said, he didn't suffer house guests for more than three nights, but he was willing to put us up, and put up with us, for as long as was required.

"However long it takes to resolve the spatiotemporal crisis," he told us, "you're welcome to stay. What, I'm going to throw out time travelers from the twenty-fifth century?"

"Twenty-second," I corrected him.

"Right, that was Buck Rogers."

Trouble was, our presence would undoubtedly disrupt his work routine. He wrote for a living, and he needed to put in a full day's work every day, including weekends. It behooved us, then, to find something to do during daylight hours, which would entail going out, which would necessitate our getting some acceptably conventional clothes. Dave came through for us again. He lent us money, enough to buy something decent for all of us at a discount clothing outlet. I told Dave that I could pay him back in gold. Carl insisted that he'd make good on the loan.

Once we'd solved the costume problem, we cast about for something to keep us occupied. Going to the local beach was out. Carl's double would be there.

"I was a beach bum, I admit it," he said. "But I know what beaches I used to hang out at. I never went to Malibu. Didn't like the kids who hung out there. Bel Air types with Corvettes and Lotus Fords and Porsches. We can go there, and my double wouldn't show up in a million eons."

Earth . . . summer . . . 1964 . . .

It was a bright and colorful and happy time, a flux of seaspray and sunlight and rock music tinny and loud from a portable radio. The images come quickly to me, along with the sounds and smells: the reek of gasoline exhaust and suntan lotion and hot dogs sizzling on the grill at the concession stand; the endless beach carpeted with seminude bodies baking in nonionizing radiation, and the roar of the ocean, rolling in and out as it has done on this planet, this home of humankind, for five billion years. Darla and I stretched out on towels beside the bright surf and let Earth's sun warm on our backs. We dozed, and the flux convolved about us. We were lost in time and didn't particularly want to be found.

. . . *summer, 1964*. It was a time of blaring news reports over the radio and TV . . . the Russians, Viet Nam, Laos, Cambodia. An election year, the Republicans nominating somebody named Goldwater, whom I had never heard of, to run against the incumbent, Johnson, whom I had barely heard of. (Hadn't there been another President Johnson, in the earlier part of the century? Or had it been another century entirely?) It was a time when the world had fallen under the spell of four young men from Britain with domed haircuts who played their electrified instruments enthusiastically, if not well, singing songs with a steady beat and charmingly simple lyrics . . .

We had some time to bask in the sun and absorb some of the backdrop of this time and place, but we had some thinking to do as well; rather, I had it to do. At night we sat around with Dave and talked, filling him in on more details concerning our adventures in the world of the future and the worlds of the Skyway, including our journey outside the known mazes —the Outworlds: Splash, Talltree, the planets of the Nogon —the chase through the Garage Planet of the Roadbugs, the wonders of Microcosmos, and other tales.

"This Culmination business," Dave said, sitting with us on lawn chairs out on a little porch off one side of the house. "Mind-boggling. From what you told me, this . . . *thing* will come into being approximately ten billion years in the future. Yet, you're dealing with it now. And you're dealing with it on a planet that you say exists back at the beginning of the universe, ten billion years *ago*."

"Near the beginning, anyway," I said. "Within a few billion years of the Big Bang, or whatever happened back then. Yes, that's the way it was explained to us. The Culmination transcends time. Once it was created, it became eternal." I took a sip of my gin and tonic. "There's a possible scientific explanation for it. If we think of it strictly on a physical plane, maybe the Culmination is nothing but an instantaneous communications device, one that makes possible the transmission of information faster than the speed of light."

"Relativity," Dave said, nodding. "I've read a dozen books about it written for the layman. The way I understand it, if you send a message that's faster than light, you send it back through time."

"Yeah," I said. "If there was an instantaneous communications device operating at a point in the far future of the universe, and if it were powerful enough, it would broadcast throughout time, and any capable receiver existing in the past would be able to pick it up."

"I think I understand," Dave said, "but something as grandiose as the Culmination . . . I mean, it's hard to think of it as nothing more than a souped-up radio."

"Right, but that may be the only handy way to think of it. Otherwise, the concept gets mystical and slippery."

"Well, seems to me it's got to get mystically slippery at some point. It sounds like what they did was create God."

"Or some approximation of Him . . . or it."

Dave whistled softly. "Mind-numbing. Way out. There're no words for it." He took a long drink of beer, looked thoughtful for a moment, then said, "I still can't grasp why the Culmination built the Skyway."

"From what we can guess, it exists as a means to bring potential candidates to a central place for processing into the Culmination," Darla said.

"I understand," Dave said, "but *why* do they need candidates? Why do they need minds for the Culmination?"

"That's what we don't know," I said. "We've some clues, but nothing like an answer. And we don't know exactly what joining the Culmination entails. Do you get zapped into a computer? Get transmuted into pure energy? Or what?"

"Maybe you just die," Dave suggested.

I chewed over the current paradox situation. Something had to be done, and soon. I talked it over with Arthur.

"Arthur, do you know any reason why Prime would abduct Carl and set him loose on the Skyway?"

"No. The notion is totally ridiculous. Prime would never do such a thing."

"Why not?"

"Why not?" Arthur laughed derisively. "Why in the name of all that's holy in the universe would he?"

"I dunno. You tell me."

"Well, I can't. It makes absolutely no sense that Prime would travel ten billion light-years to a jerkwater planet and kidnap a human being—not a very bright one, at that—give him that bizarre vehicle, and set him off on the Skyway to cause all sorts of trouble. You think of Prime as a god, don't you?"

"A demigod, maybe."

"Demigod, shmemigod. Okay. The gods—or the demigods, if you will—may be inscrutable, but they sure aren't stupid! I mean, they don't go around doing idiotic things just to pass the time."

"Then who abducted Carl?"

"I think you know the answer."

I did. However, I had a hell of a time convincing Carl.

"Carl, let me explain it one more time. . . ."

Carl covered his head with a beach towel, turned over on his stomach, and shoved his face into the sand. "I'm going bananas," he said in a muffled voice.

"It's crazy, but that's the only way it works."

"I'm going to have myself committed. None of this is real."

"It probably isn't. Look, your double—the you of a year ago—is down there in Santa Monica living the life of a typical teenager of his era. In a few weeks, he's going to be abducted by a flying saucer and taken one hundred and fifty years into the future and set loose in a strange world. That happened to you. Now it has to happen to *him*, on the same day in history that it actually happened. Prime isn't going to be around to do the deed. We have the ship, the only one of its kind in existence. Do you understand it now?"

Carl turned over again and unraveled the towel. He lay back, blinked sand from his eyes, and covered them with his arm.

For a minute, we listened to the Beatles sing of love and its loss.

"I understand," Carl said finally. "I think. It doesn't make sense, but I understand it. I'm getting used to things not making sense."

"Good," I said, "because they rarely do."

"There's only one thing."

"What?"

"I've been thinking about this for a while. If things are so screwed up, so backward and impossible, then it must be true that Lori is Debbie."

I nodded. "Again, it doesn't make sense, but . . ."

"Yeah. Besides, it works out better that way. If Debbie is another person, then I got some explaining to do."

I asked, "When did you finally convince yourself that she isn't another person?"

"The other day, when we went to the clothing store. When

Lori came out wearing that pink blouse with the white lace around the cuffs, I recognized it. Debbie was wearing that blouse when we first met. I remember because I teased her about how shocking pink it was. When I saw Lori choose it in the store, I stood there like I'd been struck by lightning, because it hit me that hard. I knew then that somehow—and don't even know how, yet—somehow Debbie and Lori are the same person. The only difference is the hair. Debbie's was darker. Not by much, either, now that I think of it, but it was darker. Seems to me that it was a little longer, too, but that may be my lousy memory. It's been a long time since I've seen Debbie."

Darla came back from a swim and lay down beside me, her skin glistening wet in the sunlight. She had bought a one-piece maternity swimsuit with a little skirt, and she'd been complaining that she looked ridiculous. She didn't look ridiculous.

I asked Carl, "Where did you meet Debbie?"

"That's another strange thing. She came right up to me on the—"

Carl sat up with a look of shocked realization.

I nodded and said sympathetically, "Yeah, Carl, it's going to be rough."

I tried to look fatherly.

Lori and I had come down into L.A. by way of Sunset Boulevard, which had taken us through Brentwood, Westwood, Beverly Hills, and into West Hollywood. It had been a nice drive, traffic on the moderate side, and I had reached a point where I felt comfortable operating Dave's Volkswagen. It was a good, economical little car. I know, because I had filled it up before we left. Gasoline was ridiculously cheap as it was. I couldn't see the price staying that low for any length of time.

"Okay," I said. "I'm going to let you off around Vine Street. Do you remember the address in Culver City?"

"Yeah," Lori said. She was nervous and a little scared.

"Dave's sister is expecting you at ten."

"Ten, right. But I don't know where Culver City is."

"If everything goes well, Carl—Carl Two, the double—should take you there. He knows where Culver City is."

We had asked Dave if he knew anyone who could put Lori

up for a few days. We couldn't have Carl Two bringing her to Dave's place. Carl One said that Debbie lived in Culver City, and it turned out, Dave had a sister who lived there. Dave phoned her with the story of a social worker friend of his who ran a shelter for runaways, and of a girl who needed a place to stay because of overcrowding. Debbie Smith—nice kid, basically, just needs a little special attention. Dave's sister said fine, send her over.

Lori was chewing her lip anxiously.

"What's the matter?" I asked.

"What if . . . ?" She shivered. "Oh, Jake, this is so scary. What if I can't get Carl to pick me up? What happens then?"

"Good question," I said, "and I'd be lying if I said I knew. I don't know what happens if you foul up a paradox. I don't know that a paradox can be fouled up. But I don't think you're going to have any trouble. Those jeans of yours look sprayed on."

"They shrank in that silly clothes dryer of Dave's."

"All to the good, I say. Just walk around looking as pretty as you are."

She frowned and flicked a hand through her hair. "I think I look horrible as a brunette. What an awful color that dye turned out to be."

"Darla did her best. Okay, what street is this?"

"Bonita."

I turned left, went two blocks, and turned right onto Hollywood Boulevard. I cruised for a few blocks, then pulled over.

"This is it," Lori said.

I looked around. "I don't see him, but our Carl said that this is one of his hunting grounds." There were plenty of kids out, riding in cars, shouting at one another, standing on street corners, and generally misspending their collective youth.

Lori got out, closed the door, and poked her head in the window, her eyes wide with apprehension. "Jake? What if there really is a Debbie?"

I smiled. "Don't stay out too late, Debbie."

A little of the anxiety left her face, and she smiled thinly. "Wish me luck," she said.

I watched her walk away. Those jeans really were a second skin. Carl Two didn't have a chance.

17

IT WAS A lovely summer with an undercurrent of suspense.

The Paradox seemed to be working out on schedule. "Debbie" saw "Carl" on the average of three times a week. They'd go out driving, cruising the main boulevards and meeting friends, or they'd go to "drive-in" motion picture theaters, afterward ingesting hamburgers and accompanying confections at various establishments offering same. Every odd day they went to the beach, where Debbie learned the rudiments of surfboarding, Frisbee sailing, and increasing the natural pigmentation of the skin by overexposure to ultraviolet radiation. All these activities, and more, we were told, were typical pastimes for young people of the period and locale. "Debbie" didn't care much for surfboarding. "I'm always hanging ten," she complained—whatever that meant.

Meanwhile, Carl (our Carl) would grind his teeth. The drive-in movies upset him especially. He never mentioned it but once, and never asked Lori what transpired when the couple visited these "passion pits," as he called them.

"I know damn well what they're doing," he told me. "'Cause I did it, too!"

But he endured it. After all, it wasn't as if Lori were dating another guy. It was as if . . . In the final analysis, the language lacked the means for accurately describing the situation.

It was good, then, that Lori spent a good deal of time over at Dave's sister's place. Shelly and her husband seemed to like "Debbie" a great deal, and didn't balk at the prospect of her staying on indefinitely.

"Shelly can't turn away a stray animal," Dave explained. "Drives Bob nuts—they must have half a dozen cats by now." The couple had no children of their own.

Dave took Lori down to the Federal Building in L.A. to get her a Social Security card, which she obtained by presenting the authorities there with a false birth certificate that Dave had conjured up. "Didn't cost a hell of a lot, either," Dave told us. "Amazing possibilities, if you think about it."

What did Debbie do, mostly, over at Bob and Shelly's? "Watch TV, sit and read movie magazines. Eat a lot. I've put on five pounds. I like TV."

She liked rock music, too. She adored the Rolling Stones.

There were dangers inherent in the situation of having two versions of the same human being running around in proximity to one another. Dave was worried that the other Carl might drop in some time, as he was wont to do on occasion. We forestalled that eventuality by having Dave call Carl up and tell him that he'd be away for a month or two—up in the mountains writing a feature film script. There was still the possibility that the two Carls might bump into each other. But the consensus was that, as Carl had no memory of encountering a twin of himself, it never happened. Ergo, it wouldn't happen. We could have rewritten the textbooks on logic that summer, if we'd have put our minds to it.

Something else was bothering Carl. I tried to sound him out on it, but didn't get very far. Obviously the prospect of reliving the abduction, compounded by the monstrous irony of his having to take part in it, was taking its toll on his nerves. There was nothing I could do except to assure him it would all go according to plan.

And I wondered myself, *Whose plan?*

The summer wore on and the crisis approached. The Paradox Machine clanked and whirred and shot bright blue sparks, its spinning sharp-toothed wheels up to full speed.

We summoned Arthur.

It was a balmy California evening. We stood in a hollow in back of Dave's house, watching the skies. There were few stars; only the biggest and brightest could make it through the hazy glare that the sprawling electric grid of Los Angeles threw back at the sky.

"I've got goose bumps," Dave said, playing his flashlight beam up into the night. "This is like a scene out of *The Day the Earth Stood Still.*"

"A movie?" I asked.

"Yeah. And if Arthur looks anything like Gort, I'm going to shit enough bricks to build a barbecue pit."

"I can't say for sure, but Arthur probably doesn't look anything like Gort. Arthur doesn't look like anyone or anything I know."

"There?" Darla whispered, pointing to a distant shape moving against the semidarkness.

We heard a low droning accompanied by a chopping sound.

"Helicopter," Dave said. "See the lights?" Dave stamped his foot. "Damn, there's a lot of air traffic tonight."

"Probably better that way," I said, wishing I had the communicator. Lori had it. She was out somewhere with Carl Two. Arthur said he already had Dave's house pinpointed and would be able to land if we stood near the site and signaled visually. Carl One was in the house, biting his nails. Would Carl Two repeat history and go up to Mulholland Drive, there to meet his destiny? Only time would tell, and time wasn't telling yet.

Dave gasped, and I looked up.

There was the ship, ghosting over the lip of the hollow, its dark ovate bulk outlined by a constellation of flashing red and blue lights. I smiled. Arthur had done a good job of camouflage. The lights were positioned to mimic the configuration of a conventional aircraft. I wondered if he'd been tracked on radar. Soundlessly, like some sort of dirigible whale, the craft eased to the ground, its immensity filling up the hollow. The main cargo bay dilated and we went in.

"*Je*-sus! This is your truck?" Dave said, awestruck.

"That's it."

"This thing's a monster! You say it's atomic powered?"

"Nuclear fusion. Want to climb in?"

"*Je*-sus."

He did, and we did. I gave him the tour, and Dave oohed and aahed for a while, then fell into silent wonderment.

"What's the matter?" I asked.

He took his hands from the steering bars. "You know, up till now, I gotta admit that there was a tiny bit of doubt in the back of my mind about all this. I was secretly hoping, desperately hoping, I guess, that I'd fallen into a group delusional psychosis thing, like those saucer cultists who camp out in the desert waiting for the aliens to come down and save the world." He slapped the instrument panel. "But here it is, in all its mind-shredding reality. You know, there were times when I thought—"

Brought up short, he stared numbly out the viewscreen. "Oh, my God," he said in a hollow voice.

I looked. It was Arthur.

"Yoo-hoo!" Arthur waved.

We got out, and I introduced Dave to our quasiandroid servant.

"Are you tracking Lori?" I asked.

"Yes, indeed," Arthur said.

"Where are they?"

He gestured vaguely. "Out there somewhere. Nowhere near the pick-up zone, which you said wasn't far from here."

"Well, we have some time," I said, then glanced around. "Carl should be here. Darla, would you run and get him?"

"Sure."

I noticed that Dave was still gawking at Arthur, who was returning a supercilious glare. Suddenly self-conscious, Dave averted his eyes.

"Dave's been a real help," I said to Arthur. "Don't get on his case."

"Well, excuse me," Arthur sniffed.

"My fault," Dave said. "I was staring. I've never seen a seven-foot tall, pink and purple person before."

"And yellow," Arthur said, pointing to an appropriate section of his plasticlike skin.

"Yeah. Sorry."

"Quite all right. You know, Dave, I'm not as strange as I look."

"That's right," I said. "He's stranger."

"All I get is abuse," Arthur lamented. "A servant's lot. One of these days I'm going to rise above my station in life and tell you how passing strange I think humans are."

"We know we're strange, Arthur," I said. "Don't forget. You may not look it, but you're human, too."

"Don't remind me."

Arthur conducted Dave on a tour of the ship.

"It's so empty," Dave remarked, perplexed. "There's nothing in here."

"Oh, there's plenty of auxiliary equipment," Arthur said. "It's all built in." Arthur went to a bulkhead and ran his index finger over its surface, outlining a simple oblong shape. Suddenly, the pattern materialized and the portion of bulkhead that it described tilted out. Arthur detached it and held it in both hands. "This is a weapon, for instance. There are lots of things hidden in the walls, everything from scientific instrumentation to—"

Darla came running in. "Carl left," she said breathlessly. "Took the Chevy."

"What?" I yelped. "Where'd he go?"

"He was raving that he'd had enough crazy stuff and that he was going to get Lori and go away somewhere and forget all this. I tried to stop him, but he was already pulling out of the cul-de-sac."

"Great," I said. "Arthur, do you have another communicator?"

Arthur crossed to the opposite bulkhead and did the same trick, pulling a smaller oblong out of the wall. He handed it to me.

I said, "Is there any way to track Carl's Chevy?"

"Do you know what type of propulsion system it has?"

"Of course not. Hell, I'd never catch him, anyway. But it's a good bet he'll find Lori. So just guide me to her."

"Should I take the ship up? I've got the outside surface tuned properly now. It should be radar transparent. And with the camouflage, we'll be fairly inconspicuous."

"Yeah, for a flying saucer. Just stand by. Dave, I'll take the VW and go after him, if that's all right with you."

"Okay," Dave said nervously. "I'll stay here in the dimension of imagination."

"Hm? Right."

A balmy, subtropical California night, traffic-choked and many-peopled. We raced north on the San Diego Freeway. By this time I could dart and weave between lanes like a native.

"I wish there were some way for Arthur to contact Lori," I said.

"It might be awkward for her if Arthur's voice suddenly came out of her handbag," Darla ventured.

"It might. Again, where did Lori say they were going?"

"Out somewhere in the San Fernando Valley, to watch a drag race."

"A which?"

"Drag race?" Darla flipped both hands palms up.

"Do you have any idea—"

"It has something to do with automobiles, but beyond that . . ."

"In this culture," I said, "what *doesn't* have something to do with automobiles?"

Traffic thickened as we got into the valley. I was used to the incessant rush of traffic by now. The automobiles no longer looked hopelessly antique to me. I rather liked their rococo flourishes and useless adornments: tail assemblies that stuck up like shark fins, massive and totally functionless chromium "bumpers," kitsch statuary mounted on hoods, white-striped tires, garish paint schemes, buffed wax finishes, radio whip antennae, blinding tail-light configurations, and other embellishments.

"Arthur?" Darla called into the communicator. "Are you tracking them?"

"They haven't moved. You are now about five kilometers west of their position."

I took the next cutoff and headed east on Roscoe Boulevard, then made a series of lefts and rights at Arthur's direction as he zeroed us in on the signal emitted by the communicator that Lori was carrying. We passed a big parking lot adjacent to a brilliantly lighted outdoor stadium.

"This might be it," Darla said.

Howling engine sounds came to us from the other side of a curving grandstand. I hung a U-turn and headed back. The sign at the entrance to the lot read VALLEY DRAGWAY.

"You're right on," Arthur said.

It cost fifty cents to park. We got out, I locked up the VW, and we jogged toward the entrance to the track, an opening in a corrugated metal fence blocked by turnstiles and a ticket booth. As we neared the booth, Darla stopped. She pointed left toward a row of cars. I looked and spotted Carl's Chevy.

"Which one is it?" Darla wondered. "The double's?"

"No way to tell. Let's look around. If we find another one, that means our Carl's here."

We searched the immediate area but came up empty. It would have taken us an hour to cover the whole lot.

"He might have parked out on the street," I said. "Let's go in."

The ticket girl said that there were only a few heats left to run, but sold us two tickets anyway. We bumped through the turnstile and walked through a concession area littered with scraps of sticky paper, coming to a passageway between two sections of grandstand. We mounted steps and came out into the seating area.

The grandstand was crescent-shaped. A long, straight strip of asphalt began in the middle of the crescent and ended about two thirds of a kilometer out in brush-covered flats. Two bizarre vehicles, which were nothing more than long, low, open metal carriages with overgrown motors mounted on them, were poised at the starting line, bellowing like dinosaurs and shooting blue flames. An array of lights on a pole changed color, and the two things took off like demons loosed from hell, trailing smoke and fire. They reached the end of the course in no time, and parachutes blossomed from their back ends. The noise was incredible. A pall of gray haze hung over the track, and the air was pungent with fuel exhaust and the smell of burnt rubber. An announcement was made and a roar went up from the crowd.

"What's this all about?" Darla shouted above the din as two more outrageous vehicles approached the starting line.

"A display of exotic automotive technology," I said, "or a circus. Probably both. Let's look around."

"What do we say if we run into Lori?"

"Nothing," I said. "We wink and act as if we don't know her. But we stick close, and if our Carl shows up, we try to intercept him. And don't ask me what we do if Carl Two catches sight of Carl One. I'm playing this strictly by ear, and my goddamn ears are killing me."

"Right."

We climbed to the last row and walked along an aisle, looking down over the heads of patrons. Besides the smoke and the fumes, I smelled women's perfume, tobacco, and cooking grease. It was a good crowd for a Tuesday night.

There were a good many young couples, some of which, at first glance, I mistook for Lori and Carl Two. Kids seemed to dress alike in this time and place. Maybe they do in all times and places. The grandstand was a huge affair and the crowd thinned out toward the far end of the crescent. No Lori in sight. We doubled back a ways, then went down steps and walked along the bottom aisle, looking up and scanning for three familiar faces, two of which would be identical.

We saw nobody.

"Where could they be?" Darla fretted.

"Don't know. It's a huge place. Maybe we just missed spotting them. Let's go back to the concession area."

The hot-dog stand was closing down for the night, and people were leaving the track in steadily increasing numbers, filing through an exit on the other side of the concession area. I sent Darla to check the women's room while I glanced in the men's. The latter was being used, but not by either Carl. Darla reported no luck. I told her to stand by the exit while I went back to search the grandstand one more time. The voice over the loudspeakers announced the last race, to be run by two vehicles which looked a shade more conventional. I walked along the middle aisle scanning up and down the grandstand.

"Jake?" came a quiet voice inside my pocket.

"Arthur?" I answered. A man in a green T-shirt turned his head to me with a curious look. "Wait a minute," I said.

I took steps up to the last row, found some empty seats, and sat down. I took out the communicator.

"Go ahead," I spoke into it.

"I'm tracking the other beacon. It has left your area."

I wondered how we had missed them. "Right. We're leaving."

Hurrying back, I spotted Carl. It was our Carl—I recognized his clothes. He was caught in a crush of people at the head of the stairway leading down to the concession area. Just as I was about to close with him, he turned and saw me, then forced his way through the crowd, plunging down the steps. I followed, leaving jostled, angry teenagers in my wake.

As he neared the exit gate, Carl saw Darla and slowed. I caught up with him. Darla ran over.

"They left, Carl," I told him.

"I know," he said, continuing toward the exit.

"Did you see them?"

"No, they weren't up in the stands."

"Where, then?"

"I finally remembered. Most of that night is fuzzy to me. We went to the races, but we didn't sit in the stands. I found out a buddy of mine was racing, and we went down to the pits. I still don't remember everything, but we must have left by the pit entrance and walked around back to the parking lot."

"Let them go, Carl," I said.

"I have to be there tonight," he said vehemently.

"Carl, you can't," I said. "Look. Forces are operating here that we have no control over. I don't know what would happen if you intervened and prevented the abduction. Nobody knows, but it's a good bet that the universe wouldn't be the same. You might throw it entirely out of whack."

We walked through the exit and out into the parking lot.

"I know," Carl answered. "I still have to be there."

"Carl, what is it with you? Something is bothering you, something you haven't let on yet."

"That night, the night it happened," Carl said. "Tonight. It's about Debbie. The way she acted . . . the way *I* acted."

"Are you worried she'll be hurt?" I said. "We've gone over that. Arthur told us that when your double pushes Debbie— Lori—out of the car, she'll float. She won't fall. She'll still be in the gravitational beam the car is in. After Arthur tucks the Chevy into the small cargo bay, he'll lower her down and we'll pick her up."

"That's just it," Carl said. "I remember now. I didn't push Debbie out of the car. That was where I was all screwed up in my memory of that night. I wasn't trying to push her out. I was trying to keep her from jumping. But there was something else—" He stopped and looked around. "Oh, God."

"What is it?"

"The car. It's gone."

We were in the general area where Darla and I had found it. "This is where you parked yours?"

"Yeah. He was parked way over on the other side, but when he was walking back this way from the pits, he must have seen the super-Chevy here and figured he remembered wrong. I do that all the time—forget where I parked. Now he's got the super car." He sighed, holding up a set of car keys. "This is the original key. It fits both cars, of course. And he wouldn't be able to tell the difference. I made the super-Chevy identical to the ordinary one."

I didn't know that to be a fact, but I did know that the vehicle he had created had been identical in every detail to the one he'd been driving when we met on the Skyway—the one I stole from him—down to the pair of fur-covered dice hanging from the rearview mirror.

"How could you do that?" I asked.

"I did the custom job on the original myself," he said. "I spent two years doing it. Bought the thing when I was fifteen, before I could legally drive. I know every inch of that car."

I nodded. "Okay, then that solves the problem of how we make the switch. Your double's already got the super-Chevy."

"Yeah. But there's one more thing I have to do."

Carl turned to leave and I caught his arm.

"Carl, don't. You're coming with us."

"Sorry, Jake, but—"

He swung a wild left. I put up my forearm, but it was a feint, and I was slow to block his quick right jab. The punch landed squarely enough to daze me. Darla rushed in, but Carl had already begun sprinting away. Darla chased after him but couldn't keep up. He disappeared into the streams of people exiting the track.

Darla ran back. "Are you all right?"

"Getting old," I said. "He suckered me good."

"Should we go after him?"

I rubbed my jaw, shaking my head. "No way to make a decision. We might screw things up by trying to prevent him from screwing things up. I'm coming around to thinking that nothing anybody does or tries to do can thwart fate from taking its course. This is turning into a Greek drama."

"I've always hated Greek drama," Darla said.

"Me, too. It's those damn choruses breaking in and yapping all the time."

We found the Volkswagen and got in. We went nowhere. The exits were jammed up, and we had to wait in line. We were held up a good fifteen minutes, and we tried to catch a glimpse of the other Chevy. Carl either had beaten the rush or was tied up at another exit.

Finally we got out. When we were back on Roscoe Boulevard, I checked in with Arthur.

"Lori is now bearing generally south," Arthur informed me. "But she's on a road paralleling that big express highway down there."

Darla leafed through the map of L.A. "Sepulveda," she confirmed. "It intersects with Mulholland about a mile south of Sherman Oaks."

I turned left at the intersection of Sepulveda and Roscoe, heading south. We underpassed the Ventura Freeway and hit Ventura Boulevard, continuing straight. Sepulveda narrowed to two lanes, winding its way up into the Santa Monica Mountains. House lights glowed in canyons to either side.

Darla turned on the dome light and looked at the analog wristwatch she had bought. "Eleven-thirty," she said, and turned the light off.

We had no timetable. Carl had said that he didn't remember exactly what time the abduction had occurred. He guessed that it had happened around midnight.

A pair of headlights grew in the rearview mirror. Carl passed us, doing at least seventy miles an hour. The original Chevy was a hot vehicle, too. I floored the pedal, and Dave's VW coughed and gave its all, which was pitifully little. We chugged along in Carl's wake until his tail-lights vanished around a bend.

"Well, hell," I said. "There goes the monkey wrench into the works." I handed the communicator to Darla. "Check in with Arthur."

"Turn west off of your present route," Arthur instructed us.

At least that much was going according to plan. Carl had pinpointed the kidnapping site as being somewhere near San Vicente Mountain, the peak of which overlooked Mulholland west of Sepulveda.

I missed the turnoff before the tunnel and had to double back. We went up a short ramp and got onto a dirt and gravel road—Mulholland Drive. It led us into a surprisingly remote-looking area. You'd never guess that one of the biggest cities the world had ever seen was just down the mountain. It wasn't exactly desolate, but you got the feeling that you were a long way from everything.

The road was edged with scrub brush and an occasional

prickly pear, and wound through groves of live oak and juniper. We drove along for several kilometers without seeing anything.

"Jake? Darla?"

"Yes, Arthur," Darla answered.

"The signal source has stopped at a point due west of you. You're almost on top of it."

I slowed, though I couldn't see thing. I coasted down a slight grade, searching my side of the road.

"Arthur, where are you?" Darla asked.

There was a slight delay, then: "Right above you. I have the phony airplane lights turned off."

"We don't see the car," Darla told him.

"It's parked about fifty meters off the road. Just to the right, up ahead."

I saw a gap in the brush—a narrow side road. I stopped.

Darla said, "Arthur, are there any other vehicles in the area?"

"None that I can see or detect."

"Let's make sure," I said, starting forward again and turning off onto the side road, which was little more than a horse trail leading us around the base of a hill. We passed under a large brooding tree and came out into a hollow.

I saw a glint of candy-apple red in the sweep of the headlights as I turned around.

"There they are," Darla said. "Unless it's Carl."

"You're right on top of the signal," Arthur said.

No other vehicles were in sight.

"Okay, this is it," I said. "Arthur?"

"Yes, Jake?"

"Are you ready?"

"As ready as I'll ever be." He sighed. "Dearie me, how do I get myself into these predicaments?"

"Did Carl ever mention another vehicle being nearby when it happened?" Darla asked with some concern.

"Not that I remember. Let's head back around the hill and park. We'll come back on foot."

I headed out of the clearing, following the trail back almost to where it made its T with Mulholland. I wedged the VW between two junipers and killed the motor.

"You got that flashlight?"

"Yup." Darla held it up.

I shut off the headlights and the night deepened around us. We got out and walked back up the trail. Insects clicked and snapped in the weeds. The city was a glow on the horizon, and a faint, distant roar. The air was dry and cool. Darla played the flashlight beam from side to side, searching. About halfway to the hollow we found a path leading up the hill, making its way among big gray boulders. Darla shut off the flashlight and we climbed up to the first switchback and hid behind the rocks. We looked down and listened.

"Carl may have gotten cold feet," I whispered.

Darla nodded. "Let's hope so."

We went down and continued on the trail, stopping when we reached the tree with the weeping branches. I put the communicator next to my lips.

"Any time, Arthur."

"Roger."

I looked up through the branches, but couldn't see anything. Nevertheless I somehow sensed the craft's descent, felt its immense bulk growing black-on-black against the sky like some dark angel auguring doom. A shiver ran through me, and I began to appreciate the extent of the trauma Carl must have suffered. I couldn't blame him a bit for having been scared out of his wits.

I heard a voice coming from the parked Chevy. It was Carl Two. A door slammed, and the engine roared to life. The back tires spun briefly, then the engine died. The starter whined futilely, again and again. There was a shout. In the dim scattered light of the city-glow we saw the Chevy begin to levitate from the ground, its front end rising. We heard Lori's voice, but she wasn't screaming. She was shouting something at Carl.

Suddenly there was a rustling in the brush above us, and the sound of running feet coming down the hill.

Darla gasped, "Oh, no—"

Carl One burst into the clearing, running toward the car, which by now had lifted a good two meters into the air. The passenger-side door had opened and Lori had one leg dangling out, holding the door open with both arms. Carl leaped and grabbed onto something—either the door or Lori's leg, or both. I couldn't see. He began to rise with the Chevy, hanging on.

Lori was screaming now, frightened and shocked and confused. Slowly, the three of them, two layers of a core sample of the same human being and the woman they both loved, floated up into the still California night.

"Jake?" came Arthur's voice. "What's happening down there? I have an extra body in the scoop beam."

"It's Carl One," I said. Darla and I hadn't moved; neither of us could think of a thing we would dare do.

"Well," Arthur said with annoyance, "I've stopped trying to figure out what's supposed to happen here. Two of them fell out, so I'm going to set them down after I've stowed the automobile in the bay."

I slumped against the tree and closed my eyes. I could hear the Paradox Machine. It howled and shrieked and it sounded like Lori's screams.

Presently, I was aware of Darla hugging me, her face against my back, and I realized that Lori's screaming had stopped.

I turned around and held Darla for a moment, then took the flashlight from her and thumbed it on. Her face was drawn and pale, her eyes frightened.

"Oh, Jake, it was so awful."

"Yes."

"And we did it. We perpetrated it. We're guilty."

"Of what?"

"I don't know."

"Of doing what we had to do?"

"Did we have to do it?"

"We thought we did."

"Jake, I just don't know. I just . . . don't know any more."

"I never did, honey. I never knew the tune, but I keep trying to hum along."

We walked out into the clearing. Two bodies came down from the sky like stage deities on invisible wires. They landed gently on their feet.

Lori and Carl.

Our Carl. He was holding her, her face pressed against his shoulder. She was trembling violently.

"Hi," Carl said as we approached.

"Hi," I said. I didn't know what else to say.

"It happened like it was supposed to happen," Carl said. "I knew something else went on that night. I finally remembered what Debbie had shouted at me when the car began to lift. She told me not to be scared. I was stunned. Here was this *thing* coming down out of the sky at us, and here was the girl I loved acting as if she knew what was happening. That's what I blanked out of my mind. It was a fact I couldn't explain. It made me afraid just to remember it. I didn't want to believe that the girl I had met and fallen in love with could have had anything to do with the kidnapping. And I could never understand why she tried to jump out of the car, like she was leaving me. I tried to stop her. But she was being dragged out . . . by someone else. I couldn't see who." He stroked Lori's tinted hair. "It was me. It was the only person it could have been."

Lori's trembling had subsided. She turned her head up to Carl.

"You did, didn't you?" Carl said. "You tried to tell him. You saw that he was scared out of his mind and you tried to tell him that he'd be all right."

She nodded, closed her eyes and rested her head on his chest.

"I felt awful," she said. "Like I was doing something evil. I set him up, I went along with it. And then . . . when you . . ." She sniffed and wiped her eyes. "And when you came out of nowhere, Carl, I thought I was going crazy. I didn't know what to do. I was so scared."

Carl took a deep breath. "It all happened exactly as it was supposed to. Everything."

I spoke into the communicator. "Arthur?"

"Yes?"

"How is he?"

"Out like a light. Fainted dead away. He's fine, though. Just frightened."

"Did you speak to him in Prime's voice?"

"Yes, but I don't think he heard me."

"Well, if he comes to, just do your Prime routine and say something comforting."

"Oh, I will, I will, but he'll still be scared shitless. I'm going to try something on him. It's a mechanism that was formerly used to tranquilize wildlife specimens. It shouldn't hurt him, even if it doesn't work."

"Okay. Meet you back at Dave's place. How is Dave, by the way?"

There was a delay. "He says the only thing he regrets is that he can't ever use this in a script. Lacks verisimilitude."

18

I'M BAD AT good-byes. But I did my best.

It was about five in the morning. Carl, Lori, and Dave saw us off.

Lori hugged Darla, then me. I shook Carl's hand and then Darla kissed Carl and Lori. Then Lori hugged me again and kissed me. This went on for some time. Dave just stood by and smiled oddly.

"Jeez," Carl said, "I'm going to miss you people."

"Us, too," I said.

"I can't say I'm going to miss being nine zillion miles from home," he added. "I'm glad to be back. You can have the future. It's yours. I don't belong there."

"Future? No such thing," I said. "No future, no past. Time is one big wide-open amusement park. We proved that."

"Yeah, I guess."

Lori was sniffling. I stroked her cheek and said, "You're sure you want to stay, Lori?"

She pulled Carl closer. "Yes. I'll put up with smog, tooth decay, and this character. There's really nothing for me back where I come from. I kind of like it here. This is a nice place . . . a nice time to be alive."

I nodded. "Yes, it is. It seems peaceful, in a way, compared with what history says about it."

The eastern sky was growing milky. A few birds were tuning up in a nearby copse of sumac trees. Behind us the ship hovered silently; Arthur was standing by to take us away from Earth in the waning summer of a year long past.

Carl began, "I wish . . ." He chewed his lip, thinking.

"What is it, Carl?" I asked.

"I wish there was some way of contacting you," he said,

then shook his head. "Somehow, but . . . it's impossible. Right?"

"Send me a letter. Mark it: Jake McGraw, Postal Slot 7836, Administrative Zone Twelve, Vishnu, Colonial Planets. That's my address. Figure out a way to delay delivery for about a hundred and fifty years. Should be easy enough."

Carl laughed. "Yeah, sure." Then he stopped laughing and had me repeat it. I did.

Arthur's voice came through the communicator. "Are you *quite* ready?"

I walked over to Dave. "Thanks," I said, shaking his hand. "We couldn't have done it without you."

"I still think there's an outside chance that I've hallucinated this whole thing," he said. "By the way, Arthur doesn't look anything like Gort." He stared at the ship for a moment, then sighed. "The future. I've dreamed about it, written about it. And here it is, right in front of me. You know, Jake—you haven't really told me much about it. Nothing about what's really going to happen in the next few years here."

I said, "You mean like stock market quotations?"

"No." He glanced at Carl and Lori, then said, "Tell me, is there going to be a—" He stopped, then shook his head. "No. Don't tell me anything. At least I know there's going to be a future. Sometimes that prospect looks very dubious. And judging from the little you've let on, it's going to be a pretty interesting future."

"Never a dull moment," I said.

"People . . ." Arthur said impatiently.

"Keep your pants on," I yelled.

"I won't say the obvious," Arthur said.

"Well," Dave said, offering his hand again. "Good luck."

"Thanks."

There was more hugging and kissing, and Lori started crying again, so I dried her eyes and kissed her and told her to be a good girl. Which was silly, for she was now a woman.

"I'll always remember you, Jake," she said.

"And how could I forget my little Lorelei?" I said.

"Debbie," she corrected. She whispered in my ear, "I *hate* that name!"

"Which one?"

"Both, actually. Debbie the most."

"It looks good on you."

Presently there was nothing more to say.

I took one last look at Earth, at Earth's sun showing its face to a new day, at the grass and the trees and the kind skies of the birthing place of humankind.

And then I left that world, that time.

Earth dwindled in our wake as Arthur piloted the ship through the gravitational vortices of the solar system and out into deep space, where we could, as he put it, "do a good clean jump."

"Where to?" he added. "Back to Microcosmos?"

"Not just yet," I said. "We have to dump Carl off somewhere. And the sooner the better."

"He'll be okay. That tranquilizer mechanism seems to have done its job. Where did you have in mind?"

"Look. This is a spacetime machine, right?"

"Right."

"We can go anywhere, any time?"

"Well, more or less. There are some limitations."

"Can we jump forward in time about one hundred and fifty years and drop him off on the Skyway somewhere?"

"Just anywhere?"

"Terran Maze would be a good idea."

"Right you are. Just point out a likely planet and I'll shoot for it."

Bruce helped him do that. We picked Omicron Eridani II, and Arthur got his bearings from the Earth-based astronomical data that was stored in that tiny but powerful robot brain of his. We picked a date that was about a year before I met Darla on the Skyway. All would go according to plan.

Arthur asked, "Are you all getting off there?"

"No, just Carl. We're going back to Microcosmos with you."

Darla drew me aside. "Jake, do you realize that if we did get off, the Paradox would be complete? You'd be back in T-Maze before you left—before any of this happened. Don't you think—"

"No, Darla. The story's not over yet. I have to go back and get Sam."

She nodded, and didn't mention it again.

* * *

We had given a lot of thought to the subject of setting Carl loose on the Skyway. Our Carl—Carl One—had tried to describe his experiences immediately after the kidnapping. But his memory of the whole period aboard ship was hazy to say the least—which accorded exactly with the way things were going for Carl Two, who was at the moment slumped in the seat of his magic Chevy in the small cargo bay. He was catatonic, and it was hard to say whether this was the result of the "tranquilizer" beam or the trauma of the kidnapping. Probably a little of both. I was worried.

Carl One had told us that "Prime" had spoken to him during this period. We induced Arthur to do his impression of Prime for Carl Two at regular intervals.

"What do I say?" Arthur had demanded to know.

"Be soothing. Be a nice person."

"Oh, great."

But he did it. We had no idea if any of it got through to Carl. I had the feeling that it did.

According to Carl's story, when the mental haze lifted, he found himself in his car on the Skyway. And when he saw a portal for the first time, he somehow knew what it was and how to shoot it.

Arthur pondered this problem for a while. Then: "I can come up with something akin to dreamteaching by modifying the tranquilizer beam circuitry. I think."

I asked, "Don't you need tools or equipment or something to do that?"

"You're thinking in terms of conventional technology. It won't be a simple task, but it's not a matter of tinkering with anything physical, at least not on the scale of ordinary objects. This ship has the capacity to reprogram its auxiliary mechanisms for any function desired, within limits. Trust me."

"Oh, I do," I said. "You exude trustworthiness."

"I'll have to change my deodorant."

So it was that we set Carl off on the road between the worlds to seek his destiny, which was to find me and go home. He had nothing more than his car, the clothes on his back, and a little over 1000 Universal Trading Credits' worth of gold (my entire stash—I was now broke) in the trunk.

It was a grungy mudball of a planet with lowering skies

and mud-colored rocks—but just beyond the portal was
Adonis, a very nice world indeed, well-populated and civilized. We landed on the Skyway a few kilometers from the
portal's commit boundary. Arthur opened the bay door and
nudged the Chevy out. Carl sat there in the middle of the road
for a minute. Then he started the engine and drove off. He
never looked back.

The Chevy dwindled to a candy-apple red dot and vanished
between the towering jet-black columns of the portal.

Carl had shot his first portal and survived. Arthur's modified dream-teaching gadget had worked.

"Good-bye, Carl," Darla said in a murmur. "For the second
time, good-bye. And good luck."

"Hail and farewell," I said.

It took us over fifty jumps and six hours to get back to
Microcosmos, which wasn't bad time when you consider the
distance. It had taken longer to get to Earth starting from a
little beyond the orbit of Pluto. Arthur apologized, though, for
the delay. Well, he didn't exactly apologize. When either
Darla or I would stroll into the control room to see how things
were going, he'd glare at us defensively and give some excuse. "I keep running into bumpy spots," he complained.
"Fouls up my calculations. Spacetime isn't uniformly smooth,
you know."

"I never said it was," I told him.

"This has to be done just right," he went on. "We don't
want to return before we left. I've had just about enough of
that nonsense."

"You and me both," I said.

Eventually we got there. Arthur turned the ship transparent, and we watched an odd little cloud of stars grow and
grow until it became the peculiar star-sphere that enclosed the
textured disk of Microcosmos. It was daylight on the Emerald
City side.

All seemed peaceful down there. Nobody threw things at
us, no mind-shaking enigmas chased us as we made a smooth
entry into the atmosphere and streaked across the sky on a
decelerating trajectory toward Emerald City. The patchwork
surface of the planet rolled underneath the ship like a giant
map on a fast scroll. Arthur broke all the speed records and

nearly scared us to death. It looked as if we were about to go crashing into one of the city's valley-side curtainwalls until Arthur suddenly veered off and took the ship in a harrowing turn around the castle. Veering again, we dove between two huge towers and came to a screeching halt above a third. The domed top of the tower opened like a morning glory and we descended into it, coming to rest on a smooth black floor. The dome closed up, and we had arrived.

Arthur sighed and took his stubby fingers from the control box. His narrow shoulders slumped.

"If I were flesh and blood," he said, "I'd be exhausted. As it is, I only need a two-day recharge session."

"Some pretty fancy flying, there, Arthur."

"Thank you. I thought it best to hurry like hell. Looks like someone called a truce, but you never can tell."

I locked up the truck, telling Bruce to keep an eye on things, and we debarked from the ship.

"Jake," Arthur said as we walked toward a nearby down-chute. "I think you have a little bit of a shock in store."

I stopped. "What?"

"Well, it's about Sam. He's no longer a computer. He's alive, Jake. He's very much alive."

19

"HELLO, JAKE," SAM said.

He was sitting at the dining room table with John and Zoya, having coffee and rolls. He got up with a smile that lived in my memory. The face was my father's face, but it was one I hadn't seen since childhood, for the man coming toward me with arms extended was my father as he had been as a young man, around thirty-five. His hair was dark brown, almost black, his eyes the color of slate. He was about six feet tall (lately I'd fallen into using that antiquated system of measure), plus an inch or two. His jaw was strong, his shoulders broad, and his hands and feet, like mine, were a bit oversized. His lips cut a thin line over a markedly cleft chin. His nose, thin and straight, was prominent but not large. Altogether a handsome figure of a man. He was dressed in a trim gray two-piece utility suit with a black belt, and he wore black hiking boots.

He embraced me, and I could not speak. Although Arthur had done his best to prepare me, there is little that can serve as an adequate buffer against the shock of your life.

"Son," he said, "it's good to see you again."

"Dad," I finally croaked. I put my head on his shoulder and shut my eyes tight against the flow of tears.

I think I was a little irrational for a few minutes; it was a total state of shock. I don't remember what was said, or who said it, but sooner or later I noticed Prime standing off to one side, observing us with approval.

"Welcome back!" he said brightly.

I nodded and looked around. Ragna and Oni were seated at the table along with John and Zoya. Ragna smiled, his wide pink eyes gleaming. Zoya beamed at me. John looked bored.

Another wonder—so what?

Darla had been standing off to one side. She walked over and said, "So we finally meet in the flesh."

"Come here, Darla darling," Sam said. They hugged.

I couldn't help keeping one arm around Sam, could not relinquish the feel of his flesh, his corporeality. If I hadn't been used to having Sam's disembodied personality around, the sight of him like this, reborn, reincarnate, would probably have been enough to stop my heart. I would have died on everybody right there.

As it was, I had trouble fully regaining my powers of speech.

"How . . . was it done?" I gasped at Prime.

"An artificial body is nothing miraculous," he said. "The problem lies merely in effecting an adequate interface between it and the artificial brain that controls it, which in this case is the Vlathusian Entelechy Matrix. You are aware of the many resources on this planet. I simply used those needed to accomplish the job. And I think we were quite successful. Wouldn't you agree, Sam?"

"I sure would." Sam slapped his chest. "Never felt better in my life." He turned to me. "I'm told that this isn't your garden variety human body."

"No," Prime said. "It doesn't have some of the biochemical subtleties of a natural organism—even science at its height can't duplicate the genius of the Creator. For instance, Sam will never have another son, nor any more progeny. But his body does have a number of advantages. Sam will never grow old. He won't suffer illness—"

"But I'm not immortal," Sam said.

"No," Prime said, walking over to us. "I offered to tell Sam the body's estimated life span, but he didn't want to hear it."

"Even if it were a million years, or only a week," Sam said, "I wouldn't want to know. I'll be damned if I'm going to spend my second life counting down the days. You can't live like that."

"I understand and agree," Prime said.

I asked, "How did you get this body to look like his former one?"

"The imaging entailed using a number of sources—but

chief among them was a three-dimensional photograph of you and Sam that was stored in the on-board computer's auxiliary memory. Did you know it was there?"

I said, "Yeah, I do seem to remember having an old holo scanned into pixels and stored away."

"Your memories of Sam also were useful," Prime added.

"Okay," I said, rather absurdly, as if we'd been talking about the weather. I sat down and poured myself a cup of coffee. I couldn't keep my eyes off Sam, who seated himself and took a sip from his cup.

He winked at me. "Who says you only go around once, eh?"

"Sam, did you have any choice in this?" I asked.

"Not in getting shanghaied out of the truck. When I came to, I found that I'd been loaded into some weird kind of computer . . . I think." Sam looked to Prime for corroboration.

"It was a computer, in essence," Prime said.

"Anyway," Sam went on, "I was in contact with our host here, and he asked me if I wanted to join the Culmination. I said thanks, but no thanks. He said, okay, then how about a new body? I said, sure, why not?"

I laughed. "Sure, why not."

"I was getting a little tired of being a trailer truck. I like this just fine."

"I can't blame you. Your turning up missing like that gave me quite a scare, though."

Prime had seated himself at the table. "Our apologies. But had I told you our intentions, I doubt you would have believed me."

"You could have tried," I said.

"I did try," Prime said, "and would have succeeded if you hadn't left rather abruptly."

Aside from pointing out about a half-dozen holes in Prime's reasoning—for instance, hadn't he ever heard of radio communication?—I had little to say to that. It seemed that in any given argument, Prime had a subtle way of manipulating the emotional tug-of-war so that he always wound up on solid ground, leaving his adversary in quicksand. I couldn't figure exactly how he did it, but you simply couldn't argue with him, and I didn't feel like going through the motions with him now.

"Where have you guys been?" Sam was curious to know.

I looked around. "How long have we been gone?"

"About five days," Zoya said. "We were worried."

Darla filled them in while we breakfasted.

"So Carl finally got home," Sam said. "Well, good. And I think Lori will be happy back there." He pushed his coffee cup away and sat back. "Imagine," he said wistfully. "Earth, way back when. It must have been something to see. Nineteen sixty-four. Let's see, that was almost seventy years before I was born."

Darla changed the subject with: "I can't get over how much you two look alike." She swiveled her gaze back and forth between us. "And with your looking just about the same age, you could almost be twins."

I was about to remark that I'd always been accused of being Sam's clone when I suddenly realized that amidst the confusion and shock I had completely forgotten about the most important topic of all.

"Where the hell is Susan and everybody else?" I blurted.

"That's hard to say," Sam said, rubbing the blue-black stubble of his chin. He had always had a heavy beard. He looked at Prime. "Do you want to tell him what you told us?"

"I'd be glad to," Prime said as he buttered a croissant. "Ah . . . John, would you please pass me the marmalade?"

John passed him the marmalade.

"Thank you. Jake, Darla . . . let me first assure you that your friends are fine. Alive and well, fit and hale, and all of that. They are under no—"

"Okay, okay," I said curtly, "I'll take your word for it. Just tell me where they are."

"That brings up the perennial problem of communication again. But let me try—"

"Look," I cut in. "I'm getting awfully weary of these huge philosophical barriers that keep preventing you from answering the simplest of questions—like, where are my friends? Are they here, or are they somewhere else?"

Prime interrupted the job of applying marmalade to his croissant long enough to turn his head and ask, "Do you want to visit them?"

"Of course."

"Then sit back and relax."

I tried.

"Open your mind and call your friends. One or all of them."

I stared at him.

"Just do as I say," Prime instructed.

I leaned back and pictured Susan's face in my mind. Nothing happened.

Prime smiled, his black eyes twinkling. "Keep trying."

So I kept trying ... to do exactly what, I didn't know. I began to feel faintly ridiculous sitting there, staring off into space, but then something began to happen. Hard to describe. The environment around me began to dissolve, like a film, into another scene. It startled me at first, and the process halted and reversed—the dining room, the table, and everyone in the room reappeared. But then I relaxed and let go, discovering that I could control whatever was happening. I let the scene around me fade again.

I found myself sitting on a ledge on a steep rocky slope. Far below was a fog-filled valley ringed by snow-tipped peaks. Above was a jagged mountaintop against a gray sky. I stood and breathed in. The air was cool, fresh enough to have been created the instant before. Looking around, I saw stunted trees clinging to the slope, along with an occasional bush. The slope was steep but not difficult to climb, set with wide flat stones in uneven steps. I hopped to a higher outcrop and looked around. Deciding to climb the mountain and perhaps get a better view of what was going on, if anything, I began the ascent.

A cold wind rose. Eventually the slope leveled off to a wide ridge graced with an occasional tree. I walked along the edge, gazing down, until the way narrowed to a ledge just big enough to walk on without having to turn and sidestep. I paced slowly along it. The ledge narrowed some more, and I considered going back; but I kept on. Soon the ledge was barely as wide as my feet were long. I inched along sideways, the wind strong enough to tug at my open jacket but not enough to unbalance me. Far below a lake of mist swirled at the bottom of the cliff.

Eventually I came to a crevice splitting the wall behind me

in a crooked V. I stepped back into it. It was a corridor cut back into the mountain, widening into a descending pass. I walked for a few minutes, came out the other side of the mountain, and found a gentle slope leading down to the edge of a forest. I took a path that led me down through tall conifers bearing enormous cones. A soft trilling came from the treetops; birds, maybe. Maybe something else.

I came to the bottom of the hollow and found a swiftly running brook. I turned downstream and followed it, jogging over the smooth boulders that lined its banks. When the forest thinned out, I left the rocks and took a path that paralleled the stream and wound amongst miniature trees and tended shrubbery. The path became stone-paved and bore away from the main stream, following a small tributary and cutting through rock gardens. A dwelling lay up ahead: a cottage, done in a vaguely oriental style, fronting on a quiet pond. Susan was there. She was sitting on a stone bench near the edge of the pond, reading from a slim volume bound in blue cloth.

She glanced up and saw me, smiled, then got up and ran to me.

We embraced. Her brown eyes shone.

"Jake! It seems like years," she said, beaming.

"It does seem like it's been a long time," I said, running a hand through her straight, light-brown hair.

This was all very strange. It wasn't a dream, but it couldn't be real, I thought. Not altogether real, at any rate.

"Where are we?" I asked. "What is this place?"

"This is a place where I stay . . . sometimes," Susan told me, taking my hand and leading me back toward the bench by the pond. "It's quiet, and I can think here."

"About what?"

"Anything that I think is worth thinking about."

"I see."

We sat. Pink and yellow flowers floated on the pond's surface, bobbing gently, and reflections of overhead boughs shimmered deep within. Rushes grew at the pond's edge. A trilling cooing sound came from the trees. Other than the murmur of a brook, all was quiet.

"Where are we?" I asked again.

"It's a space and a time I sort of like," she said. "Isn't it nice?"

"Very. Tell me—does joining the Culmination mean that you can never give a straight answer again?"

She laughed. "No. Jake, I really don't know where or when this is, exactly. It's somewhere and when outside of all space and time—or maybe I created it. I don't really know. I haven't given it much thought. Does it matter?"

"Maybe. Maybe not."

"What was that about straight answers?"

"Sorry," I said. "Fair is fair. Okay, it doesn't matter. But how did I get here?"

"I gave you access to the Consensus Metaphysical Substratum. Go ahead, ask what that is."

"What is it?"

"I'm still learning, but basically it's a reality that everyone can agree on. But it isn't necessarily the true reality."

"The true reality of what?"

"Of everything. Real reality."

I nodded, then turned my head and stared into the pool. There was something dark at its bottom.

"It's hard to explain," Susan told me.

"I'm sure."

She patted my hand, and I took hers in mine.

"Are you real?" I said. "Are we really here, or is this an illusion?"

She pinched the back of my hand. "Feel that?"

And I did. "Yes. But it occurs to me to ask what that's supposed to prove. A pinch can be dreamed, too." I looked into her eyes.

She said, "I'm really here, Jake. And so are you."

I had never noticed that there were little flecks of green in her irises. "I must be," I said.

A ripple crossed the pool, and a faint reflected wave flowed back.

"Where have you been?" Susan asked. "You guys took off the other day."

"Earth," I said, "for a vacation."

She nodded as if she understood. "Did everything work out?"

"More or less."

"Good."

She was wearing what she always wore, her gray and

brown survival suit with soft gray deck boots. Her hair was a little mussy, as always.

I said, "I guess it wouldn't do any good to ask you to tell me what the Culmination really is, or what it's like being part of it."

"Would you like to be a part of it, Jake?"

I shook my head. "No."

She nodded again, smiling, and again she understood, this time only too well. "It's not your kind of thing, Jake. You're not a joiner. The idea of it goes against your grain."

"I guess so."

"But you're wrong, Jake. The Culmination is nothing like anything you've ever experienced before."

"There's something in me that dreads the loss of individuality."

She took both my hands and gazed at me intently. "Jake, look at me. Am I any different? Do I act differently?"

"No, you seem fine."

"I am. I feel wonderful. And I'm the same Susan you knew before. Nothing's changed. I haven't lost myself in some endless ocean of consciousness. It isn't like that at all. It's . . . it's like being reborn."

"I've heard that before."

She let go my hands, leaned back and sighed. "No. You see? I'm as inarticulate as ever."

"I understand," I said. "I think."

"It's not all that difficult to grasp."

"By the way, where are the others?"

"Oh, they're around." She looked over my shoulder. "As a matter of fact . . ."

I turned to see Sean strolling down the garden walk.

"Jake, me boy!"

We shook hands, and he slapped my back. He seemed substantial enough; he almost fractured my spine.

"I knew you'd be back," he said. "We were a mite worried, though."

"I was worried about all of you."

"No need. We're getting on rather well." He glanced around. "Nice place, Susan. Very nice indeed."

I said, "Oh, you don't hang out here?"

"No, I have my own place. So do the others, I suspect."

Susan nodded. "I've been to Roland's. It's on a mountain-top."

"Roland's a philosopher in the grand tradition," Sean said, grinning. "Waiting for his Zoroastrian flash of understanding. Mine's a shed in the woods. So's Liam's. Loggers to the last."

"So," I said. "What you people do basically is hang out and . . . what, have each other over for tea?"

Sean chuckled. "Among other things." Sean walked to the pond's edge and surveyed the scene. "Very nice place indeed."

Susan and I reseated ourselves.

"Tell me something, Suzie," I said. "Why did I have to climb a mountain to get here? If this is some Neverneverland, why couldn't you have just materialized me right here?"

"I didn't materialize you, I just let you into my space. I want people to have a sense of having traveled some to get here. Next time, though, I'll eliminate that part of it, if you like."

"No, no," I said. "It was interesting. Beautiful, actually."

"Yes, a journey is always beautiful."

"Some of ours haven't been."

"There've been some bad things," she admitted. "But it's all been an experience."

"I suppose you can say that about anything that happens."

"You can, but it's true."

I looked off into the quasi-Zen rock garden. I wasn't learning much. But then, I really had stopped caring so much about finding the key to all this. I was convinced that Susan and the rest were okay, were under no compulsion or duress, and that was all I needed to know. I decided right then that if the four of them wanted to stay, I wouldn't argue with them. I was going home; if they wanted a lift, fine. If not, fine.

Still, I wondered what would become of Susan, and felt obliged to find out.

She seemed to be in tune with my thoughts. "Jake, would you like a small taste of what it's like?"

"Is that possible?"

"Sure. I don't see why not."

"A free home trial, no obligation?"

She giggled. "So to speak."

I nodded. "Let me ask you this: Were you offered this sort of thing?"

"Uh-huh."

"And you took Prime up on it, right?"

She nodded.

"Was everyone asked to take a trial run?"

"Yes, I believe so."

"And did anyone besides you four take it?"

Susan chewed her lip. "You know, I don't believe anyone but us did."

I bent over, rested my elbows on my knees, and watched a circular wave propagate across the pond. Well, I had at least one piece of evidence, circumstantial though it may have been.

"He's thinking we were hooked, Suzie," Sean said.

Susan nodded solemnly. "Funny that it worked out that way. But it's not true, Jake."

After a long moment's contemplation, I said, "There's only one way to find out."

But I thought, should I risk it?

I turned and looked deep into Susan's eyes, trying to see through to some core of her that might have been hollowed out and filled with something that was not Susan at all. I searched, but saw nothing but the warmth, affection, and trust I had come to know was there.

"Take me for a ride," I told her.

She smiled and took my hand. "Let's walk," she said, rising.

20

WE WALKED PAST the pond and through more oriental gardens. Sean accompanied us.

"I'll go along with you a bit," he said, "if you don't mind. Then I'll be on my way."

"Come with us, Sean," Susan said. "By all means."

The gardens gave way to forest, and we climbed out of the valley. Reaching the timberline, we broke into alpine meadow. The air grew chilly, but I wasn't cold. The meadow sloped upward and ended where patches of snow lay atop gray-brown shelves of rock. We walked laterally along the slope, crossing through colonies of mountain wildflowers, their stems bending in the wind. Cold breezes from the summit blew about us, and puffs of misty cloud scudded through a bright, silver-gray sky. The grass fluttered in waves up and down the mountain. A streak of sunlight fell across the high part of the meadow, then faded. Clouds grouped and broke apart, chased by icy fingers of wind. The smell of heather and wildflowers rode on the lean, bracing air.

Susan and I walked hand in hand, Sean to my left and a little behind us. Susan didn't seem to be leading me anyplace in particular, yet her stride had purpose in it.

"Beautiful, this place," I said. "Where is it? Is this someplace in space and time, or is this the Substratum?"

"This is the Substratum," Susan told me. "And most of what's around us now is due to you."

"Huh?"

"This is basically your show now, Jake. My turf petered out a little ways back."

"Yeah?"

I didn't know what to make of that. I didn't feel in control of the situation. This place was as real as any I'd ever seen, and just as responsive to my whims and desires as the rest of the universe was, which is to say not at all.

We had traversed the windward face of a huge mountain whose peak was unseen, lost in clouds above. Now we came to a pass cutting between it and another mountaintop. We climbed a steep grade which gradually leveled off into a gravel-paved path between two steep slopes. The wind pushed at our backs, but as we began to climb again up the rock-strewn face of what apparently was a still higher mountain, it abated, replaced by stiff, cold breezes blowing down the slope and into our faces. The going was tough; huge masses of rock reared up in our path, and we had to skirt an occasional deep crevasse.

I was beginning not to like this one bit. I was in no great physical shape, and was beginning to get tired—although, strangely, not as tired as I should have been. It was getting a little too chilly for comfort, now that I thought about it.

"Where the hell are we going?" I asked.

"As I said, Jake, this is your show," Susan said. "If you don't like the metaphor, change it."

"This is a metaphor?"

"A common one. Scaling the heights, that sort of thing. Change it. Find a new way of getting to where you want to go."

"Where—" I began, then stopped and looked around. Everywhere the earth seemed to run up to a ceiling of cloud. What to do? Go back down?

So I pushed on, leading Susan by the hand. Sean took up the rear. We trudged up the slope and entered a bank of fog. Wet mist enveloped us, and rocks glistened underfoot. I was fine, except for feeling a little chilled. Susan didn't seem to mind the cold at all. We broke through the fog and the ground leveled off abruptly. We had come up to a broad level plateau populated with dark monoliths. I looked up and saw a brightening sky painted in swirls of gray and silver, shot through with luminescent streaks. A fine icy rain fell, cold and bracing on my face. The clouds roiled and billowed like milk poured in water.

"What now?" I asked, stopping.

"I think you want to make it warmer," Susan suggested.

"Yeah."

The clouds parted and a golden sun broke through with shafts of cathedral light.

"Religious symbolism?" I commented.

"Maybe."

"Pretty," Sean said.

It did warm up a bit, and very quickly, but up here lay a high windswept plateau, and I turned my collar up against a breeze blowing sand from the direction of a ruined city far out in the flats—Broken towers, tumbled walls, sand drifting against a shattered dome. To our right, nearer, another ruin was wedged into a box canyon, stone dwellings pressed together under the eaves of a sheer cliff.

"This gotta be someplace," I said.

"It is," Susan said. "Everyplace is someplace."

"Penetrating philosophical insight."

"Thank you."

Hills in the distance, and somehow we reached them in a very short time. The wastelands dropped behind us as we followed a twisted trail upward through scrub brush and browned grass.

"California," I said.

"Hm?"

"Reminds me of southern California."

"I've never been there. I'll have to go sometime."

"It was a good place circa 1960. Except for the smog. I've heard it was very nice between 1919 and 1940."

"I'll have to go, then," Susan said.

We reach a ridge. The path snakes down a hill and into changing terrain. The sky changes, and it becomes a star-dusted night, low half-moon hanging to our left, another moonlike body—a tiny disk—speeding along the ecliptic. At zenith a river of stars . . . strange shapes in the darkness at either hand, moving things, hulking things. No trace of fear in me, just resolution. I'm searching for a particular place. I don't know what it looks like, or where it is. A meteor shower, brilliant points of green fire falling out of the night, vanishing almost as soon as they appear. Glowing filaments radiating from an area of sky to our left, galaxies pinwheeling overhead—to the right, an aura of zodiacal light at the horizon. A night wind rises, and the star-rivers flow.

"Beautiful," Susan comments.

"Thanks," I say, understanding that she means it as a compliment, not comprehending why I'm accepting it.

A violet sun comes up and chases the glory away. Another city to our right, a grouping of crystal bubbles sitting on a vast empty plain. This world stays with us for a short minute, then dissolves into a seascape at twilight, breakers pounding a porcelain-white beach. Shells crack under our feet as we walk the strand. The sky churns with grays and blacks. There is no color in this place—if it indeed is a place, and not a phantasm conjured by Prime or some hidden deceiver. No life here. The sky is dishwater gray fading to charcoal, and the bits of shell underfoot are chalk white, gray, and black. Sand dunes to the right bristling with stalks of dried beach grass. In the distance a line of low hills.

"Great place for a beach house," I say.

Susan nods. "Sure." Ironic agreement.

Sean says, "Don't much care for the look of this place, Jake."

I say, "Neither do I."

What to do? We step out of that place and into another. It didn't occur to me to ask how we had done that.

Night again here. A moonlit necropolis, a ruined temple, a mound of debris, truncated columns, a half-buried plaza. We walk in alien moonlight. Stars again, a gaseous nebula glowing above. Where are we? The question goes unspoken.

I stop and gaze at the time-swept city around us.

"The ruined cityscape motif again," I comment.

"Time," Susan says.

"Yeah. Great big gobs of it."

Whispers from the darkness: ghosts. A shadow falls across our path, thrown by a communion-wafer moon backlighting a blasted tree. The shadow looks like a wild dancer. A temple sits on a hill up ahead, its riven dome no longer sheltering the statue of a tall alien deity. In a crypt somewhere a mote of dust falls and the heavens are disturbed.

"I'm spooked," I said. "Let's get out of here."

Over here, Susan says, so I follow her over there, wherever it is. It's not in any particular direction, really, just a slightly different frame of mind. It's a soothing emotional shade, a combination of restful contemplation and wistful nostalgia. It's more than a state of mind; it's almost a smell. I tell Susan that I'd rather see/feel something, and if she could do that for me, would she? Yes, I can, she says . . .

. . . and we're in another world, this one swampy and wet, so I can it and get into another, then another, then a fourth and fifth. We linger in this one, for it's a little like the place I'm looking for, a little, not much, because it's much too warm, so I take the temperature down five degrees and change the color of the sky to blue—I like blue skies—and shade the grass so it isn't so blindingly, feverishly green, and I make the trees taller and give them fuller foliage, and perhaps touch up that bark to look a little less like cancerous leather, and what I'm looking at now is a planet under a kind sun, a very nice place indeed for good old-fashioned dirt farming, which is the sort I like best. The terrain rolls gently, not too flat like some places I'd seen—the tornados wouldn't be totally implacable here. There are some mountains in the distance; good, if you want a change of weather, you don't have to go very far. And there's a cute little farmhouse under some poplar trees, and a barn, and sheds, and a chicken coop, a corn crib, a granary, a cattle pen, and other outbuildings and accessories, all you'd need.

"Like this place?" Susan asks.

"Yes," I say. "Yes, I do. Very much."

And I do, because, although it's not a lot like our place on Vishnu (which is a much less benevolent planet than this one), it comprises all the elements that I require for a sense of well-being and peace: space, quiet, green things, more space. The clouds are white and puffy, and whoever had painted them had first laid down washes of pure Earth-sky blue underneath. It did look a lot like Earth. Maybe that's where all we humans belong, after all.

"Nice little farm," Sean said approvingly, grabbing up a fistful of black sod and smelling it. "Fertile."

"Great, I've found it," I said. "What have I found? What am I supposed to do?"

But I knew the answer. Susan told me, anyway.

"Your body can stay here while other parts of you roam wherever you want. No matter where you are or what you do, you'll always have a sense of being home. Just like now—I'm still back at the cottage by the pond, even though I'm here at your place, too."

"Makes sense."

"No, it doesn't." Susan laughed. "That's why it's so neat. It doesn't make any sense at all. But it's wonderful."

"This is it, then?"

"Of course not. It's only the beginning."

I knew that, too. I knew a lot of things, then. What this was, was a new form of existence. Exactly what kind of existence, I didn't know. The answer was part of what lay at the end of the long road ahead.

I thought about it for a while, and when I snapped out of it, I was back on the farm again. Susan was there, but Sean had left.

"He says he wants to visit again sometime," she told me. "He told me to tell you good-bye. Someone else is here, though."

I was already shaking hands with Prime.

"We should talk," he said.

"I'll be going," Susan said.

Susan and I embraced. We parted, and I looked into her eternal brown eyes and saw that we would never meet again.

"It was wonderful, Jake. Knowing you. Loving you."

"I love you, too."

There were no other words to speak.

"You won't join, will you, Jake?"

I turned my consciousness to Prime and said, "No."

The corners of his lips turned up into a knowing smile. "You are a remarkable individual."

"Thank you. I must go back."

"Of course."

"You gotta tell me about the cube, though. I'm not sure I understand everything. You took the first one, the one I brought from the Skyway."

"Yes."

"Why?"

"We opened it," he said.

"And?"

"The results were ambiguous. Not surprising, since the experiment sought to answer an ultimate question. Those rarely admit of unequivocal solutions."

"What ultimate question did the experiment pose?"

"It is perhaps the only ultimate question—the only one that

matters. And that question is: Why is there something rather than nothing?"

I found a nearby tree stump—somebody had cleared this land—and sat down. I watched clouds for a moment, then said, "That *is* pretty damn basic."

Prime paced in front of me. "Oh, it can be formulated any number of ways, and it has a million corollaries. Did the universe come into being spontaneously, or was it caused by something else? If the latter, what does that do to the concept *universe* itself? And on and on and on."

"So," I said, "the results were ambiguous."

"Let's say that the data will be a long time yielding conclusive results. Very difficult to tell at this point."

"Okay. Tell me this: In all of space and time, no one ever thought of constructing this experiment?"

"It had long been known to be theoretically possible. For some reason, it was never done. At least, there is no record of it ever being done. We don't know everything that ever happened."

"You're not omniscient?"

"Not quite."

"Uh-huh. You're not a deity—in the sense that beings of my time and space and culture understand the term."

"No. That is a very curious concept, by the way. Intriguing, though."

"Do you think there is such a deity?"

"It may yet be true," he said.

"The jury is still out on that one."

"I understand the allusion. Yes."

"All right." I took a deep breath. "All right. The cube created itself, didn't it?"

"It seems to have done just that. Remarkable. Possibly recapitulating the history of the universe it modeled."

"Possibly?"

"Very possibly."

"Why couldn't the Culmination have created the experiment?"

"We don't create. We don't do science. Science is knowledge. We seek wisdom. In the final analysis, science gives answers which lead only to more questions."

"But what does wisdom lead to?"

"Ultimately? Perhaps only to a state of mind . . . or a state of being in which a question is its own answer."

I got up. "Well," I said. "Thanks a lot. I have a load of goods in my truck that I have to deliver. I'm running late."

"I understand."

"Thanks for all your help."

"You're very welcome."

I turned to look at the farm one last time. Nice place. I could have stayed there for a million years or so.

But I have to get out on the road once in a while.

And I really did have a load to deliver.

21

DISSOLVE TO:

INTERIOR—EMERALD CITY DINING HALL—DAY.

A lap-dissolve from one scene into another, just like in mopix.

And there I sat, in my free-form sculpted chair at the table. Everyone was looking at me.

"Jake?" Sam was eyeing me curiously.

"Yeah," I said. I shook my head and rubbed my eyes. "How did I get back here?"

Sam arched an eyebrow. "What makes you think you've been anywhere?"

"Huh? I must've been gone for hours. Days maybe." I glanced around. Everyone was puzzled. Me, too. "Wasn't . . . I mean, didn't I—"

"You've been staring off into space for the last minute or so," Sam told me.

"What?" I sat back and exhaled. "Holy hell."

"It must have been quite a trek," John commented.

I looked at him and nodded. Then I noticed Prime was gone. Inclining my head toward his empty seat, I said, "What happened to . . . ?"

"Hm?" Sam answered. "Oh, he just got up and left. Said he had some pressing business. Probably was double-parked."

I took a long drink of coffee. It was still warm. I began, "How long did you say—" I stopped and put my cup down. "Never mind."

"Jake, what happened?" Darla asked.

"Huh? Nothing. I mean . . . I'm not really sure. Tell you later."

Darla shrugged. "Okay."

And I wasn't sure at all, now, what had happened. It had been something outrageously wonderful, mysterious, and sublime—that much I did know—but exactly what had happened was unclear. I might never really know for sure. I did know that all of a sudden I felt extremely depressed. It was a crashing to earth. A letdown, a feeling of great loss. The sense of bereavement was profound.

"Jake? Is something wrong?"

I didn't answer. I sipped my coffee and stared at the table. Conversation started up again, but I didn't listen.

I thought I heard Susan's voice, far off, faint. I cocked my ears. No. Just wind, maybe. Or a castle ghost.

"Jake?"

It was Darla, again. I turned my head to her.

"Are you all right, Jake?"

I nodded. "Yeah. I'm . . . fine. Fine."

The feeling passed quickly, leaving a wistful longing for something I couldn't name. That gradually faded, too.

I sighed and sat up, drained my cup, and stood.

"We're going home," I announced.

We hunted up Arthur and found him fiddling with the controls on the back of his little helper robot, which looked like a mobile gum-ball machine.

"What's gotten into you?" he was asking it as we approached. He looked up. "Oh. Hello, there."

"We're leaving, Arthur," I said.

"Want a lift to the exit portal, or are you taking the scenic route?"

"What you said."

"Right. Dearie me, this little guy's innards are all cockeyed." He flipped the access plate up, and it clicked into place. He tapped the robot's transparent globular head. "All right, Edgar, run along."

The mechanism rumbled off on wobbly wheels.

"'Bye, Edgar," Darla said, waving. "Nice meeting you."

"Whirrclickbeep," Edgar said, swiveling his head around and raising a mechanical arm.

"Nice kid, but from a low-tech family, if you know what I mean," Arthur said. "Okay, I'm your chauffeur again."

There wasn't much to fetch from our quarters. John, Zoya,

and Darla had a few things to pack, Ragna and Oni next to nothing, and I rounded up my toothbrush and an extra shirt. I didn't see anything belonging to Susan, Roland, or the Talltree boys. Sam had nothing but the clothes on his back.

Our host made no appearance as we made our way to the tower. I didn't expect him to show, but for some reason I doubted we'd seen the last of him.

Emerald City's glossy green walls remained mute; the empty chambers were as silent as they had been for the last million years. What events had transpired in them, long ago? What plots had hatched, what scenes had unfolded? Don't ask me. The place had made a fair motel, as motels go.

We took an up-chute to a higher level, walked down a hallway, then climbed a spiral stairway to the tower.

"Good Lord," Sam exclaimed. "You weren't kidding about a flying saucer."

"Would I kid you about a thing like that?" I said.

Arthur dilated the saucer's main hatch and we boarded.

By the time we got our gear stowed in the truck, Arthur had taken off. As I stepped into the control room, the walls de-opaqued and I could see the tower's top closing behind us. Emerald City dropped away, and we shot out over the valley.

Sam was mesmerized as he watched the terrain of the diskworld slide beneath us.

"This is pretty weird," he finally decided.

"You think?" I said.

"Most spectacular!" Ragna exclaimed, his pink oval eyes wider than usual.

Oni's pale blue hands were up over her mouth in a very human gesture of amazement. She uncovered to say, "It is indeed magic, or something verily like it!"

"Verily," I agreed.

"I am almost sorry to leave this place," Zoya said quietly.

I regarded her for a moment. There hadn't been time to discuss what effect Yuri's decision was having on her. She looked relieved. Perhaps it had been for the best.

We were heading for the dark face of the planet—it was still broad daylight on this side. I scanned all around, trying to catch sight of anything coming our way. And sure enough, slowly gaining on our tail . . .

"Arthur—"

"I saw it before you did," Arthur said as he stood at the control panel. He hadn't moved his head.

Darla searched the sky and saw the glittering many-colored phenomenon behind us. "I wonder what it is this time."

"I know what it is, and I'm scared," Arthur said. "And I'm not even *alive*. In the conventional sense, that is."

"What is it?" I asked.

"What's the conventional sense of being alive?"

"For God's sake, what's chasing us?"

"I don't have a name for it. You'll soon see."

The glittering vortex grew until it became a rotating wheel of fire that stretched from horizon to horizon.

"Oh, my God," Darla said, clutching my arm.

"Arthur," I said, "you had better reach deep, *deep* into that bag of tricks of yours."

"What bag is that, dearie?"

The rim of the wheel was a ring of golden fire braced by hundreds of green luminescent spokes that spun about a ruby-red, star-bright hub. Cascades of pyrotechnics spewed from the rim at various points along its circumference. The spokes shimmered and left blue smoky trails as they rotated. The phenomenon wasn't a physical object in the conventional sense—the spokes and the rim seemed to be turning in opposite directions.

"Pretty," Sam said.

"Deadly," Arthur said.

"What's it do?" Sam asked.

At that instant the ship was enveloped in a brilliant fireball, and we were thrown to the deck by a terrific concussion. I rolled and got to my feet, helped Darla up, but another shock wave hit us, and we went down. This time I waited for a moment before trying to get up. I asked Sam if he was all right.

"Never better," he reported. "What hit us?"

The walls had opaqued instantly, but now they were partially transparent again. The wheel was radiating dazzling purple energy beams from at least a hundred points along the circumference of the golden ring, and they were all focused in on us.

"Whew!" Arthur said. "For a couple nanoseconds there we were actually subject to the normal laws of physics! Any more of that and we'll turn into vapor. But I have the energy pretty much neutralized now."

We all got up and looked back. We seemed to have put some distance between us and the wheel. Not much, but we were slowly pulling away. There was still a faint aura surrounding us, gradually fading.

"I think we can outrun this thing," Arthur said.

"Can you do a continuum jump?" I asked.

"Not with that thing chewing on our tail, and certainly not this close to the planet. We lucked out last time I did a blind jump. Our fortune might not be so good the second time. Just let me get some distance first, and then we might be able . . . uh-oh."

"There," Darla said, pointing to starboard.

A V formation of glowing red disks was coming abreast of us, having just darted out from a suspicious-looking greenish cloud. Arthur steered the ship to port, but we were met by another V, this one made up of a squadron of pulsating blue cubes. Arthur veered off again.

"Cubes," Arthur observed. "Well, at least that's in keeping with the minimalist style they seem to be fond of. Dodecahedrons next, I bet."

"They can give us trouble?" I wanted to know.

"Maybe. They don't seem to want to close with us — which means . . ."

"They're herding us somewhere," Sam suggested.

"Yes," Arthur said, "but I can't imagine where or why."

The interceptors kept feinting at us, pinching us in, forcing Arthur to adjust and readjust our heading. They obviously had some specific course in mind for us.

"Very effective ploy," Arthur commented admiringly. "We can't outrun them while we're neutralizing the wheel's energy, nor can we outshoot them. I'm betting they can't outshoot us, either, but all bets are off when we get to where they want us to go."

"We're coming up on the edge of the world," John informed us solemnly.

"That may work to our benefit," Arthur said.

The curve of Microcosmos' rim swept under us looking like an LP record covered with moss and lichen. We flew out into space following a trajectory that kept us at a fairly uniform altitude above the bulge of the cross-hatched, metallic disk edge.

That's where they got us. A blinding blue-white flash enveloped the ship.

"Oh, dearie me."

The ship wobbled, then shuddered, then wobbled again. The walls went opaque, and the interior lighting went off. Strange forces pushed and shoved at us. The lighting returned.

"Everybody up against the bulkhead!" Arthur yelled. "Strap in!"

I stepped back and leaned against the bulkhead, which immediately threw out rubbery tentacles that snaked around my thighs and my chest, wriggling under my arms.

"Merciful deity-types!" Ragna exclaimed as the same happened to him.

The next minute was disorienting. We went into a tumbling fall, then straightened out and dove in a tightening spiral. G-forces tore at us, but the straps, marvelously resilient, cushioned the shocks, and the bulkhead behind me seemed to have turned soft and mushy. I wondered if there were anything in the infinitude of possible universes that this craft could not do.

Besides making a claim of absolute invulnerability, that is. It couldn't do that.

"They caught us in a cross fire," Arthur said after he had regained control of the ship. We seemed to be flying fairly straight now, though still descending. "I was wondering if there was a weapon that could bring this ship down. And there isn't. But they maneuvered us exactly into a position so that three of the defensive batteries along the rim could get off shots at us simultaneously. That did the trick, at least temporarily. The main propulsion system is inoperative. It can fix itself, but it'll take time. Meanwhile, I have to set her down, like right now."

There was a gentle bump. The ship skidded a couple of dozen meters, stopped, rocked back and forth a few times, and came to rest.

"Whew," Arthur said. "Crash landing."

I said, "Any landing you can walk away from is a good one, I always say."

"They'll be here any second," Arthur said. "There should be a tunnel entrance around here someplace. Our only chance is to get in the truck and get underground right away."

The rubbery straps retracted, disappearing into the bulk-head. I looked around. It was dark outside. We had come to rest on a flat metal plain whose only nearby discernible feature was a reticulated cube glinting in the starlight about fifty meters away.

I took a step forward, bounced up about ten centimeters, and floated gently back down.

"The only gravity here is what the mass of Microcosmos generates naturally," Arthur warned. "It's about one twentieth of what you people are used to. Watch your step."

"You coming?" I asked.

"If there's any time, I'll deflate the ship and stow it in your trailer. Get going."

"Looks like we're back in the trucking business," Sam said.

We ran to the rig and piled in. I turned her over, and by the time I had the engine squeezing hydrogen, the door to the cargo bay had dilated. I backed out, slipping and sliding. The gravity was just barely enough to allow the rollers to grab at all. I juiced them up to maximum traction.

"No need to brief me on the current situation," Bruce said. "I have been monitoring."

"Good boy, Bruce," I told him.

Sam was staring at the dashboard camera, which had once been his eyes. "Who the hell is Bruce?" Then he figured it out. "The Wang A.I.?"

"Right," I told him.

Arthur followed us out. As soon as he stepped out onto the blue-tinted metal of the surface, the ship began to shrink. I cycled the trailer and opened the rear door. There was no air out there. When the spacetime ship had become a miniature of itself, Arthur picked it up and galumphed around back. Arthur could move when he wanted to.

I scanned the dark sky. One of the blue cubes was hovering off to starboard at about a hundred meters off the surface.

"Damn!" I said. "We've had it."

I checked the trailer camera. Arthur was aboard—

—and I saw something back there I couldn't believe, but now was not the time to ponder it.

I gunned the engine and shot forward, making a sharp turn

toward the cubical structure. A pink flash stabbed my eyes.

Sitting in the shotgun seat, Sam looked back. "It's the cube," he said. "Firing at us."

Green spots chased each other in front of my eyes. "Are they hitting us?"

"I guess. Can't tell. I don't see how they could miss at this range."

Another flash lit up the metallic plain, but by this time I had the ports polarized.

"Did you have this rig retrofitted with some kind of super-tech defensive screen or force-field?" Sam asked.

"No—I never thought of it. Should have. Had the opportunity, in fact."

The cubical structure was big, its surface running with pipes and conduits. Antennalike projections bristled here and there. It had no opening, however. I swerved away from it, rolling over the smooth featureless surface. The cube got off another shot at us, and this time the rig shook a little with the impact.

"Hm," Sam said. "They're not missing."

There was an obstacle up ahead, a pipeline or something of the sort, running across our path. I turned left and ran along it until it ended at an elbow joint curling into the ground. There were other structures to the left, and I turned and scooted toward them, rolling in and out of one of two shallow troughs on the way. I ducked into the midst of some oblong buildings, shooting up and down the alleys between them, finally exiting the miniature town and heading for another just like it which lay across an obstacle course of valves and pumps. I nearly flattened a few of these; it was dark out here on the edge of the world. The flashes were getting more violent. The cab shook and buffeted more with each new assault.

"They're getting through to us," Sam said worriedly.

"I wonder what's been holding them back so far," I said.

I shot through another whistle-stop town of mechanical structures. At the other end I found a ramp leading up to a wide raised slab which cut across our path—a sort of elevated roadway. I had to get up on it or double back, so I gunned the engine, sent the rig thumping up the steep ramp, and turned left on the roadway, looking for a way down the other side, because we were sitting ducks up here. The star-filled sky crawled with red disks and blue cubes, most of them shooting beams of pink fire at us. Colorful bastards, I had to give 'em that.

I floored the power pedal and got some speed up. The roadway was wide enough to permit cautious evasive action —the edge was difficult to pick out. As we made our way down the level road, I could see that the ground below was dropping away. Then all of a sudden the ground left off entirely, the road having become a bridge over a deep pit, at the bottom of which lay things that looked like cranes and wrecking equipment. There was no guardrail, and although being up there would have been scary under any circumstances, getting shot at into the bargain provided that certain zest, that sharp experiential tang, that . . . *je ne sais quoi* which makes life worth living. He said blithely.

There was something lighting up the murk at the other end of the bridge, something familiar yet frightening.

"What the hell is that?" Sam demanded, and I realized that Sam had never seen what Carl had named a Tasmanian Devil.

"It's a real pain in the butt," I answered, braking hard.

Looking like a swirling tornado of red-orange fire, the strange phenomenon slowly but steadily advanced toward us, strange shadows writhing at its center. I slid the rig to a halt —it was hard stopping in this gravity—and switched all the monitors to rearview. The roadway wasn't wide enough to execute a U-turn, and there wasn't time to back and fill, so I slammed the transmission into reverse and floored it. This is just the sort of thing you don't want to do with a trailer truck. There was a very good chance that we'd wind up at the bottom of the pit. But we really had no choice. I knew what that thing would do if it caught us. When it caught us. I had first seen a Devil back on a planet called Splash—it seemed a thousand years ago. Roland and I had inadvertently unleashed one by fiddling with the weapons controls on Carl's Chevy. This one, and the one that had chased the spacetime ship, looked about the same. There was something absolutely implacable about it. It gave the impression that it would not stop until its assigned task of the complete destruction of its target was accomplished.

The trailer was already angling toward the edge of the roadbed. I cut the front rollers to the right, compensating and straightening it out.

We didn't get very far back up the road. Something came out of the pit and picked us off the bridge.

"Some kind of crane," Sam said, pressing his face against the port and trying to look straight up. "Don't know what the hell—some kind of magnetic gizmo."

Reeling us like a fish on a line, the gizmo or whatever it was swung the rig out over the pit, dangled it there for a moment, then began to lower it swiftly but carefully down. A hole opened up at the bottom, and we descended through it. The trailer hit the floor first, then the cab thumped down, not ungently. There came a loud, echoing clang above us. Then there was silence.

I looked around. In dim light I could see outlines and shapes of things—machinery and the like. We were in a large chamber, its farthest corners hid in shadow. The darkness was a little unsettling, even though the scanners showed nothing stirring out there.

"What now?" Sam wondered.

The engine was still running. I eased forward a mite, peering into the gloom. "I don't know. Can you see . . . ?"

The scanners went crazy as a towering dark shape outlined in flashing lights came out from a hole in the wall. I focused the rig's spotlights on it. Rising to about thirty meters, it was an asymetrical structure composed of interconnected components, and taken as a whole it appeared to be some sort of mobile wrecking crane or other piece of heavy equipment. It was jagged with mechanical arms and appendages, some of them very wicked-looking, all of them capable of opening up the rig like a hotpak dinner.

And it was coming for us.

22

"JAKE, I AM receiving a query," Bruce informed me, "presumably originating from the Artificial Intelligence in control of the mechanism which is advancing toward us."

"Tell it we come in peace," I said lamely.

"I do not think that is the issue. It is asking why we have not been assigned a Disassemble Order Number, and demands to know what sector and subsystem we have been decommissioned from."

"Tell it to stand by for data transmission!" Sam barked.

"Done," Bruce said.

The hulking thing stopped in its tracks, lights flashing, its Shiva-arms waving threateningly. Motes of light flickered on a pyramid-shaped component at its top.

"Go to address 0000H to 0002H!" Sam ordered.

"Done."

"Restart and move Source Library to Working Storage!"

"Done."

"Download!"

A minute later, Bruce said: "Done. Receiver acknowledges."

Sam exhaled, looked at me and grinned. "When the checkpoint guard asks for your papers, give him everything you got. Swamp the bastard."

"Good move," I said.

"Let's hope it works."

The huge thing chewed the matter over for a moment, standing there in the darkness. Then a grouping of lights realigned itself along the monster's left flank.

"The mechanism informs me," Bruce relayed, "that it is

219

having very little success in processing the data it has received. It demands further data and clarification."

"System reset," Sam said.

"Done."

"Select datapipe B. Begin moving entire contents of Auxiliary Storage to CPU."

"CPU at capacity," Bruce stated.

"Download, then reload."

"Downloading."

Sam crossed his arms and snorted. "That ought to hold it."

It did for about thirty seconds. Then angry red lights blared on the pyramidal structure.

"The mechanism informs me that it is not capable of processing the data we are transmitting," Bruce said. "It instructs us to follow it to a place where such a thing may be accomplished."

"He's taking us to see the Commandant," Sam said.

Some of the robot's components swiveled about, a few lights changed pattern, and the thing began moving away. I followed cautiously. The hulking contraption led us into the high-arched tunnel that it had come out of, and as it entered it reconfigured itself, reducing its height slightly. The tunnel ran for about a quarter klick, debouching into a dim spacious cavern full of gigantic equipment. I tagged after our robot captor down a wide central aisle that ran straight through the chamber and ended at another tunnel, this one shorter than the first. It fed through into a smaller chamber clogged with pipes and machinery. The aisle here branched at a Y, the left leg leading to a tunnel mouth which looked small enough for the robot to have a hard time squeezing into.

It didn't take me long to arrive at the decision. I had no desire to see the Commandant. When we got to the Y, I gunned the engine and swerved left, racing down the branch and into the tunnel. The robot either hadn't noticed we had gone the other way or wasn't willing to chase us; it showed no reaction.

Maybe, I thought, because this tunnel is a direct chute to the discombobulator.

But it wasn't. We came out onto a high suspended metal ramp that curved through a perplexity of multicolored pipelines, cables, and exotic technology. It was at least a ten-story drop off the edge, and overhead the tangle of conduits and titanic machinery continued up out of sight. I slowed and drove carefully; there was no guardrail, and it was a long and very unpleasant way down.

"Sam, was that too easy, or am I just paranoid?" I said.

"Seemed just a tad too easy," Sam allowed.

We moved on, soaring through congested and confusing spaces. The ramp took odd bends, banking crazily as it swooped and swerved. Then it did something that made me come to a full stop.

"Either this roadway has artificial gravity, or it's for flies only," Sam deduced.

A few feet ahead the ramp did an outside loop, curving under itself and doubling back. It then twisted and spiraled downward, finally leveling off a dozen stories below. I looked at Sam. He shrugged. I shrugged, too. Why not?

It was the best roller coaster I ever rode. A little disorienting, though, as there seemed to be about four equally valid centers of gravity to contend with. As we came shooting down the final dip, my stomach was debating whether to turn itself inside out or plant soybeans this winter.

We moved on, encountering more nonsense. I could have sworn that at one point we were crawling across the ceiling, instead of the floor, of a huge compartmented chamber. I became convinced of this as loose debris in the cab began to fall up. Then it all fell to the driver's side. I peeled a dirty sock off my face and considered taking a Dramamine pill. I had a headache, and the contents of my stomach were sloshing about. Darla looked a little green.

"How long do we do this," Sam asked, "before we admit to ourselves that we're lost?"

I looked back and forth between two branches of a diverging ramp, considering the choice. "We were lost when the saucer crashed," I said. "Now we're just making a proper job of it."

"Maybe Arthur knows how to get out of here," Darla said.

"Holy heck," I said, "I forgot all about him." Switching a mike to the intercom circuit, I called, "Hey, Arthur! You okay back there?"

"Wonderful," came the robot's voice.

"You don't sound happy."

"Things could be better."

"Do you want to ride up here in the cab?" I asked.

"If you want me to."

"As a matter of fact, you might be of some help." I scratched my beard stubble. "Trouble is, you probably can't squeeze through the access tube."

"If you're talking about that hatch at the front end of the trailer, you're probably right," Arthur said. "Actually, I may be able to do more good back here. I have some of the ship's sensors activated."

"Do you know where we are?"

"Only generally. What we want to do is to find an access terminal that will allow us to plug into the computer network that runs Microcosmos."

I looked at Sam, who chuckled. "Uh, I think we were on our way to one when we got lost," I said.

"I know all about it, I was listening in. Yes, that's where that maintenance robot was taking us, I think, though you were probably wise to play it safe, even if we did get lost. No matter, there must a terminal around here somewhere."

We meandered for a while longer, touring the guts of the machine that was Microcosmos.

Presently Bruce announced: "I have made contact with an Artificial Intelligence who seems to act in the capacity of a supervisor, of sorts."

"I'm linked with it, too," Arthur said through the intercom circuit, which I'd left open. "It's a subsystem coordinator. Get off the line, Bruce. I'll handle it."

"Very well," Bruce said.

Moments passed until I grew impatient. "What's up, Arthur?"

"Hold your pants on," Arthur said peevishly. "I'm being routed up through the hierarchy."

More time passed in silence.

"Okay," Arthur finally said with a sigh. "You may find this hard to believe—I did—but the artificial brains in charge of running the machinery of Microcosmos don't seem to know about Prime. At least I couldn't get any sort of recognition out of them. However, they do seem to know about the Goddess. She seems to swing a lot of influence around here—which makes sense when you think about all the trouble we've been having."

"Exactly," I said. "And that may mean we'll never get off this pancake alive."

"Don't give up hope, dearie. We do have some friends on this world. I've managed to get a message to the industrial facility where we hid out before. I got a reply. It looks like they'd be delighted to have us back, and we can travel there under their auspices."

"They can guarantee us safe passage?" I asked skeptically.

"Practically. The situation has grown into a sort of an internal political tussle. I don't think the Goddess will want to interfere, at least not at this point."

"Okay," I said. "How do we get to the plant from here?"

"I've arranged for transportation. We're taking the train. And if you take that ramp to the right, we should reach the station in about ten minutes."

I followed Arthur's directions, and ten minutes later on the dot we entered a high-ceilinged chamber bathed in red light. The layout of the place was complex, but you could see that a wide, slightly concave track or raised platform ran through the middle of it all. Suddenly things started shooting by at phenomenal speed—odd machinery, huge wrecking cranes like the one that had collared us, unidentifiable gadgets and doodads, all skimming along and levitating slightly above the track.

"What do we do now?" I asked Arthur.

"Sit tight."

A few moments later a gigantic crane arm reached out of a crimson shadow, picked the rig up, swung it out over the track, and lowered it down. A force caught us, and we were whisked away along the track at tremendous acceleration. It nearly broke my neck.

Eventually the G-forces fell off and our speed steadied.

"I nearly got killed back here," Arthur complained over the intercom. "All this loose junk . . . and that stupid damned automobile!"

"You okay?" I asked.

"I'll live."

"I thought you weren't alive in the conventional sense."

"I wouldn't be able to stand it."

Our speed was fantastic; everything outside was a blur. We shot through another huge chamber in the blink of an eye, entered a tunnel and sped through it, hurtling toward a mote of pink light.

"Jake?" It was Darla.

"Yeah?"

"Did Arthur say what I thought he said?"

I nodded. "Yeah, it's back there."

Darla was thunderstruck. "Jake, *how?*"

"I don't know," I said.

"But . . ." She groaned, exasperated. "Which one *is* it? The one Carl created, or the one . . . ?"

"You were saying?"

"Oh, Jake, I'm confused."

"You're confused." Then I remembered something Prime had told me. *Everything will be returned to you.*

We plunged headlong into darkness, periodically flashing in and out of eye-stabbing light. Our speed must have been something close to five hundred kph, but I didn't feel like asking Bruce to confirm it. I kept my grip tight on the control bars and my left foot heavy on the brake pedal; there was no telling when I might suddenly regain control.

"Arthur," I called. "How far?"

"How far to the plant? Oh, I don't know. At this speed we'll be there in a few more minutes."

He was right. It wasn't long before we began to decelerate at a mercifully gentle rate.

"Now, if I can't get the spacetime ship started again," Arthur went on, "you can make a dash for the central portal. The plant is about a half day's drive from it, as the crow flies."

"We'd never make it," I told him. "Any chance of taking the train to a point near enough to the portal so that we'd have at least a fighting chance?"

"I'll work on it," Arthur said. Then he heaved a mortal sigh and lamented, "This was a peaceful world before you humans arrived."

I asked, "Was anything at all going on before we arrived?"

"No. And that's just the way I like it."

"Sorry, but coming here wasn't our idea."

"I know, I know," he acknowledged grudgingly.

We had come to a full stop inside another station, and another crane lifted us off the track and deposited us on a high ramp. I started the engine and drove off, again following Arthur's directions.

"How the hell can you see outside?" I interrupted.

"I told you, I'm partially hooked into the ship's sensorium. Seeing through walls is child's play."

"Oh, sure," I said.

"Never mind. Make the first right."

I did, running up a wide ramp that went through a large rectangular opening. We entered an area that looked like a loading dock, and something about it was familiar.

"We should be here," Arthur said.

"I am in contact with the plant foreman," Bruce said.

"Put him on," I said.

There was a pause. "Some difficulty in audio reception," Bruce informed us. "Possibly due to our position. I suggest proceeding directly to the Display Area."

"Um . . . Jake?" It was Arthur.

"Yeah?"

"Is there—" The intercom went dead.

I tested the intercom switch, found nothing wrong with it. "Bruce, do we have problems here?"

"Yes, Jake, a short in the circuit. It will take a few minutes to locate it."

"Not important. Just get me to the showroom."

A huge sliding door was opening to our right. "That way," Bruce said.

A few more turns and we were back where Carl and I had first seen our respective dreams made real. Still no plant foreman, though.

"Bruce, what's going on?"

"Sorry, Jake. We seem to have sustained some damage to our communications hardware."

"You should have reported it before this," Sam said, his eyes suspicious.

"First opportunity," I ventured. "Right, Bruce?"

"Don't make excuses for him," Sam snapped. "He doesn't need them, anyway. He can't—"

"Sam, hold it," I said, cocking my ears. A sound was conducting through the bulkhead, faintly.

"I guess that's the foreman," I said. "Jesus, Bruce, are the outside mikes dead, too?"

"I'm afraid so, Jake."

"Damn it, anyway." I groused, popping the hatch.

"Jake, wait a minute!" Sam shouted, too late, as the hatch hissed upward.

"Don't twitch a muscle," said the man who was pointing the gun at my face. I recognized him as Geof Brandon, one of Zack Moore's gunsels. "Not one move, mate," he growled, climbing up one more rung of the mounting ladder and shoving the gun barrel under my chin. "I owe you," he rasped. "I'll pay you back later for sure, and I'll burn your fucking face off *right now* if you blink a bloody fucking eye."

Zack Moore himself walked into my field of vision. He smiled. "Hello, Mr. McGraw. I do believe we have you."

And from the computer's vocal synthesizer came the voice of Corey Wilkes.

"That's right, Jake," he laughed. "And this time it's for good."

23

THERE WERE FOUR left out the original band of nine men. Krause had told me about the two who had succumbed to the hardships of the grueling trip to Microcosmos, and Moore now informed me that three, including Krause, had perished in the road battle. Of the survivors, I knew Brandon, of course; him I had shoved through the access port of an outhouse back on Talltree. Apparently he was still rather miffed about that. The other two I recognized from the little tussle we had had on the Roadbug Garage Planet. Zack Moore was the leader. He was a big man, large-boned and tall, thick-limbed and unyielding, like the massive trees of his home planet. His roots went deep; they were like braided iron cable, and they were tough, and mean. He looked as though he'd lost some weight. His face was thinner, paler. It made his eyes more intense, two motes of fire in a pale cinder of a face.

Arthur was outside—Moore had asked him to leave, and Arthur was only too willing to oblige, with the proviso that he be allowed to take the collapsed spacetime ship with him. After examining it, Moore scratched his head and reluctantly agreed.

Arthur was apologetic. "This is a strictly human affair, Jake. It's not my place to interfere."

"I understand," I told him.

"No, you don't, but I don't blame you."

Sadly, Arthur left through the rear door. It closed behind him.

This was a reunion of sorts. Everybody who wanted a piece of my carcass was there, including the late Corey Wilkes. He attended by proxy, of course—that being a rogue Artificial Intelligence program imbued with his memories and

227

personality traits. A while back it had invaded the rig's on-board computer, at one point managing to wrest control from Sam himself. Sam had fought back and eventually prevailed, but apparently with Sam out of the picture there had been nothing to prevent the Wilkes program from breaking out of its restraints and regaining control, this time disguising itself as the A.I. operating system that had come with the computer's software package. "Bruce" had played his role well, biding his time, fooling the hell out of me.

Joining in on the fun was another nonhuman being who wanted a pound of my flesh, Twrrrll the Reticulan, former leader and sole surviving member of his Snatchgang. A tall, gaunt nightmare in pale green chitin, he stood in a far corner of the trailer, his zoom-lens eyes focused on me. After all this time, he was still hot on my trail, and wouldn't give up the chase until either or both of us were dead.

A cozy bunch. We'd been through a lot together. Old friends.

Moore whirled and hit me across the mouth hard with the back of his hand. "That's just to start," he said.

Tasting blood, I tugged at the cuffs binding my hands at my back. I hadn't gone down, and could have kicked at Moore's crotch, but I didn't, for fear he might have killed me right then and there.

"You can have the cube," I said.

"Decent of you to offer," Moore said. "We accept."

A dull, hollow thud came from inside the cab.

"That'd be Murray blowing the safe," Moore said.

"I would have given you the code," I said.

"And have us set off a booby trap? Not likely. Besides, you'll have no further need for the safe. Or this lorry. In fact, you won't have much need for anything at all, by and by."

"I don't understand you, Moore," I said.

"How so?"

"All this trouble, all this effort. All for a dead Corey Wilkes—or is it George Pendergast who's calling the shots here?"

"I'm not quite dead," the voice of Corey Wilkes said through the trailer speakers.

"Corey, you died years ago," Sam said, shifting his weight. He and the others—John, Zoya, Darla, Oni, and Ragna—

were sitting cross-legged in a circle at the front of the trailer.

The voice giggled. "Sam, I'm still not used to addressing you in the flesh. I assume that *is* flesh, or some reasonable facsimile. When I first saw you like that, I nearly blew my cover. Quite a shock. But to answer your accusation, Sam— no. I didn't die years ago. We simply began to think differently. Rather, I did. My worldview diverged radically from yours. And, of course—"

"We don't have time for this," Moore barked.

"I think we do," Wilkes said evenly.

"Guv!" Murray came crawling through the connecting tube. "Guv, there're *two* of the buggering things!"

Zack eyed me, then looked at Murray. "What are you blathering about?"

"There were two cubes inside the safe. Here!"

He threw one out, and Moore caught it. Then he threw an identical cube. Moore caught the second, dropped the first, picked it up, and stood staring at both.

"I'm buggered and damned," he said.

I laughed. It hurt, so I quit.

"What's the meaning of this?" Moore demanded.

"Two cubes," I said, my fattened lip moving painfully. "One I came with, one I created here, in this industrial facility."

Moore snorted. "You don't say." He tossed them both to the third gunsel, then sidled between two crates and walked over to where the Chevy, in one of its many incarnations, was parked. He grabbed one of the door handles and yanked. The door didn't give. He thumbed the little cylinder on the lock, pushing it in and out.

"Now, this thing," he said. "You *will* be kind enough to give us the key."

"Don't have it," I said.

For that I got a whack on the head with something hard but not too damaging. I turned to see Geof Brandon brandishing a length of thin, hollow titanium pipe—a tent pole, probably. It had stung.

Moore smiled pleasantly. "Want to amend that answer?"

"No."

I ducked this time. Geof missed, but got me on the backswing.

"Sure?"

"Yes."

Geof whipped me across the backs of the thighs.

"Look, you can *have* the car, God damn it, but I'm telling you I don't have the key!"

Moore raised a hand to stay Geof's. "Forget it. Murray, take a look at this lock."

Murray rummaged through a tool kit he'd brought on board, selected a flex-torque wrench and a long thin metal rod that looked good for picking old-fashioned mechanical locks, then sidestepped his way to the Chevy.

"You never answered my question, Moore," I said,

"What question was that?"

"Who's pulling your strings?"

That got me another whack across the cranium.

"Nobody pulls my strings," Moore said mildly. "Or hasn't that been clearly established? I have been *misled*, though." He scanned the trailer and caught sight of one of the computer's camera eyes. "Misled. Hoodwinked. Led down the garden path."

"If I had ears," Wilkes' voice said, "they'd be burning."

Moore snorted.

"Then what's your motive, Zack?" I persisted, my ears ringing from the last blow. "Don't tell me your beef against me was what made you chase us to the end of the universe."

"Why not? I've been known to bear a grudge for far less than what you did to me . . . but you're right. My motives were strictly patriotic. We had to get that map from you, or the Outworlds are sunk."

"Oh, bullshit." Another stroke of the tent pole creased my back. Wincing and blinking back tears, I rasped, "Moore, listen to me. Hasn't it sunk in yet? The cube isn't a map. It never was!"

"Of course it's sunk in. It's branded in my hide, advertising me as the biggest fool in the cosmos. But now I need the blasted thing—both of them, I guess, though I don't understand that part of it. I need the cubes to buy off this insane planet."

"So you've got 'em. So get the hell out of my truck!"

Before Geof could lay on another stroke I pivoted sharply, brought my knee up waist high, and struck out with a kick to his chin, leading with the side of the foot. It caught him squarely, and he went flying into a pile of loose junk, out cold.

The third gunsel swung his weapon around to me but held off firing. I could tell by his eyes that he was very close to just letting me have it, but I'd frozen immediately after delivering the kick, and was far enough away to give him time for second thoughts.

I stood, unmoving, looking at him. A chuckle from Moore broke the tension, and he relaxed.

"Very good move," Moore said. "I was wondering when you were going to get a belly full of old Geof." He sighed. "Poor Geof. Dim as they come, I'm afraid." His expression turned wistful. "I wish Jules' heart hadn't given out. Jules had a head on him." He sighed again, and turned toward Murray, who was probing the lock with the metal rod. "How goes it?"

"It looks simple," Murray complained, "but it isn't."

"Zack," I said, "do you really want that vehicle, or will you settle for an exact duplicate?"

"Eh?"

"This factory can turn out a thousand copies of that automobile in ten minutes—will, if the plant takes a liking to you. That thing was designed and produced here."

"What are you talking about?"

"Didn't the Goddess tell you? This is where we got the car in the first place."

Moore scowled. "But you had it before you ever reached Microcosmos. How could it have come from here?"

"It's a paradox. Ask the Goddess."

Moore grunted. "Try to get a straight answer out of her. You haven't had to deal with . . . with that *thing*."

"You don't need the cube, either. I know a way back. I have a map. The real map. It's yours if you leave the others out of it."

Moore gave me a level stare. "Where?"

"In the computer."

Moore slowly turned his gaze toward the camera. "True?"

"Absolutely," Wilkes' simulacrum said.

Moore smiled thinly. "You were waiting for the perfect moment to tell me—is that it?"

"Of course."

"Of course." Moore walked slowly, arms akimbo, toward the tiny box-and-cylinder affair of the camera, looking into the lens. "It's painfully obvious that you want something, Wilkes. But for the life of me, I can't understand why you think you're in a position to bargain for it."

"Think again."

"I can just take that map. Murray knows computers."

"I'll erase it before you can pull my plug."

Moore stopped and stamped his foot. The trailer shook. "Damn you! You're dead. I saw them bury you. And here you are, scheming your way through eternity—"

The Wilkes program laughed.

Moore sighed again. He looked tired, very tired. "What do you want?"

"Well, this is a little embarrassing . . . but I don't quite know. Um, let me put it this way—I know what I want, but I don't know who exactly to bargain with. That is to say, I have an idea of who to dicker with, but the notion won't—"

"What do you *want*?" Moore said tightly.

"Why, a fine new body, like Sam's."

Moore was exasperated. "*I* certainly can't give it to you!"

"No, you can't. But maybe Jake can."

Moore's eyes grew wary. "Oh?"

"Sure. I know the plant, what it can do. It can manufacture almost anything. It surely could fabricate me a body as good as Sam's. I'd be willing to bet that Prime had Sam's built here. Now, I don't think the plant would do it for me—in fact, I'm fairly sure they wouldn't. But Jake's got a rep as something of an artiste around here. Right Jake? They'd do anything you'd tell them to do."

"Why not?" I said. "Sure, Corey. It's a deal."

"Wait just a bloody minute here," Moore said. "There's no deal unless I'm in. Now, is that understood?" He waited. "I *said*, is that underst—"

There came a flash of light and a loud crackle from the rear of the trailer. Moore jumped back and dropped to his knees, gun drawn. A column of blue smoke rose from where Murray had been standing. I looked. A pile of carbonized matter lay on the deck—a blackened thigh bone, a rib, a shard of skull. There was nothing else but a heap of ash.

Moore rose slowly. He stepped cautiously toward the car, peering at the charred remains of his employee. The stench of burnt flesh filled the trailer. Moore's face drained, then filled with cold anger. He turned his gun on me.

"God damn you," he breathed, then screamed, "God *damn* you!"

He drew a bead on my forehead.

"No."

The word fell between us like a carcass dropped from the ceiling. The voice that had uttered it was not human.

Twrrrll stepped out of the shadows. He held a small hand weapon, and it was trained on Moore.

"No," he repeated. "The Sacrrred Quarrry cannot be damaged."

Moore didn't move, keeping his deadly aim.

"Don't, Zack," Wilkes' voice warned. "Wouldn't be wise . . . just now."

Time passed, a short eternity or two.

Slowly, Moore let the gun drop. "Tie his feet, Darrell," he told his only conscious helpmate. "Then see if you can bring Geof around."

Darrell had me sit. He was very careful not to give me an opening for a move. He tied me with more of the plentiful rope they had brought.

Geof finally came to. I hadn't broken his neck, much as I wished I had. Rubbing his chin, he picked up his gun and stood up shakily.

"Bring her over here," Moore then instructed, pointing at Darla.

I strained against my bonds. There was nothing I could do.

"She's pregnant, Zack," Darrell said uneasily.

"So?" Moore thundered. "If you haven't the balls for it . . ."

Darla didn't look at me. Her face was grim, but resolute. I was glad she didn't look at me. It would have been worse.

They had her down when something happened outside. There was a light so intense that, somehow, it seeped into the dark of the trailer.

Moore rose, cursing. "It's her," he said.

Suddenly the back door flew up and white light flooded the

place. To me it was a divine presence, a deliverance.

"SHOW YOURSELVES, MORTALS," came an amplified voice. I recognized it.

Moore debated with himself before taking only one of the cubes. His face was pale, but he steeled himself and moved forward, squeezing around the Chevy. When he reached the opening, he dropped to his knees.

"We hear, Great Lady," he said, shielding his eyes from the source of divine light high above. "We have the object you desire."

There was a slight hesitation before the voice answered sharply. "YES. YES, VERY GOOD. IS THAT IT?"

"Yes, Great Lady."

"GOOD. TELL YOUR COMPANIONS TO COME OUT. I WISH TO SEE THEM. NOT YOUR CAPTIVES—THE OTHER ONES IN YOUR BAND."

Geof and Darrell began moving, but Moore waved them back.

"See here . . . Goddess," Moore said tentatively.

"WHAT IS IT?" The voice was impatient.

"We had an agreement. Here is the cube, the object you told us to obtain for you. We did so, at great peril . . . we paid a dear price." He grunted in discomfort, and rubbed his eyes. The light was much too bright to bear. "I . . . can't see you, Great Lady," he said.

"NEVER YOU MIND. I GAVE YOU AN ORDER, AND I EXPECT IT TO BE CARRIED OUT. PRONTO. ER, RIGHT NOW."

"What order?" Moore said suspiciously.

"I TOLD YOU TO COME OUT OF THAT TRUCK, THAT'S WHAT ORDER. AND LEAVE YOUR WEAPONS BEHIND, TOO."

"What? I—" Moore strained mightily to see through the blinding glare. "Look! If you'd cut out the bloody theatrics for a moment—"

"DON'T USE THAT TONE OF VOICE WITH ME, SLIMEBALL! WHEN I SAY *RABBIT*, YOU HOP. UNDERSTAND? AND FURTHERMORE—"

Moore was beside himself. "Just a bloody minute!"

Sam chose that moment to move. I didn't have time to wonder how he'd gotten free of the extra-sturdy lumberjack rope, because things started happening very quickly. He came running out of the front of the trailer, slamming into Geof after delivering a neck chop en passant to Darrell, who fell over. Sam and Geof tussled on the floor for a moment, then the gun popped out of their combined grasp and hit the floor. They both dove for it. Next thing I knew, John was cutting me free; I hadn't seen where he'd come from. As I clawed free of the ropes I heard the sizzle and saw the flash of energy discharge. John ducked. I crawled over to Darrell to look for his gun. The voice was still booming outside. Inside, shouts and general commotion. Glancing up, I saw Zoya on her feet, wielding a hunting knife. I found the gun and rolled toward the back of the trailer, coming to my knees beside the right rear tire of the Chevy. I popped to my feet, saw Moore aiming over the automobile's roof. I raised Darrell's machine pistol and let loose about ten rounds at him, then fell to my knees again. It was quiet toward the front of the trailer. I glanced back. Everyone was down. I could see Darla—she was huddling behind some empty food cartons; she was okay.

"Sam?" I called.

"He's hit, Jake," I heard John say.

There was no movement at the back of the Chevy. I decided to risk it and charged to the rear door. Moore wasn't visible. Outside, the light had dissipated.

"John!" I yelled. "Can you see him on the other side of the car?"

"No, he must have jumped out."

I heard running feet out in the showroom. I poked my head out the rear opening and looked toward the front of the truck. Moore was running full tilt across the glossy blue floor. I brought the pistol up and got off a few rounds just as he disappeared through the entrance to a tunnel leading to one of the main factory buildings.

I went back inside.

Sam's eyes were closed, but he was breathing, which was miraculous in light of the massive chest wound he'd sustained. The energy bolt had seared a twisted black burn from his abdomen to the base of his neck.

"Do what you can," I said to John quietly. "I'm going after Moore."

Darla was at my side, her grip tight on my upper arm.

"Don't go, Jake," she said. "Let's get out—let's leave."

I took my jacket off and covered her. I kissed her.

"He must die," I said.

Zoya was standing over Geof. There was a hunting knife in his back. I put one arm around her and hugged. She was stiff, unyielding. "Good work," I said.

"I have never killed before," she said.

"How did you get the knife?"

"It was right next to me, under a loose piece of paper. They didn't bother to check. And they sat us so that we could pass the knife back and forth." She ran a hand through her chestnut-brown hair. "Stupid of them."

Darla said, "Our last joyride really messed up things back here. That's Sean's knife, I think. I remember putting it inside this tool case. See? It fell and popped open."

I hugged Zoya again, then checked Darrell, who hadn't moved since he'd gone down. His neck was broken, and he was dead.

"Where's the Reticulan?" I asked, suddenly remembering.

Ragna said, "The beast left in all hastiness when the shooting is commencing." He pointed to the access tube.

"Damn. We'll have to check out the cab and aft-cabin."

"Hi, there!" came Arthur's voice from the back of the trailer.

I went back and lowered the lift for him. He stepped on and came up.

"Did you see the Reticulan out there?" I asked.

"That ugly one in the chartreuse chitin? He took off after the other one. Did you like my little show?"

"Show?"

"I thought my performance was especially brilliant in light of the fact that I've never really heard the Goddess speak in person."

"That was you?" I said in astonishment.

"Sure was. Tell me I'm not a true thespian."

"You're a genius."

Arthur feigned protest. "Oh, really, it was nothing."

"Thanks," I said.

"Thank the plant people. They handled the special effects. . . ."

"Only too happy to oblige," the plant foreman said, its voice as usual coming out of thin air. "Issue was debated, and was decided that some form of indirect intervention was required."

"Again, we owe you," I said.

"Small matter."

I went back to check on Sam.

"Strangest thing," John said. "The wound is healing. See?" He ran his hand very lightly along Sam's wound, brushing away crumbs of fried, charred flesh. Underneath was whitish scar tissue. "Remarkable. He's still out, though. Pulse good, and—"

Sam's eyes fluttered.

"Sam!" I said, kneeling beside him.

He opened his eyes and looked at me. "Yeah?"

"You okay?"

"Feel okay." He began to scratch his chest, but John stopped him. "Itches like hell," he complained.

"I think you're going to be fine," I said.

"Would you believe I tripped over some junk and let him grab the gun? If you'd clean up this damn place once in a while—"

"Sam, shut up."

"You talk to your father like that?"

"Rest up and you can chew me out later. Moore got away —I'm going after him."

"Don't be a fool."

"I do believe he's left the plant by now," Arthur said. "Their vehicles were parked in a loading dock not far from here."

"What about the Reticulan?"

"The security systems are reporting that two 'life-units' have 'exited facility,'" Arthur said, apparently hearing a report on the electromagnetic wind.

Sam got to his feet, John helping. "There's something I have to do, Jake. No, I'm okay."

He crawled through the access tube. I followed. When I got to the aft-cabin, Sam was standing at the bulkhead, undoing the plate over the CPU housing.

"Hello, Jake," said Bruce's voice. "Sam here seems to

think that we need a complete reformatting of auxiliary storage. I was trying to explain to him that that action would necessitate—"

"Forget it, Wilkes," I said. "We're not falling for it."

"Jake, I don't think you understand. The mole program you call Corey Wilkes has relinquished control to me. There is no need—"

"SHUT UP!" I said, then took a deep breath. "It's over, Corey."

A pause, then: "Sam, please." It was Wilkes' voice.

"No, Corey," Sam said, lifting the protective lid over the RESET switch. "Time to call it a day."

"I see," Wilkes' voice said quietly.

Sam stood, poised with his finger over the red switch. "I should hate you, Corey. But I don't. I've always felt sorry for you. I don't think you've ever enjoyed one minute of your life."

After a long silence: "Push it, Sam." There was a sound not unlike a sigh. "I'm . . . I'm really very, very tired."

Sam pushed the switch. A few red lights appeared on the CPU.

And another human life ended. Somehow, it's always sad, no matter what.

24

WITHIN AN HOUR, Sam's wound had reduced itself to a long, thin white crease. A little later, you could barely see it.

"Damned efficient body you got there," I said.

"Isn't it, though?" Sam concurred.

It took some time to get the computer back into shape. We had to load all the software back in, using the master pipettes, then run checks and so forth. We called up the real Wang A.I. and set it to work. It takes a fully sapient and very versatile computer to monitor and control a vehicle such as the one we drove. I didn't give the A.I. a name this time. Didn't much feel like it. "Computer" was good enough.

Arthur told us that the spacetime ship still wasn't functioning. "Oh, it's repairing itself, but the job is going very slowly," he said. "It really got messed up. Don't worry. You can take the train to within three-hundred kilometers of the master portal."

"That's not close enough," I said. "We have at least three enemies left on this planet—Moore, the Reticulan, and the Goddess, if she's still bent on our destruction. Pretty formidable alliance, there. I think I'd like to wait for the spacetime ship to get itself squared away."

"Perhaps you're right. Okay, we'll wait."

"Anything the factory can do?"

Arthur shook his head. "I doubt it. This is a manufacturing facility, not a fix-it shop."

Even though we'd completely erased all data in auxiliary storage, we hadn't lost the Roadmap. I still had the pipette the Goddess had given me. I hadn't even bothered to put it in the safe; it had been in a storage box all the time. It was a job loading it back in, but we did have some time to kill.

A day passed. Then we got a report that a "life unit" had entered the plant.

"Does Security have any idea who?" I asked Arthur.

"They say that this life unit is one of the same sort that left yesterday—beyond that they don't say. I don't think they're really equipped to tell the difference between life forms. The plant is very light on security. After all, it's a showcase operation, not a top-secret project sort of thing."

"It's probably Moore," I said, feeling my stomach tighten. "I'm going after him."

"No, you won't," Sam declared, "even if I have to hog-tie you."

"There's no other way," I said. "He has an all-powerful ally, along with an armored van and who knows what else. He'll harass us all the way to the portal. I've got to deal with him now."

"Why do you have to deal with him? I'll go." He put up a hand. "Okay, okay, we'll both go."

"Are you insane? No way I'll leave the truck with only John to defend it."

"Then stay here," Sam suggested.

"No. I have to go and settle this once and for all."

John said mildly. "There's no dilemma if I were to go with you, is there? That way the lorry will be in good hands and you'll have at least some backup."

I winced. "Sorry, John. I didn't mean it the way it sounded."

John smiled, his light-brown face looking tired and drawn. "I understand. You're quite right, too. Sam can handle it. And you're doubly right on our going out to meet him. I don't relish sitting and waiting for the next lightning bolt to strike. No telling what Moore's doing, skulking about the place. We must take the offensive."

"Then it's settled," I said.

Sam nodded, shrugging. "I'll have to admit, John has a point or two." He crossed his beefy arms and sighed. "Oh, God. Right, go ahead. And for my sake, at least, be careful. I'm an old man. This constant excitement is bad for my constitution."

"What, is your atomic-powered heart beating too fast?" I

scoffed. "Look at him. He's twenty-five if he's a day. Has more hair than I do."

We devised a foolproof plan. Arthur would keep a line open to Security and relay the intruder's position to Sam, with whom I'd stay in radio contact. I took the last of our supply of button transponders along; a few of those placed strategically at various points along our planned route of attack would satisfy our signal-bouncing needs.

John and I armed ourselves and set out into the plant. We had the intruder pinpointed. He had entered the building housing the Monomagnetic Mirror Array and had stayed there. John and I planned to surprise him, chase him into a blind alley, and get him in a cross fire. When we got as far as the Submicron Fractionating Assembly, we split up.

The place was quiet once again. It had buzzed and howled for us, but now there was no one to work for, no new designs to think through, no prototypes to test and evaluate. Had the plant ever operated on a regular basis, or had it always been, as Arthur had said, a showcase, a world fair (universe fair?) exhibit? No matter; it was silent now, and would be, possibly, for the rest of its existence. Or until more candidates arived on Microcosmos. If any. I wondered about that. Were we indeed the first? Nobody had said for sure. When were more intrepid explorers expected? Week after next . . . or in two million years? But time wasn't an element on Microcosmos. It didn't matter. They would come, surely.

I walked through the quiet and the shadows. There was a dry, clean, industrial smell in the air. A shaft of light from a lone high window speared the gloom, and where its end touched the shiny green floor, an array of monoliths sat in a pool of sunlight. On banks of control instruments, a few lights glowed—all this equipment on standby, ready at a moment's notice to come to life, to work, to get out the product, fill the quota, produce.

I stopped and put what used to be Sam's key close to my lips. It was now just a computer terminal, but it could be used as a walkie-talkie as well.

"Intruder still stationary," Sam said. "Where are you?"

"I'm just about to cut through the machine shop that abuts on the north wing of the Mirror Array. Once I get through there, I'll be practically on top of him. John should be coming through the Diffusion Ring complex now."

"Check. Be careful."

"Will do. Over and out."

I walked on. Robot arms, poised to do someone's bidding, reached out of shadow at me. They would work at blinding speed to make anybody's dream a reality, if they were given the right instructions. I passed a mobile worker-robot—a subsystem engineering supervisor, probably—dormant, standing by, waiting silently at its station. Farther on, a tall shadow in an alcove startled me—but it was only a maintenance robot.

The key's call light blinked. I answered.

"Jake, intruder is moving. Repeat, intruder is moving."

"Acknowledged," I said. "Which way?"

"Toward you."

"Great. I'm keeping the channel open."

I proceeded slowly, staying in shadow and moving as silently as possible. I stopped, listened. Nothing. I moved on, pausing every few meters, ears cocked.

Suddenly, a beeping tone. Somewhere behind me. Then another. A faint whirring sound. I froze. No. Just some machine clearing its circuits, draining off a buildup of static charge. Besides, wrong direction. He should be coming from the north. I wondered where John was.

The key again. "Still moving toward the machine shop," Sam informed me. "Where are you?"

"I ducked into the little workshop or whatever it is adjacent to it."

"Wait a minute . . . here it is on the map. Okay. Hell, looks like the intruder is vectoring there."

"Then that's where I'll get him," I whispered.

"Stay put until you see him. He'll have to pass by the door if he wants to get to the showroom."

I waited, watching, listening.

A few minutes later, Sam called again. "Anything?"

"No," I said whispering. "No sign."

"He should be on top of you."

I waited a few more minutes, then got impatient. "Are you sure about intruder's position?" I asked.

"Yes."

I looked around. Silence formed a wall around me. "I'm

moving to get a better angle on the doorway."

I crawled down a narrow aisle between two gigantic machines. There was only one door to the place, the one I'd come in. Poking my head into the clear, I brought the machine pistol up and aimed. I wouldn't fire when I saw him, but when he passed, I'd move out and follow him. He wouldn't get away. If he got anywhere near the truck, Sam would burn him down. Good. We had all the angles covered. We'd thought of everything.

Wrong. I hadn't thought that there might be an another entrance to the workshop. And there was one, high up in the wall, through which a suspended ramp passed. The ramp continued its way into the shop, winding amongst the rafters, overhead beams, and the clutter of suspended machine tools. I craned my neck. A ladder. There was a ladder connecting it to a lower ramp, this one passing directly overhead.

I sprang to my feet, tried to run . . . too late. Something slammed into my back and sent me sprawling. The pistol skittered across the floor and disappeared under a workbench.

I rolled, sat up. I was cornered, nowhere to run. Twrrrll stood blocking the way. He wielded his ceremonial dagger, with its black curving blade and jade-green hilt.

"Jake-frrriend," he trilled. "Sacrrred Quarrry. I bid you grrreeting."

I got up slowly. I had no weapon, but I would have to fight him. This would be the second time I would be forced to fight a largely ceremonial battle with a Reticulan hunter. I had won the first round, defeating two opponents, Twrrrll's companions, in hand-to-hand combat. I didn't think I would be so lucky this time. He could just shoot me, of course. His gun was hanging from the leather harness he wore over his thorax. But that wouldn't be honorable. He had to do me in with the dagger for it to be an honorable kill. Rather, the usual technique was to hamstring the quarry, then gut it while it still lived. Vivisect it. Flay it alive. The more the victim screamed, the prettier the sacrifice.

"Long have I stalked you, Jake-frrriend," Twrrrll said. "The trrrail was long and arrrduous. Many times the spoorrr was lost, then found again."

I looked past him, hoping to see John at the door. No such luck. Where the hell was that tall skinny black guy?

"Okay, Twr—" I spat. "Twer . . . Twrrrll." It was hard to say his name under any circumstances, let alone when I was scared witless. Never could trill the R just right. But then, I was always terrible at languages. "Okay. I just want you to tell me one thing."

"Yes?"

"Why do you do this?"

"Hunt? Because the . . . you would say, the blood. The blood tells one."

"But you're civilized. Intelligent. Very intelligent. You speak our languages well, while we can barely manage yours. You have a technological civilization, advanced science, the whole bit. Why can't you overcome the need to kill in this manner?"

The big alien took a step forward, moving his huge bare feet slowly. "Humans have no need?"

"Well . . ." It was hard to concentrate on winning debating points.

"Do not humans kill theirrr own kind? This is something we almost neverrr do."

"Bullshit."

"A denial? No, it is not usually necessarrry."

Maybe he was right. Reticulan societies were very rigidly stratified and very stable, though top-heavy with useless nobility, of which Twrrrll was probably a sterling example.

"Your race is very unpopular. You spread ill will, resentment toward your people."

"That is the way it has been, and must be."

He took another step forward. The smell of his pheromones—turpentine and almonds—filled my nostrils. I gagged.

There was nothing to do but rush him, try to duck through those thin legs of his. No possibility of tangling with him; his strength was phenomenal.

He stepped forward.

"You have become the most Sacrrred Quarrry of all, Jake-frrriend. Thrrree times the nets caught you, thrrree times you fought and escaped. The hunted has vanquished the hunterrr. So be it."

I stood there with my mouth open. The alien was offering the dagger to me, presenting it to me.

"Take this weapon. It now belongs to you. You have surrvived, and I have failed. I ask only that you turrrn it against me, hunted against the hunterrr. It is the only honorrr of which I may still be worrrthy."

I overcame my shock and took the dagger.

"Does this mean I won't have to fight you?" I asked.

"The time for combat is past. Time now to end the hunt, and the hunterrr." He crossed his forelimbs; it was a sign of submission. "Do honorrr to me."

I stared at him.

His eyes—cylindrical camera-lens affairs—rotated back and forth. Presently he said, "You will not do me the honorrr?"

"Yes, I will," I said.

I approached the alien, knife in hand, looking for an appropriate spot on the shiny chitin of his abdomen. I had no doubt as to his sincerity. Stabbing underhanded, I plunged the blade of the knife into his body and yanked upward. The exoskeleton was tough, but capable of being cut; however, I was in a bad position for leverage.

"Difficult?" the alien asked. "May I assist?"

I nodded. Twrrrll took the hilt in both hands and jerked the knife upward. The carapace split like thin plastic. He ran the knife up to the middle of the chest, pink froth oozing from the wound.

Suddenly his head exploded in flame. An energy bolt had come from the direction of the door. I looked.

It was John. He got off another shot, this one missing, just as the alien fell. Then he came running over.

"You got him," he said breathlessly. "Thank God. And with his own knife, too. Dreadfully sorry, but I looked all over for you. How did you manage to corner him in here?"

I told him of Twrrrll's surrender. He could scarcely believe it.

"Incomprehensible," he said, gazing at the alien's prostrate form. "We'll never fathom the alien mind. Never."

"I'm not so sure it'd be a good idea if we did," I said.

25

IT FELT GOOD to be back on the road again.

We'd decided to take our chances at ground level. The spacetime ship was still on the mend, and there was no telling when it would heal itself. (Strange how easy it was to think of the process in these terms). Besides, there was no guarantee that we'd be safe in the ship. There were other reasons. I didn't like being a passenger, being chauffeured about. It made me feel vulnerable; I hate being helpless and not in control. Moreover, as we were now down to two enemies— Moore and his puppet-mistress—I decided that keeping to the ground was a calculated risk we could afford to take. It might even be the best way to go . . .

. . . I thought, grinding my teeth.

Of course, we all knew very well that it wasn't over. It was only a matter of time before our enemies would move against us once again.

The train let us off in an unusual region of Microcosmos— unusual in the sense that we'd not seen terrain like this before. It was mostly flat grassland, relieved here and there by sharp low ridges proliferating in networks like wrinkles in a bed sheet. Visibility was unlimited, and the master portal was a vast gray smear on the "horizon."

"Well, we'll be able to see 'em coming for kilometers," Sam said.

"Miles and miles," I said.

Sam looked at me askance. "How much time did you say you spent back in 1964?"

"About a month and a half, maybe less."

"Sure rubbed off. 'Miles' indeed."

This wasn't exactly sparkling conversation, but it filled in the lulls. We were nervous and trying to make the best of it. It

is profoundly disquieting to know that somewhere out there is
an all-powerful deity who wants to cancel your season ticket.
We talked about this. It was a way of relieving the psychological discomfort.

"But if she's that powerful," Sam argued, "why can't she
just swoop down any time and pound us into hash?"

I said, "You should have been a theologian. John, this is
right up your alley, isn't it?"

John said, "My suspicion is that Prime is somehow inhibit-
ing the Goddess from making an overt move. I think that's
why she finds it necessary to work through human agents."

"Makes sense," I said, "until you try to speculate as to why
the Goddess has it in for us in the first place. And what is it
she wants to do, exactly? Wipe us out, or just prevent us from
going back? Or both?"

"That's a good one," Sam said. "You say she originally
asked you for the Black Cube?"

"Yeah. But now she has it. Or one of them, anyway."

"Maybe it was the wrong cube."

"There's only one cube, Sam. You've got to understand
that basic fact."

"Oh, I understand that basic fact, all right. I just don't want
to *deal* with the sucker."

I thumbed the intercom switch. "Arthur, old buddy! How's
it going back there?"

"Please, I'm nauseated."

"Now, just hold on a minute. Tell me how a robot can get
motion sickness. You're really not a robot, are you?" I had
suspected as much all along.

"Of course I'm a robot. Why can't a robot get motion sickness?"

I grunted out a derisive laugh. "It just doesn't make sense."

"Nonsense. I feel pain, discomfort, the whole thing. In a
somewhat subdued form, though. Don't ask me to explain."

"For pity's sake, why? Why would your makers go to the
trouble of wiring you with pain circuits?"

"For the same reason you got wired with 'em. Excellent
mechanism for automatically protecting the organism. You in-
stinctively avoid pain, ergo anything that would tend to damage you. *Quod erat* whatever. Wake me when we get there."

It was Arthur who had insisted on coming along. He maintained that he was responsible for us and wouldn't feel as though his obligation had been properly discharged until he'd seen us safely through the correct portal. Besides, the space-time ship might come in handy at some point, if and when it cured itself of its ailments.

We were about two hours from the portal. I wasn't rushing, just maintaining a steady speed. There was no use in hurrying. They were out there, and would make an appearance at some point. Count on it. For now, it was simply a matter of watching the road and waiting, keeping one or two extra eyes on the sweep scanners, wondering when some innocuous gray dot swimming in the murky stuff at the extreme range of vision would suddenly turn into something wickedly sharp and well-defined, move in at you and strike. No telling what it would be: an armored car, perhaps, or a shimmering cube or other shape, or maybe something you could barely comprehend, some monstrous mind-denying unreality. It didn't matter. We were dead no matter what. Because I had the feeling that we had long ago scraped bottom, run out of tricks. We had dodged one too many bullets. I was very worried.

Something else was bothering me.

We had already located the portal that led back to T-Maze, and mapped a route to it through the congeries of highways that twined among the forest of towering cylinders. But judging from what Arthur told us and from what we had learned from the map, this portal would *not* send us back in time. We would not arrive back in T-Maze paradoxically before we left. This was not a "backtime" route, as Skyway travelers were wont to say.

"The system's just not built that way," Arthur told us. "It was designed to eliminate the possibility of a paradox."

"How was it done?" I asked.

"Dearie me, I couldn't give you specifics, but I do know this. There is a sort of standard, objective time observed along the entire length of the Skyway. It works so that the 'present' always moves with the traveler. You'll never get ahead of it or behind it. When you return to the place you left, the stretch of time that has passed there is equal to the time you spent away. Don't ask me how it's done. Actually, if you *really* want to get technical about it, the time flows aren't exactly equal. There is slippage, for some esoteric reason, but it amounts only to nanoseconds. Due to quantum uncertainties, I think."

After all this time, after all the legends, the tall tales, the stories told about me, the fact was that the way back still was not clear. When I'd first laid eyes on her, Darla had acted as though we'd met before, a meeting I knew very well never occurred. She'd stuck to that story ever since. I'd come to believe her, and my belief wasn't based entirely on my growing love for her. Other facts, other observations had persuaded me. But now doubt gnawed again.

But no. How could it be? The Paradox, a creation of one woman's harebrained scheming? I couldn't accept it.

Fine. So what was I telling myself? Were we headed for an alternate reality, a universe where I didn't do my time loop, my temporal backward somersault, where Darla and I had never met the "first" time . . . a place where *none of this had ever happened* . . . ?

Or were we never going to make it back at all? I gritted my teeth. No, damn it. I would not permit myself to think that way. It was up to me. Somewhere up ahead, one of those roads led back through time. I had come here by way of the Red Limit Freeway, and now I would have to find the shortcut, the little side street that led directly back to where I started. I would have to find Paradox Alley.

Red lights yelled at me from the instrument panels.

"Looks like we're suffering high radiation losses in the plasma," Sam said. *"Bremsstrahlung* reading is way up, and electron temperature is dropping."

"Kink instability?" I asked.

"Looks more subtle than that. Just guessing, but we may have a software foul-up here."

Which meant that, although the engine was probably fine, there may have been a problem somewhere in the megabytes of programming that controlled and monitored the engine. Software difficulties can arise from any number of causes, indigenous bugs in the original coding being only one of them. However, as we had just flushed out and reloaded the entire operating system, I was more inclined to suspect that we may have screwed up somewhere.

I pulled off the road as the engine groaned and complained. By the time I stopped, we had lost controlled fusion entirely.

"No cover," Sam said looking around. "Well, it probably

makes no difference anyway. They'll know where we are no matter what."

I said, "How 'bout we fire up the auxiliary engine, shoot up that side road, and hide out among those pyramids out there?"

"What pyramids? Oh, those. Looks to be about five kilometers." Sam studied them. "By God, those look familiar."

"I was going to say that they looked like Egyptian pyramids. The ones at Giza."

"Yeah, and right next to it . . . is that the Sphinx? Little too far away to tell."

"Darla and I have seen other earthly structures here, so maybe they're the genuine article."

They weren't. Close, but no papyrus scroll. The pyramids had a four-sided base and went up at an angle that looked right, but they were constructed of some off-white seamless material, not stone block. The sphinx was properly enigmatic; it simply wasn't the famous Terran one. The nearby mortuary temple, though, provided us with cover. It was big enough to hide a fleet of trucks.

"Let me try to wrestle with this," Sam said, flipping down the computer keyboard terminal.

"I can't think of anyone more qualified than you," I told him, "seeing as how you used to be a computer." I looked at Sam and he looked at me. "Are you still a computer?" I asked.

Sam seemed a bit concerned. "I don't know. I don't feel like a computer. Do I look like a computer?"

"You don't look like a computer. Can you do ten million arithmetic operations per second like you used to?"

He squinted his eyes and looked far away. Then, with some relief, he said, "No. Definitely not. I'm no longer a math wiz. I can't tell you how glad I am of that. Never really took to being a computer."

"Well, I always thought of you as sort of living in one," I said, "rather than being one."

"But the real question is this: Am I the same person who was your father when he was flesh and blood?"

"Sure you are, Sam."

"Am I? I don't have one cell of that body in me."

"I don't see what that has to do with it."

"No? Am I really Sam McGraw, or am I only an Artificial

Intelligence program that's putting on a good show?"

"Both."

Sam rubbed his jaw thoughtfully. "Interesting notion."

"Here's the way I see it," I said. "When you get right down to it, a human being is not a physical entity. A human being is a piece of software. Body cells are constantly dying and being replaced. Over a period of time, there's a complete change-over, right?"

"Brain cells, too?"

"I don't know. Doesn't matter, because the essence of what you are is really just information. The body dies one cell at a time, and is replaced at the same time. But the information stays, and that information can be stored any number of ways and in any number of different containers."

"You may have a case," Sam said. "Still, I often wonder if I've died and gone to heaven and don't even know it."

"Maybe you're lucky. Maybe you didn't go to heaven."

"Oh, ye of little faith. Well, we're wasting time."

An hour went by. By this time Sam was deeply annoyed, swearing under his breath and stabbing at the terminal with his long fingers.

"Why do they insist on making things unnecessarily complex?" he was muttering. "Who the hell coded this crap? God-damn Egyptologist couldn't decipher this."

In the meantime, I had checked the engine and found nothing I could see, which is usually how it goes. I got out what testing equipment we carried and attached leads all over the damn place, but got told nothing. Sam was right—it was probably a software glitch. That wasn't good. It might take forever to find it.

I got restless and went back to the trailer. I opened the back door, let down the ramp, and walked down it to the floor of the temple, thinking to take a quick walk and study the archi-tecture of the place. I didn't wander very far. It would be a quick dash back to the truck in the event of trouble. The place was shadowy, though, and made me a little nervous. I was just about to go back when I heard sounds behind me—a shoe against stone, the intake of breath. I froze.

"Jake?"

I whirled around and went into a crouch.

"It's me. Roland."

He came out from behind a column. He looked the same, dressed in his shabby survival suit and scuffed hiking boots. He looked very calm, almost detached.

"Roland," I breathed. "Where the hell did you—" I stopped myself, and chuckled. "You shouldn't oughta do that."

"Sorry. I couldn't think of a way to announce myself without startling you anyway, so . . . How have you been? I didn't get a chance to say good-bye."

"I'm fine. Just fine. How are you?"

"Great. You ought to know."

I put the gun on safety and put it away. "I did know," I said. "Hard to remember . . . to recall the experience of what it was like."

"You've forgotten completely. You wouldn't be able to go on living if you had to carry the memory around with you."

"It's that powerful," I asked, not really asking.

"Of course."

"I have . . . *some* memory of it, though. I mean, I haven't blanked out any of it. The mountains . . . the way the air smelled . . . the different landscapes. The heights."

"You only remember the outward forms, not the substance of the experience."

"I guess." I took a deep breath. "So what's up?"

Roland crossed his arms and began to pace slowly. "We've given it a lot of thought. We must help you. There's no other way."

"Thanks. We need it. Can you fix the engine?"

"That's really not an area where we could have much input."

"What did you have in mind?"

"Difficult to discuss details at the moment. You'll be doing most of it, Jake. But you need a slight nudge, an encouraging word, maybe."

"I don't want to sound unappreciative, but I'd rather have a hot engine," I said.

Roland stopped pacing and gave me an impish grin. "I enjoy sparring with you, Jake. You give as good as you get. Better." He chuckled again. "You're really a very remarkable chap. Did I ever tell you that?"

"You never tell anybody anything, Roland."

He nodded. "You're right. I do play it close to the vest. But—" He dismissed the subject with a wave. "We don't have time to discuss Roland Yee."

His use of the third person didn't quite leave the impression that he was speaking of someone else . . . but there was a hint of that.

"Jake, I really can't give you details, but we will help. In fact, I'm coming along with you. If you don't mind."

"You're going back with us? Giving up the Culmination?"

"Oh, no. Not at all."

I shrugged. "You're welcome, of course."

"You're probably a bit confused."

"A little." I slapped him on the back. He seemed substantial enough. "Come on. Darla will be glad to see you."

We walked back to the trailer and mounted the ramp. I stopped to look at the Chevy once again. We had disposed of Darrell's remains. A bit unceremoniously, but then, he hardly deserved better.

Mysteries concerning Carl's magical vehicle still remained. Here—again!—was one of its many doppelgangers. This edition was, ostensibly, the one Carl had arrived on Microcosmos with, the one that had been stolen out of the truck. Prime had taken it, probably because he was curious about it, and had put it back. For the sake of my sanity, I decided that this was the best way to explain why Carl's automobile was still in my truck. For the sake of my sanity, I would avoid dealing with the notion that, after all, there really was only one Chevy. But if I took this one back to Terran Maze . . . ? Well, really, I didn't want to think of that either.

Carl, or the design chief, had really gone overboard with the antitheft mechanisms. I wondered how we were ever going to get it out of here. Would using a crane or a winch activate the booby traps? Possibly, though they didn't seem to be especially touchy. Darrell had jiggered the lock for quite a while before incurring the lethal penalty.

Gingerly, I put my hand on the door handle.

The door came open. And I heard Carl's voice: "Jake. You'll hear this if you try to get in when the door is locked, so listen up . . ."

I clambered in, listening.

"...this is kind of strange," Carl's voice went on. "I'm recording this as I look at you. You're stretched out, asleep, here in the Ideation and Design Facility. I thought about it, and I figured I had to find some way of allowing you to use the car while making sure it's otherwise theft-proof. The design chief says it'll be simple. If anybody other than you tries to steal this car, or even just fiddle with it, it's curtains. Deathsville. That's if they try to break in. If they do get in somehow and try to hot-wire it, or even start it with the key in it ... or get this—even if they try to drive off when the motor's running, they won't get far. That device isn't deadly. I don't want a goddamn mess in the front seat. I just makes you want to get out of the car in a hurry."

As I well knew. I had tried that once.

"So, listen. You're right here, so we can get readings on you, and feed them into the design specs. The car will know you, Jake. It will let you get in, start it, and drive it. Without a key, too, since I won't give the key to anybody. In fact, if anybody other than me tries to start the car *with* the key, it'll trigger the nonlethal mechanism. I figure, if they've got the key, they've killed me to get it. Okay. I hope I've covered everything..."

It seemed to me that he had overlooked a few possibilities, which possibly explained why I was able to steal the car with the motor running, yet got zapped with the nonlethal device when I tried to start it with the key. Why had the Chevy refused to recognize me then? Possibly because Carl had made the proscription against unauthorized key-starting a blanket one, just to be safe.

"...but if I haven't, well ... hell, I can't think of everything. I'm not sure I understand what the hell this is all about, or all the flip-flops and crazy reasons for everything, but I do know that at some point you've got to steal my car. And maybe you'll need it if anything happens to me. But nothing's going to happen to me, so you'll never hear this." He laughed. "This is nuts. I'm nuts. Getting a little daffy, anyway. Okay, that's it. I hope you never hear this, but if you do ... oh, hell, I guess I should erase this and just tell you. I don't know. Maybe I shouldn't. When you get right down to it, maybe I don't trust anybody. Not even you, Jake. I've learned, believe me. You can't trust anybody in this stinking world. Universe.

Yeah, the whole universe is pretty undependable, when you get right down to it. Okay. I'll decide later whether to tell you. See ya."

And that was it.

Sitting beside me in the front seat, Roland chuckled. I couldn't recall him opening the other door and getting in.

He said, "I remember us sitting here, trying to figure out how this insane vehicle worked. Little did we know it had been designed by a paranoid teenager from the distant past, who had the help of some of the most advanced technological intelligence of the far future."

"Funny how things work out," I said.

"By the way—there was a reason for my suggesting you try the lock."

I looked at him. In my version of reality, he hadn't said a thing.

The key beeped in my pocket. I took it out.

"Jake, something coming. I think it's that dust-devil business that chased us a while back."

Roland was smiling as though he'd just brought off an elaborate practical joke.

"I see what you mean," I said.

26

I SPOKE INTO the key.

"Sam, I'm in the Chevy. I'm taking it out against that thing."

"What?" Sam came back. "How did you— Never mind. All right, I guess it's the only superweapon we've got."

"It's the *only* weapon we've got. Over and out."

The ignition lock was set into the instrument panel on the right-hand side. There was no key, of course. "Damn it, Carl," I muttered, "you forgot to tell me how to start this thing without a key."

"I'd suggest putting your hands on the wheel," Roland said.

I did. And the engine roared to life.

"Roland, how did you know that?"

"If the Culmination's good for anything, it's good for knowing things. Most of it's useless, but now and then . . ." He laughed.

I depressed the clutch pedal and fiddled with the floor-mounted "four on the floor" gearshift until I felt the transmission settle into reverse, then craned my head around and backed out of the trailer. The Chevy hit the temple floor with a slam and a jolt. I jerked the gearshift lever around again, this time finding the top of the left upright on the semi-imaginary H, and rammed it into first gear, my arms and legs and reflexes quickly remembering all the coordinated movements. Once you learn to drive a standard transmission, you never forget.

I peeled out around the truck and weaved in and around the many supporting columns, heading for the outside. I slid into second and popped the clutch, and the tires gave a short chirping screech like a yelp of pain from a small animal. I swerved around a sacrificial altar, dodged a partition, and hit an open area of polished salmon-pink floor that led to the vestibule. The place was immense, and there was plenty of room to maneuver. By the time we hit open air the Chevy was screaming for third gear, which I gave it, prematurely, because now I had to slow down to make the turn onto the side road. I downshifted, wound out of second gear, shifted to third.

"There," Roland said, pointing to the left.

The Tasmanian Devil was coming at us, following the broad curve the side road took from the highway. It had lost no energy; the pale orange fire and luminescent yellow smoke of which it was made still swirled furiously about its spar-kling, molten, ever-changing center. Shadows moved within it, the suggestion of a living thing, its shape constantly shift-ing, ephemeral, now a manlike form, now a winged demonic thing, now something else, some nameless terror, a shape out of the night, out of the deepest core of the ancient mind of man. My stomach coiled and quivered, and the taste of iron sat bitterly on my tongue.

Roland was busy with the car's weapons control panel, which had materialized automatically on the dashboard.

"Roland," I said calmly, "Carl never showed me how to fire it, but there's a weapon on this buggy he called the Green Balloon."

"That's exactly how he marked it," Roland said, peering at the board. He pressed a switch.

A spherical object whooshed out from under the car—it was green, about a meter across, and it sparkled like the Fourth of July. It streaked directly toward the approaching tornadolike phenomenon.

The Tasmanian Devil came to a full halt, still spinning. It seemed to sense what was coming, moving quickly to one side, scooting off the road and up a grass-covered hillock. Its course unchanged, the balloon went flashing out over the plain, missing its target by a wide margin.

"Interesting," Roland said.

"At least we know it's afraid of the balloons," I said, not very thankful for small favors. "Damn. I would've thought they could seek out a target."

"Maybe the devil is doing something to confuse it."

"Maybe. Try it again."

Roland launched another glittering green ball. The devil retreated again, this time ducking behind the hillock and disappearing for a moment. When the balloon was gone, it came out of hiding, rolled down the hill and got back on the road.

"I wonder who or what it's programmed to kill," I said.

"Go off-road and see," Roland said.

I steered to the right and ran up a shallow grade, bumped down into a trough and ran up onto level ground. The devil crossed the road to follow us.

"So, it isn't the truck, and it isn't the spacetime ship," I said. "I was hoping it was the ship."

"No, Jake. I'm afraid it's after you and you alone."

"Fine. Why should it be different from everyone else?"

I floored the pedal. Streamers of dust trailed from the back tires. I ran the car up another gentle grade, this time turning sharply to follow a ridge that paralleled the road and eventually curved back toward it. I didn't know the top speed of that thing, but I was willing to bet the Chevy could outrun it, providing the race were run over the highway. Off-road, all bets were off. That horrible whatzis didn't have wheels and didn't need them. If we could dodge around the thing, though, and make it back to the road, we might have a chance.

But what about Sam?

Roland seemed to be reading my thoughts. "Sam's coming out of the temple," he told me, looking back through the rear window. "I don't think the devil will give him any trouble."

But it was giving us a truckload, racing to cut us off. I floored the pedal and immediately hit a rough spot that wrenched the wheel to the right. I countersteered, but saw that we'd never make it. I wheeled right again, and we rolled down a little hill, hit bottom and bounced. I bounced, my head hitting the mercifully padded roof. Roland lost his seat and wound up on the floor. I stood on the pedal, aiming up the opposite slope. The devil came over the ridge behind us. The slope was steeper than I had thought; the rear tires started spinning and throwing dirt; the back end began to fishtail. We made it to the top and rolled onto level ground, but the devil had gained ground and was now sniffing at our tail. It was all I could do to keep ahead of it.

"Jake, did you know that it was possible to drive the Substratum as well as walk it?"

"Um . . . no," I said. "I get the message, though."

And so I turned the wheel so that the front tires were aligned—as my friend Dave Feinmann would have put it—with a dimension as vast as space and as timeless as infinity. I floored it, and we went somewhere. It was a sort of shortcut between here-and-now and there-and-then, with a stopover in hither-and-yon. Angry clouds appeared above, and a spatter of rain hit the windshield, briefly—then bright stars came out and something trilled a night song in a wood off to the right. Quiet. The smell of autumn leaves . . . And then all that disappeared and we came out into bright sunlight back on Microcosmos, back to the here-and-now, only now we were *here*, on the side road, racing for the main highway. The devil was far behind us, whirling its dervish and wondering what the hell had happened.

"Neat trick," I said. "How did you do it?"

"You did it, Jake."

"Yeah, I know. It makes me feel creepy."

"Better creepy than dead."

The speedometer read over a hundred miles per hour, which was just cruising as far as the Chevy was concerned. We could outrun the devil, beat it to the portal, but Sam wouldn't be able to keep up. And I wouldn't be able to find the right portal without Sam. That meant it was best to deal with the devil now. I had no reason to doubt that it could follow us through a portal. But how to deal with it?

My mind raced furiously. Maybe I could lead the devil a merry chase until Sam caught up, then . . . But any ploy would call for close timing.

The side road diverged. I took the right branch, which swung us back onto the main highway.

"Roland, what the heck *is* the Substratum, anyway? In twenty-five words or less."

"It's the metaphysical base of the universe. It underlies everything."

"Who discovered it?"

"No one. It was agreed upon."

"Thanks, Roland. That helps a whole hell of a lot."

He guffawed. "You're welcome."

"No, really. You mean to tell me"—I glanced at the rear view mirror and saw that the devil was still well behind us, but keeping pace—"that consciousness can create a new universe?"

Roland looked at me; his eyes were limitless. "It's a good universe, Jake. But it could be better. Lots better. Don't you think?"

"I think it could be a whole *shitload* better, Roland. But that don't mean..." I checked the mirror again. The truck was a gray dot way back up the road.

Metaphysics 101, three credits, Monday, Wednesday, Friday, 1500 hours. Kantian rationalism. Jesus, mercy, let me out of here.

"Why did you guys build the Skyway?"

"For those who're dissatisfied with the way things are, a path to follow."

I nodded. "And why the bloody hell did you make that path so *difficult* to follow?"

"You know the answer to that. A quest is never easy. Although there is a more mundane reason. If we'd handed out roadmaps, we would've had the biggest traffic jam in the universe on our hands. The real candidates would have been trampled in the rush."

"And that's why the White Lady wants me to have the Roadmap."

"Oh, that's part of it, I suppose. She has her reasons."

"Roland, answer me one more question. Will I ever understand it all?"

"No."

"Thanks, Roland."

"No problem. Why don't we try to deal with the Tasmanian Devil now?"

I said, "Suggestions?"

"The first devil we saw was generated by this automobile."

"Are you proposing we fire a devil at a devil?"

"Precisely."

"Oh, good. I always wanted to find out what happens when the proverbial irresistible force meets your average immovable object. They probably sign a nuptial contract and invest heavily in tax-free provincial bonds."

Roland bent over the weapons panel. "I have it set up here.

It might be best to lure the things away from the road. There's the chance Sam might get in the way."

"Looks like suitable terrain up ahead," I said.

The creases had been smoothed out of the land. The road ran straight over a world-sized tabletop landscaped in cropped grass. This part of the planet had the look of extra space set aside for expansion. It was raw and undeveloped. The portal was ahead, its hundreds of black cylinders taking form out of the gray mist of distance. They looked like impossibly tall skyscrapers, a ghost city on the plains.

I veered off the road and onto the turf. It was smooth going; we hit only an occasional bump. The TD followed.

Roland said, "There is the chance that when the two devils meet, there'll be a terrific explosion."

"You don't know for sure?"

"It's never been done before, so there's no way of knowing."

"You guys are timeless and eternal. Why can't you look into the future and see?"

"We did," Roland said, "but it has to happen first."

"Huh? Whaddya mean?"

"Well, if we *knew* what happens when one of these things meets another, then there'd be no reason to try it and see. In which case, when we looked into the future, we wouldn't find out anything. Would we?"

"Oh."

There are some days when it's useless to argue. This was one of them.

"Well," Roland said, "here goes nothing . . . and I don't mean that in the phenomenological sense."

He jabbed a switch, and a gout of orange fire leaped out from the underside of the Chevy, immediately coalescing into a twin of the phenomenon that was showing as a fuzzy purple splotch on the aiming device of the weapons board. The new devil rotated in place for a second, revving itself up and emitting a howl the likes of which are not heard in places where mortals dwell. Then it shot forward.

I yelled, "Go get 'im, boy!"

Roland said, "I'd suggest getting well away from them."

I was already doing that enthusiastically, heading back for the road. When we got there, Sam was nowhere in sight. I slowed, stopping completely when I got back on the pavement. I looked back through the rear window.

"I gotta see what happens," I said.

The devils met. They appeared to absorb each other, blending into one cyclonic cloud that stood still but rotated twice as fast. Then something began to happen at its center. The writhing shadows faded, supplanted by an ever-brightening star of white-hot intensity. The nova grew and grew until it was impossible to look at. I shut my eyes, then opened them again as the light began to fade. The star collapsed in on itself as the whole structure fell apart into streamers of fire, swirling about the dimming nucleus. Then, slowly, the Devil began to reform, finally solidifying into a cloud twice as big as either of the originals, this one darker in color. It wasn't stable. Parts of it kept radiating away in flaming auras, and chunks of energy flew off constantly, dissipating into the air.

"It's not going to last long," Roland said. "The resulting explosion might wreck the planet."

I whacked my forehead. "Great idea you had there, Roland. When you looked into the future, was there any future at all?"

Roland rubbed his chin. "I think what we have to do is give it something to focus all its destructive force on. Something almost indestructible that will absorb most of the devil's energy before being destroyed."

"Not the Chevy," I said, hoping against hope.

"I'm afraid so."

So I turned Carl's magical horseless carriage around and steered for the gates of Hell itself.

The devil met us halfway. The boiling cloud enveloped us, and we baked in radiation until the windows darkened and cut most of it off. It was like sitting in the middle of a nuclear fireball.

I said, "I presume you have a way of getting us out of this."

"We'll have to leave the car," Roland said, putting a hand on my shoulder. "Get ready."

It got awfully hot inside the Chevy. Very hot. The seat was beginning to burn the backs of my legs when Roland slapped my shoulder.

"Now," he said. "Get up and walk."

I did. The car was gone. We were walking down a country road. It was dusk, late winter. The road was red and cold, lined with the dried stalks of last summer's weeds. There was a bare-limbed forest off to the right, to the left a meadow of browned grass with half-buried smooth gray stones sticking up here and there. The sky was gray. It was Pennsylvania.

"Very nice," Roland said. "But a little too cold for comfort."

A chill wind blew through my jacket. Brown leaves lay trampled in the gravel underfoot. The sun was an orange smear behind the clouds on the horizon. There was the smell of an early spring in the air. The call of a blue jay came from the hills beyond the meadow as the wind stirred the tall brown weeds.

"You've never walked a specific part of the Substratum," Roland said, "just your wants and desires. It's endless, you know. Not like the 'real' universe, which has limits. But you can walk the real one, too."

"Yeah? Isn't this Earth? It looks like it to me."

"Maybe, but it's probably a generalization of many places that you knew at one time."

"You may be right. This looks like Pennsylvania, but not any specific part that I remember."

We continued walking. For some reason, I felt obliged to keep moving. The air was pure and I filled my lungs with it.

"This is great," I said, "but I want to get back to Sam."

"We have all the time we need," Roland said. "Don't worry. Find the road you want. If this isn't the one, find another."

I found roads, all right. Roads that led through places I didn't want to see, let alone spend a weekend in. It seemed as though we walked for days.

We came to a wide highway of silver metal sweeping over a plain of blue rock. I looked up and down it. I didn't know where it came from or where it was going.

"Roland, where the hell are we?"

"Don't know. Find another road."

I found more. None of them were of any earthly use to me.

I found another, and it was fine, except that it didn't go anywhere I wanted to go. Another, and I left immediately.

"I give up," I said.

"What about over here?"

It looked promising, so I followed it, and it turned into something that looked like the Skyway, but not much, so I changed it, and it looked a little closer. Then, all of a sudden, I understood how to do it and we were there, back on Microcosmos, and the truck was braking hard behind us. We moved to the shoulder. Sam brought the rig to a crackling stop and popped the hatch.

"What happened?" he asked as I climbed up the mounting ladder and got in. He got up and gave me the driver's seat.

I turned around to see Roland walking away, looking back, waving.

"Good luck, Jake. Stay well," he called.

I watched him go. He didn't disappear. He just kept walking.

"I wonder if he'll be all right," I said, closing the hatch.

"Who?" Sam asked.

"Roland."

"What made you think of him?"

"What made me— Are you telling me you didn't see him?"

"Didn't see anybody out there but you."

"But he's right over—"

He was gone. Or was that moving dot out there him? The sun was low, and I couldn't tell.

"Never mind," I said.

27

I TOOK THE controls and got us moving again.

"Anyway," Sam said, "you're just in time. We're tracking a blip on our tail."

"No flying cubes, no wild stuff?"

"Looks like your average road buggy."

I picked up the hand mike and switched the radio to the skyband. "What's wrong, Moore?" I said. "Had a fall from grace? Tough luck. That Goddess is one harsh mistress. Never came through with doodly squat for you, did she?"

After a moment of silence, the radio sputtered once, then: *"No, she's not been especially benevolent."*

"What's the game now, Moore?"

"Game? No game. I'm going home."

"Oh? And just how do you propose to accomplish that?"

"Follow you," Moore said simply.

I threw the mike down. "Not if I can help it," I said. "Sam, got any ideas?"

Sam shook his head. "We can't outrun him on auxiliary power, and this isn't exactly the sort of terrain you can lose somebody in."

"So all he has to do is tag along and get a free ride home. That sticks in my craw. I want him to rot here. Or better yet, to shoot a portal that'll send him to some horror of a planet six billion years from last Wednesday, with no way home."

"We can turn and fight."

I thought about it before I said, "No. We'll have to deal with him on the other side. Wherever that is. Computer? Oh, hell, what's the warm boot command?"

"Ticonderoga."

"Hello," came the flat, colorless voice of the A.I. "I am an

267

artificially intelligent, high-performance multiaccess operating system, and I am at your service for a variety of data process-ing functions—"

"Shut up. Sam, find out exactly how we get to the portal, will you?"

"Will do."

Sam set up the run, the A.I. did its table lookup function, and some lines on the map lit up in yellow.

"This is going to be tricky," Sam said. "The aperture is right in the middle of this big mess here." He pointed to the tangle of intersecting roads on the screen. "We'll have to walk on tippy-toes every step. Cylinders every which way in there. In fact, I don't understand how we're going to do it. I didn't think you could put cylinders this close together without hav-ing them all mush into one another."

"I hope they behave themselves until we get through."

Sam grunted. "I'm not worried about that. What bothers me is shooting any portal, let alone this monster, on an auxil-iary engine. It's good to have extra power if you need it."

"No luck tracking down the software problem?"

"I was on to something when that business with the dust devil started. And that's what I should get back to." Sam flipped down the terminal. "We might be able to lose our friend Mr. Moore if I can coax this rig into squeezing hydro-gen again."

"That remark about your being the best qualified still goes."

"Thing is," Sam said ruefully, "to err is human, and the more time I log in this new body, the more human I get. Just a few days ago I think I could have solved this thing in a min-ute. But now . . . hell, I never even liked computers."

"Do your best."

Darla had come up and was standing behind my seat, her hands on my shoulders. "Jake, are you sure you're okay?"

"Yes, darling."

"We saw flashes up ahead—and then there you were. What happened? Where's Carl's buggy?"

Just as she spoke I saw something about a quarter klick off the road. I pointed. It was the burned-out hulk of the Chevy, its shape still recognizable. Thin black smoke rose from it. There was no sign of the Tasmanian Devil.

"There," I said. "It's come to the end of this cycle of the loop. Now it all begins again, somewhere in time."

"But what happened?"

Sam said, "I've stopped asking him that. He goes off into Neverneverland, then comes back and asks if it's lunchtime yet, like nothing's happened."

"You'll read all about it in my memoirs," I said.

"I'll stick to whodunits. Those I can figure out. Bingo!"

"What is it?" I said.

Before Sam could answer, all the gauges went green and the main engine kicked in with a whine and a surge of power.

"Hooray," I said. "Now let's see if we can lose our dead-head passenger."

"I can take a hint!" Arthur yelled from the aft-cabin.

"Not you, Arthur dear," Darla said as she went aft to strap herself back into her seat.

"Thanks, sweetie."

I floored the power pedal. The main engine was operating, but somehow it didn't feel quite right. A brief image came to me: inside the engine, atoms whacking into each other with astonishing violence—but they were hitting off center, not head-on.

Nevertheless, it was too much for Mr. Moore. He began to drop back.

I laughed. "He's on auxiliary power. His Goddess won't even fix his wagon for him."

On the rearview screen, Moore's battered armored vehicle dwindled to a gray dot.

"He can still track us," Sam said. "He may be able to tell what portal we shoot."

"Not if we get far enough ahead of him," I said, reaching to switch the auxiliary engine back on. I watched the velocity readout edge up.

"There we go," I said. "Even if he's at full power, we'll lose him completely."

We watched Moore's vehicle become vanishingly small.

"Good," I said. "Good."

Sam bent over the computer terminal. "Getting back to the map—Jake, it looks like the minimum speed requirement for this portal should be a little higher than average. Just guessing from the number of cylinders and their placement, the conflicting stresses should be horrendous. Shooting this thing is going to be like trying to walk an elephant over a rope bridge."

"What do you figure?"

Sam's long fingers darted over the keyboard. "I'm estimating over fifty meters per second. Say fifty-five to be safe. That's 198 kilometers per hour."

"High," I said, "but we can make it. As long as there're no hairpin turns."

"Well, that's exactly what I'm looking at here."

"Oh."

"No problem for a Roadbug, probably, but for us—tricky, to say the least. Going to call for some fancy driving. Computer assistance, maybe."

"Piffle."

"Piffle, is it? Hey, Arthur! Why the hell is this portal so screwed up?"

"How should I know?"

"I don't know who else to ask."

"Well, neither do I. I do know that washouts don't usually shoot this portal all by themselves. They go back with a Roadbug escort."

Sam was astounded. "What do you mean, 'usually'? You mean to say there've been other washouts?"

"No, you're the first. You were also the first group of candidates. What I meant to say was that it was my understanding that a Roadbug escort through the portal would become standard procedure."

I said complainingly, "Why the hell didn't you ever tell us that we were the first? And if you say we never asked, I'll dismantle you with a rusty powerdriver."

"You're not giving me much choice, are you? Okay, I never told you because I'm a rotten s.o.b. Satisfied?"

Darla said, "It's true. We never asked him."

"Thanks again, honey," Arthur said.

"How come we don't rate a Bug escort?" Sam wanted to know.

"Nothing with you people has gone according to standard procedure."

"I believe that," Sam said. "If it weren't for bad luck, we

wouldn't have any luck at all—"

"Alert," the computer said offhandedly. "Incoming ballistic object. Take evasive action."

I wheeled hard to the left and went into the grass, taking the rig in a wide parabolic arc away from the road. It wasn't wide enough. There was a hollow explosion to the rear, followed by a steady rumbling, scraping sound.

"What's the damage?" I asked as I steered back toward the road.

"Looks like an encore of the last performance. Rear door is sprung, no pressure seal..." He bent forward to peer at a readout. "Jesus. Looks like the lift is down. Blast must have activated the servo."

"That's bad," I said. "I can feel it. It's dragging and making it difficult to steer." I looked at the velocity readout. "Well, it won't hamper us too much."

"I'll go back and crank it up. Can't have that thing banging around back there."

"Sit tight a minute, Sam. He may have a missile left."

Darla said, "Moore wants us dead, even at the price of his own life." There was a disturbing sense of fatalism in the way she said it.

I was worried. If Moore was doomed to be stranded here, he'd try his damnedest to see that we never made off the planet either. I hadn't helped the matter any by rubbing his nose in it.

The portal was coming up fast. A forest of black towers thrusting at the sky, it looked like the skyline of a city of dark gods. Not exactly the kind of place for a getaway weekend. But I just wanted to pass through, if they'd let me.

Then, suddenly, the main engine died again and our speed dropped precipitously.

Sam slammed the terminal down and frantically jabbed at it. "The program's looping," he said grimly. "My quick fix didn't fix."

"What a time," I said, looking downroad and seeing our doom. Two solid white lines began demarcating a lane in the middle of the road. It was the guide lane, the safe corridor, and once we got into it, we were committed. Once committed, straying out of that slot was a very bad idea.

But stopping was worse, and there was no time to avoid committing, even if Moore hadn't been back there. I looked at the readouts. Our speed was still dropping, and at this rate, we would soon fall below minimum speed. It was the dragging lift platform. The auxiliary engine wasn't powerful enough to compensate.

"John!" I yelled. "Do you know where the manual crank on the load lift is?"

"I'm afraid not," John said as he unstrapped, "but I'll find it."

"On the right-hand side at the rear," I said. "There's a panel, and there's four toggle bolts."

"He'll need me," Darla said.

"No, Darla—" I began, but knew unmechanical John would need help. "Be careful!"

Even though we had passed the commit point, the portal proper was still some distance away. I hoped that meant that we had a bit of leeway, that speed and direction wouldn't be hypercritical until we neared the edge of the forest of cylinders. But this was a portal unlike any of the Skyway. No telling what it demanded in the way of portal-shooting expertise. I knew that it was not for amateurs.

"Sam, how's it coming?"

He didn't answer.

Side roads began shooting off to the left and right with increasing frequency.

I said, "Computer!"

"Acknowledged," the A.I. answered.

"Display planned route, show present position."

"Done."

"Assist navigation, stand by to take control in the event of emergency."

"Orders acknowledged."

Even though its voice was a little too cold-blooded, I was glad that Sam had shut down most of the A.I.'s "personality." I, for one, was a little tired of disembodied intelligences, friendly or otherwise, hanging out in my truck.

"Prepare to bear left," the computer warned as we approached a fork in the road.

I bore left. We were well into the maze of roads now. An

array of cylinders stood off to the right, the road I had taken skirting them by an ungenerous margin. The sky was murky now, and it seemed that the sun's light had dimmed. There were no clouds—the darkness was a result of the intense and focused gravitational fields distorting and refracting the space around us.

"Keep left," the computer instructed.

I chanced a fleeting look at the small monitor that showed the trailer interior, but couldn't see anything. Then I noticed that our speed was still dropping, but not as fast as before. Nevertheless, accelerating or decelerating whilst shooting a portal were not recommended procedures.

"Sam?"

"Almost," Sam answered.

"Alert," the computer announced. "Incoming projectile. Possible missile. Take evasive action. Defensive firing has commenced."

Which wouldn't do us much good, as Moore's missiles had been too tricky even for Sam. And I couldn't take any evasive action, none at all. Unless the computer got in a very lucky shot, we would have to eat that missile. As soon as the warning came, I was on the intercom to the trailer.

"Darla!" I screamed. "Take cover! Incoming missile—get to the front of the trailer and get down! Repeat, get—"

A horrendous explosion sent shudders through the rig. The trailer yawed to the left and I did everything I could to keep it from wandering out of the guide lane. I could see smoke streaming from it and pieces dropping off.

I was on the intercom as soon as I regained control. The trailer monitor was showing nothing but noise.

"Darla! John!" I yelled. "Report!"

No answer. I looked back. Zoya was on her feet.

"I'll go back," she said.

"No! Strap in!"

She did, and it was all I could do not to countermand my own order. But I didn't want to lose Zoya, too.

"Airborne object tailing," the computer announced.

"What?" I croaked. "Another missile?"

"Negative. Unidentified object, possibly hostile."

I didn't know what it was talking about, and didn't have

time to look. The blast may have played hell with the scanners.

Sam's face was drawn into thin, grim lines, and beads of sweat had sprung to his forehead like a sudden dew. His fingers worked furiously yet efficiently, accurately.

"Prepare for tight turn to right," the computer droned.

If I slowed for the turn we would drop below the minimum speed, so I took it with fully juiced rollers, hoping the trailer wouldn't slide out and end it all for us. It didn't. I checked the speed readout again. We were holding steady. Maybe the blast had ripped the lift completely off. A bit of luck if it had.

"Darla, answer!" I shouted into the mike. "Report!"

Again no reply. I didn't want to think about it now.

I checked the sweep scanners again. Moore was gaining. I could see nothing that could account for the computer's warning about an airborne bogey. The forest of cylinders grew thick. I drove among them, my heart a ball of ice, the gloom of the distorted spaces around me reflecting my fear, my despair.

The Paradox Machine was working fast; its wheels had sharp, shiny blades that whirled and whirled, and they were coming straight for me.

We were in the heart of the black city now, and light was scattered and dim. The road was lost in the murk, but the white guide lane was still visible. The rig's running lights had come on automatically, but there was almost nothing to see except the guide lane and a fuzzy patch of road. The cylinders were vast walls of blackness in a landscape of gloom and obscurity. And . . . quite suddenly, a crazy funhouse apparition, a view of the land surrounding the portal, refracted and distorted wildly out of shape as if by a fish-eye lens . . . then, darkness again. Gone. Nothing left but gritty road rolling underneath us, a circle of light leading us farther into a strange dark night.

"Extremely sharp left turn ahead," the computer told me.

It was, but I made it.

"Estimate ETA to aperture," I instructed.

"ETA three minutes thirty-two seconds, at present speed. Stand by to bear to extreme right at next intersection."

Ahead the road branched off at weird angles. The extreme right was almost too sharp a turn to make without slowing down. But you can't slow down in the middle of a portal, so I juiced up the rollers, swung the control bars hard to the right, and prayed. We almost tipped over.

"Sam, we have to get our speed up." I figured I had enough time here to increase speed slowly enough to avoid surging, which made a vehicle unstable when in the grip of extreme tidal forces.

"Almost, almost, almost," Sam breathed as he continued to punch madly at the keyboard.

So I drove on through the streets of the dark city.

Then came a hand on my shoulder, unexpected, improbable, a calm hand, and a calm voice, saying, "Jake."

I knew who it was. For some reason I wasn't surprised. "Yuri," I said, without looking back.

"Think of it, Jake," he said. "Each corner here a gateway to different eras of the history of the universe."

"You think of it, Yuri. I'm busy."

"Of course. But you'll be needing the Substratum again."

"Sure could use it."

The rig lurched as something smacked into us from the rear.

"Jesus," I said, "he's gone completely nuts. Trying to kill us all."

Moore's buggy gave the rig a further nudge, backed off, then smashed into the back end. The trailer gave a shudder, slid out a bit, then swung back into line.

"Sharp left ahead," the computer said phlegmatically. "Very dangerous under present circumstances." It could have been giving a weather report.

"Not just yet, Jake," Yuri told me gently.

"No?"

"GOT IT!" Sam shouted as the main engine kicked in.

I surged, preferring to take the awful risk rather than let Moore keep trying to knock us into a cylinder. But I lost the gamble. Something took hold of the rig, lifted us right off the road . . .

. . . then had second thoughts and let us drop. Part of the trailer landed outside the safe lane, and the cab set down at a forty-five-degree angle to the trailer. I fought at the controls as every safety servo in the rig struggled to straighten us out. The rear of the trailer floated up again like a paper in the wind, set gently back down, this time within the guide lane, but jackknifing to the right. I wrenched the control bars to correct. The trailer wafted back into line, then rebounded to the left, which I corrected for as well.

The rig was squirming now like a snake wriggling out of an old skin. It wouldn't stop. Every correcting maneuver seemed to generate an unexpected new counterforce, offsetting and negating the correction. It seemed there was nothing I could do to make the rig stop swaying, swerving, shaking, buffeting this way and that, nothing I could think of doing that I hadn't already done.

"You have missed the left turn," the computer informed me.

We were not going back to Terran Maze. We would never go back.

"He's coming alongside!" Sam shouted, looking out the port to the left.

I couldn't see, but felt Moore banging his armored buggy against the rig as he edged his way toward the front. There must have been at least some space to squeeze through on the side. I had no control over the rig, and couldn't make a move against him.

"He's not in the safe lane!" Sam said. "He's—"

Then I saw Moore's rig as it rose from the road, lifted by an unseen gravitational hand. And for just the barest instant, I saw Moore's face through the small front port of his doomed vehicle. He looked right at me, and his ghastly smile chilled me to the core.

I'll see you in Hell.

Then the vehicle was gone.

"Cover your eyes!"

Strange thing to say to a starrigger while he's operating his vehicle, but I knew why. The atoms of Moore's vehicle, after being torn one from another, would make a few orbits about a cylinder before being sucked into it, and would in the process release synchrotron radiation, along with a lot of light.

The flash didn't blind me, but it left sparkling dots chasing each other in front of my eyes. Perhaps that's why I didn't see that the road made a sharp right up ahead. The computer saw it, tried to warn me, too late. Sam leaped out of his chair and tried to take the controls.

Too late. We were out of the safe lane, off the road completely, but still on the ground. Giant fists batted at us, and invisible forces pushed and pulled at us. I became increasingly amazed that we were still alive, still traveling. I was still in my truck, my rig. My senses were heightened now, here in these last moments of my existence. I was still where I wanted to be, doing what I wanted to do, what I had always wanted to do. Sam was with me, and we'd had a good run.

Then Yuri said to me, "You're about to make history, Jake. In a very real sense."

Suddenly the rig was airborne, rising into the dark sculpted spaces of the portal like some ungainly, impossible aircraft on its first and last flight, hurtling through the darkness toward a hole in the sky—a hole with blurred edges, and as it loomed near, about to suck us up, I remarked to no one in particular that it looked like an aperture—the hole in space that a portal creates. And it *did*, it did look like an aperture; I made a mental note to someday look into the mystery of what an aperture would be doing this far off the road's surface, as they were usually lower down, like right off the road, so vehicles could drive into them. I was thinking this as the rig somehow, miraculously, straightened out and entered the aperture in a more or less head-on manner.

And then there was nothing. Absolutely nothing at all.

28

NOTHING. WHICH I thought rather impossible, so I filled the void with something. "Let there be anything," I said.

And lo. Yuri beside me. "Consider the following events as happening in no time at all," he said.

"Hey, I'm easy," I said.

He laughed. "I've known you for only a short while, Jake, but I can say that you're one of the most remarkable individuals I've ever met."

"Everyone tells me that."

"As well they should. Shall we go?"

"Where? There doesn't seem to be anyplace to go around here. Fact is, there doesn't seem to be..." I put an arm around his shoulders. "Hey, Yuri, old buddy, listen. You're not going to tell me that you're the Ghost of Christmas Past or something, are you?"

He hesitated for a moment. "Dickens? Dickens. I'm rather weak in English literature, I'm afraid."

"Now, I've always loved Dostoevsky. I can quote you chapter and verse of *The Possessed*."

"I've never read him."

I was shocked. "And you call yourself educated?"

"Hardly. The universe must be protected from scientists with literary pretensions."

"Well, you've done your duty, Yuri, old pal. Now. What did you have in mind?"

"Let's walk, Jake."

"On what? I don't see— Oh." I felt a floor underneath my boots. Smooth, a little slippery, as if freshly waxed. I looked. There was a bit of a gloss to it.

We walked. As we did, I got the impression of a huge

interior space surrounding us. A vast hall, dark, its features black-on-black, unseen, yet somehow felt. The roof soared kilometers above. Our footsteps echoed.

"Is this my show?" I asked.

"Partially. I like the sense of space you've conjured up."

"Big place," I said. "What is it?"

"A meeting place. Perhaps. Perhaps something more."

"I have a question."

"Go ahead."

"It's rather mundane. It's about portals. Do they create more than one aperture?"

"Oh, are you referring to the one you're in the process of shooting?"

"As a matter of fact . . ."

"Yes, there usually is more than one. A cylinder array creates a whole host of distorted spacetime effects. Most of the secondary apertures are not penetrable. Not usable. That's been known for some time. The research hasn't had much circulation among the general public, of course. As you know, the Colonial Authority censors all scientific publications. The secondary effects are rather difficult to see if you don't know exactly what to look for."

"Oh. Thanks."

I saw something in the distance. We approached, and saw that it was Prime, or some oversized statue of him. If the latter, it spoke.

"Now we come to the conclusion," it said, its voice sounding like Prime's. The image must have been two kilometers high.

"Indeed," a voice answered, and it sounded like the Goddess.

Prime said, "Are you satisfied with the construct? Do its logical elements still offend you?"

I turned and looked. The form of the Goddess came to us from across a distance so vast that I could have reached out and touched her.

"Not so much its logic as its lack of elegance," the Goddess answered.

"What is more important, then? Elegance or actuality?"

"Both are supreme."

"There is truth in what you say. Yet I find fault in the color of your volitional thought-branching."

I leaned toward Yuri's ear. "The who and what of your which?"

"Not every concept can be rendered linguistically, I'm afraid," Yuri said in something like a whisper. "Well, not easily, anyway."

"Generally speaking, what the hell are they gabbing about?"

"You."

"Oh."

Again, Prime's voice rose in the dark hall. "Is the resolution so difficult to accept?"

"Absurdity is unpalatable."

"So is inflexibility, rigidity, and blind refusal to let the waters flow where they must." (This last was probably linguistically fudged.)

"So, too, is unregenerate profligacy. The strength that flows through our minds yields to the channels that contain it. The strongest stem bends in the wind."

I leaned and whispered, "I know what she means. The force that through the green fuse drives the flower drives my trailer truck every other weekend."

Yuri winced. "I'm sorry this isn't better. It is fairly awful, isn't it?"

"Oh, this isn't my show any more?"

"Well, not entirely. At least not the content. Perhaps . . ."

The apparitions faded.

"So, what's it all about, Yuri?"

He laughed. "That's the question, isn't it? Perhaps it's about the universe coming to grips with itself. As for the Skyway—my own personal preoccupation—suffice it to say that in a universe of mysteries, here is one more. The Skyway didn't exist, and it was necessary to invent it. Millions of intelligent races spread throughout the universe, separated by unimaginable distances and immutable laws which rendered those distances unbridgeable. The loneliness! An impossible problem, which the Road creatures solved with science that took ten billion years to develop, a science that bent those unalterable laws to the breaking point, that—"

"Yuri," I said, "let me tell you something. I've had it with metaphysics. Totally uninterested. What I want to know is: What happened to Darla?"

"I'm sorry, Jake. I feel your grief."

I wanted to punch him. "Do you feel my anger, too?"

"Yes, of course. But . . ."

Yuri's face became indistinct, then came into focus again. "There is no need for either, Jake. Can you believe me?"

"What? She's okay?"

"Let me use an expression that is, I think, American in origin. 'It will all come out in the wash.'"

"That's comforting. I'll ask again: What happened to Darla?"

"That's all I can say for now. Jake, have a little faith. A *little*. If you have a fault, it's that you can't *believe* anything."

I nodded. "I'm like that. I also pick my nose and flick the snot onto the ceiling."

"You also lack a sense of reverence."

"No, life is holy to me."

"Of course."

"Another thing. If I didn't believe that existence was *totally meaningless*, I think I'd go crazy."

"That's very interesting," Yuri said. "Few people think like that."

"I do. Now, listen. I have a life to get back to—rather, a death. I was just about to cash it in when you dropped by. Now, I hate to be rude, but I really have to get back to business."

Yuri smiled cordially, offering his hand. "I wouldn't think of keeping you. Best of luck, Jake. It's been a pleasure knowing you."

I shook his hand. "Thanks, and write when you get work."

I turned, walked away. But there was nowhere to go.

There was nothing at all out there.

The truck was not moving, not a centimeter, nor an inch, either. There was no sound except a faint throbbing coming through the floorboards. The engine, I guessed.

"What the hell happened?" Sam asked. "Where are we?"

I turned around. "Is everybody—"

And there was Sean, of all people, sitting in Darla's seat. He grinned at me.

"We're fine," Zoya said. "A little shaken."

"Was great fear, there, for the moment," Ragna said. Beside him, Oni nodded. "But now, okeydokey."

I couldn't take my eyes off Sean. No one else seemed to acknowledge his presence.

"Yeah," I said. "Fine. Um . . . good."

"You forgot me," Arthur called from the aft-cabin.

"I can't figure it out," Sam said, pushing his face against the port and trying to peer out. "I can't see a damn thing out there. Nothing."

"Are you okay, Arthur?" Arthur asked himself, and then answered with mock cheer, "Fit as a fiddle! Don't worry about me!"

I tried looking out. I could only see my reflection. I doused the lights in the cab. It didn't help. The strange stars glowing out there were only reflections of the instrument lights.

Sam said, "Well, we've done it. We shot a portal to no damn where at all."

"There have always been road yarns like this," I said. "Shoot a portal the wrong way and you wind up in nonspace, or somewhere in between universes. Something like that."

"Yeah, something. Trouble is, where do we go from a place that isn't even here?"

I shut my eyes—and only because I really wanted to, I saw a road in front of me.

"That's it, Jake," Sean encouraged.

But before we left that nonplace, that nowhere, a furiously intense pinpoint of light sprang into existence somewhere outside. The light flooded the cab—a blinding actinic flash, a burst of transcendent radiance. I ducked my head, pushing my face into the soft leather of my jacket. Then I felt the wave of heat ebb, and looked up. The nothingness was gone . . .

. . . and we were on a road like no other I'd seen. It was wide as a dream, and silver—all silver—shining in the light of ten billion stars. It was a world of silver night under the most breathtaking sky of any planet in the universe, and the road ran straight and true through a pass between two black mountains silhouetted at the edge of the heavens, out there at the rim of infinity. I floored the pedal, and eons flowed beneath the rollers.

"You've found it, Jake," Sean laughed. "The Backtime Route."

"I love it," I said.

Strange omens streaked across the skies—comets, motes of fire. The cycles of the universe beat in phase, pulsing out the years, the centuries, the millennia, marking off the ending of things from the beginning of things, keeping a steady tempo.

I was looking out at all this. Sam wasn't. Ever the practical sort, he was checking instruments.

"Jesus, did we all get a dose," he said. "The dosimeter is way up. Not lethal, but we'd all better get some sulfahydrite in us." He unstrapped and got up.

"Sam, get back to the trailer. See if—"

"That's where I'm going right now. Son, you've got to prepare yourself for the worst. You can't see most of the damage from your side. It's a mess back there."

He left me to drive through time, which I did. I didn't think to ask Sam about Sean, and I didn't want to look back now. I just drove. And drove. It seemed like a long time. Then Sam returned.

"John's alive," he said. "Second-degree burns, concussion, but he's basically okay. Jake, Darla's not back there. She's just not in the trailer."

I nodded. "It was meant to be, Sam. From the beginning. Written in those stars out there."

"No, no, you got it all wrong. It was my fault," Sam said. "Don't blame the stars. I—"

"No, Sam. I blame no one."

He didn't know what to say. I didn't either. I just kept driving.

Presently I got the feeling that I had driven as far back as I wanted to go, as I needed to go. I needed a new road, so I tried to put the Skyway out there, but it was no go.

"You know where the Skyway is, Jake," I heard Sean say. "It's your home, the only home you feel at home in, or on. Find it."

I looked. I searched here and then there, this highway and that byway, high road and low, but none of them were it. I riffled through a million landscapes, seascapes, starscapes, one after another, flashing onto them, discarding them in one smooth mental notion. Universes flickered by. Roads diverged, and I took both of them.

Finally, I found it. The impossible Skyway, eternal mystery, as hard and as real as the doorjamb you stub your toe on—there it was, out there, whizzing by underneath the rollers. But I wasn't through changing worlds. I had one in mind, and I had certain chronological coordinates pinpointed, and I drove until I reached that world and that time.

"You surprise me, Jake," Sean said. "I think I know, but I don't think I like it."

The world was Talltree, Sean's world.

Sam injected me with the tickler, then looked out. "This place looks mighty familiar," he said.

It was a forest world, the trees immensely tall, their foliage brightly and strangely colored.

"Well," Sam said, "with the Roadmap, we can get home from here."

"I don't need the Roadmap," I said.

It was near dark. The planet's sun, a bronze-colored star, had left pink and purple streaks along the horizon. A few kilometers farther down the road, a dirt trail intersected the highway, and I turned off and followed it. I had followed it before. But now I had to be careful, because my former self was here, my past self. I was now a time-traveling doppelganger, a ghost from the future. Perhaps from a future that never would be—if I had anything to do with it.

John was fine, really. He remembered nothing after the missile hit, but he could tell us this: he had started running toward the front of the trailer when my warning came, turned around and saw Darla still struggling with the lift crank. He yelled for her to get back; she started running, and that's when the missile hit. It blew off the back door and tore a huge hole in the left bulkhead, right where Darla had been standing. As it was, she must have been blown out of the trailer, or had fallen out. We had been traveling at a speed in excess of two hundred kilometers per hour. There was no question of her surviving, even if the blast had not killed her instantly.

I parked the rig in a clearing which I estimated to be about a kilometer from the Frumious Bandersnatch, Moore's inn and restaurant. I went back and inspected the damage, then went to the aft-cabin and rummaged for a change of clothes. There wasn't much, but I did find an old pullover sweater, a ratty thing with leather shoulder patches, and some blue jeans. Possibly Carl's.

I wanted a disguise, of sorts. I pulled out a knitted longshoreman's hat, this from under the cot, dust balls clinging to it. I looked and looked, and in the bottom of the clothes locker I found a pair of polarizing goggles—it makes the fuzzy nothingness of an aperture easier to see when shooting a portal. They're rather useless, really, because if you're not already dead on target by the time you can see the aperture, being able to pick it out isn't going to do you much good. But now these specs would suit my purposes nicely.

I chose a gun, a twelve-shot burner, from the ordnance locker.

"What are you up to?" Sam wanted to know.

"I'll be back in two hours. If I'm not back in four, you have the Roadmap."

"Jake, I think you're insane."

"Possibly. I'll be back, Sam."

Arthur looked at me strangely. "I can't imagine what you're up to."

"I'm Master of Time and Space."

Arthur slowly nodded. "Uh-huh." He looked to Sam for help.

He didn't get any. I went through the cab, climbed down the mounting ladder, sealed the door shut, jumped down and walked off into the woods.

I remembered these woods well, remembered well the cries, the noises, the night sounds. I heard them now. The first time had been a little frightening. More than that, I must confess. Some snarling horror had chased me—I got away, but never saw the thing. But that had been in deep woods, on a back trail. This was a good logging road, probably well traveled.

And I wasn't alone. I grew aware of Sean walking beside me.

"Ah, Jake. You've got the divvil in ye."

I said nothing.

"You'll be havin' to go to confession this Saturday, for sure."

"I hate to be curt with a demigod, Sean, but punk off, okay?"

"Ah, Jake, Jake, Jake."

I left him behind.

It seemed a very short walk. It was dark now, but the warm lights of the Bandersnatch glowed ahead. I could hear sounds of partying. I stopped, hid behind a tree, and looked out over the parking lot. And there was the truck. My truck. This was the night, our first night on Talltree. Sam was in that truck, in his second incarnation, as an arrangement of magnetic impulses. What was he now?

I skirted the lot and went around back. There had been a window. . . .

Someone was coming out the back door of the place.

Lori! And Carl! And Winnie, too. I ducked behind an immense tree trunk. They walked by, hand in hand. I leaned out and watched them. They stopped while Winnie examined a leafy bush. I stared at them. The old saw about staring at the back of someone's head proved true—Lori abruptly turned her head. I leaped back behind the tree, cursing myself, then remembered that it was dark and I was in semidisguise.

I remember that Lori and Winnie had gone off foraging for vegetation that Winnie could eat, but that had been earlier, if memory served. Later on in the evening, the three of them had been jumped and Winnie kidnapped. Well, if I could do what must be done, that would never happen. I went to the back window of the bar.

Just a look, just a peek. I couldn't bring myself to do it. Couldn't force myself to look at her. She was in there—drinking, having a good time, watching me go through the good-natured nonsense of the initiation rituals of the Brotherhood of the Boojum. She was probably stifling a giggle right now. Or had she gone upstairs by now? Or had Moore already . . .

Maybe I didn't want to look, for fear of seeing myself. For fear of becoming the demon that glares at you from the other side of the looking glass. I didn't feel real. This couldn't be happening.

Exactly. The whole of my experience since this paradox

thing had started had been the longest nightmare on record. I could not believe in any of it. It could not be part of the stream of existence—it was a bubble in the continuum, a glittering, shimmering bubble that threw back false reflections from its prismatic surface. Prick it anywhere, and it would burst into a billion sparkling motes and vanish into the void.

Kill Moore here, now, interrupt this turning of the cycle, and it all would end. Darla was gone—no way to retrieve her. But she wouldn't have to die if she didn't meet me—if she never met me. And that's what I would do. It was the first time in my life that I was gripped by such a terrible resolve. I wanted to see Moore's blood, and I would before the night was through.

I stalked through the shadows at the rear of the Bandersnatch. I found a door with an exhaust fan over it, cooking smells coming from within. The door was unlocked, and I opened it quietly and stepped in. A man in an apron and cap was chopping cabbage at a counter along the far wall. He was preoccupied and didn't turn around as I walked through the kitchen. I stopped at the swinging door and looked out before I went through into a corridor that eventually led me to the lobby of the inn. The place was empty, and no one was behind the desk. Shouts and general jubilation came from the bar. I went behind the desk and saw a door, slightly ajar, at the end of a little hallway through an open door against the side wall. Voices within. I crept down the corridor, flattened myself against the wall, and listened.

". . . Pendergast . . ."

It was Moore's voice. I strained to hear, inched closer to the door.

". . . on the ship, but they got away. Says the monkey-looking animal has the Roadmap—has it or *is* it, I couldn't understand which. At any rate, he wants our help. Big money, possibly. Very big."

"And he's right under our noses?" Another voice.

"Checked in this afternoon. Answers to the description."

"The cops—they'll take him, then?"

"Not if we can help it. We might have to keep him on ice for a while. Thing is—there's seven of them. We can't bag them all. . . ."

Someone was ringing the bell at the desk. I stiffened,

brought the gun out of my pocket and flicked off the safety. Now was the time. But—

"I'll get it, Zack."

"Forget that," Moore said. "This is important. I want you and Geof—"

The bell rang again.

"Forget it, I said! Listen to me. He'll be going through the Brotherhood ceremony. When he's out in the brush . . ."

I crept away. Better get rid of the customer first, then go back and do the deed.

I came out from the doorway. "The clerk's busy now," I said. "You—"

It was Darla. "I just wanted to ask—" Her mouth sagged open as the recognition slowly grew on her. "Jake! What . . ." Bewildered, she looked back at the door to the bar, then at me. Her mouth closed, and she looked at me soberly, a little fearfully. "Jake," she whispered. "It's . . . *you*."

I had frozen. Time stopped for the briefest quantum moment, and all I could see was her face, which seemed the most beautiful thing that had ever been created.

I unfroze, jumped over the counter, took Darla's arm and led her back out through the kitchen. The cook noticed this time, and muttered something about this place not being a tram station.

Outside, I crushed Darla to my chest and kissed her. She was surprised at first, then responded.

"Darla . . . love," I said.

Her eyes grew fearful again, and she drew back. "You *are* Jake. You're him—I mean, it's you. You're traveling through time, somehow. Like the stories say." She glanced back toward the inn again, then said, "It has to be. I just saw you in the pub. I walked out, and fifteen seconds later there you are, in different clothes. I almost didn't recognize you." She shook her head, and leaned against the trunk of the tree we stood under. "It's almost impossible to believe."

"One thing—remember," I said. "You can't say anything to—" I didn't know how to phrase it.

She nodded. "I understand. No. He wouldn't believe it, would he? How could he, now, after I lied to him . . . so many times. But you know, Jake. Don't you? You know so much now. You must. And . . ."

"And I love you."

She smiled and embraced me. We kissed again.

She clung to me. "Jake, I'm scared. We're lost, Jake. But we will get back, won't we? You're back, you came back. We will get home again."

"We're almost there, Darla, my darling."

"Jake, dear. So short a time. I love you. I loved you from the first. You know that, now. We're caught up in this awful thing, and it just seems we'll never get free."

"We will, we will," I said.

"I believe you. I can't imagine how it will happen, but I believe you."

We stood there in the enchanted night, holding each other, not speaking.

There were footsteps behind me. "There you are," somebody I didn't recognize said. "Well, this is cozy. Who's this cobber?"

It was somebody vaguely familiar. Another lumberjack— possibly one Darla had been talking to in the bar. I really couldn't be sure. I had been so drunk that night . . . this night.

"I'll be back in just a minute," Darla said to him. "See you back in the Vorpal Blade."

"Take a walk, mate," the guy said to me.

I punched him squarely in the chops, and he went over backwards into the weeds. But I should have looked the other way.

That's always been my problem.

29

IT WAS LIAM who picked me up and shook me awake.

"Been in a punch-up, eh, Jake?" He laughed.

My head hurt like hell. I said, "Wha?"

"You all right, man?"

"Yeah," I said, leaning against the tree, holding my head. I couldn't believe it. This was the second time that I'd been knocked cold, on this planet, on this night. Good thing Liam had come along—what would Moore had done with *two* Jakes? That would have disrupted the cycle in a way that I didn't want at all. Good thing. But hadn't Liam just come from the bar? Hadn't he just seen me in there?

"Looks like it was a good whack on the head," Liam said. "Are you sure you're all right, Jake?"

"Yeah, just give me a minute."

Maybe they'd already taken the other Jake out into the woods on the snipe hunt, and Liam just figured I got lost and wound up here. But how to explain the different clothes?

Suddenly it dawned on me.

I looked at him. He smiled back and I knew.

"You're Liam of the Culmination, aren't you?"

"The same. Sean thought I could give you a hand. I chased Moore's lads away. I don't think they recognized you. It's dark back here."

I nodded. I had been lucky.

Liam chuckled. "Have you had your fill of tampering with the warp and woof of the universe?"

"Yeah. I'm leaving that warp and that woof the hell alone."

He laughed. "There was no need of it. All's well, Jake. All's well."

"But you can't say *how* all's well."

"Not really. I couldn't give you the specifics."

I straightened up. "Well. Listen, thanks."

"Are you going home now?"

"Yeah, if I can get back. Have to drop Ragna and Oni off, though."

"You still might need help."

"I might. If we go ahead and shoot the portal to their world, they'll get back before they left. That business again. Can't have that, can we? I'm the only one who has the Pope's dispensation."

"I'll send someone, if you like," Liam said.

"Fine. Appreciate it. Good-bye, Liam."

"Good luck, Jake. Be well."

I got away from there. I felt remorse—not for wanting to kill Moore, but for not thinking. Pricking the bubble would have meant undoing Sam's good fortune, canceling his new life. Had I thought of that? No. And Carl? Disrupting the cycle would have spared him, but what about Lori? She had been an orphan here in the Outworlds. A hard life. But now she was . . . No. Now she was long dead, wasn't she?

I walked on through the woods, small things greeping and borking at me from every bush and weed.

I really didn't know. What about Darla? Would her fate have been different as a fugitive from the Colonial Authority? Would she have died in a shootout with the Militia, died for her cause, the dissident movement? I didn't know.

To say nothing of Susan, Sean, Roland, Liam, and Yuri.

And what about you, Jake? What about the person who experienced all this, who lived inside the bubble for a brief moment or two. What would become of those memories? What would become of your love for Darla? Would the slate be wiped clean? Would the moving finger erase a line and move on?

How the hell should I know. I'm no goddamn demigod.

I did know that Darla and I were possibly the only human beings in the history of the race actually to have communicated across the chasm that separates the living from the dead. In that sense, our love was immortal.

A small voice in the forest: "Jake?"

I recognized it, but I could scarcely believe it. "Winnie?"

It was she, stepping cautiously out of the shadows. "Hello,

Jake," she said in the clearest voice imaginable. Not a trace of her usual garbled enunciation.

"Hi, Winnie," I said.

"Can I walk with you?"

"Of course, honey. My, you've changed a great deal."

"I'm still me, Jake. How are you?"

"Still having problems, Winnie. Still having problems."

"I grieve for you, Jake."

Her double-thumbed hand in mine, we walked along the moonlit path.

I asked, "Tell me about the Guide Races."

"They were seeded along the Great Road to act as guides and travel companions. An individual of these races does not know himself for what he is until he reaches Home."

"I see. And you reached Home."

"With your help, Jake. Thank you very much. George thanks you, too."

"You sound like Winnie, even though I can understand you now," I said.

"But I am Winnie, Jake."

"I think so, but I think you're something more."

"That is also true."

She took her hand away and stopped. "I will help you later, Jake, if you need it. I will be there."

"Thanks, Winnie."

"Good-bye, Jake."

"Good-bye, Winnie."

When I got back to the truck, Sam greeted me with a frown.

"That pink and purple spook took off after you," he said.

"Arthur?"

"Yeah, he fretted and fretted, then said he couldn't let you upset the apple cart, in so many words, so he lit out into the woods. Without a flashlight, either. Nothing I could do to stop him."

I knew exactly where he'd gone. And I didn't know if I wanted to stop him. But I took a torch and dashed back toward the Bandersnatch, hoping the warp and the woof would tolerate a little more tampering.

A half hour later I was creeping through the undergrowth, the torch doused. Familiar voices all around. I was somewhere near the 'Snatch, but I didn't know where.

I knelt under a sapling and listened. There was some thrashing off to my left.

I waited. More thrashing in the bushes.

Then I heard, "Oh! Dearie me! Goodness gracious!"

A short commotion in the undergrowth, then something big came running down the trail at me. I turned on the torch, briefly.

"Yawp!" Arthur yawped.

"Ssh!"

"Jake? Is that you? I mean, the real one. I mean—"

"Yeah, it's me. Shut up. This way."

We got away from there. When it was safe enough, I turned the torch on.

"Oh, dearie me, that was horrible!" Arthur wailed. "I thought it was you, and it turns out to be your double! I knew my mistake the moment I got close to him! You left in that rag of a sweater and that tatty cap—"

"Are you kidding? This is the new look for fall."

"Oh, my. Do you think I screwed it all up? I mean, he *saw* me."

"Forget it. I saw you. I remember."

"Well, of course, you should remember it, but what I mean is—"

"Forget it. I have."

"You found him," Sam said, his tone implying that he maybe wished I hadn't.

"Let's blow this mudball," I said.

We drove all night and blew that mudball, which left us still in the Outworlds, where we didn't want to be, so we left by a potluck portal and used the Roadmap to find Ragna's planet. Before we shot the portal, I got back in the driver's seat—Sam had been relieving me and conjured up the Backtime Route again. As I drove, I sensed Winnie's presence in the truck. I didn't turn around to look.

We arrived in bright desert daylight.

"Is best to be playing it safely," Ragna said to me. "There is an alternate entrance to our caves which we should be using. I, for one, am not fond of meeting myself and passing the time of day withal."

"Withal?"

"So to speak. Be making a right up here, if you please, Jake."

I went off the road onto loose sand, and had some trouble until the ground firmed up. Then we hit rock and everything was fine. The alternative entrance was at the base of a sheer cliff. You could hardly see it, but Ragna picked it out. He said that he knew the route back to the main *Ahgirr* living areas, and I believed him. There was a problem, though. We had no idea what time frame we were in. Ragna couldn't come up with a way to find out without going up to somebody, tapping them on the shoulder, and asking the date—and that would involve the risk of paradox.

"We will stay in the lower caves for a good while, then will come up and risk."

Sam suggested we drive to the local faln and find out the date—but that might have been a risk for us. We'd had trouble the last time we'd visited one of those immense desert arcologies. No, Ragna felt more comfortable in his caves. I couldn't help, because my time traveling was purely intuitive. I had no accurate way of measuring how far forward in time we'd gone. The slippage factor involved, if memory served, was only a matter of a month or so. We'd left Talltree a few days after our troubles there, spent a day or so traveling, then had come here and stayed five weeks. It turned out that I still needed some practice driving the Backtime Route.

Sam stayed in the truck with the recuperating John while Arthur and I entered the caverns with our *Ahgirr* friends, carrying what supplies and equipment we could. We walked for kilometers, it seemed, but it was pleasant. The caves were cool and quiet, and as beautiful as I remembered them to be. Susan and I had spent some pleasant times in this subterranean world.

Susan. I missed her sorely.

Ragna chose a charming little grotto near one of the underground streams that flowed through these caverns. We set up camp. There wasn't much to do, but there were two army cots to put together—they came in the box disassembled. (They must have belonged to Sean and Liam, as those two had taken along just about all their worldly possessions. They'd cleaned out the farm. The trailer was still full of their junk.) After I got them put together, I noticed that Arthur wasn't around.

"The creature is going off in that general direction," Oni said. "But it is not taking a light with it."

"It's really a robot, not a creature," I told her. "He can probably see in the dark pretty well. I wonder why he took off." I scratched my head. "Oh, well. Ragna? What about these emergency food stores you were telling me about?"

"They are being hidden in various parts of caves. Is old custom among *Ahgirr* in case cave is invaded by unfriendly sorts—retreat and survive."

"Oh. And you know where these stores are?"

"Assuredly."

"Good. Well, I hope you'll be comfortable here."

"We will be jim-dandy, and we will be thanking you."

I laughed and took Ragna's smooth-skinned hand. I had come to know and love these aliens, and I would miss them, too.

We hard a squawk. Turning, I saw Arthur rushing out of the darkness. He looked flustered.

"I don't *believe* it happened again!" he shouted.

"What?" I said.

"*You're here*. You. Again, it happened. He saw me."

"Yeah, I know," I said. "I remember that, too."

"Well, for pity's sake, this is getting ridiculous."

"Why did you go wandering off like that?"

"Just wanted to explore. This is the first vacation I've had in six million years. I'm loving this little jaunt, and I wanted to see the sights."

"Well, you saw another ghost. Consider yourself lucky. Hard to book a tour with those on the itinerary."

Ragna and Oni accompanied us back to the entrance. They now knew exactly how long they would have to lay low. When they finally showed themselves, they would have some explaining to do, though.

"Everyone will be listening politely," Ragna said, "then will be thinking, Ragna has finally attained craziness. But Oni and I will be writing our memoirs and be selling them to publishers for big bucks."

We said our good-byes. They cried, I got a little damp-eyed.

What could be more human?

30

THERE ISN'T MUCH left to tell.

Among the loose ends, there was the matter of rescuing myself from the Colonial Militia on a planet called Goliath. I remembered seeing someone who had my face standing over me in the cell, administering a shot of a drug that would bring me out of the quasihypnotic state I was in.

Here again was an opportunity to mess things up. We could simply decide not to do it. That would, theoretically, snap the whole chain of events that led up to and proceeded from the rescue . . . but no. I couldn't resist thrusting a hand through the glass to help my mirror twin. After all, he was in a bind, and he just might be in a position to do the same for me some day.

But there were problems. I didn't know how we could do it at all, much less do it quietly, efficiently, and without causing unwanted paradoxes. We had the means: the Reticulan dream wand, the mind control device that I'd taken from Corey Wilkes aboard the *Laputa*, which still lay almost forgotten in the glove box under the dashboard. It was a good guess someone had used the wand, or one like it, to knock out everyone in the Militia station.

But just how were we going to juggle all the balls?

The answer came when Arthur announced that the space-time ship had completed its repair work.

"It's fine now. I've run some tests, and it's working very well."

We discussed the rescue operation, and Arthur had plenty of suggestions.

"Well, adapting the ship's auxiliary systems to duplicate

297

the effects of the wand wouldn't be a problem at all," he said, "if you want to do it that way.''

"That'd be swell," I said. "There're a few problems. We'll have to be in the vicinity, and we'd be vulnerable to the effect, too. The only antidote I know of is a good dose of a moderate tranquilizer—and the medicine chest is just about empty."

"Oh, that's no problem. I said we could duplicate the effects, as you've described them. That doesn't imply we have to use the same means, although they'll probably be similar. I'll just tune the beam so that it won't resonate with your particular brain scan. You'll be immune, and you can go in there and do your duty."

"Well, that's fine I guess," I said, then snapped my fingers. "No, it isn't. Then my double will be immune, too. And history says he succumbed to the effect."

Arthur shrugged his negligible shoulders. "So, can't history give us a little break? The universe won't miss a few historical facts here and there."

"I dunno," I said, scratching my beard stubble. I was also running out of razor blades. "I really have no idea."

"Arthur," Sam said, "you must tune that gizmo to my brainpan and I'll go in and do what has to be done."

"No, Sam. It won't work. I didn't see you at the station."

"Wait a minute."

He went into the aft-cabin for a moment, then came back. He had done something to his hair, parted it differently, combed it to the side, something. I couldn't tell exactly what.

Zoya studied him, then looked at me. "You could pass for twins."

I conjured up the memory of the rescue, tried to see the mysterious face hovering above me. How could I have not recognized my father's face? Or was it that I could not bring myself, at the time, to believe it? Perhaps the explanation simply was that my recollection wasn't very clear. After all, the memory was half concealed in a hypnagogic fog, and always would be. So be it.

"What about the tranquilizer?" I said.

"We won't need it," Sam said.

I said, "Then why do you have to go in at all?"

"Oh, your double will need something to pep him up,"

Arthur said. "I don't know about that dream wand gadget, but my technique is going to call for some chemical relief, if you want your double to be up and about, doing things."

And he would have things to do, to be sure. We did have one ampoule of amphetamine sulfate left. That would do nicely.

Still, there was the problem of getting there, and getting near enough to the station without causing no end of paradox problems. Arthur suggested we make the trip in the spacetime bus, and we took him up on it. I did not feel up to trying the Backtime Route again. Besides, I felt my connection with the Culmination growing ever more tenuous.

On a dusty planet with no name, Arthur unloaded the spacetime ship and inflated it. I drove the truck in, and we took off.

We had spent some time giving Arthur the most accurate temporal data we could, and with the help of the Roadmap, we were able to pinpoint the spatial coordinate exactly. Goliath was part of Terran Maze, and the planet's star was known to Terran astronomers, albeit only as a catalogue number. It was enough; by the time we'd locked up the truck and gone to the control room, we had arrived.

"That fast?" I said in some amazement.

"Well, the ship makes all transitions—jumps—in zero time. What takes time is making successive jumps and setting up for them. However, Goliath wasn't all that far away, and I did it in one clean transition." Arthur looked proud.

I gazed at the dun-colored world turning below. It looked huge, untamable, and cruel; a big sprawling monster of a planet.

"Now I have to search for that city," Arthur said, his stubby plasticine fingers feeling the control box. "Oh, there it is." He laughed. "Well, of course. It's the only one on the planet. What's it called?"

"Maxwellville."

"A real cultural mecca, huh? Okay, here we go."

The dun-colored ball rushed to meet us, then became the vast arid world it was, its sky coloring to hazy blue, the various shades of its surface separating and becoming features, the most salient of which was a high plateau ringed by dark jagged mountains. Maxwellville sat up here in the cooler air. The surrounding plains were uninhabitable. We could attest to that—we'd nearly died out there.

We were a little hazy as to what time of day we were aiming for. As I remembered, I was interrogated sometime in the early morning, made an escape attempt, and got thrown in the jug around dawn. I spent maybe two hours in there before blacking out, and I estimated I was out for only a few minutes.

We seemed to have hit it right on the button. Goliath's fierce sun was still low in the sky. Maxwellville came into view, a raw, ugly little burg of quickie buildings and pop-up domes. It looked like any pioneer settlement. It took us a while to pinpoint the Militia station. The city was bustling with early-morning traffic, and there were a good number of pedestrians up and about at this hour. Everything would have to be done in broad daylight and in front of witnesses.

"Can the ship be seen?" I asked.

"Only if you look *real* hard," Arthur said. "Don't worry. Sam's going to raise a few eyebrows when I levitate him down, though."

"Can you extend the effect to cover a few blocks?"

"You mean so it will affect people outside the station?"

"Yeah, the less witnesses, the better."

"Well, sure. Any way you want to work it. But everybody is going to wonder what the hell happened."

"Let 'em wonder. I just don't want them to *see* anything."

"Can do, dearie."

I was ready to draw a map, from memory, of the inside of the station, but Arthur magically produced a piece of flimsy material on which was inscribed what looked like an architect's floor plan.

"The ship's probing devices don't miss much," Arthur said.

Sam familiarized himself with the layout. Then he crumpled the clothlike artifact, which had been extruded from the bottom of the control panel, and shoved it in a pocket.

"Well, I'm ready. Do I need burnt cork on my face? How 'bout I just take a bottle?"

"Wait a minute," I said. "Arthur, don't human brain scans change over time?"

"A little. Why?"

"Can't you tune the effect to exempt me but not my double?"

Arthur scowled. "Can't make it easy for me, can you? Well, I'll see."

Sam was eyeing me dubiously.

"I'm going along, Sam," I told him.

"Whatever for?"

"Something tells me I should. Darla's down there."

"Okay. I guess you know what you're doing."

"Oh, sure," I said, wondering what the hell I was doing.

Arthur found that he could indeed do what I had asked. We were ready.

Sam and I went out to the cargo bay and stood in front of the puckered valve that was the door. I held the communicator up and spoke into it.

"Any time, Arthur."

The door dilated. The city spread out before us, bright and busy in the morning sun. The smell of brewing coffee came to my nostrils on a fresh, cool breeze. We were about a hundred meters above the Militia station.

"We gotta jump, don't we?" I said.

"That's what the spook said."

We jumped. It was a fast trip down, and I nearly swallowed my heart. But we hit gently enough to take the impact with nothing more than a bend of the knees. I looked around. We were in the parking lot behind the station. Three pedestrians were sprawled on the near sidewalk. There were two Militiamen passed out in a parked police vehicle. Another constable had wrecked his bubble-topped interceptor into a heat pump, apparently having succumbed as he was driving into the lot.

We dashed in through the garage.

"What are you going to do?" Sam asked when we were inside.

I looked around at the blue-uniformed bodies slumped over desks, lying on the floor, collapsed in swivel chairs. "Go do it, Sam. I'll meet you here in five minutes."

I walked through the white, aseptic hallways. I knew where I was going, and didn't tarry. I had seen this movie before.

Darla was there, in Petrovsky's office. But there was something different. She was seated, her head down on the desk, her outstretched right hand seeming to reach for something in Petrovsky's left. It was Sam's key.

Details, details. Now I knew what I was here for. I took the black and orange plastic box from Petrovsky and slipped it into Darla's pocket. I lifted her head and held it in my arms.

"Hello again, darling," I said, after kissing her flushed cheek. Her eyes were open but unfocused. I looked into them, and they looked through me. Except for the briefest instant. Her lips moved almost imperceptibly. She moaned softly.

I looked at her for a while, then kissed her again. I rested her head on the desktop, trying to fashion her body into the position I had found her in, but her body seemed to have gone slack, and she wouldn't stay up. I checked my watch. I was running late, so I stretched her out on the floor in front of the desk, face down, head resting on her right arm.

"We'll meet again, darling," I said.

I left. Sam was waiting for me.

"C'mon! H. G. Wells I ain't!"

We ran out into the lot. And there, standing almost where we'd landed, were two strange beings whom I knew to be members of a race called the Ryxx. It's a sort of combination whistle, chirp, and click.

"Greetings, Roadbrothers," one of them squawked through his translator box.

Sam tweeted a greeting, then said to me: "I guess Arthur's gadget doesn't work on nonhumans."

The other was holding a strange-looking weapon on us.

The first looked up at the sky, its two round sad eyes searching. Finally its eyes fixed on something—the ship, presumably. I looked up and saw a shimmering in the air, nothing more.

"Superior technology," the first one said. Its fat ostrichlike body seemed to heave a sigh. "Very, very superior. We are puzzled and vexed."

"It's pretty hard to explain," Sam said. He whistled something.

The second birdlike creature said, "I am of her nest, although I am not an issue of her egg."

"Well, please convey my warmest compliments to *(chirp-*

whistle-click) for me. Tell her that the straw of my nest is always fresh for her visit, and that I hope the issue of her egg will be many and prosperous. That comes from Sam McGraw."

This seemed to impress the hell out of them.

"So, it is true," the first one said. "The many strange tales told of you and your egg. Is it true that you have the Roadmap?"

I said, "It is true. But hear me. You will never get it. No one will. *I will never give it up, not to anyone in the universe.* It is mine, and I will keep it."

"Hello?" came Arthur's voice from the communicator, which I held in my hand. "Hell-o-o?"

"Yeah, Arthur?"

"Um . . . want me to make fried chicken out of them?"

I glared at the two ungainly bird creatures. Their faces were impassive behind transparent atmospheric-assist masks. The one holding the weapon lowered his winglike arm.

"No," I said.

"Upsy daisy."

We rose into the air. On the way up, Sam said, "I've always wanted to start a religion, and God forgive me, if this keeps up, I just might."

We tacked against the wind of time once more. The displacement was about eight months this time. We directed Arthur to a farm planet on the outskirts of Terran Maze. People I knew and trusted lived here.

Arthur landed on a deserted road, and I backed the rig out of the ship.

"Time to say good-bye," Arthur said. "It's been interesting, to say the least."

"Yeah," I said. "Thanks for everything, Art, old boy."

"Boy? You know I'm sexless. They say I'm missing a lot, but what the hell. Anyway. . ." He put his absurdly small hand on my shoulder. "Listen, I'm sorry you lost so much. There wasn't much I could do about it. . . ." He seemed to drift off into thought.

"Here," I said, handing him the communicator.

"Uh, no. No. You go ahead and keep it. The ship has

plenty. Keep it as a souvenir. Besides, you might want to call me someday."

I shrugged and put it in my pocket.

We watched the ship rise and become an olive drab dot in the sky. Then it was gone.

Sam slapped me on the shoulder. "Let's go see if Gil Tomasso is home. I hope his heart is strong."

Gil's heart was plenty strong, but he fainted when he saw Sam.

Our next few months weren't very busy. It was just a matter of laying low and waiting for the paradoxical crease in our universe to work itself out. Right now my double was on our farm back on Vishnu. On or about the fourth day of April, he would pick up a small shipment of astronomical equipment from an importer on Barnard's III and set off on a trip to deliver his cargo to Chandrasekhar Deep Space Observatory on a planet called Uraniborg. He would never deliver that equipment.

Actually, that was wrong. We would deliver it for him, more or less on schedule, and we would do that when my double disappeared through a potluck portal on Seven Suns Interchange.

I had a duty to perform as soon as possible, though. I had to get rid of the cube. I still had it. (Was there a single person who coveted it now? Depends on what *now* means.)

Darla said that I had given the cube to a member of the Colonial Assembly by the name of Marcia Miller. She said I had simply walked into her office and plopped the cube down on the assemblywoman's desk.

I disguised myself, borrowed Gil's four-roller, got on the Skyway and drove to Einstein, the capital planet.

The Assembly Office Building was big and neoclassical and cost too much money, just like every other governmental barn in the cosmos. I strode down a carpeted, marble-walled corridor, looking at nameplates on doors. Most of the names were eastern European, a few oriental, one or two or three Anglo-Saxon.

"The Honorable Marcia B. Miller, Member of the Assembly," I read aloud, then opened the heavy blond wooden door.

There was a human receptionist, a young woman. I smiled as I stepped past her desk.

She looked up from her console and did a double take. "*Kamrada?* Sir? Do you have an appointment?"

"Honey, I've had an appointment for ten billion years."

"Sir, you can't go in there!"

I was through the inner door before she could extricate herself from her huge work station. I clucked at the lack of security in the place.

An annoyed Marcia Miller looked up from the screen she was reading. "Who the devil are you?"

"Does the name Daria Vance Petrovsky mean anything to you?"

Her face tightened, then slowly relaxed.

"Marcia, I'm sorry!" the receptionist wailed. "I've called Security!"

"No! No, cancel the call."

"But—"

Miller rose from her desk, still looking at me. "It's okay, Barb. Cancel the call."

Mystified, Barb retreated, closing the door.

Miller sat back down. "Of course I know of Daria Vance Petrovsky. Why shouldn't I recognize the name of the life-companion of a high-ranking Militia officer?"

"One who is a subversive and a fugitive from justice?"

"That is none of my—"

"Listen," I said, "I'll make this short. You'll think I'm a crank at first, but in time you'll know I'm not. I'm Jake McGraw, and I've lived what most people dream. I've driven to the end of the Skyway and met the Roadbuilders. They gave me a map. Here it is." I drew the cube out and held it in my hand. "It's the key to the Skyway system. You'll be hearing about it, and me. Roadbuzz, road yarns, stories, rumors. They're all true. You'll hear my name spoken in bars and roadhouses. They'll say I drove into the fireball of the birthing universe, and they'll be right. It's true, and I even got a bit of a sunburn doing it. Everything they'll say about me will be true—so damn true it'll drive you crazy. And here's what I'm going to do. I'm going to give you this map, and I won't be doing you a favor. What you'll have to do is see that the dissident network protects Darla—Daria—at all costs. She is the key to this whole affair. Exactly how, I can't say. But you must do all in your power to protect her."

She began to lose patience, and I silenced her. "I know all about the dissident network," I went on, "and I know all about your involvement in it. Don't worry, I was told this office is debugged. It makes no difference if it isn't. I'm just a crank, right? So, forget it. Here."

I dropped the cube on her desk. "Happy birthday, honey."

And then I left. The security guard at the front entrance smiled at me on my way out.

It was a pleasant few months. Gil Tomasso was a gracious host, and then Red Shaunnessey offered to put us up, so we drove over there. Sam and I passed the time repairing the trailer. John recuperated from his burns, and Zoya fell in love with Sam. It was inevitable, I thought. I remembered how well they had hit it off thirty years ago.

But eventually it became time to perform another duty, one I both dreaded and craved.

The trailer was fixed. I climbed in, and Sam saw me off.

"Do you know where?" he asked. "Exactly?"

"No, but there are only a few places on the starslab where hikers can hope to get a ride."

"True. Well, good luck."

"There's no such thing, Sam."

I found her on a planet called Monteleone. She was standing in front of a Stop-N-Shop on the Colonial highway, looking very pickupable. She was wearing her silver Allclyme survival suit and stood with her backpack parked at her feet. She was beautiful, young, thin, unpregnant, and I was a total stranger to her.

I slid back the port. "You look like you're going somewhere," I said.

But she knew who I was. In fact, she was here for the specific purpose of getting picked up by me. I had acquired a shadow two days back, a blue-seater driven by a dark-haired young man. One of Darla's dissident comrades, probably. The dissidents were probably very confused by now, because they were getting conflicting reports that made it look as though I could be in two places at one time. They were also following my double. But I made it easier to follow me. And so I had swung by this Stop-N-Shop a few times over the past few days. And sure enough . . .

"Matter of fact, I am," Darla said, picking up her pack. "Are you going where I'm going?"

"Where is that?"

"To the other side of T-Maze. Here, there . . . everywhere." She smiled, and my heart melted.

"Sure. Hop aboard."

There was nothing strange about it. It was something I had to do. I had to meet Darla, for we had never been properly introduced. And she had to fall in love with me, because she said that she had, once, a long time ago, but I never remembered it, because I wasn't around at the time. It makes sense to me.

We drove around, not aimlessly, just unhurriedly. We toured Hydran Maze, then came back, spent some time on a park planet, camping out in the trailer.

Darla met "Sam" for the first time. "Sam" was the result of my dad's fiddling with the Wang A.I. He tuned up its personality programming and gave it a voice that pretty much could pass for Sam's former computer voice (which never sounded like Sam himself). It was a pretty good approximation—it spooked me. Mostly, the computer kept quiet.

We fell in love. I don't know where we were when we first made love. "Sam" was driving. You ought to try this sometime.

There was one planet . . . it was green, and it looked like Earth (but not really; they never do), and the sky was scrubbed so squeaky clean that sunlight just slid right down it, spilling into the clearing of a forest of quasioaks and maybe-maples and making the fuzzy seedpods on the tops of tall weeds look like a cloud of ectoplasm at the tip of a magic wand—or halos on angels—steeping the grass and trees and Darla and me and our love in the light of a faraway star, a warmth and a power that has lasted five billion years and will last five billion more. It was a nice place to eat a picnic lunch.

And there were motels—cheap ones (I was just about

broke), the kind that have the state-of-the-art entertainment gear and beds that squeak and smell of mildew and faintly, ever so faintly, of urine. And have bad water. And a broken ice machine. And a robot desk clerk that nearly pokes your eye out when it hands you the lock pipette. If I had a nickel for every one of those I've stayed in, I could go back to 1964 and spend them. But we made do, and made love. Mostly we kept to the truck, and kept on the road.

Soon, the time drew near to when we would part. She said nothing about it, but I knew. Her mission was not to fall in love with me, but gather information. Roadmap? Cube? Find out. On at least two occasions I heard her rummage through the cab and aft-cabin as I feigned sleep in the bunk. She asked "Sam" leading questions when I was supposedly out of ear-shot. She did her best, but got nothing. She would have to duck out, her mission a failure. But she would be back for a second try, that I knew. However, next time "I" would not be here.

Last chance, Jake, a voice said. (The divvil's, as Sean would say.) Last chance to smash the bubble. Take her, tell her, even if she doesn't believe. Point the rig toward the nearest potluck portal and put the pedal to the metal. Exit hero with heroine.

But I couldn't. Because, somewhere out there, there was a kid in a '57 Chevy who was lost and needed to get home. Because somewhere in the Outworlds there was an orphan girl who worked for coolie wages on a strange ferryboat and who would fall in love with the kid in the Chevy. Because Sam was right now lying in bed with a beautiful woman who loved him, and you can't do that sort of thing when you're merely coughing up a little blood, much less when you're dead, which is what Sam used to be, but isn't now . . . and because if I did, the whole damn universe just might blow a converter manifold and wind up having to be towed home. And some-where, *somewhere,* there were five gods who used to be human beings. What would they have to say about upsetting the whole apple cart? Bolts from Olympus I could do without.

But mainly I didn't because I had faith. Where I got it, I don't know. Faith in . . . what? I don't know. I think it was just an unspoken certainty that the universe has a purpose, despite all the reasons for insisting that it can't, and that this purpose is a good one. It was absolutely absurd of me to think that.

I didn't know exactly when she would leave. So I couldn't linger in a last kiss, a last embrace, couldn't know when such was happening. And I didn't know until one morning I got up and she wasn't there. Her pack was gone.

And so was Darla, gone for the last time.

Sam must have done more than he knew, because the computer kept saying "There, there, son." It said it over and over as I cried.

At last, we could go home. There were still a few loose ends, though. Gil Tomasso and his driving partner, Su-Gin Chang, would be at Sonny's Restaurant on Epsilon Eridani 1 to back my double up in the confrontation with Corey Wilkes. (God, Corey, you never die!) So would Red Shaunnessey. That would take care of . . . that.

Before we went to Vishnu, we delivered our load to Chandrasekhar Observatory. We were only a day late.

There was a problem with John. He was fine physically, but emotionally he was foundering in deep water. Guilt was the obvious ballast, and he had a ton of it. Even confession didn't do him any good.

"You've known that I've been an Authority informer," he said to me in Red's kitchen before we left.

"Really?" I said.

"Yes. Of course. You knew that. I reported regularly on the activities of the Teleologists."

I told him that I really didn't know that.

"I made my report to Colonel Petrovsky on Goliath, the night our camp was raided. I had to. No choice. I've never had a choice. It's my brother. Did you know he was a political prisoner?"

I told him I hadn't known that.

"Didn't you ever wonder why the Militia let us go that night?"

"Yes, I've wondered."

He stared at the plank tabletop for a full minute. "I'm a fraud, Jake."

"Because you gave into fear?"

"Because . . ." His face had tightened into a knot of pain. "Because I—"

"Take it easy, John. You were under no obligation to become a light of the universe."

"After a life of seeking the truth, trying to find some answer..."

"Forget it."

"And now what? The Militia will want my report! And I'll have to tell them you have the map!"

I laughed so hard I nearly choked on the sandwich I was eating.

It got to John; he laughed in spite of himself, then faded to depression again.

"You'll have to kill me," he said.

I shook my head. "John, give it up. Go home, make your report. Tell them that your group disappeared through a pot-luck portal on Seven Suns. That's the truth. Or tell them I have the map. It really doesn't matter, John. It never really has mattered."

It didn't help him. He rose slowly and went into his room.

The next day he was gone. His clothes, his toilet kit, everything was still there. We never found him, never saw him again.

Home.

The farm was fine. After all, we had just left.

There was work to do; the fish tanks were foamy with algae, the paddies were dry, the reactor was on the fritz— everything I had been putting off for a year or so.

Sam was in disguise, so as not to terrify the neighbors. A pretty good one, too. Rumors were thick, though. The stories about us were at the peak of their circulation—but they would eventually die down. We hoped, but didn't know.

"Time to get off this mudball," Sam said. "Time to pick up and move."

"You're right, Sam," I said. I called a real estate agent the next day.

And one day I got the strangest, most miraculous letter of my life. The cover letter was from one Ernest P. Blass, Esq., of the firm of Dolan, Musico, Shwartz, and Blass. It read:

Dear Mr. McGraw,

As I am informed that you are primarily an *Inglo* speaker, I will write this in English instead of Intersystem (which I must confess I prefer myself).

The enclosed letter, addressed to you, will no doubt cause you as much bafflement as it has to us. It was discovered among the assets of a holding company which a corporate client of ours has just acquired. To trace the long history of this letter, and the long and circuitous route by which it came into our hands, and thus into yours, would be tedious and time-consuming at best. Suffice it to say that, on the face of it at least, this letter had been held along with other papers and instruments in a fiduciary trust, which itself can trace its history back at least over a hundred years. Now, Mr. McGraw, let me tell you straightaway that what I believe we have here is a hoax, pure and simple, for there is no possible way for . . .

Inside the manila pouch was a yellowed envelope with my name and address on it. I tore it open and saw it was a handwritten letter. It was from Carl Chapin. It was dated November 6, 2005.

Dear Jake,

There is no possible way I can ever know if you'll receive this, of course, but just writing it is giving me chills along with a warm feeling of nostalgia for a time long past and an experience that I've often suspected might have been just a momentary hallucination. But no. Deborah remembers, too, so it must have been real. Our life together has been overall a pleasant one, and we owe to you the fact that we are together. We have been married for over forty years. We had four children, three boys and a girl, and they are all grown up now, and two are raising families of their own. I don't want to bore you with statistics or a recitation of the events of our lives, but we do want to assure you that we are fine, and that the decisions we made back then have proven out pretty well.

    Shortly after the last time we saw each other, I went to college and majored in electrical engineering. The years ahead saw a growth in computer technology (I still think of Sam even to this day!) and that's the field I chose to go into. I did pretty well, and wound up managing my own company for a while, until we were bought out, and then I went into consulting. Well, I said I wouldn't bore you with details. I'd love to ask how you are, if only I could believe that there was even the slightest chance that you could answer. But I still think of you, Jake. You were a hero to me. I was young, and looking back, a pretty stubborn kid. I must have been hard to handle at certain times. But you helped me, Jake. You took a lost kid and helped him get home. And I'll never forget you. Debbie has something to say to you, too, so I will turn this over to her.

Hi Jake!

Carl said everything I wanted to say, except for this. Over the years I've sometimes stood out on the back porch looking up at the stars, on summer nights, just looking, wondering. Are you out there somewhere, Jake? Or was it a dream? So many years and miles separate us, but I'll never forget the crush I had on you. Carl was my age, and I loved him from the very first, but you were a knight in shining armor. Oh, I guess that's as romantic as you can get, isn't it? But I look up and I think and I wonder. Will he get home? Will he and Darla be happy? I hope you are well, Jake. I'll always love you. Good-bye.

And then, again in Carl's hand:

Me again. I guess that's it. Nothing more to say, except that over the years I've kept asking myself this question: What was it that we found at the end of the Skyway? I'll never know, but I'll never stop thinking about it. Good-bye, Jake, and good luck.

                                        Carl W. Chapin

P.S.—My lawyers have devised a pretty fancy scheme for seeing that this letter has a chance of getting to you. They think I'm crazy, but I pay them enough money to build several mental institutions.

Hail and farewell, Carl. Hail and farewell.

Home. We sold the farm very handily, turning a nice profit. After thirty years of sweat and strain and broken backs. So we packed up the truck and made ready to move. We would stay well away from Terran Maze for a while; maybe for good. I'm not political, but on a bad day my opinion of the Authority was about as low as it could get. Governments just don't come much more odious. Well, with any luck, the dissident movement would one day change things for the better.

But there is always hope, as I found out on the day we were to leave. Sam was out in the truck with Zoya, going over our itinerary (we were going to take a little vacation, visit a few nice spots), and I was in the farmhouse looking for things that we may have left behind. It was a nice day, and I was sort of taking my time saying good-bye to the place, when I heard, of all things, Arthur's voice coming from the cutlery drawer in the kitchen. I opened the drawer and saw an oblong piece of olive drab material. The communicator, and I had forgotten all about it.

"Jake? Come in, Jake. This is Arthur! Can you read me?"

"Arthur!" I yelled. "What the hell? Where are you?"

"Oh, good," Arthur said. "I have someone here who wants to see you, Jake. I'm hovering at about half a kilometer. That's your house down there? The tacky yellow one?"

"Get down here this instant!" I shouted.

I raced outside just in time to see the ship land. "Darla!"

"Jake! Jake, darling!"

And again she was real in my arms, warm and real and alive. And not pregnant any more.

"You'll be wanting this," Arthur said, handing me my infant son.

I couldn't speak. Sam said, "The spitting image of somebody."

"Well, it was like this," Arthur said, "I was on my way back to Microcosmos, and I said to myself, you big idiot, here you are with a time machine—"

"The airborne bogey that was tailing us when the missile hit!" I blurted.

"Yeah, that was me. I got back a little before I left, is all. Nothing unusual. But what a mess! Darla was in bad shape, and I very nearly lost her to the cylinders! You can imagine what it's like flying near those things! Why, I almost lost the ship. Would Prime have been pissed! *Anyway,* so I snatch Darla up, and I *streak* back to the plant, and those darlings whip up a minihospital cum maternity ward in a blink of a gnat's eye, and . . ." Arthur slumped against the ship. "I'm pooped."

The road shot over brown sand and pink rocks, bisecting the plain and racing toward the potluck portal. The cylinders rose against the yellow sky like dark angels on judgment day, and through them lay all of eternity.

"How's our speed, Sam?"

"Don't ask me, I'm diapering a baby."

"Darla?"

"Warming this bottle, Jake. Just a minute."

"Hey, you people know I can't drive and read instruments at the same time. Zoya?"

"Thirty meters per second, Jake, and holding steady."

"Good. Can't you keep that kid quiet, Darla?"

"He takes after his father."

"And his grandfather," Zoya added.

"Son, we shoulda never allowed womenfolk aboard this vessel."

"Yeah, you're right, Sam. I've always said—" I took a better grip on the control bars. "Commit markers coming up. Everyone strap in! Now!"

Everything was right. The board was green. This was going to be the longest trip, and the best. The markers shot past—I looked back to see that everyone was strapped in tightly, even the baby, Samuel Jacob, in his little crash seat.

We shot into the portal, and the gates of eternity opened. . . .